I0708600

WHERE

THE LIGHT

SHINES

Published in Australia by
Beachcomber Books
5 Hotham Road, Sorrento, VIC 3943
Email: anne.olle.author@outlook.com
Website: www.anneolleauthor.com

First published in Australia 2025
Copyright © Anne Olle 2025

All rights reserved. No part of this publication may be reproduced, stored in a retrieval system, or transmitted, in any form or by any means without the prior written permission of the publisher, nor be otherwise circulated in any form of binding or cover other than that in which it is published and without a similar condition being imposed on the subsequent purchaser.

National Library of Australia Cataloguing in Publication entry

A catalogue record for this book is available from the National Library of Australia

978-1-7643662-0-5 (paperback)
978-1-7643662-1-2 (hardback)
978-1-7643662-2-9 (epub)

Cover design by Neat Design
Layout and design by Sophie White Design
Printed by Ingram Spark

This is a work of fiction. Names, characters, businesses, places, events, locales, and incidents are either the products of the author's imagination or used in a fictitious manner. Any resemblance to actual persons, living or dead, or actual events is purely coincidental.

WHERE THE LIGHT SHINES

Just Because You Are Lost
Doesn't Mean You Won't Be Found

ANNE OLLE

For those who see the light in us

even when we don't see it in ourselves.

WHERE ARE YOU,
MY DAD?

Where are you, my dad,

Where have you gone?

I've been so lonely and sad.

For far too long.

It's not the same here anymore,

Without your smiling face coming through the door.

A big hello from Mr Moon

I pray every night to see you soon.

Dad you were my sun, and you were my laughter.

I hope so hard that we meet in the hereafter.

I love you forever and ever and ever.

You were my greatest treasure.

ONE

The morning felt light, leisurely, as if it had all the time in the world to appear. Lily lay in bed longer than usual, not because she needed to but because she could. She could hear her mother, Meredith, humming along with the radio, and she could smell the bacon frying. Eventually lured out by the promise of breakfast, Lily skipped into the kitchen and hugged her mother from behind.

"Morning, Mum. God, how I love holidays!"

"Yes, darling, me too," she said, flipping the eggs.

"Ah, sleeping beauty has arisen," Frank, her dad, teased. "And what a bloody beauty she is, too," he said, tickled his daughter, and she said, "Oh, Dad, are we swimming or what today?"

"You bet your sweet bippy we are! Picnic, beach, swims... oh God, I love not having to keep a schedule. Especially not a railway one."

They all laughed as they set the table and ate.

They spent the day at the back beach. Her Dad said, "With the amount of gear we take, you'd think we were going to move country." He had a point. They had their umbrella, a full Esky, towels and change of clothes. They would get there early, set up camp, and position and reposition the wind break and umbrella throughout the day. Lily would swim for hours with Frank. Meredith liked to paddle and then back under the umbrella to read and wave, especially when they landed a good wave and body-surfed it to shore.

It was a mild, grey day. Hard to distinguish the bobbing black bodies out behind the breakers.

"Dolphins, Lily-pily, dolphins!" Frank was yelling breathlessly and pointing. "Oh my God, there's so many of them."

Lily and her dad were treading water and watching the forms slowly swimming around each other.

"Maybe they're gathering up dinner. They move as a family, you know. Even have their own unique language."

After their swim, huddled under their green-striped umbrella, eating their ham and salad sandwiches, and sipping their iced orange cordial out of tin cups, Lily asked her dad about his ever-present notebook. He said it was his friend; he could capture snippets of nature in it. He read: *Grey weather was ideal for the eye, gentle enough to absorb the beauty and easy enough to observe all within sight.* Frank took the notebook wherever they went. Lily asked him if he was writing about the people he met or conversations he overheard.

"People are unique. No two people are the same. Not even identical twins. They may look the same but in their souls they're different. I can't copy a person and then write about them, that's not cricket. I can listen to them and observe them – now, that's interesting. I can make up why they say what they say, do what they do, what their motivation is, what drives them. That's where the juice is."

Lily's mother, Meredith, was a tall, strong woman with large soft brown eyes. She had shoulder-length brown hair that bounced in the sunlight.

Her dad was tall and slight. He walked fast, talked slowly, and loved to stop wherever the view was best. He'd always tell Lily to never miss nature, *because it comes tapping on your shoulder and if you're too busy, it will go away, and you'll miss something very beautiful. That's how I met your mother.*

Lily knew the story. One autumn day, Frank was nestled into a magnificent view, watching the water with the big ships in the distance. It was peaceful and quiet, just the way he liked it, when a large black shaggy wet dog came bounding up to him from nowhere. Peace and quiet well and truly destroyed, Frank's lunch and drink-bottle went flying.

"Percy, Percy, come back! You are driving me nuts, Percy – you bloody stupid animal. Percy!" A bedraggled girl with wet curls, wearing a dark swimsuit and a towel around her neck, came running up to him.

"Have you seen Percy? My sheepdog? I've lost him, again. Oh God, there he is near the edge of the cliff!"

Frank lunged towards the dog, scrambling to grab him as he bolted in the opposite direction. Percy was scuttling over the edge and Frank was dragged along on his knees as the girl ran towards them, tripped, and fell on to him as she tried to grab Percy's collar.

"And that was the beginning of a beautiful relationship. See, if I was too busy doing something else and not just viewing the water, maybe I would have missed my opportunity to meet your mother."

It always struck Lily as odd that her dad thought it was so great to meet that way. It sounded like a disaster to her. Her mum, on the other hand, had a different version.

"I was wandering around the coastline, quite high up, on a beautiful day, when for no apparent reason Percy took off. We'd been swimming earlier, and I was in no mood for running. But run I did because the edge of the cliff was close and I loved Percy, as naughty as he was. I was calling his name and panicking, when I thought I saw his dark tail go scurrying in the undergrowth.

I ran through the bushes and there was this handsome young man, sitting with his lunch and drink-bottle splayed everywhere, smiling at me. I felt like an idiot. I was yelling and talking rapid-fire and there was Percy launching over the edge of the cliff. Your dad jumps up to grab him, I lunge to get Percy, lose my footing, and fall on top of this stranger. How embarrassing is that?"

Her mum and dad would belly-laugh as if they were reliving this story every time they retold it.

Later, the wind picked up and the sea chill filled the air, and they reluctantly packed up and left. Once home, de-sanded and warm, Frank lit the wood-fired barbecue ready for his favourite meal of chops for dinner whilst The Eagles' *Take It Easy* wafted through the house and yard.

As he took a beer from the fridge, tea towel over his shoulder and tongs in his hand, he said, "Life doesn't get any better than this." He said this to no one in particular, James Taylor's *How Sweet it is to be Loved by You* on the stereo as the flywire screen banged.

That was the last family day Lily could remember. It was also one of her happiest.

TWO

Lily's dad was excited when he accepted the promotion to Spray Point. Meredith was so happy for him. Lily was nervous about having to change schools – not that she was happy at Cremorne High, but at least she knew the place. They'd lived in the city, but now they were a four-hour drive from there, at Spray Point. They went to an orientation day at the end of the fourth term. Lily was smiling at all the kids she saw as the principal took her and her parents around the senior school. No one smiled back except a tall boy with olive skin and silky, dark wavy hair.

Lily said, "Hi. I'm Lily and I'm starting here next year in Form Four."

"Good. I'm starting Form Four next year too. See ya then." He waved to her as he headed for class.

Three weeks after her dad died, Lily started Form Four at Spray Point Secondary College. She had begun the summer holidays with Mum, Dad and Bessie, their trusty golden retriever. She started the school year with Meredith, her grandmother Nini, and Bessie.

The walk to school should have taken twenty minutes along Shearwater Road. It took Lily thirty-five minutes, more like a trudge, a motion akin to trekking though minestrone, disentangling the residue to move forward. Her resolve evaporated. Survival kicked in. Keep your head down, do not make eye contact, shut up in class, speak to no one in the playground and just get through the day. She had started the term hopeful of making friends. She came to understand that Spray Point Secondary was not the place to do that. Do not look scared and never, ever, find yourself alone and out of sight.

It was a wet February day with a sultry, stormy sky. At lunchtime, finding shelter was like winning Tattslotto. Lily tiptoed around aimlessly. No point loitering in the school doorways for shelter; the yard teacher would sharply usher you on. On to where? That was the student's problem. Lily wrapped her arms around herself and tried to hop from tree canopy to tree canopy.

"Where do you think we should shelter, Mr Lightfoot?" asked Nastacia Smythton.

"Find a tree."

"Looks like they're all taken."

"Not my problem. You're young and a little bit of water won't kill you." Mr Lightfoot, in his neck-to-knee clear plastic raincoat and huge blue umbrella, walked on unperturbed.

Nastacia and her cronies squealed as they ran to the only empty canopy at the end of the yard. A deluge dropped from the soaking branches and the shrieks from the group were unbearable.

Lily thought that if you don't get killed at school, you're doing okay. Physically, you may survive, but not to be crushed mentally was quite an achievement. She wanted to ask her dad's advice on that one. She trudged on. *If only I could give that moron a piece of my mind.*

Better not, Mum always said, *Play the game Lily. Play the game. On the outside you can look as though you agree with whatever ignorance they throw at you but, on the inside, you can really tell them what you think.*

Dad would laugh hard. *Never get your insides confused with your outsides, or you might turn yourself inside out! We love you and that's all that matters.*

It *was* all that mattered, until he was gone.

THREE

The air was listless; there was no sea breeze. It was as if the weather itself was exhausted. The heat wave engulfed Spray Point. The dawn's tendrils were merciless. The birds were limp and languid, their chirps diluted and pathetic. Lily felt aimless, heavy and drained. She lay damp and overheated in bed, delirious from sleep deprivation and tears. Her eyelids slowly prized open, the familiar tautness in her stomach morphed with the ironclad headache that consumed her, and she knew it was true. She'd been dreaming of when she was four and saw all these amazing magic characters dancing across her window and waving and laughing and all for her. She sat up in bed as their tinseled shoes with golden bells, flower wreaths on their heads, brightly beaded vests and skirts spun, whirled, and dazzled. She heard beautiful, fluted dancing music coming from outside the window.

Lily called to her dad and told him what she could see. He sat next to her and said, *Tell me everything you see, darling.*

She told him in the greatest detail.

He said, *Well, isn't that something? You are very special, Lily. Always look for the magic. It's there, we just need to look.*

Lily used to look for the magic in life. Not anymore.

Her dad had only infrequently complained of a sore back and stomach. Her mum, Meredith, thought he'd strained himself in the garden. She'd told him to go to the doctor. He refused. *It's no big deal. Docs just inflate things. This'll right itself soon.* Except it didn't. Over the months it intensified, until Meredith insisted that he get in the car.

She rang from the hospital. "Dad's been admitted, darling.

The doctor's running a few tests. Nothing to worry about. Keep Bessie inside with you. I'll be home soon."

Except there was everything in the world to worry about. Their whole world was about to implode.

The next day, Lily's nana, Enid (*Nini* to Lily), arrived with a little suitcase. The phone broke the heavy silence and Lily raced to answer it. She could not make out who it was. Her mother's voice switched from a dying animal's wail to spurts of incoherent words and, finally, descended into guttural sobs. Nini gently took the phone – until they both understood. Enid's voice soft and tender, "Oh, my darling girl, oh my darling, I'm so sorry. Oh darling…"

That was all Lily remembered. They collapsed onto the floor and stayed in a hugging, rocking motion until it was dark. Bessie, too, started to wail. She came and placed her paws across the bodily heap.

That night, Lily and Nini slept in the same bed or, rather, they lay in the same bed. As the black sky lightened, they fell into a fitful sleep. When they awoke, Meredith's door was closed. Lily knocked a few times and when there was no answer she went in. Meredith kept her back to Lily as she knelt, weeping, by the side of her parents' big bed. She stroked her mother's back for hours. Eventually, Nini came in, kissed Meredith on the top of her matted hair and took Lily's hand to leave.

On the day of the funeral, Lily's clothes were lain out for her. Nini had washed and ironed her navy gingham dress with the white sailor's collar: the one her father bought with her for her fifteenth birthday. That was in December, when he said they'd go into town for lunch and buy her a dress for her birthday. Everything about that day was bright. They had driven to

Melbourne early. They had walked around the Botanical Gardens, and Frank had regaled her with tales of all his pranks as a teenager.

"Wow, Dad, I reckon you were what they would've then called a tearaway."

Her dad had laughed. "Yeah, I certainly wanted to tear away from those brothers – that's for sure. Some of them were vindictive bastards. Old Brother Mack was a good one, though. Fair to say, Lily, I've always enjoyed a healthy dose of disrespect. And a bloody good sense of humour. Thank God for that!"

Afterwards, they went to the Myer food hall for lunch, found the Miss Shop and, with the help of a friendly assistant, found the dress. Her dad had said, "You look beautiful, Lily-pily. A dress fit for a princess."

They had finished off at the Block Arcade chocolate house for afternoon tea.

But today, her beautiful birthday dress was a funeral dress. She bitterly thought her English teacher would say that was a good example of irony. Her black patent leather shoes were glaring up at her, shiny as mirrors, and her pristine white socks seemed to be mocking her. All she had to do was shower and dress. It took her all morning. Her body was not willing to move; it didn't have the energy. It felt wrong – disloyal to be in her best clothes, the ones her dad bought her, when all she wanted to do was curl up in bed and never go outside again.

As they entered the stuffy church, there was already a sea of mourners, dressed in their solemn funeral attire. Lily noticed some distant relatives, a couple of her parents' friends, but most of the congregation she didn't recognise. Her eyes drifted over the mourners until they settled on the worn timber path beneath their feet. People who'd gone to school with her dad, played sport with him, worked with him, some family, and friends and, of course, *the local professional funeral goers,* as he liked to call them.

Years later, Meredith told her: "There wasn't a soul from Cremorne or beyond that knew Frank who wasn't at his funeral. Shows what people thought of him. Doesn't make the day any easier, but it's a mark of respect for such a wonderful man."

Old Saint Jude's Church was packed. Lily thought of her dad chatting to her, the night after she received her Confirmation sacrament.

"Lily, you can believe or not. I'll never ram religion down your throat. This is something for you to work out as you grow older. Either way, it doesn't make you a better or a worse person. Only what's in your own heart and how you treat others does that."

As he kissed her cheek goodnight, he said, "Don't be conned that you can only speak to the Almighty in a church – that, I know for sure, isn't true. I speak to the old boy whenever I bloody well want to. Mum's only doing this to please Nini, 'cause Nini thinks religion gives you an entry into heaven. But I also know, when you're very, very, very old, you'll have an express pass in because you're beautiful and full of goodness."

Frank never went to church unless he had to. Meredith took Lily to receive her sacraments. He said that, for him, church brought back bad memories from his youth when he was a boarder. He was usually jovial and ready to talk about anything; however, he was silent on this subject. Only to say, *No child of mine will ever go to boarding school.* Lily never found out why. Meredith said he wouldn't discuss it with her, only saying, *Some things are better left unsaid.* Nini said she didn't know why either.

Mum eventually agreed with Nini that the local church was the most practical place to hold the funeral. Nini told them she was relieved that Frank would be receiving his final blessings and that he'd be straight into heaven.

The walk up to the old bluestone entrance was excruciating. It was still morning, but the sun bore down on their heads like a punishment. Lily glanced around momentarily; her throat constricted like a chokehold. She kept her eyes on the asphalt steps until the darkness of the narthex consumed her. Meredith was being held tightly by Nini. Lily dragged behind them. Down the aisle, the organ hymn filled the void. Nini reached around, midway down the aisle, and with her pale, plump arms guided Lily towards her embrace. Nini was now keeping both her daughter and her granddaughter upright. The indecipherable dirge played, and Lily felt they were walking a death march.

Pitying faces stared at them as they inched towards the front empty pew. The centrepiece, the sole reason they were all here, the concealed content of the shining mahogany varnished casket with its shocking silver handles, dominated the end of the aisle. Frank's smiling photo, the one Meredith took of him last Christmas, sat together with his St Kilda Football Club scarf and books – *To Kill a Mockingbird, Australian poetry, Banjo Patterson* – on top of the coffin.

How can my beautiful dad be lying in that box? Lily thought. She averted her eyes to the flaking fresco ceiling with its cherubic babies floating aimlessly around the saints. The service dragged on, aching silence in between prayers, hymns and the eulogy, the priest in his white regalia swishing around as if performing a Shakespearean tragedy. Except this was real life. The end of their lives as they'd known them, interspersed with Meredith's wailing. Lily and Nini cried quietly, their handkerchiefs sodden. Nini held Lily's hand; the heat and sweat stuck them together. Lily did not remember anything that was said.

Apparently, Frank's best mate Gilbert spoke of mateship, football, family, and good times. Lily heard that part and nothing else. *What about the bad times now?* Lily wanted to scream at him. The sanctimonious priest, Father Archibald Demazzoda, scattered incense over the coffin. The dusty, pungent fumes sucked what little oxygen there was left from the church like a vacuum, as the light seeping through the stained-glass windows covered the congregation in a sickly purple hue.

The organist finally lurched into an unbearably morbid hymn. Meredith had to be assisted by Nini and Lily to stand. After Father Demazzoda pranced in front of the coffin, carrying a huge silver crucifix aloft, the pallbearers staggered, tearful, behind him. Nini and Lily supported Meredith's collapsing body down the funneled aisle as onlookers stared, sorrowfully. The organ stopped and Frank's favourite song belted out, *What a Wonderful World* by Louis Armstrong, as the procession left the church.

Lily was outraged. *What a cruel joke. Who in their right minds would play that, today of all days, when today is proof that the world is not wonderful but a tortuous hell-hole?* Lily's anger rose as she fought her way to the fresh air, intent on not speaking to anyone. *I do not believe either, Dad. They can all go and get stuffed. And if that bloody priest comes near me, I'm gunna tell him what a load of crap it is.*

As the unforgiving midday sun seared down upon her, Lily refused to go to the burial, the argument the night before still raw in her mind. Her last word to her mother, *You can't make me go. I won't go. Dad wouldn't make me.* The compromise was that Lily stood outside the cemetery and, when it was over, she left with Nini and Meredith.

The airless parish hall made of tin, security-latticed windows, and white plastic and brown vinyl everything, was unbearably sickly, stale and smelly after the moderate cool of the church. Lily drifted through a throng of *deepest sympathies, how terribly sad,* and *dear, dear girl from* concerned adults. They offered her unwanted hugs, kisses, pats, paper plates of dehydrated food, lukewarm drinks and, after a lap of the hall, the walls started to close in and her aching head felt as if it could explode.

Next thing she knew she was halfway home. Paulo, a boy she barely knew from school, was running behind her, dripping sweat like he'd just had a fully clothed swim. His dark locks were plastered to his face when he called out, "Hey Lily, wait!"

He ran up to her, panting hard, took off his school blazer, caught his breath, and asked if he could walk her home. She didn't answer but he kept walking alongside her. She remembered that everyone in her year level had to attend the funeral. *What for?* she thought. *Doesn't make this any better.*

Once home, he followed her in, made her a cool drink, got her a sandwich, suggested she kick off her shoes. He hosed down Bessie and let her in. That night, Nini asked her how she got home. Lily vaguely remembered Paulo being there. She noticed that Bessie had been let in, had been fed, and lay contentedly next to her on the paisley couch. Her James Taylor cassette, *Fire and Rain,* was on. When she woke up, *You've Got a Friend* was playing. Paulo's presence had such a dreamlike quality it was as if he hadn't been there at all. But, in time, she came to know that it *was* Paulo.

Meredith lay motionless on the couch, her thin pink petticoat stuck to her body like plastic wrap. Nini placed the fan nearest to Meredith, then silently placed sandwiches and tea on the coffee table between them. But nothing was touched. Silence consumed their home; only the whirr of the fan and Bessie's breathing broke the stillness. Nini stroked Lily's hair. That night, she suggested that Lily do some writing. Lily went to the back step with the diary her grandmother had given her and wrote poetry. Her poems were sad and strange, as if from another world. It felt as though her heart were a purse and she'd emptied the contents onto the page.

The days and nights after the funeral were a blur. Nini moved around, cooking, washing, answering the phone, and taking food deliveries from the neighbours. Most people did not come in. They were not invited. When the phone rang, or the doorbell sounded, Meredith went to her bedroom and firmly closed the door. Lily often stared at this door, but less and less often did she try to go in. Meredith assumed a ghost-like quality about her. She hardly ate, she hardly spoke, and she drifted as if not connected to where she found herself. Lily kept to herself and became withdrawn. Her only comfort came from Nini's constancy and soft, frequent hugs. And, of course, ever-faithful Bessie.

Then, one day, Nini took the train home. She rang them several times a day. Six weeks later, she sold her house and moved in with them. Permanently.

In Lily's mind, the deep sadness, fear, and uncertainty had culminated in: *What now? How will I survive without Dad?* Some days, she had trouble breathing. Especially if she woke up in the night.

Your troubles are much worse in the night, Lily-pily. Remember that, and you can deal with them better in the morning.

Not this time, Dad. Her chest was like a vault – heavy and locked. Lily took to lying across the back porch swing and watching the clouds for hours. Sometimes she fell asleep, other times her happiest memories with her dad ran like a movie reel. Christmas day last year, with Frank singing and belting out at the top of his lungs, *That's the Way I Like It* by KC and the Sunshine Band and *Stayin' Alive* by the Bee Gees. Frank was goofy and his feet moved out of beat with the music while his arms did this wild cartwheel motion. He threw his dressing gown over his clothes and put his sunglasses on to be the real rockstar deal. He always sang into Lily's hairbrush. He never cared how crazy he seemed; in fact, the crazier and zanier he was, the better. It would've been embarrassing, except she laughed so much she had to join him. He was out of control and Meredith and Nini joined in too.

The best memories were of him reading with her. He worked at the railways, but his passions were reading, and writing in his notebook. Whatever she was reading at school, he'd read with her. If there was a funny part, *Oh God, you've gotta love writers, Lily-pad! Their imaginations are endless.* Safely tucked under his arm, everything was better – happier, safer. Her dad smelt of velvet soap and a manly warmth.

The first couple of years of secondary school were hard and she could tell him. He said he'd go and give them *the old one-two or tweak their noses.* But this would only make Lily laugh, and that was the end of it. She believed he'd always be there to protect her, but he lied. He lied the cruelest lie. *How could he just disappear? He didn't even say goodbye. He should have gone to the doctor; Mum should've made him go earlier. Why did he have to get sick? Why?* She snuggled her head into the cushions and held her chest in a vice grip to stop the chilling pain. She knew what a broken heart was now. No one would sit next to her and read to her, and tuck her in, say goodnight to old Mr Moon – even though she was far too old for that. No one would say, *Good night, my Lily-pily girl.* No one.

Her life and memories had gone from a glorious spectrum of colour to a monochromatic grey. The cards, the flowers, the funeral, the wake, the endless phone calls, the making and serving of tea and cakes, the food parcels left at their door, none of it made it any easier. An elderly relative insisted on calling in, as a couple of the pushy ones did. She expressed her sympathy to Lily, but Lily didn't want to listen to her. She wanted to slap the woman's face. She'd never experienced unexpected rage like it. She turned her back as the aunt was mid-sentence and dashed outside, the door slamming hard behind her. *She doesn't know how I feel. He was my dad. I've lost my everything. She says how sorry she is. That doesn't mean anything. She should just shut her mouth. Her life will go on; mine won't. He's gone and I'll never get over it.*

FOUR

Footprints in the sand stretched haphazardly in front of Lily as she walked. Bessie bolted ahead, her blonde tail swirling like a willy-willy. Some days there were several footprints, some early mornings there were none. Only in the summer were there always plenty. They fascinated Lily. *Who were these people, what did they believe, why were they here?* She traced them with her own feet, trying to get a feel for their stride, how it would be to walk in someone else's shoes, pretend she was inserted into their lives. Had any of them lost someone they loved without warning too?

She thought back to the night Meredith told her about losing her own father. They sat together in Lily's bed while Meredith stroked her hair. She told how devastated she was to lose her dad suddenly, and how angry she was. She was crying, telling Lily how mean she was to Nini, but that she couldn't help it. She was heartbroken and needed someone to blame. She sat with Lily and cuddled her, telling her that a broken heart has a mind of its own. Especially if it is sudden. Then she kissed her goodnight and said, *At least that's something you'll never have to go through.* Another shot of rage pierced Lily's heart like a lightning rod. Even though Meredith hadn't known that she was lying, the fact remained. Everything Lily thought about life and her life wasn't true. She wasn't safe. Her world wasn't secure. But that was then when they were close, and affection and long chats were part of their everyday.

Lily thought, even if she did have warning, her father's death would've been devastating, but at least she could've said goodbye.

Her dad had this thing about not leaving the house without saying goodbye, which she mostly adhered to; and never going to bed on an argument, which she wished she did. He said that when he was young, he'd had a mate, Brian, whose mother was strict, so he often argued with her. To avoid a confrontation one Saturday afternoon, he slipped away to hang out with Frank and his mates at the beach. That evening, while she was out looking for him, Brian's mother drove through an intersection and was t-boned by another driver. She died at the scene, but no one could find Brian. The first he knew about it was later that night when a neighbour tracked him down. Frank reckoned the poor fellow never forgave himself.

FIVE

It was a mild afternoon with intermittent sunshine, a soft breeze filling the zone between work and rest. Lily walked along Tea Tree Road to Point Boulevard and all the way to Spray Point Cemetery. It was in the furthest corner of the town, nestled between the ocean and the tip of the point, directly behind the lighthouse. The lighthouse was derelict, defunct and decaying. It weathered the worst of the storms, faced full frontal into the Great Southern Ocean, and was a reference for all the Spray Point townspeople.

Today, the surf whimpered behind the scrub and the protection of the dunes. Birds flitted in and out of the Tea Tree bushes. Lily tiptoed past the dedications, the dates, the name, the tombstones, the epitaphs, the graves under the casuarinas, until she found her dad's, fifth row down, half-way along on the right-hand side of the cemetery, the white marble tombstone inscribed: *In loving memory of Francis Arthur Mango, 28. 1. 1934 – 7. 1. 1976, Beloved husband of Meredith and devoted father of Lily. May the words flow freely darling and the music play, until the sun rises, and we meet again. Rest Peacefully*

She walked lightly; her feet hardly made a sound on the gravel path amongst the hardened grass. She was silent as if the world had stopped, as if she'd taken a deep inhalation and held it and the earth had too. She read other epitaphs – *In loving memory of my dear husband; my dearest wife; our dearest father; my beloved sister; my little brother* – until they blurred into one. Meredith told Lily that her father had the best position because it caught the afternoon sun; he faced the ocean and could view the beach scrub amongst the sand dunes. Lily wondered why this mattered when you were dead but thought maybe it made Meredith feel better. *Rest in peace* was on many tombstones, which made Lily question whether life had been peaceful for most.

The names of the deceased floated across her eyes. She didn't remember many names, but she did picture what some of them loved to do in their lives: *gardening, socialising, golfing, fishing, sailing, flying.* Her dad loved to read, write, and listen to music. He got to write his own story in the end, but not his own ending. Lily never thought he could die; never thought he could leave them without warning. A magpie came swooping into view, hovering before it landed behind Lily on a silver cross etched into a tombstone. It stayed there, turned its head to the side and watched her leave. Once she reached the large black iron gates, she saw it soar way out towards the Great Southern Ocean.

As she trudged towards the exit, she passed a tiny ancient grave with a crumbling stone border. She could only make out some of the writing: *Beloved one may sleep take you in its arms, until you soar with the angels our darling child. Bertram Clive Embrenderich aged 5 years old. Forever loved.* Lily had never considered young children passing away. From then on, whenever she visited her dad's grave, she also paid her respects to the long-lost little Bertram.

That night after her first visit to her father's grave, Lily asked, "If there is a God, why is he so cruel?"

Meredith placed her cutlery together across her unfinished chop and mashed potatoes.

Nini looked to Meredith and after a while said, "Cruel, Lily? Hmm, I don't think God means to be cruel, even though sometimes it feels that way. I think it's more that death is a natural part of life. It is one of the few certainties in life. If you are lucky enough to be born, one day you will die." Nini ate another mouthful of her meal.

"That doesn't mean he's not cruel, Nini." Lily said.

Nini smiled and said, "I know that losing someone you love feels cruel. There's nothing harder in life than to lose someone you love." She leaned across and squeezed Lily's hand. She watched dolefully as Lily left her unfinished meal and went to her room.

Meredith got up and slammed her plate into the sink. "She's right, Mum. God, religion, it's all a sham. You have faith – God knows it's been challenged – but I don't. Frank's gone and that should never have happened. Never!" She shouted, "He had everything to live for."

Meredith returned to the table, snatched up more plates and attacked the sink with them. Lily heard the sound of china breaking.

Nini nodded her head slowly and got up to join Meredith. As the water sloshed around the sink, she said, "I know, darling. He shouldn't have been taken so young. Nor your dad. I have faith because it got me through. I understand that's no comfort to you." Nini put her arm around her daughter's slumped back. "I'm so sorry for you, and Lily. I feel your pain deeply, my love. It's a terrible loss. The only thing I can say is, it takes time. The pain doesn't go away but, in time, it eases." Nini patted Meredith's back. "If I could do anything to change it, I would."

Meredith turned and looked at her mother. "But you can't," she said wearily as she staggered to her room, wrapping her arms around herself. "Nobody can," she added, silently disappearing behind her closed door.

In the weeks and months that followed, Nini started to open the curtains and windows. She sometimes answered the front door. She played music on the wireless. Trying to entice Lily and Meredith to eat, she roasted meat and vegetables, fried onions and bacon, let the waft of sponges or scones fill the house to greet them when they'd return. In time, it worked. Little by little, she'd take small plates of treats to them in their rooms, or to the porch, or join them at the kitchen table. Always, always, with the obligatory pot of tea. Slowly, it began to feel like home again for Lily. Before Nini had come to live with them, it had felt as if she and Meredith were floating aimlessly in a vacuum. Nini was their safe harbour.

One lifeless grey afternoon, Lily joined Nini on the back porch. Bessie snuggled her head into Lily's lap. Nini poured the tea as Lily cut a wedge of strawberry sponge oozing with cream. At the back of the yard, between the apricot and lemon trees, two rosellas darted in and out as if dive-bombing each other, their shrieking squeals interspersed by the rustling leaves.

"Have you ever been sad like mum and me, Nini?" Lily's face flushed from the hot tea.

"Oh, yes, darling, I have. I've been so sad I couldn't get out of bed. When your pa died suddenly all those years ago, I was a relatively young woman. It was his ticker, bad hearts run in his family. Poor Alf. I was sad to the point I started to question if there was any point." Nini gazed at the pale sky.

"What helped you get better, Nini? What helped you see the point?" Lily placed her plate down gently and held Bessie close.

Nini took her time and looked at Lily. "Time, my darling Lily. Only time. In time, the harsh, unbearable edges of our pain soften. They never go away, for that is the measure of our love. They stay as a part of us, but eventually we adjust and we carry that pain, loss and grief with us more easily." Nini poured more tea.

"Nini, will I ever get better? I mean, I'm so angry now. Inside my heart I'm a raging fire that could burn me up. I want to smash something, someone, I don't even know what I want, but underneath it all I'm furious. All the time." Lily's translucent blue eyes glistened.

"Of course, you are. I know that feeling. Lily, I believe your dad has passed from this life into the next. That he's not here as he used to be, but he's not gone just the same. The spirit never dies. It comes to you in its own way, in its own time. Alf has come to me in dreams, in visions, in clouds, in the sky and in birds. And, my darling, it's good to have faith. In times of need, He's good to have on your side." Nini patted Lily's knee.

The next afternoon, Lily walked to the lighthouse. Since Frank had passed away, she found herself drawn to this old relic more and more. She sat on the northern side, where its white walls were grasping the last rays of warmth. She closed her eyes, crossed her arms, and thought of Nini sitting on the back porch night after night, listening to the birdsong. She had once told Lily, *If you're not mesmerised by nature, you're not looking or listening. Where does the breeze come from? Why does each cove, each beach, smell different? How can the sky keep changing as we're looking at it? Do birds think?* Many afternoons they'd sit and ponder these questions.

"Nini, why can't God be a girl?" Lily had asked her grandmother the day before.

"Well, now, that's interesting. Maybe He is. I mean, maybe *She* is. Why not? I've just never considered it." Nini drained her tea.

"You've got a wonderful, curious mind, Lily. Keep asking the big questions. It's people like you who make people like me use our brains. I love the way your mind works." And she padded off to the kitchen humming the Al Bowley song, *I'll Be Loving You Always.*

SIX

Lily was drawn to the sea. Often, she'd find herself there, not knowing how she arrived or when she'd decided to come. Perched up on the highest crest and folded into herself against the whipping wind, she imagined being way out at sea on a yacht, screaming, with no place to land. In that vision she was the wind, the tide, and the heaving heart of the ocean. With her senses tingling, the light would tantalisingly dance across the water, luring her along. She dreamt of a place not of this world, another world just out of her reach but there, nonetheless. The ocean, her heartbeat floating freely over the rise and fall of the sea.

A squawking seabird's incessant call broke her reverie and the pain punched her gut. With her eyes still closed, she remembered Frank was gone. She sat with her pierced heart until the dimness forecast it was time to go.

Wandering along the solitary windswept ocean, her arms firmly dug into her coat pockets, she tried in vain to push away a recurring dream. In it, she was running down to the surf, ready to plunge in, and the closer she came, the further the sea receded until it became a black, roaring shadow obliterating the sun and leaving a gargantuan wave racing towards her. There was no time to turn and run, and as much as she tried with all her might, she could gather no traction. She'd be cowering in the wet sand as the lip of the peeling mountain started to curl. She'd wake up screaming, sweating and shaking.

Meredith would run in. "Lily, Lily, it's only a dream. There, there, love."

Lily would rest in her arms thinking, if only that were true.

At night, if she couldn't sleep, she would drop back inside the hum of the ocean and the wind would lull her rhythmically into deep slumber. The sea and the freedom of it. Just a run, a swim, a walk away. Beauty demanded her attention; she never let it down. No matter what she was engaged in, she would take a moment to drink it in. The sweet reflection of what had been would linger in her mind. She felt richer for it. It helped to soften the brutal moments at school.

School was not for the timid. School was not for the meek. School was definitely not for the fearful. Lily steeled herself for another day, determined to appear brave, unaffected by their snide remarks and deliberate exclusion. Even when she was crying on the inside, she would try to smile on the outside. Sometimes she'd laugh back at them. It was her protective layer, her only form of defence, and she wore it like a cloak every day as she walked through those steely iron gates.

She walked to school the usual route as the salt breeze caught in her throat. She desperately wanted to turn and run to the open arms of the bay. But, instead, she thrust her hands deeper into her worn maroon blazer and strode towards the overbearing concrete buildings. The harshness of those walls prickled her skin, her heart felt heavy, and her stomach churned as she entered the gates. The Latin alma mater, which she could not say, meant *Through Learning Thou Shall Grow.* She didn't believe it. Not when learning was so hard and the breaks between even harder. It was endurance, as her mother told her. School did not suit everyone but, unfortunately, she had no choice. The battle began again, another exhausting day to survive. The sickly cream walls chilled her, and the screech of the incessant bell jarred her into reality.

In the evenings, Lily shuffled around in her green dressing gown. It was too small for her, but it was a precious gift from Nini when she turned twelve, so she kept wearing it. When she was nine, Nini took her into town for lunch. While they were there, Nini asked Lily if she needed anything. Lily took a while to answer and, after much deliberation, said, *I would like a dressing gown*. After lunch in the store's massive cafeteria, they went on their expedition to search for the perfect gown. Her nan, being a practical woman, wanted one that Lily could grow into. In other words, she wanted a long one, which she could take up now and then each year let down an inch or two. This is exactly the one Lily wore daily nearly four years later, replete with the obvious stitch-lines from having been let down again and again. The dressing gown, that is – never the person. Little could Lily know that it was to become her daily attire in years to come. When Nini had come to live with them, she had not been pleased to see Lily getting into her dressing gown earlier and earlier each afternoon. Nor did she like the fact that Lily would wrap her arms around herself, keep her head down, and wander morosely through their small rooms.

"Lily come and sit with me and have a chat."

Nini expertly poured the tea. Once the tea and homemade rock cakes were strategically placed, she asked, "How is everything, Lily?"

"School?" Lily looked into her mug, spinning it around on the table.

"Well, yes, school, friends, study, teachers..."

"Pretty lousy," Lily answered as she kept spinning the cup. "I mean, school would be bearable if it wasn't for the kids. Most of the teachers are okay, one hates me. Study I'm doing alright." She looked up at Nini's soft crinkled face.

"So, let's break it down. It's the kids that are causing you the most grief? Which kids?"

"Yep. There's the mean, pretty group; there's the sporty, bossy group; and then there's the dumb boys who like to put girls down in general to make them feel not so dumb. I'm over them all. I try to ignore them and see it as their problem, like you tell me," she said, still looking down at her cup, "but it's... hard." Lily watched as the teardrops fell into her teacup. She wiped her eyes with her sleeve.

Nini took her hands and said, "I'm sorry, love. Meanness is hard to take. I wish I could do something to make it stop. Is there something you'd like me to do? Could I talk to your year-level teacher?"

"No, Nini. That'd make it worse. I have to tough it out. Anyway, they're worse to Paulo. He's gentle and they give it to him non-stop. I stepped in for him the other day. He was happy. He's such a good guy."

"Good on you, darling. I bet he'd do the same for you if you needed it."

"Yeah, I reckon he would."

"Promise me you'll tell me if it gets too much? I'm always here and we stick together – thick and thin." Nini took both of Lily's hands in hers.

"Promise – thick and thin."

"Do you think it would be good for us to go for a little walk together?"

"Sure." Lily laughed, looked down at her fluffy slippers and dressing gown and went to change. She smiled to herself as she went to put on her walking shoes. Nini called them her strollers, as she didn't walk these days, she strolled.

SEVEN

School is a punishment for something you don't remember doing. Day after dreary day. It is a highly effective punishment because it is so constant. Lily asked herself, *I know it won't be a good day, but how bad will it be? Please don't make it as bad as yesterday. Head down, head up, look straight ahead, look sideways, sit still, speak up, don't say anything, answer the question, don't make eye contact, stare straight back at them, hold their stare, don't you stare at me young lady, pull your socks up, your hair looks unkempt, this homework is not good enough, pay attention, I don't like your attitude, you lack originality, concentration, imagination, who do you think you are, don't be impudent with me, answer me when I speak to you, sit down, stand up, look at me when I speak to you, get moving, hurry up, don't be lazy, ignorant, dull... The rules for inside and the rules for outside, keep to yourself, if they surround you – run, run fast, if they trip you up remember to put your hands out, eat with your back against a wall to see them coming, when you see them get up, move fast, never walk out of sight, never go behind the shelter shed, never go to the toilet block, or behind the science department alone.*

Each morning, Lily kept her gaze down, so much so that she often tripped over her own feet or walked into another student. One morning, as she dragged herself with her laden bag down the squeaky corridor towards Room 4B, she heard Stacey Middendorp lording it over her friends. *I don't intend to do well this year; I intend to excel.*

Lily thought Stacey was a stuck-up prig. What a big-noter. She had the urge to whack her, deliciously satisfying impulses that she barely contained.

By the time Meredith came home from work, Lily was ready to unleash. "Oh my God, Mum and Nini, you're not going to believe what stuck-up Stacey did today. Old Mr Bisogni was so annoying! He's an old fart, plus he's bloody deaf. Then Mrs Melviney gave out all this homework, which I don't understand, and Felix Mentenberry had a fight at recess and big Boris Yepping belted him one for falling on his food. God, boys can be stupid. Look sideways and they want to punch each other's lights out. Speaking of which, I nearly did. Well, not really, but I wanted to. Stacey is the most stuck-up snob I've ever met. She's literally in love with herself. She plays with her long golden locks when she's speaking. You know, like she rolls her plaits over her hands like she's coiling a snake." Lily imitated her with her own hair. "She's a selfish snake and she brags about herself non-stop. She always looks me up and down and then frowns as if my presence offends her. Today she's lecturing her group of *so-called friends* and saying how she intends to excel. Oh, I wanted to whack her one so badly. Just to see her surprise and shut up that big fat flap-trap of hers."

Lily paused for breath.

"Well, my darling heart, you've had quite a day," Nini said, and placed her arm around Lily's shoulder. "School is not for the faint-hearted, that's for sure. I know this move has been an adjustment for you. I'm sure it'll get better in time. Let's face it, most of us don't like school."

Meredith sipped her tea as she leant on the kitchen bench, listening, and said, "You know, I wouldn't be a nurse today if it hadn't been for Nini's encouragement. When I matriculated, I wanted to throw study in. I was sick to death of regimented learning. I wanted to be free. Imagine that – no prospects, no career, and no good income. Lily, you just have to endure it. I know it's hard, but it'll be worth it in the end."

"Well, the bloody end can't come quickly enough." Lily went to her room and slammed the door.

The second-best thing to door slamming was running with Bessie to the beach. She'd bolt out the back door and Bessie would charge after her. There, they'd run hard until they had nothing left. Then the anger would subside, and Lily would walk up the sand dunes, calmer, and wind her way down the dusty road home.

That was before she and Paulo Rotondo became the firmest of friends.

EIGHT

The sea mist had settled like a veil across a woman's face. Lily could not clearly make out the boats bobbing in the bay. The misty rain came sideways in sheets. She did not bring a raincoat and the salty dampness gathered around her mouth. The sky was a pallid grey, an indistinguishable line between the sea and sky. She walked the known pathways, only seeing several feet in front of her. Like the day that lay ahead, she could only concentrate on one step at a time.

The thrum of the ocean, present and pleading, filled her senses like a trusty piece of machinery humming and hovering, calling her. The familiar smell was acrid and biting yet brought her no comfort today. With the heft of her school bag, she felt the heaviness of autumn. The light was softer, and the air was thicker. A tightness took hold of her chest as she laboured through the gates and into the schoolyard. There, they were huddled in their nasty little groups, gossiping, sniping, sneering, and ridiculing. She didn't know what they said, but she knew what they meant. She tried to ignore them and walk steadfastly to class, but occasionally she would catch their eye and the meanness of their look weighed down her every step.

At the screech of the recess bell, she grabbed something from her lunchbox and escaped out into the yard. She tiptoed past the usual prissy gangs of girls in their territorial spots, tentatively smiled, which they ignored as they turned to face their leader. Sometimes their circles shrank, like an anemone at the approach of an outsider. She took a deep breath and tried not to care, but her gait, her stance, her expression said otherwise. Exclusion was like an old coat that stuck to your body, it went everywhere with you, irrespective of the weather. It singled you out.

One breezy June day, as she looked for somewhere innocuous in the yard to hide, she ruminated. *Why do they hate me? What have I ever done to them? Why have I become persona non grata across the board? Why will no one be my friend? There must be something wrong with me. I'm just not good enough.* Bewildered tears filled her eyes, and she rubbed them hard with the backs of her hands. The screech of the lunch siren sliced through the wind, and she dragged her feet towards the entrance doorway.

"Hey, Lily." Paulo's soft voice broke her memories of last night's dream.

"Hey, Paulo."

"How you doin'?"

"Good. Yeah, I'm good." She looked at her shoes. He sounded like he was glad to see her. She told herself to smile.

"Oh, good. I'll see ya round."

"Yeah. Yeah, of course."

Paulo looked relaxed. She wished she felt that way too. He beamed a broad-faced smile and she tried to smile back. He wandered on ahead.

"It was good to see you," she yelled clumsily after him. Then regretted it. *How embarrassing,* she thought. *What a dick I am.*

"Yeah. Me too." He turned and waved back. Hmm, maybe he meant it. Maybe.

She hung around the corridor, to catch him after school, but she'd missed him. She fought her way through the usual scurry of kids screaming out banalities. None of which involved her. Loaded bag on her back like a pack horse, she trudged the slow march home.

"Hey, Lily."

Lily scanned the fleet of buses and cars and saw Paulo waving. He weaved his way laconically across the road to her.

"You wanna go for a walk tonight?"

"Hey. No, I can't – I'm meant to help Nini, my Nana." She chewed her lip, deep in thought. "But maybe I could help her and meet you after?"

"Yeah, no worries. Tell me a time and no sweat, I'll be there." His chestnut eyes sparkled like chocolate gems with gold flecks.

That night, as she strolled to their meeting point at the end of her street, a tiny bluebird caught her attention. It landed on a tree stump, looked away, looked over her shoulder, and then, finally, directly at her. After a few seconds, it darted off as if it had never been there, but its presence lingered long after it had disappeared.

Lily and Paulo wandered to the beach. They talked and complained about the kids at school and the meanest teachers and how they hated school and the funniest things that happened. They left the beach at dusk when the chill was biting. The crashing waves quietened, and the moist sea air wafted in drifts. There was no awkward silence. No hunting for things to say. They told each other they'd do this again.

At home, Nini asked how her walk went.

"Well, Nini, maybe I've made a friend."

"Good for you, darling. All good things come in time."

"Took a bloody long time. Anyway, I was down today, but after talking with him, I realise he's going through a lot of crap at school too. It's not just me."

"As long as you've got one friend Lily, that's all you really need. Other friends will follow, but you do need one." Nini tossed the vegetables in the oven and a whoosh of steam escaped. "Is he a kind person?"

"Yep. He looked after me after Dad's funeral."

'Oh, yes, of course."

"I think he sensed I was having a tough day. I reckon that's why he asked me for a walk."

"Well, they're all the credentials you need in a friend. Everything else is just window dressing." She gave the roast potatoes a good shake. "I look forward to meeting him."

"Yeah, you'll really like him, Nini." She gave Enid a big hug and breathed in her rose water spray.

NINE

After Lily's father died, Lily started to dream of the ocean. In some of these dreams she'd be frolicking with him in translucent, calm water. Slowly, steadily, stealthily, the waves would lift like blue whales rising to their peak, until she'd look back and her dad would be gone. She would dive down to the gritty ocean bed, hanging on with her fingernails bleeding, oxygen deprived as the explosion of water rumbled above. Exhausted, breathless and broken from her fruitless search, she'd eventually find herself washed ashore like discarded kelp. *I knew you would make it.* Unmistakably her dad's voice. *I always knew.*

Many mornings she'd fling herself out the door, down the well-worn track with Bessie, and find herself at the beach. Initially, she'd run to the end of the cove. Gasping and panting, she'd hold on to the undulated rocky outcrop until she regained her breath before returning homeward. Over weeks and months, she graduated to climbing to the furthest point on Durga Rock. First, she had to climb the sharp ridge she called the 'tiger's back' that led there. And then she screamed her father's name over and over to the depths of the cascading sea.

One afternoon, the rhythm of the waves held her attention as if in a trance – melodic and repetitive, *Come, come Lily. Come to me.* Transfixed, she stripped to her underwear and dived in. The ocean's heartbeat held her, propelled and numbed her frozen heart. Gradually, the pain of her grief seemed to melt slightly. She swayed and bobbed with each unfurling wave. Calmer now, she swam steadily until she was at the shore.

From that day onwards, she swam a few days per week –

irrespective of the weather, and often in spite of it. The icy shards pinpricked her body like electric shocks, the force of the waves pummeled her. *If you're here, Dad, I want to be where you are.* With each new wave crashing unforgivingly into her, she thought, *I can do this.*

On other days, she just sat still on Durga. The climb along the tiger's back was jagged, unstable sandstone. Once seated, with the wild spray in her face, she felt part of something greater than herself – something majestic and true. Many times, she'd be howling her sadness and rage to the wind, the water, or the sky, as a flock of ibis, pelicans and other sea birds would float and swirl above the breaking waves. The cloud-filled sky would suddenly lift, and a blazing streak of silver light would beam towards her; or the sunset would linger, a bedazzling burnt orange, for the longest time. On other days, dolphins would frolic and play. They would surf right up to where the wave was breaking just past the rock. She watched their shiny, sleek bodies thrust themselves along wave after wave. It was as if the pod was putting on a show solely for her.

During these times the heaviness lifted, and she knew that she was not alone, that her dad was nearby watching over her. Somehow, whenever she was at the beach, she was not alone.

TEN

Lily woke up early with the chorusing magpies outside her window. Insistent, Bessie was panting and scratching at her door. Within minutes, they were marching up the dusty bush track, the sweet wetness of the night filling the sea laced air. The morning chill was bracing, even though the sky promised a warm day. Once they reached the top of the rise, Lily's breath was heavy. Bessie bolted ahead, tail spinning in ecstasy. Lily's pale face was prickled by the finest needles, which left her cheeks rosy and made her fully awake. The coastal scrub was all rolling greens and browns hugging the undulating dunes. Bessie flew straight into the frothy edge of the waves. The darkness of the sand, still wet in the shadow of the dunes, contrasted with the brilliant sunlight dancing leisurely across the waves. The briny air had hints of warmth as she ran to the point, with Bessie charging to catch her.

Once there, Lily threw her arms out wide and yelled, *Please make today better than yesterday*! And that's what she believed, and she didn't know why. She just knew that everything always seemed better at the beach.

When she returned, no one mentioned that she'd been gone. She got away with flying out the door because Meredith often wasn't there, and even when she was there, she wasn't fully there. The house was quiet when Lily wasn't home; but it moved, creaked, moaned, and slammed when she was. No matter the noise, her grandmother loved the sounds that Lily made – happy, exasperated, sad – to Enid, they were a reassurance of life. And Enid knew silence. She also knew no one had exuberance like the young.

Enid spent more and more time with Lily. She felt close to her. Over time they shared their sorrow. Lily shared her loneliness, her anger, and her pain. She tried to imagine the pain that Enid had gone through in her life; some of it she understood.

Her grandmother believed that if it saved you mentally, it had to be done – whatever 'it' was. Lily often thought about what her Nini meant by this. *Saving yourself mentally. I want to find out what that means.* She also told Lily, "When you need a life buoy, you'll find one. Life is strange like that."

The more Enid got to know Paulo, the more she liked him. He would often call in and have a chat, a cup of tea, something to eat. Enid thought he was good for Lily and, even though Lily was a capable swimmer, she felt relieved once Paulo started to join her at the beach. Until Paulo made up three, Bessie was the sole lifeguard. Once he told her, as he was running, that he wanted to head towards his future. Lily responded that she was running away from her past. She told Enid, "When I'm swimming, Nini, Dad talks with me. He says, *Don't give up, Lily. You're in pain, but in time it will ease, and the joy will come back. Remember, little one, I'm always with you. Always.* Do you think that could be true, Nini?"

"Of course, Lily. It's very true."

The next week, Lily raced down to the sea and threw herself at the rolling waves. Paulo watched as she swam hard beyond the breakers to where the ocean was flatter. Rising gently, she floated as if lying on grass. As her starfish shape swayed, she watched the sun sneak through the cumulonimbus clouds. In her head, the dreamy lines: *I drift. I float. I'm free.* Over and over this played in her mind. She swam hard to catch a long peeling wave, green and glistening with change. Once inside it, she bounced along, feeling her hair pulled in all directions, until she panted up to her laid-out towel, collapsed and closed her eyes.

I am a piece of seaweed, loose-limbed and laconic.
I move in all directions.
The heartbeat of my home carries me, holds me.
Once in the sand my body is held warm, hugged.
The sun kisses my drying skin,
As the breeze reassures me,
I'm alive.

The sun filtered weakly through the clouds. Intermittent moments of warmth hit their drenched bodies. Paulo did not swim far, often standing at the water's edge as his friend swam a long way out.

One afternoon, a rogue wave loomed up and crashed down over the top of him. That changed Paulo's ideas about trying to swim out beyond the break. When Lily finally came out of the water, she was thrilled to see him wet. Paulo, on the other hand, was not so thrilled. She shared her towel with him, barely drying herself, preferring to put her clothes on top of her wet body, though she didn't know why. Maybe it reminded her that she'd been with her dad again, or maybe the chill reminded her that she was like her dad.

ELEVEN

A sonic ray hit as Lily pulled the doona over her head. Bessie's bark was becoming more agitated, until he wore Nini down and she rewarded his bad behaviour yet again, letting him in. Lily could hear Bessie bound up their linoleum hallway, and in record time the dog was spraying her rancid breath in Lily's face. Just as Bessie was leaping rocket-style onto Lily's head, she surrendered and jumped up. The salty lure enticed her down the gravel road to the narrow winding path like a hooked fish trawled behind a boat. Bessie tore down the path with her tail flailing, sand spraying golden stars in her wake. Lily hastened and free-fell down the sand dune as the sun cast a burnt pink that beamed spectacularly across the water to greet them. Bessie's fawn coat morphed into the beach as she vaulted airborne towards the sea.

Yesterday evaporated in the slipstream behind her submerged body as she thrashed along Driftwood Beach. The swim seemed to wash her new. Its bite pulled her cheeks as taut as freshly picked apples, expanded her lungs, and wiped her mind clean. All the accusations, insinuations and injuries from school were faint memories now. Twenty-four hours ago, who would ever have thought she could feel like this? But, then again, who would ever have thought the unthinkable could happen.

Yesterday, the alarm had screeched as Lily's hand fumbled to flick it away like an unwelcome fly. Nini could be heard padding around in the kitchen, the whistle of the kettle gathering momentum on the stove, competing with the background hum of the radio. Bessie's bark ceased simultaneously with the familiar slam of the flywire door. Today, her bounding was to no avail – Lily had beaten her. As per their usual morning routine, Lily had dragged herself towards the front door as Meredith air-kissed her head on the way to work, and Nini saw Lily off with a kiss and a *Have a good day, darling.* Nowadays, after school, rather than fill Nini in with the usual torrent of complaints and problems, she often said that she was tired and went straight to her room, only reappearing briefly for dinner, where she sat half-heartedly picking at her food while Meredith and especially Nini coaxed her to eat more.

Last night, when she was meant to be at basketball practice, Meredith had asked Lily why she hadn't gone.

"I'm not interested in basketball anymore. I'd prefer to walk with Bessie instead."

"But you can do both. What about team sport and friendship?"

"Mum, when you will get it? Friendship is hard for freaks like me. I'm not going. They think I'm weird."

"Why didn't you tell me? I'm going to speak to the coach. It's her job to ensure everyone has a go and has fun."

"No, you're not going to see her. This is my life, Mum. This is how it is for me. I have to go to school, but anything extra, I'm not doing it." Lily got up and slammed her bedroom door.

School was as predictable as a snake: drama would ensue somewhere, somehow, often at her or Paulo's expense. Lincoln Simon Addlingson and his cool mates lined up and, as she passed, their snide comments engulfed her like toxic fumes. She kept her head down, inspecting her worn runners as if they revealed a hidden escape route, and pressed forward. No eye contact – so much so, that she suffered severe headaches from her permanently sore neck.

Lily kept her answers and opinions to herself in class, only speaking if directly asked by the teacher and, even then, reluctantly. She felt herself disappearing, trying to make herself as small and inconspicuous as possible. This proved difficult, especially when the other kids tried to trip her without warning. This ended when she reached the sanctuary of the classroom, only to suffer the indignation and general disapproval of the teachers. Lily arrived at school later and later. Only Paulo or Mot Wheatleigh arrived later than the bell. Alexa Kaklamanis was on time; punctuality was insisted upon in her family. Mrs Kraveen had no tolerance for tardiness. Little did she know – it took everything Lily had just to leave home in the mornings, let alone arrive at purgatory on time.

Mrs Kraveen was like a glass of whisky. She looked like sweet tea, but one sip and it was flaming fire all the way down. She tolerated Alexa, ignored Paulo, loathed Mot, but now she hated Lily, too. Every day, when she slunk into class, Mrs Kraveen would swivel on her chair like a roulette wheel. Lily routinely disappeared beneath the desk lid to dodge the blowtorch of her searing stare.

Recess and lunchtime were the highlight in the dim tunnel of the school day. Her lunchbox held the comfort of Nini's food and was duly shared with Paulo. His lunches were light on, or nonexistent, depending whether Ronaldo had spent all the weekly budget on booze, which was often the case recently. Paulo would stuff his face with whatever Lily offered.

When Lily had told her this, Nini had exclaimed, "That poor boy! How embarrassing it would be for him to admit there wasn't enough food at home. Breaks my heart." Once she knew, she packed extra so there was plenty for them both.

Yesterday, the usual argy-bargy gathered as Lily approached Form Four Blue's classroom. Once she was framed by the doorway, however, the silence was deafening. The steely stares confronted her, a punch to the stomach, a full body-blow, and the students didn't even need to leave their desks to deliver it. She remembered her dad's advice: *Look them straight in the eye, Lily. They're like dogs, they smell fear. Never let them know you're scared. Stare them down and act strong.* She tried to do that. But her face burnt red and, once at her desk, her sweaty hands shook all the contents of her school bag across the floor.

Mrs Kraveen looked up and stomped several paces towards her.

"What on earth do you think you are you doing, Lily? My, my, you're one of the most disorganised students I've ever taught."

Lily continued to scurry across the floor like a field rat. The room smiled smugly as Mrs K resumed her seat for roll call in her beige and pink suit, her neat maroon bob swinging.

Paulo slunk in with his curls swaying loose where he had tried to hide them in his collar, late as usual, and crept to his desk.

"Paulo, Paulo, Paulo, late again, are we? Glad you were able to drag yourself out of bed before lunchtime to join us," the teacher snarled.

Paulo's soft, sad eyes lowered, and his smooth olive face turned the deepest scarlet. The students nodded. When Mrs Kraveen's head was down, he turned to Lily and mouthed slowly, "I hate that woman."

Lily mouthed back, "So do I."

He stifled a laugh with a fake cough and turned to the front.

At recess, Paulo and Lily resumed their usual position high on the red brick shed wall. Through a delicious mouthful of

Nini's bacon and egg pie, Lily said, "We are at war, Paulo, and it's not a war we started. There's no choice but to fight. I know this goes against your grain, it also goes against mine, but we must defend ourselves." Lily looked hard at her friend's sweet, concerned face. "They can't make this any worse for us. We have to stand up. I'm not scared, Paulo," Lily lied. "Don't you be, either." He stopped eating and looked at her apologetically.

"It's just not me, Lily."

"We can do it, if we do it together," she pleaded.

"Sorry, buddy. I won't fight. I'm a pacifist."

"I don't even know what a pacifist is."

"It's someone who's against war. My dad went to war. He came back a different person. I can't fight. I won't."

Millicent-Mae Munroe was the leader of the girl pack – petite and pretentious but, most of all, malicious. Every command she issued, her band delivered, and every day, as Lily walked past, the class was told to silently stare Lily down. Millicent-Mae had a way of seeming friendly while stabbing you in the back.

Lily knew she had to fight Triple M. As small and delicate as she was, Lily was strong and statuesque. Lily was as kind as Millicent-Mae was mean. She'd met her nemesis.

The next morning as she ate breakfast, Lily ruminated on how to get even. She remembered Nini's advice; there had to be a way. She knew Millicent had a sensitive sense of smell. So much so that she doused herself in vanilla musk daily. Wherever she went, the sickly waft trailed behind her. Her band would put their collective noses in the air and sniff to find their leader.

The game plan came to her when she looked out of her kitchen window to where Bessie had deposited her morning ablutions on the nature strip. Pure joy surged through Lily's veins like a floodtide, and adrenaline propelled her along as she packed her bag with military precision. She was on a mission to sweet revenge.

Once at school, the usual stare down, freeze out and sniggers greeted her. But that day, Millicent's recruits were lined up near the front gate. Today, not only did Lily not feel sick with dread, but she also felt light with anticipation. She moved with purpose and poise straight to her room and Millicent's desk. There, Lily put on her mum's dishwashing gloves, took out Bessie's foul-smelling contribution and smeared it carefully over Millicent's seat. Being a timber chair, the colour blended in exactly. By the time the clamour and chaos of the ensuing herd approached, Lily was concealed in the sanctuary of the toilets, where she deftly disposed of her weapon, washed her hands meticulously, and swiftly returned to class.

Paulo raced in as the last bell drilled and took one look at her. "What's up Lily?" he whispered.

"Nothing's up; something's *on*," she said with a wink.

He shook his head. "You're one crazy cat, Lily Mango."

"You better believe it, my friend."

Millicent-Mae glared as she sauntered past and swung herself onto her seat, her perfume hanging thick in the air. Shortly, she started to fossick frantically, lifting her feet to examine the soles of her shoes, looking in and under her desk, behind her seat, and accusing Bertie Davies of vile bodily actions and emitting fetid, putrid smells.

Mrs Kraveen asked the class what the ruckus was all about.

"Someone has let off the most disgusting smell, Mrs Kraveen. I heard Bertie Davies do it." Millicent stood and pointed her dainty hand towards his face.

"Bertie!" the teacher cried. "I will not tolerate foul behaviour in my class. We are not animals. Remove yourself immediately and come back when you can behave like a human being."

"But I didn't do nothin'. I didn't fart, Mrs Kraveen. She's lying,' he stammered.

"How dare you accuse Millicent of lying! You have detention for that disgraceful comment."

Bertie left, muttering. "That's so unfair. I didn't do nothin'."

As Mrs Kraveen's polished voice punched the air with the roll call, Millicent stamped her feet, and rummaged noisily around her desk.

"Sit down, Millicent!" she said.

"No, Mrs Kraveen, I can't. The smell is still here. I feel nauseated. I think I'm going to vomit."

The students nearest her sniffed the air and there it was, mixed with the lingering perfume but undeniable: a pungent, vile stench lingering around Millicent. They turned their heads to where the air was breathable, holding their noses.

Mrs Kraveen opened the window and stomped over to Millicent's desk.

"For goodness sake, Millicent, sit down, please. There is no smell now, I've opened the window for you..." and with that she convulsed in a coughing attack, took several large steps backwards and tripped on her peach pumps.

Millicent screeched through her tears. "I can't tolerate this disgusting smell any longer."

As she stormed out of class, the back of her pristine dress displayed an enormous brown patch, in line with her bottom. The architrave shook wildly as she slammed the door and bolted from class with her hand covering her mouth. This was met with explosions of uncontrollable laughter throughout the room. In the ensuing mayhem, students rolled on the floor, pounded their desks, or stood laughing, holding their stomachs as tears streamed down their astonished faces.

Mrs Kraveen clapped her clipped hands hard and yelled furiously. "Class! Millicent! Class! Stop this immediately. I'm warning you, there'll be detention for the whole class."

It took a long while for some order to be reinstated.

"I can't smell anything now," Paulo said to the students nearest him. "Maybe it was Millicent who farted? I mean, what else could it be?"

The rest of the class were postulating and saying. "Yeah. Had to be her. It still smells around her desk. She stinks like dogshit."

One of her closest allies, Zarsha, said, "No amount of vanilla musk's ever going to cover that smell."

Later, Paulo said he couldn't believe Lily had come up with that and called her a "magician". She said daydreaming at breakfast and Bessie's daily deposit on the nature strip were the magicians.

After Millicent's classroom meltdown, the frosty receptions ceased. The students had moved on, but they still had it in for Paulo.

On a blustery Friday afternoon, with her stuffed bag over her shoulder, Lily fought her way through the throng of sweat-laden bodies and out into the fresh air. Carried on the intermittent breeze, rap music floated in snippets of jarring chords, indecipherable lyrics, and the aggressive, monotonous tone that Lincoln Smyth-Addison and his gang played constantly. The only other thing Lily ever saw put a smile on LSA's dial was his fastidiously crafted, fragile, massive, iridescent green model airplane. It took pride of place in Mr Romertson's woodwork room.

Without warning, a baying, bloodthirsty crowd was running to the furthest part of the yard. As she approached, the din of "Fight, fight, fight!" reverberated like a tribal beating drum.

She pushed her way to the front where Paulo was on his knees, both arms held protectively across his head, while LSA and his four thug mates circled him like salivating sharks.

"Get up and fight, you fat fag! Get up or we'll drag you up, you lowlife faggot." Lincoln was kicking Paulo, whilst his jeering mates landed the odd kick themselves.

Instinctively, Lily sprinted to Mr Romertson's room and grabbed LSA's airplane. She shoved and elbowed her way into the center of the crowd and screamed, "Stop! Stop, you filthy coward, Lincoln! Stop, you thugs."

Lily kept the airplane above her head, circling towards them. Everything was in slow motion: the chanting ceased, and the stunned perpetrators paused. Lincoln pushed his chest out and stuck his repugnant face in hers.

"Give me my plane, you ugly freak." His mean beady eyes disappeared into his fleshy face as his spittle peppered her with a combination of fish and chips doused in foul breath.

Every insult, slur, slant, rumour, exclusion and taunt they'd received that year culminated in a tsunami of rage within her. Lily felt stronger and fiercer than ever before; the anger she felt was frightening. Her intense eyes bored into his like a nail-gun hitting dry wood and she spat at him. "Oh, I'll give you your precious plane alright, Lincoln. It'll be in a thousand pieces, but I'll give it to you." She sneered at him, shaking the airplane hard.

Paulo stood close behind her.

"Don't you dare, you mad freak, Lily," Lincoln said.

"I'm only going to say this once," she responded. "You piss off now, you pathetic punks, or not only will I smash this" – swirling the model airplane close to their frozen faces – "right over your heads! You'll get to see firsthand just how mad and maybe bad I am, LSA."

"Don't call me that. My name is Lincoln!"

"Have as many tantrums as you like, LSA. I couldn't give a rat's arse what you want to be called. This is only the beginning. You want a war with us. We say, bring it on!"

Paulo jutted his clenched fist towards Lincoln's face.

"Remember, you started it, so we get to finish it," Lily said. "Your choice. Either leave now with your idiot mates or – starting with you, LSA – we say, let the fun begin."

Once again, the airplane whizzed and dove like a World War 2 bomber. The fluorescent green streaks made spectacular swirling ribbons in the air, moving closer and closer to their faces. Lincoln staggered backwards as if hit, nearly falling over his own legs, as his petrified gang grabbed their bags and fled.

"Piss off before we change our minds. And don't ever mess with us again or you'll live to regret it," she roared.

Paulo threw his clenched fist into the air behind them, shouting, "Yeah, you will."

The crowd peeled open to create a pathway for the skulking LSA.

"You haven't heard the last of this. I'll get my dad to come to school. I'll show you, you ugly freaks,' he stammered and blubbered from the other side of the circle that had formed around them.

"Oh, piss off, you baby," Lily said. "Got to get Daddy to fight your fights? You're an absolute embarrassment."

The mesmerised onlookers fixated on the vanquished leader, then started in fits of laughter, interspersed by wolf whistles and slow claps, yelling, "Yeah, LSA, you baby. How embarrassing. Pathetic. Piss off!"

The alarm for the last bus screeched, everyone grabbed their bags and ran to catch it. Everyone except Paulo and Lily. They gathered their belongings and meandered home the long way, guarding their precious new possession, discussing where they'd keep it and how handy it could be for any future negotiations.

To celebrate, they walked to the beach kiosk and bought two dollars' worth of hot chips and two potato cakes. Then they walked to the end of the pier with their newspaper parcel and sat with their legs dangling as they recounted their win. Blow by blow. Paulo let Lily attack the food first for once.

"We've got each other's backs," Paulo said.

"Always and forever."

They smacked each other's salty hands in exultation and watched the gliding pelicans swoop in for scraps.

TWELVE

Lily sauntered along the foaming edge of the spitting sea. The waves dumped angrily onto the shore, and she zigzagged her feet to stop her runners from getting soaked. The further she went, the less she concentrated on avoiding the spewing froth; soon her runners were sodden and squelching. Nonetheless, she continued. Most of her lank hair was dragged into an unruly ponytail, leaving irritating wisps of hair around her face. The wind pushed hard against her back, and she thought, *The sea is like the most alluring beast...* Her English teacher, Mrs Wyndthorpe, had written that across the board for the creative-writing session earlier that afternoon. Lily remembered the times she came close to being mauled by it, sucked into its lethal force, and that helped the words flow. The deafening rhythm of the crashing waves also dulled the frustration in her mind.

Lily knew she should be at home continuing her English essay or starting her larger history assignment. She also knew that the longer she walked, the less inclined she'd be to start it tonight. She breathed out hard, laboured breath and turned around at the chunky sandstone outcrop that had cut her foot so badly last year. Facing the full strength of the sea-drenched southerly, she pushed her head down, digging her arms into her windcheater pockets. Her feet felt numb with the damp chill. *If only Dad was here, he'd help me. There's never anyone at home to help me now. Poor old Nini doesn't know anything about schoolwork and Meredith, well, she's away with the fairies.*

A lone and noisy sparrow darted in front of her, hovered on the strong southerly and did a huge and uneven loop above her head like a shaky cracking of a whip. She bent backwards trying to watch the bird as it lingered unsteadily in the gusting southerly assault. It came back three times. On its last spin, its friend joined in. They watched her with their black, beady eyes. The dumping waves cast an icy spray that resembled fog as the sky darkened. The air was a stew thick with chill. Lily turned and saw the sparrows dance one last joint flutter before one darted out towards the lonesome sea and one flew north, far beyond the rocky outcrop.

"Do you believe in birds?" She peered at Paulo the next day after school as they headed home.

"What, like, that they're birds?" He rearranged his overloaded school bag on his shoulder.

"No. Like the reassurance of them; that they're visiting you to reassure you that your loved ones live on. Your dead loved ones."

"Nup." He shook his lustrous mane for emphasis. When he saw her perplexed expression, Paulo added, "I reckon they're just birds."

"Well, Nini does," Lily ploughed on. "She told me that Grandpa comes back sometimes, and she reckons Meredith sees Dad..." Just as she was gathering momentum she stopped and cleared her throat. "You reckon I'm nuts, don't you?" Lily dropped her gaze.

"Yep, probably," he answered without hesitation.

"But don't you reckon it could be true? Just maybe...?" Her pale eyes implored him.

"Sorry, buddy, I don't reckon." He grinned. "But, hell, what would I know?"

"Last night, I went for a long walk along the back beach because I'd had a gutful of thinking about that stupid history assignment, when a sparrow came to visit me, flew over my head three times. Then its mate came. They hovered, stared at me, and flew off in different directions. How cool is that? I mean, what do you reckon that could be a sign of?"

"They're just doing bird stuff."

"I don't reckon. I think they were giving me a message from upstairs or heaven or wherever and telling me that I'm not alone. I mean, I know that I'm not alone 'cause I've got you and Nini and Meredith – sort of – but you know what I mean."

"And Bessie."

"Yeah, I know, but I just think weird stuff happens with birds and they look intelligent, and they sing and talk, and dance and they know stuff. The other night, when I put out the bin, it was dusk, and these red finches kept darting in and out of the shrubs in front of me like macrame. It was incredible, as if they were playing a game with me. Like they wanted to have fun with me. Do you see what I mean?"

"Nup."

"Why?"

"Dunno. I don't believe in stuff like that."

"Why not?"

"I just don't."

"But don't you care about what they could mean? Like signals or messages or…"

"Nup. I don't care."

"Do you care about anything?"

"Hmmm… not much." Paulo scratched his head. "I care about my dancing. And food – big time."

"Dancing I get, but food – oh, that's hilarious. *That*'s what you care about?"

"Yep. Nini is the only good cook I know."

"She should teach me. But she's so good at it, I just let her do it. All I can cook are eggs and toast, French toast, or toasted cheese. Maybe I'll try pancakes soon. She reckons they're easy."

"Not for you, they wouldn't be. Eggs, toast, French toast… you don't even do *them* well."

"Shut up." She pushed him harder than she intended to. "You're no better. Burnt snags and chops in the vertical griller. Last time I was at your joint, I was going to call the fire brigade. The smoke was disgusting from that fat-ridden thing. Nearly set the house on fire."

"That's true. The snags were bad, but the chops were okay. Covered them in tomato sauce – no worries." He rubbed his face. "Yeah, the fire part wasn't good."

"That's for bloody sure." Lily shook her head.

They were nearly outside Paulo's place at 39 Southern Ocean Road. The nine only had one nail holding it in place and it had tipped sideways, so it was difficult to tell what number it was meant to be. Just the way Ronaldo liked it. Reckoned he'd get fewer bills that way.

"Seriously," Lily asked, "do you reckon I'm nuts?"

"Maybe."

"Yeah, because I probably am. But, still, I believe in that stuff."

"Nup, that's not why. I reckon maybe you're nuts, or you could become nuts, 'cause you cram too much stuff in your brain." Paulo looked satisfied.

"You look like you've just invented Pythagoras's theorem or the true meaning of life. You haven't solved any of life's great mysteries, no offence, mate. I mean, I do want to know everything, but it's so I can make sense of something. I'm not actually wanting to make myself crazy, I just really need to know stuff. Otherwise, what's the bloody point?"

"Of what?" He looked puzzled.

"Life."

"To have a good time." Paulo hunched his shoulders.

"When? School? Homework? Chores?" Lily crossed her arms and lifted her eyebrows.

"No. Sometime, maybe, good times are a-comin'." He did a few twirls.

"Good thing you're patient." Lily laughed. "Anyway, I think we're meant to question things to try and work it out. Life, I mean. It's good you don't care, but I do. Life, to me, is this gigantic puzzle that needs to be figured out." She hugged the air expansively. "I don't know much about anything yet, but I'm curious. All the time. I guess we're just different."

"Bloody oath we're different."

"Like the north and the south pole. Maybe we get along because sometimes we meet at the equator." She dropped her arm across her friend's broad shoulders, and they dawdled along together. "Don't know what I'd do without you."

Two magpies flew passed, squawking and nagging at each other. As Paulo pushed the squeaking gate open with his shoe, he said, "Hey, there we go." He pointed to the sky and grinned his big open-faced grin.

"Haha. And you reckon I'm the one squawking?"

"Too right." Still guffawing at his own joke, he turned his back to her and did a soft-shoe shuffle towards his side gate. "See ya." His arm threw a wave behind his back.

"Yeah, see ya. Wouldn't wanna be ya," Lily responded.

As she walked away from number 39, she did a skip and a pretend hopscotch, and she didn't know why.

THIRTEEN

Beyond the screech of the back flywire door, Lily could smell the sizzling roast lamb and instantly felt famished. Nini cooked the best roast, followed by her own sumptuous apple pie, covered with plaited golden pastry, oozing with sugary apples and thick cream on top. Lily narrowed her eyes to Meredith's closed door.

"Hi Nini. Is Mum sleeping again?"

"Yes, darling. She's tired. She's had a big day at work. Best to let her rest." Nini wiped her hands on her paisley apron.

"God, that's the fourth night in a row she's come home and gone straight to bed."

Nini kept peeling the apples. "Oh well, she needs to do what she needs to do."

"Yeah… but sleeping your life away doesn't seem right. Like, apart from work, all she does is sleep." Lily guzzled milk straight from the bottle. When Nini turned to look at her, she burped, wiped her mouth, and said, "Sorry."

"It's tempting, I know. Meredith's resting is like your running and swimming. We all cope with grief in our own way." She turned and gave Lily a smile that was so kind it hurt.

"What do you do for your grief, Nini?"

"I sing, I cook, and I garden, darling."

"Sometimes you close your eyes when you're in the garden," Lily said as she closed the fridge. "Why is that?"

"Yes, I do that sometimes." Nini closed her eyes now and said, "I can listen better when I close my eyes. So, if I'm thinking of your Pa, or maybe the good times we shared with your dad, I close my eyes. My mind fills with the sounds of nature, then I don't feel as sad, or as lonely."

"I might give that a go."

"I think you're glad I cook, too, when I feel sad."

"Your sadness makes me happy. I mean, your food sure does."

"Good for you, darling. Nothing better than to cook for people you love."

"I sure do!" Lily headed for the shower. "Love you and love your cooking." The bathroom door slammed. "Although the singing, I could probably do without," Lily called out from the bathroom door. "But you love it, so that's a good thing."

"Indeed, I do," Enid said to herself and started up one of her favourites, Gene Kelly's *You Were Meant for Me,* a melancholy song of love, loss and longing. Lily had watched *Singin' in the Rain* with Nini. Her grandmother had sat there, sipping her brandy, and held Lily's hand. She seemed to be transported to another time. Later, she told her it was an old crooning song that she sang when Alfred was away in the war. A small line of tears wove down her well-lived face, as she plaited the pastry on top of the apple pie.

FOURTEEN

"Do you reckon sound has layers?"

"Oh God, buddy, how the bloody hell would I know?"

"'Cause yesterday I was waiting for Nini to help her with the shopping and I'm on the back swing-seat, I closed my eyes and, boy, I heard so much – like, in layers."

"Really?"

"Yeah. I heard the thumping waves, some kids playing down the street, all these different birds chirping and some cars way off in the distance. I even reckon I heard the wind. Maybe even my own heartbeat." Lily took the elastic band out of her ponytail, combed her hair with her fingers, scratched her head and let her hair fly behind her. "Do you even think that's possible?" Her long slender legs were sliding along the sandy pavement.

"You know what I know?" Paulo asked. Without waiting for an answer, he did a twirl and continued. "You really need a smart friend. 'Cause I can't answer anything you ask me." He grabbed mounds of his hair and twisted them hard in his left hand. "I'm a pretty shit friend."

"No, you're not!" She nudged him. "I mean, if I couldn't run all these crazy ideas by you, what would I do? Except I'd probably drive myself totally nuts." Lily grinned. "Well, maybe I am a bit nuts already, but I could be worse."

"You are. Nuts, I mean." He pushed her arm gently. "Seriously, I'm more interested in how you think of these bloody stupid questions than the answers to them."

They dawdled on in comfortable silence. Well, Paulo dawdled in between dance moves, and Lily skipped. She was thinking of her next line of enquiry as the clouds rolled into a ball in the mauve sky. Paulo was thinking of his next meal as his worn-out Dunlops scuffed the pavement, and he trialled a shoe-shuffle that he had seen on one of Nini's Fred Astaire movies.

"What were you like as a little tacker?" Lily asked as the clouds above her took the shape of a child. She watched their drifting, changing forms.

"Dunno. Can't remember." Paulo scrunched his locks once more and twisted them into a ponytail.

"Yeah, sure you do. Think!" Her eyes drifted to his head as if prompting the memories inside to reveal themselves. "Like, when you were three or four or five – something that made you really happy or excited."

He shook his head and ran his fingers across his face. "Hmm. That's hard."

They skirted the old cemetery with the white picket fence on the way to the point and went straight to the rocks. Paulo jiggled his knees. "Oh, well, I remember dancing in the backyard to Mum's music – like a Rogers and Hammerstein... hmm, I'll try and remember its name."

"Okay. How old?"

"Maybe four or five. I used to watch Shirley Temple every Saturday morning. Mum would do the ironing and I'd be glued to the TV until it was finished. Sometimes, she would be singing in the backyard and hanging out the washing and I'd be tap-dancing on the concrete pathway. You know, pretending I was Shirley Temple on stage with the whole world watching me because I was so good. Then Mum would applaud, and I'd take a bow." He started to sing and tap dance. *"I'm gonna wash that man right out of my hair..."* He swirled with his arms outstretched, reminding Lily of Cyd Charisse in a movie Nini had been watching.

"That's ridiculous. Is that really a song?"

"Yep, and Valerie used to belt it out every Saturday at our clothesline."

"That's hilarious. No wonder you can sing and dance. It's in your genes."

"And I love washing my hair."

"You love washing your hair, and you really love your hair."

"Why?"

"Because you play with it all the time."

"I do not."

"Yep, you do. Was your hair loose when we left school, then it was in a ponytail, and now it is loose again?"

"Maybe." He tied it back in a ponytail again. "What about you?"

"I was sitting in Dad's lap. I was about three and he was reading me *The Magic Faraway Tree* and I was in that tree with those kids. Every night, when he'd read a little bit more, my adventure went further. I never wanted him to finish. Sometimes he'd read *Winnie the Pooh*. I could smell the soap on his skin, and the woollen jumper he wore, and I was living in that book. If we were going out, I could smell aftershave. Something really pongy, like Old Spice. It felt exciting, safe – a magical adventure." Lily put out her arms as if to hug the world. "See, this shows us our true personalities!" She hugged herself and then reached her arms up to the sky.

"Who says?"

"Well, we had a session with the year level counsellor, and she said that your early happy memories tell you a lot about yourself.

Also, by the time you're seven your personality is formed. Now we're ducking for cover in case someone has a go at us or, you know, hiding ourselves – usual shit. Back then, we were just being who we are."

"Hmm, by the time we're seven?" Paulo asked as the water shimmered, smashed, and was sucked below. The small rockpools overflowed, and the water cascaded over the jagged edges and out to churning sea. "So now we are, or we aren't, being us?"

"Life can make us hide who we are. It's interesting to think who we could be if we weren't afraid of anything – other people, their opinions of us, how scared we are of stuffing up, being dumb, lazy, stupid, small, tall, ugly, thin, fat, crazy..."

"God, sounds like Ronaldo speaking to me last night."

"Bullshit. He doesn't speak."

"True. But if he did, that's what he'd say."

"He's not mean, he's just..."

"Not there. Poor bastard. I feel sorry for the old boy sometimes."

"Fair enough. I feel sorry for myself having to do this crap for homework. Three major assignments due in a week."

"I feel more sorry for how you badger my little brain with questions I could never in a million years think of, let alone answer." Paulo stood up, stretched and rubbed his temples dramatically. "Sometimes you make my head sore."

"Bad luck. I'm just saying it's interesting to consider."

"Okay. Considered." He turned to walk towards Beach Street. "Gotta hot-tail it. I'm famished," he called back.

"Check ya later," she said, as she headed down Tea Tree Road alone.

FIFTEEN

Lily thought about how she would describe school in an essay or, better still, describe her school experience in three words – glum, grubby and grating. Plus, she thought, even with the windows open, it stank. She tried to search her brain for what made school feel so horrible: the stench, the meanness, the monotony, the rules, the bells... The way her stomach tightened when she walked through the gates. Or maybe the way she sweated so much that it was humiliating; sometimes she smelled herself and she was off, too. The whole place made you off. Off in your body, off in your stomach and off in your mind.

She and Paulo shared thoughts of wagging after school on the slow march home. The only reason Lily couldn't bring herself to follow through on it was her knowledge of what Nini would've given to have an education. The long discussions with Nini, and the longing look on her grandmother's face all these decades later, made Lily think it was Nini's biggest regret. And that made Lily feel sad and guilty for hating school so much. Guilty enough not to wag, but not guilty enough to stop hating it. The only reason Paulo wouldn't do it, he said, was because if he started, he wouldn't stop. Then he'd be a schoolboy dropout and end up in front of the TV in a darkened room with a stack of newspapers and empty beer cans for company. Nup, they told each other they were stuck there and there was no way out but to finish the bloody thing. But they could keep hating it, which they did.

Lily and Paulo walked hunched over as if still carrying their weighty school bags on their backs.

"Somedays are so friggin' shit," Lily said.

"Yep," Paulo agreed.

They walked on, not speaking. Not because they were angry with each other, but because there didn't seem like anything to say. Nothing to say that would make either of them feel any better. Lily walked on with a scowl that betrayed her brooding thoughts about the week. Her mind wandered back to the girls at the tuckshop. She was waiting in line and then, just as she went to order, she was elbowed out of the way, Nastacia calling, "Hey, Lily, no pushing in. We've been in this queue for ten minutes. Sir, she pushed in..." Then her chorus of mates joined in, and Lily was told to go to the back of the queue, her protestations ignored with the threat of detention from Mr Gallstein. The fury she felt having to trudge to the back of the queue churned her stomach.

To top it off, in Maths she needed to ask some questions to understand the worksheet they were given.

"Look, Lily, if you concentrate on what I'm saying fully, then you won't need to ask for further explanations." And with that, Mrs Relsh turned and started writing the next work on the blackboard.

Lily was ropable. A mantra played over and over in her head: *How can I do the work, you stupid idiot, when I can't understand what you're asking me to do?* By the time the bell rang at the end of the day, Lily was dripping with perspiration, her cheeks were ablaze, and her aching stomach was as tight as a drum.

Paulo scuffed his shoes along the path and thought back to last night. It was his mum's birthday – or it would've been, if she had been in his life. He mentioned it to his father. Ronaldo went bloodshot red. "Don't mention that woman's name in my house. Ever." Paulo thought, *What a dead-set prick. What if I wanted to talk about her – after all, once upon a time she was my mother?*

Lost in their ruminations, they walked along the boardwalk towards the lighthouse when Lily shouted, "Oh my God, mate, look! It's dolphins."

There, just behind the breakers, was a pod of dolphins. At first, they saw a few black fins, then there were several, ducking and jumping and just having a blast together.

"You know they travel as a family. They have their own language. It's incredible, isn't it?" Her words fell out of her mouth, and then she was running.

"Nuh," Paulo said, doubtfully. "Really?"

"Yeah, they do," she yelled back at him. "Look – they're all just hanging out together. Just for fun."

"Hey, look!" Paulo gestured towards the point, where a huge rolling black mass, way out to sea, had the indisputable spout of water shooting way into the air... and another, as he tried to catch up.

"This is incredible," Lily squealed, jumping up and down. "Whales to the left of us, and a pod of dolphins to the right. If I wasn't here, I wouldn't believe this could happen. This is the most magical thing I've ever seen."

The light danced between the teal grey of the bay and the stark silver where the blackness of the mammals broke through the water. The gleaming white of the whale's fins flashed each time they rolled over.

"Whoa, look at that big boy go," Paulo shouted out to sea.

"Nah, she's a girl. All her calves are following her." Lily beamed as she pointed.

Paulo shielded his eyes, trying to spot the smaller dark shapes beneath the surface. "Not always," he said.

Lily noticed her friend's wistful look. "Sorry, mate. I didn't mean..."

"Nah, it's okay." His eyes drifted back to the dolphins. "Well, I love that those guys stay together."

They stayed and watched until the dolphins disappeared, and the whales moved further into the black of the bay.

"If reincarnation is true, what do you want to have been or what do you want to come back as?" Lily asked, as they meandered around the rocks leading back to the lighthouse.

"Hmm," Paulo halted for a moment. "A dolphin."

They continued on.

"Why?"

"Because they always hang out in a pod. There's no one left out, or lonely."

It was the first time Lily considered that maybe, sometimes, Paulo felt lonely. She thought back to the months after her dad had died and how she'd cry herself to sleep with loneliness. But now she had Nini. Not that Nini could replace her dad, but she was always there. She always listened. She wished Paulo had a Nini.

"You want to know what I'd be? A soaring majestic pelican overseeing the world." And then she added, "Or a dog, like Bessie. She has a good life and she's always loved."

"Yeah, a dog like Bessie I get. But, nah, if you were a bird, you'd be a sticky-beak, for sure." He smiled at his joke. Lily didn't, giving her friend a shove.

As they reached the lighthouse, she asked, "Where are your grandparents? You know that my dad's died young, and what happened to my pa, but I've never asked you about yours."

"Don't have any. Ronaldo's are still in the old country, in Italy. He doesn't speak with them."

"Why not?"

"'Cause when he finished school, he was expected to work on the goat farm, but instead he went travelling. He was told by his old man, 'You think you're too good to work the farm like the generations before you, you go to kangaroo country and you never come back.'"

"Shit. What sort of father says that to his son?"

"His. When he said goodbye to his mum, who he loved, she kept her head down and said nothing. She cried but didn't hug him goodbye. He went to say goodbye to his dad, but when he saw Ronaldo coming, he turned and walked in the other direction. He reckons he said 'Goodbye Papa' to no one. Then he came to Australia and met mum and you know the rest."

"Oh my God, that's so sad. Were there any other kids?"

"Yeah, he had three older brothers. They all live over there. Dad lost touch with them after he left. Two stayed and worked the farm, but the middle one moved into the city nearby. He still helped out, though. None of them were allowed to be in contact with Dad. Because his old man said, *You cannot talk to the dead.* He reckons his old man was the boss and his mother did what he said. Except Ronaldo reckons its unnatural for a mother to cut off her own kid."

"Wow, that's bloody sad. He's had a tough run."

"Yeah, come to think of it, after Valerie left, he said, *It's history repeating itself.* I didn't know what he meant, but now I do."

"Valerie's folks?"

"They were great, apparently; they were around when I was little. I've got a couple of photos of them. They were like gypsies. They'd live six months here, six months there. When I was about five, I came home, and Mum was howling. They'd flipped their car on a curve on some winding road in New South Wales. And they died."

"Your mum lost both her parents at once? It's bad enough to lose Dad, but to lose Mum at the same time... I can't imagine how sad that would be."

"Yeah, probably. I mean, I was only a little tacker, but I remember her wandering around the house crying."

Lily put her arm around Paulo's shoulder and said, "Well, at least you've got me and Nini."

"You bet. She's the best, Nini, the magnificent. *Woo*!" He gently whacked her arm. "Oh, and you too, buddy."

SIXTEEN

Dragging herself to school, and then enduring the cruel remarks and vicious actions of Triple M and her hangers-on, became a massive Sisyphean task. The harder Lily pushed, the more mammoth the job became.

She asked her dad for strength. Nini suggested she pray, but as Meredith never did, she thought it best to go directly to the source. And since her dad had come to her as birds, rainbows, sunshine on the water, she felt it was more expeditious to go to him. When she would talk to him, either in her head, or as she did at Durga Rock, or walking along the beach alone, she'd unexpectedly start sobbing. She'd struggle to get coherent words out, which she later found strange, given that he could hear her whether she uttered the words or merely thought them. The more she articulated the depths of her despair, the more it would pour out. She could not predict what she would say, she just said it.

At times when she felt utterly bereft and lonely, she would ask him to answer, to give her a sign. Always, eventually, it would come. It might take minutes, or hours, or days, but it always came and he, in death, just as in life, never let her down.

The only one who knew about this was Paulo. She didn't want to make her mother any sadder than she already was, even though Lily thought that this probably wasn't possible. Apart from the birds, she didn't want to tell Nini that prayer wasn't her thing. Of course, Bessie knew, and understood. Because whenever she was having these inter-terrestrial conversations with the other world, or with her dad, Bessie would come and nuzzle against her, and stay there until the conversation had finished.

Lily would start in a deep, dark hole, and by the time the conversation was over, she felt lighter, less burdened, and maybe notice a rainbow, or the drifting clouds, or the changing colour of the sea. She would smell the air, feel the breeze, and breathe.

SEVENTEEN

Cosy in bed one night, Lily awoke to a steam-train of wind buffeting their house. The drone lasted well into the early hours. Every time the wind picked up, Lily tossed and turned, before plummeting back into sleep.

The next morning, the sky, a blanket of mauve outside the window, rumbled and pulsated with silver flashes of lightning. Lily struggled to hear the preceding thunder, but Bessie certainly did. Bessie was like a crazed creature – running around in circles, barking at nothing. The wind whipped up a frenzy before the deluge of rain, hard and relentless against their tin roof. The drumming blocked out any other sounds.

Lily trudged to school across the sodden ground, the trees drooped and glistening overhead. Droplets of rain clung to the larger leaves like dollops of glue. The air was pungent, sweet, and clean, the sun warm upon her face amongst wafts of damp air. The road ahead was blindingly glary.

Entering the school grounds, Alexa Kaklamanis strolled casually up to Lily.

"Hey, Lily. How goes it?" she boomed. The scent of musk sticks, hot pies, and malted milks wafted around her.

"Good," Lily said reluctantly, wary of Alexa's intentions. "How about you?"

"No problem, my friend, just hangin' round, waiting to get out of this hell-hole."

Lily was surprised to hear this confession and glanced across at her classmate. "Ha! Yeah, me too. Catch you later."

"Yep. See you round like a donut." Alexa's long frizzy mane

swung rhythmically as she bounced off towards 4C for Maths.

Alexa's family owned the local milk bar. Every time the buzzer went – which was often, especially before and after school, or if people were on their way to the beach – Lily thought of Alexa's family running into their shop. It reminded her of mice darting in and out of holes.

Alexa hung out with Mot Wheatleigh. Mot was her physical opposite. He was solid, stocky and strong, with dense curly red hair, startling electric blue eyes, deep freckles that merged into each other, and skin that went pink as he walked from the shade of the school to the water-taps and back. He moved in a disconnected way, as if he was constantly in the wrong place at the wrong time; his body was there, but his mind was always somewhere else.

Most classes started in the same way, with the teacher reprimanding him, along the lines of: "Mot Wheatleigh, why are you late?" Today it was Mr Gallstein's turn.

"I didn't know I was," Mot had responded.

"Ever heard of a watch?"

"I haven't got one."

"A clock?"

"Yeah, there's one in the old dear's room, but I don't go in there."

"I'm not interested in your family dynamics. You are tardy, insolent, and ill-mannered. Use my name when you address me, boy."

"Oh. Sorry," Mot said, face flushed bright red, adding too late, "Mr Gallstein."

"My class starts at nine am, as you know. You've got three after-school detentions. And if you are late again for my class, I'll double it." Mr Gallstein's stick-figure body lent towards Mot's desk as his thin face closed in upon itself. "Do I make myself clear, boy?"

"Yes." Mot's face had dark crimson patches, and the sweat dripped down his forehead.

"What was that?"

"I said yes, I understand," Mot stuttered. "Sorry, Mr Gallstein."

"Get out. Sit in the hallway. You've already wasted ten minutes." The teacher turned his back on Mot and addressed the class.

Mot clumsily gathered his things as Alexa shook her head and mouthed to him, *He's such an idiot.*

At recess, Lily and Paulo overheard students saying what had happened to Mot. They went searching for him.

"Hi, you two. What a pig that man is," Lily proclaimed as they got close to where Alexa and Mot were huddled, cross-legged under the pines.

"Hi guys. Yeah, he's a pig alright. He hates me and I hate his guts too. If only he was a mind-reader then I'd be expelled once and for all, put me out of my misery."

The others laughed and formed a tight circle; everyone except Mot.

"Why do they pick on us all the time? He does it to me too," Paulo said.

"Hmm. Pigs always act like pigs, no matter who they're picking on," Mot responded, between mouthfuls of peanut-butter sandwich.

"What a jerk. Maybe it's because I'm small, he doesn't single me out." Alexa sat up straighter and put her shoulders back. "But he's a bully. Bullies are the biggest cowards of all. My brother, Dimitri, is a dead-set bully. Whenever I threaten to tell Mum or Antonio what he's done to one of us, he breaks down and sobs like a baby. Bullies don't frighten me. You've just got to find their weakness. That's what I do with him. Then, when they're least expecting it – wham! Get 'em and get 'em good." Alexa's emerald eyes narrowed as her tiny arm jutted out and punched the air.

Lily and Paulo nodded in solidarity.

"Yeah, but some bullies aren't worth hitting," Mot mumbled as he looked away.

The mood shifted, until Paulo said, "Gallstein, Broadwater, Kravo – they're bloody rats, too."

"Pigs and rats. One day, we'll get even. Ah, the taste of sweet revenge... One fine day," Lily said with satisfaction and expansive arm actions.

EIGHTEEN

Alexa was elfin – tiny and quick with her movements. The long, black frizzy hair that haloed her face was a third of her entire height and accentuated her expressions. Her hair and her hands had a life of their own. Moving, bouncing, and darting in unexpected ways, even to her. She was the youngest of six children and the only girl. She told Lily that her brothers fought a lot, especially when her parents were serving in the milk bar. On bad days, they'd have an all-in brawl. She learnt first to hide, or to return with a broom or a hose, depending on where the madness erupted.

She developed a strong voice and an imposing attitude. Antonio, the eldest brother and the largest, didn't fight. He'd call over his shoulder to the others – "Shut up! Shut up, you idiots" – and lope off to his bedroom, slam the door, and turn the music up to fever pitch to drown them out.

When Alexa was younger, she'd creep into Antonio's room and hide under his bed. He knew she was there but chose to ignore her. He always let her hide. As she grew older, she learned to use her tongue as a weapon. Antonio told the brothers, "You hurt Alexa and I'll smash your heads in." They all knew that he meant it. Alexa became a force in her own right. Something she frequently relied upon as the years unfolded.

The milk bar was an old two-storey pale-blue building. The older boys helped with deliveries and sometimes worked on the weekends. Alexa was mainly given domestic duties and serving in the shop when needed. Two of her brothers ducked and weaved to avoid work, but often their father would clip them over their heads and tell them to come and serve. The smell of the lollies and milkshakes permeated Alexa's very being. Her lunchbox was filled with chocolates, lollies, or anything else she could grab on her rush out the front door, as well as the Greek food her mother made.

The day after she learned about the fight – what Lily and Mot did, and how Paulo stood up for himself – Alexa went to congratulate them. Bouncing over, she reached up and high-fived the three of them in turn, saying, "Your reputation precedes you. Congratulations for taking those thugs down. I'm sorry to have missed the theatrics. I hate missing a good show."

"Thanks. They had it coming," Mot said.

"That's for sure. I've had a few stoushes with them myself."

They looked askance at her.

"I had a full-on barney with Jake," she insisted "I told him what a weak shit he was, and he threatened me – said if I told the teachers what they'd done, they'd get me good, just before he yanked me by the hair. He loosened his grip on my hair and gave me the break to do my loudest scream. Something I've practiced at home after years of my brothers' warfare. Want me to show you?" And before they had a chance to say no, she let it rip. A scream that bounced and echoed off the stone walls of the school in an unnerving reverberating jolt.

Teachers put their heads out of windows like tolling cuckoo clocks, students turned and pointed, the principal came out of her office and searched for the invisible melee that must have ensued.

Meanwhile, happy with the reaction she'd caused, Alexa kept talking. "Anyway, I threatened him back by saying my brothers would kill him. They probably wouldn't bother, but they'd bother to inflict pain." At this juncture she drew breath, and continued, "I've had a gutful of them and that shocking piece of work, Nastacia; as for Bomber Thompson and LSA – huh!" She looked around to see people pointing at her and laughed. "You've dealt with them all, Lily. If ever you need a hand with these lowlifes, just tell me. They don't frighten me. I think they're weak as piss." Her impish face was animated. It was good to see her having so much fun.

"You're in, comrade." Lily smiled. "Sometimes you need a backup, and vice versa. We've just about put up with all the crap we're going to. Haven't we, Paulo? Better to get even than get angry, we reckon.".

Paulo laughed. "Dunno. Lily can get angry and even. I'm just better backing her up and getting even that way."

"Sounds good to me. See you round." Alexa flitted off, her delicate feet hardly touching the ground as she walked. She moved like Tinkerbell and spoke like a Mafia boss.

Most students liked Alexa's sparky ways. Some days, there was a crowd of friends around her. Even though it was a long time coming, the prospect of Form Five was looking up.

NINETEEN

The whole day turned silver. The bay blended with the sky. The town was a dirty grey, covered in lumpy clouds. It was as if there was a dark secret that had been shrouded; a memory not to be given the light of day. Slowly, there it was a slip of dazzling light way out at sea – shining, alone and lonely.

Sometimes, Mot, and later Alexa, started to join Lily and Paulo for recess or lunch. Occasionally, even on the weekend. At first, Mot was shy, nearly apologetic for being with them, never accepting any of the food Lily brought. His own paper bag scrunched over the old sandwich. Alexa brought donuts, sandwiches, or yesterday's pies. Mot was also the most uncoordinated person they'd ever met. He had more bad luck and accidents than anyone they knew.

"Why do you always have so many bruises, Mot?" Lily asked him one day.

"I'm unco. Just born that way."

"Yeah, I know, but geez you must have bad luck."

"Yeah, he does," Alexa said.

"Our place is crowded," Mot said. "Last week I walked into the hallway wall, this week the back door, tomorrow I'll probably fall down the steps. I've always been like this – just the way I am."

"Well, maybe if you tell yourself that you'll concentrate more, you might have a better outcome," Lily suggested.

"Yeah sure." He rolled his eyes and shook his head. "The fat pig's still breathing, bad luck for me."

"Oh, who's the fat pig?" Paulo's dreamy eyes narrowed.

"His dad," Alexa said.

"Yeah, we don't get on. Never have, never will." He punched his freckled hand into his other palm like a baseball player about to launch. "At least the old girl isn't all bad. I dunno why she stays with him but, then again, with so many kids…" Mot's voice dropped, and his voice trailed off, as if someone might overhear him.

"That's sad, Mot. I wish every day my dad was still here." Lily looked up through the canopy of the elm tree and watched and waited. "He was really good." The little blue wren was there, nestled halfway up, staring down at her.

"I just wish my old man would speak," Paulo said. "He's not a bad old bastard, but after Mum left, he went… um… silent. He nods when I come in, he nods when I leave. Sometimes he cooks a meal and when I say thanks, he makes a grunting sound. It's like speaking now is too much of an effort, or maybe he's forgotten how to. He hates answering the phone. I try to speak with him, but it gets weird when I do all the talking and he looks away, or nods: *Righto, okay then, yep, nup, dunno or don't care.*"

Mot, Alexa, and Lily laughed. Paulo eventually did, too.

"Mine's not a father, he's a bloody tyrant. He rants and raves and thumps the table with his fist. Last night, the pot with the meat and broth in it spilled over because of him. Bloody idiot."

"Suffice to say, fathers are in short supply between the four of us," Lily said.

As they strolled back to class, Lily cast her eyes around for the blue wren. It had gone.

TWENTY

The first half of lunch went quickly, Lily or Alexa sharing whatever food they had with Paulo and Mot. But the second half dragged on.

As Alexa opened the bag of lollies she had pilfered when her dad and mum were unloading the Tarax truck, Lily was hit by the waft of vanilla. The church bell heralded some saint's mass in the distance.

"You know what I really hate?" Alexa said as she offered the bag of lollies around.

Lily thought, the more stories she heard about Alexa's siblings – and Mot's, for that matter – the happier she was to be an only child. Alexa only had one good sibling. Mot had two decent ones, but they were babies. Pretty bad percentages given their families were so large.

"I hate bells," Alexa said.

"Why?" Lily devoured another milk bottle.

"I wake up to them in the shop. I go to sleep with them. You're watching TV, eating dinner, in the bath, and that friggin' bell goes… it drives me crazy." She grabbed piles of her wild hair on both sides of her head and yanked at them. "This place is full of them – *go to class, get out of class, go home*. Get stuffed, I say. *Arrrhhh*, then the church has bells – for what? No one knows, and no one cares. Like, maybe for some poor sucker saint or a wedding or a bloody funeral. Who gives a shit? I hate 'em." She let out a large sigh and her shoulders dropped.

"Wow, I never really thought about them before. I hate brussels sprouts." Lily pegged her nose with her fingers and looked to the sky. "I hate the look of them, the smell of them, the way they taste. Disgusting."

"Oh yeah, they're foul," Paulo agreed. "I hate burnt Coles snags. I hate the look of them raw – like someone's floppy weak fingers. I hate them cooked. I even hate them rubbery and black. Although covered in tomato sauce is okay,"

"Yeah, burnt's bad," Mot said with vengeance. "I hate pigs."

"Really?" Lily asked. "God, I love roast pork at Christmas, or crisp bacon, or ham on the bone."

"Nup, pigs are the worst. Human pigs, I mean. I really hate them." Mot looked away.

The bell screeched for the second half of the day.

TWENTY-ONE

The morning was mild, and the wind had not yet gathered strength. The crunch of the gravel road was familiar; the kookaburras' laughter was not. Lily saw the pair perched next to each other on the overhead power lines. On closer inspection, one looked slightly meatier than the other. The larger one cocked his square head at his friend, as if appreciating her song, until it was his turn to chime in. Their joy echoed down the valley and bounced off the scrub. Nini called kookaburras the birds of happiness because "who could not smile when they heard that happy sound?" It vibrated through Lily's body. *Oh, what I'd do to be a bird and sit with them laughing, instead of being here.*

At school, it was Friday rush hour, rank with sweat, off fruit and disappointment, only to give way to students clamouring for their lockers and the brief reprieve of the weekend. The push intensified towards the concrete stairs to the exit. Paulo loped towards them as Jake Hensley stuck his leg out, sending Paulo hurtling down the stairs, crashing to the first landing. Bag, books, and body splayed in all directions. Alexa, who had forgotten her flute, was racing back up the stairs and witnessed Jake's act. The only sound camouflaging Paulo's shock and agony was the hyenas' laughter streaming past them. Alexa crouched by Paulo, collected his belongings and, with the assistance of a lone straggling student, dragged him to the sick bay, where the school nurse took over.

Alexa bolted to the bus line and yelled, "Hey, you! Jake!" She was standing about a metre away from him. "You're not getting away with this."

"Shut up, you scrawny scrag. You wanna keep that big mouth of yours shut or Jakey boy here will just have to shut it for you." He spat at her with his rancid breath as he lunged forward and grabbed two fistfuls of her hair.

"Let go, you filthy pig." Alexa proceeded to emit the most blood-curdling scream, which ricocheted around the quadrangle. Jake retaliated by putting his filthy fingers into her mouth. She bit down hard. He screeched like an alley cat. The yard teachers ran to the scene and pulled them apart. As they approached, Jake whispered to her, "You mention Paulo to them and you're dead meat."

She stared hard at his mottled wet face and replied, "And you touch him again and my brothers will kill you. No problem."

She didn't mention Jake to any teacher, but she did tell Lily and Mot. Paulo wanted to let it go. They argued. Paulo turned puce. "You're not listening. I don't fight. I just don't." It was the only time he stormed off on them.

"Shit. Didn't see that coming," Mot said, rubbing his wild hair for answers. "Maybe *he* doesn't, but *we* do," Alexa said with satisfaction on her face.

The next day, Alexa kept the oily dressing from her eggplant lunch and poured it liberally in front of Jake's locker as he was approaching from the other corridor. Mot kept the look-out and gave her the thumbs up for the exact moment to pour. As expected, Jake had to change his books for the next period and sauntered over to his locker. Reaching up to unlock the door, he slipped backwards, whacking his head on the greasy floor. Moments later, Alexa strolled around the corner with Mot and looked down at Jake, who lay sobbing and crouched over, holding his head. Together, they gave an insincere grimace, and

Mot said, "Oh! Couldn't have happened to a nicer guy."

"Karma," Alexa added as they strolled on by.

Alexa and Mot didn't tell Paulo as, in their minds, there was no point. He did not believe in retribution, whereas they lived by it. "Listen, Paulo the pacifist, I wouldn't be around if I didn't believe in an *eye for an eye*. We Greeks have form you know; something to do with the ancient centuries of wars – like the Persian Wars or some bloody bullshit – and, anyway, if you live where I live, you get it. Sometimes, I escape. Besides, Antonio protects me – when he's there. Without him, and my sense of cunning, it wouldn't be good." She spoke rapid fire, as if she'd become someone else, ready to flee, as if she needed Lily and Paulo to understand. Mot shook his head knowingly as his face grew dark and his expression fierce.

"She's right," he said, nodding. "You get biffed, you biff back. The pig starts the fights and – wham! – out of nowhere, it's on. The old girl doesn't start it, but she doesn't stop it. When it starts, you need to think fast, but you can't always do that, if you get dragged from bed..." Mot stood abruptly and stormed off as the school bell blasted.

Alexa maintained her 'not to be messed with' reputation. She loved the power that it afforded her. She said she learnt a lot from her Alsatian dog. Alexa would cross her arms, plant her feet, and blast the bullies with her withering look. They'd scamper – swearing, stuttering and stumbling to get away. Paulo felt safer when he was with her, even though she was the same height as girls in Form One and he was the same height as a tall grown man.

TWENTY-TWO

Lily's bleary eyes made out 4:10am on the travelling clock that Nini had given her. She rolled over, tossed and turned, and curled herself into the familiar embryonic ball she'd become attached to since her dad died. Sleep did not return. One advantage of being awake in the middle of the night was that the nightmares could not invade her mind. No terrifying images of drowning, Lily trying to reach her dad, or him trying in vain to reach her. The aftermath of these dreams was to wake up sweating profusely, shaken and disturbed. The dream was not only a nightmare; it was real. He was gone, she wanted to save him so desperately, but failed – and now she had to make it on her own. Once the clock reached six am, she was up, bathers on, towel grabbed from the bathroom, and Bessie loyally in tow.

The sea mist morphed with the softest rain – the beach was in full fog with sweet, salty air. It was the lull of the tide, with all the boats floating freely, facing every which way. The dull hue of the water was indiscernible from the sky. Beyond the boats and the old timber pier, there was a smudged nothingness – a stillness, a silence.

She hurled her body in and swam hard. Bessie came in but could not keep up. Lily swam until she could not breathe, until she thought she'd forgotten. She swam to numbness, stopped, and floated, looking at the infinity of the sky above her. The soft blue of the water, the sky, the paleness of her eyes reflecting the blue around her, as if they'd all become a single entity. The village was just a diluted outline in the distance. It was eerie, looking at the spires of the sandstone towers and the chimneys of the bluestone cottages. There was no movement. The sea was an oily, creamy consistency and Lily felt as if she had dropped back in time, to a deserted village where all the inhabitants had fled.

Once home, with Bessie dripping wet, Lily watched Meredith in the kitchen, a shadow passing over her face like the sun's rays leaving for the day. Lily glanced out the opened window at the swaying branches, the whacking of the leaves. It smelt of crisp rain. Meredith's face wore the weary expression of someone wishing to be somewhere else. She rested on one foot and her arms kept a tight grip around her chest. Meredith was still a daughter and a mother but since no longer being a wife, the lines on her face had become deep grooves. The lightness as well as the laughter of Meredith had been suctioned out of her. If she smiled, it was so fleeting that Lily wondered whether she'd merely imagined it. Meredith loved conversation but, without Frank, it was as if she had nothing to say. The only conversation came with Nini. She tried to engage Meredith, but it only came with short answers, and the usual half-eaten meal, before a long bath and the gravitation to her bedroom with the closed door.

TWENTY-THREE

Her breathing was raspy and grasping, as if each breath was simultaneously vital and laborious. Lily ran all the way to Paulo's place as it was a rare Saturday afternoon when Ronaldo was out. Lily hadn't quite got it; she wanted him to watch Grace Kelly in *To Catch a Thief,* but he refused and said he wanted to watch Fred Astaire in *Shall we Dance.* "I love the way he dances. I gotta watch it."

"But the Grace Kelly one would be romantic," Lily argued.

He laughed and said, "My place, my choice!" Ignoring her protestations, Paulo put the movie on.

Strangely, for her, Lily liked the dance moves, and Ginger Rogers was amazing, as was Fred Astaire. Paulo was tapping his feet and swirling his body in Ronaldo's chair. Lily wondered if he even knew that he was doing it.

After the movie had finished, she said, "Well, I didn't think I would, but I really liked it." She stood up and stretched after being cramped on the broken couch.

Paulo reclined in his dad's worn-out chair. He looked so strange in it, like he'd entered someone else's home and not his own. Lily thought he looked somehow older in the faint light.

"You?" she asked as he opened the blinds. The dust fell like the icing sugar Nini sieved over her cakes. The sour air made Lily want to hurl the window open, but Paulo frowned at her the last time she did that.

"Yeah. It was good. He's a star. She was good too."

"I thought you were going to jump up and join them. You were tapping your feet and jigging in your chair... oops,

Ronaldo's chair."

"Was I?"

"Yep. Big time."

Lily wondered if there was anything to eat. In the kitchen, she could feel her friend's discomfort. He opened the fridge and immediately closed it again. He went to the cupboard and shuffled around a few boxes of cereal and a Milo tin. He shook the Milo tin. Not much noise came from it.

"Sorry, there's no milk, anyway."

"Oh, no worries, I'm not hungry," she lied and walked to the backdoor. "Do you wanna come over and see if Nini's been working her magic?"

Before she'd even finished the sentence, Paulo had grabbed his runners and was putting them on, grinning.

The smell of Paulo's home always lingered with her after she'd left. Lily didn't know what it smelt of but the next morning when she was walking Bessie, she thought, "It smells of neglect and sadness."

When they'd walked from his house to hers, entering the back door she smelt scones. But, more than that, she smelt Velvet soap – Nini's Garden of Eden lavender dusting powder – and that familiar sense of welcome. There was no hint of welcome in Paulo's home. Lily wondered if there ever had been. She reckoned there probably was, once. Lily's dad had made everyone feel welcome; he had whistled and laughed. She never heard that whistle anymore. Meredith didn't laugh now, but Nini hummed and sang – boring old war ballads that Lily couldn't admit she found comforting. But she did.

TWENTY-FOUR

Lily could feel her stomach drop as she approached the concrete steps. The jarring noise, the stifling sweaty stench and the hostility combined to a toxic level. *Keep your head down, look at your feet and don't respond, no matter what.*

She edged her way into the pack and kept up, her face burning, her hands curled into fists in her jacket pocket, as her heart pounded hard. *Just breathe.* She thought of Nini last night with her steaming tea swirling in her floral Royal Winton cup, saying, *When they mean nothing to you, they can't hurt you.* Lily searched along the unfriendly stretch of linoleum corridor and saw a group of glaring faces, crossed arms, lined up like century guards. Her breathing became shallow. She chose her path carefully, almost making it the full length, until Bomber McNeally stuck out his leg-of-lamb calf and she flew face down onto the polished linoleum floor, folders, pencil case and lunch-bag spilling out in all directions. The din erupted into raucous laughter, only quietened by the bell. An assortment of runners, school shoes and scuffed boots kicked her belongings. Lily crawled around, smelling the dirt and dust as she searched for her belongings. The cramp in her stomach tightened and she fought back the threat of tears.

"What on earth do you think you're doing, Lily Mango?" Mrs Kraveen barked. "You've only just arrived and you're already making an embarrassment of yourself. Get up and get to class, you strange, strange girl."

Staggering into class, Lily tried to suppress the nausea and her raging emotions. Bomber was high-fiving his mates before turning his rotund face towards her and whispering, "Speak and you'll get it." He ran his pudgy pink fingers across his freckled neck in a slit throat gesture. "Squashed mango."

Lily sat down, disheveled, and distraught. Her sweaty palms and shaking hands made it impossible to sort her books for class.

Paulo looked at her with his soft brown eyes. "Are you okay?" he mouthed.

A fat silent tear gave her away as she dipped her head. She wiped her eyes hard with the back of her jumper. Paulo shook his head. "Bastards," he muttered.

The morning's classes were a blur until recess arrived.

After school, Paulo found Lily and they walked, his arm gently draped across her shoulder. "I'm useless, buddy," he said. "I wish I knew how to stop it."

The next morning, Lily told Nini, "I don't belong. The other kids know it, the teachers know it, and now I know it."

Nini was in the bathroom getting dressed after her shower, liberally patting herself with her favourite lavender dusting powder. Lily was waiting for her turn at the sink so she could clean her teeth.

"You most certainly do belong, darling. You have just as much right to be there as they do. In fact, with their horrid behaviour, you have much more right to be there than they do."

Nini gave Lily a long hug. All day, Lily smelt of Nini's warm, lavender-scented body, even though she'd brushed the white powder marks off her uniform the whole way to school.

As she approached the cold school fence, her mouth dry, Lily watched a blue wren land on the wrought-iron gate and wiggle its tail back and forth. Her sweaty hands started to disentangle as she stared silently at the fluttering bird. The triumvirate of 'punks' were in the distance. Across the oval, Bomber was yelling orders to some of his cronies. His face was crimson and shimmering with sweat, exertion, and the obvious need to control. Lincoln was hiding, lurking in the shadows as usual, and Nastacia the nasty was holding court with her sycophantic mates. All through the morning Lily tried to obliterate them from her mind.

Paulo squeezed her shoulder as he sat next to her on the asphalt, ready for lunch.

"I can't stand them. I'm so friggin' angry," Lily said, unpacking her lamb and chutney sandwich.

"Okay, I'll take them on, because that's what a best mate should do. I'll start with that bad-arse Bomber. I'd like to smash his face in. I want to see that prick suffer." Paulo did some dramatic hand actions that looked like a poor take-off of a *Get Smart* episode. "Then I'll move to Lincoln, the pockmarked punk. I'd like to give him a taste of the old *one, two*." Paulo belted his left hand into his right like a pro baseballer.

Lily's face brightened into a grin. "Yeah, that was good mate. You nearly had me fooled."

"Shit, I nearly scared myself." Paulo cleared his throat. "You know how you said you're angry?" He didn't wait for her to answer. "I reckon you're pretty angry most of the time." He took the largest half of the sandwich.

Lily stared wide-eyed at his impassive face. "Really? What, like, every day?"

"Yeah. I'm not criticising you; it's just that you seem angry a lot. Like it might eat away at you and make you sick, or something..."

"What about you?" Lily shot back. "You should feel angry too. Don't you want to get even, bring the pricks down?" Lily looked perplexed.

"Nah, what's the point? I'm not gunna change them. Won't make any difference. I just avoid them."

"Mate, that's the whole point. If we take it to them – you know, scare them, threaten them, I don't know – they'll back down. Your whole pacifist stand doesn't work. Look at all the wars. Did they win by backing down? No. They had to stand up and fight to the end." Lily stood upright like a warrior.

"Nup. I reckon war is shit and makes people do things they'd be ashamed of. Look at Ronaldo. I reckon the war stuff did his head in. When war comes on the telly, he turns it off."

"Hmm, for someone who doesn't say much, you've got some good theories. But I still reckon you should *fire up*. I just loved you pretending to get all fired up back then – ready to give them a red-hot spray – even if it's just to me. It feels powerful." Lily put her hand on Paulo's shoulder. "Anyway, I've got enough shit in me for both of us."

"Bloody oath you have – more than!"

"Shut up." She pushed his shoulder and burst out laughing.

"See what I mean?" He smiled. "Let's eat."

"From full-on violent thoughts to food – that's a classic."

They laughed, overcome by a tsunami of joy, neither having any idea why. Alexa and Mot heard them and came over to where they were rolling around on the ground, crying, guffawing and holding their bellies.

"What's so funny?" Alexa said.

"Lily is one crazy cat," Paulo said as his laughter descended into hiccups. "She's planning revenge on the punks and it's wild. Under this sweet exterior lies a heart of stone."

"Huh! No, it was not me! For once, it was you. Cruel and calculating – even if you're pretending. You're no cream puff.

You'd give it to them, given the right opportunity and lots of encouragement from yours truly."

"I'm in, and ready for a fight. Ready, waiting and at your service," Alexa said to Paulo and did a curtsy.

"Shit yeah. Let me at 'em! All those scumbags. Don't worry – we'll back you up. Deadshits, every one of them. We'd whip 'em," Mot said as he punched his hand into his palm.

Mot and Alexa sauntered off.

"He's a good guy – Mot," Paulo said as their friends walked away.

"Sure is. You know how you reckon I'm angry?" Lily kept her eyes on Mot. "I reckon he's *sad*." Lily turned back, adding, "And being sad feels worse than being angry."

"Maybe. Both are pretty rotten."

"Well, anyway, you, my friend, are one of the most insane, gentle, sweet boys that ever lived."

Paulo's olive skin turned a deeper shade. He shook his head in wonderment. "Here you are, telling me all these despicable things you're going to do them. I mean, as if. Don't you think that is just a little bit funny – coming from you?" Lily beamed. "Of all people."

"Okay then, smartarse. It's funny. But at least I can act."

"No, you can't. You didn't get me scared one little bit. Me, on the other hand, I had you nervous and I wasn't even having a go at you."

"Yeah, well, you get this ugly look. I mean not *ugly* ugly but *scary* ugly."

"Okay, enough. I give you compliments, and you slap me one right across the kisser. Listen, you'd impress me by firing up. If we keep dealing with it your way, they're pulling their heads in, shutting up and not causing us any grief, huh? Nup, enough's a-friggin' enough." She shook her head back and forth. "I reckon it's time to play the Joker."

Paulo scuffed his feet back and forth on the asphalt. "The only thing Ronaldo told me about the war was you've got to look like you mean business. Even, and especially when, you don't. I can't whack them. Maybe I can just abuse them?"

"Yeah, that's the spirit. Mate, we've got to scare them. They need to think we can turn feral. That's all they understand. Sad but true – huh?"

She looked at her friend's kind, implacable face with its large hazelnut-brown eyes. *He is one of the finest boys ever to live.* She knew it and she loved him for it.

"You're right. It can't go on. Something's got to change, but how? We need to think it through, to outsmart them."

"After all, you're the one who told me I'm the smartarse in this duo. Right? You're a bit of a smartarse yourself, mate." She poked his arm. "So, how do we do it?"

The wail of the bell sounded for round two. She thought of the little blue wren. She looked for it in the sky, and thought she saw a flash of electric blue in the ghost gum. Lily stood up, shoulders back, and said, "Okay. Let's get them." She put up her left pinkie finger. "Challenge accepted?"

He gripped her finger with his as he twisted his mouth.

TWENTY-FIVE

Lily waited outside the boys' toilets for Paulo – which was hard to do without looking conspicuous. When he finally came out, he was red-faced, and wiped his eyes on the sleeves of his jumper.

"What's wrong?'

"They've written *Paulo Rotondo is a stinking FAG!* on the wall above the urinal…" His voice trailed off. He had both hands on his head in disbelief.

"They what? They'll be sorry." Lily thrust open the boy's toilet door and saw the words scrawled in indelible red Texta large and angry, for everyone to see. On the way out, she smashed the door into the wall.

"That's it! That's the end of the line, Paulo. You either stand up to these gutless punks or this won't end. Don't you see they've got you running scared? They do something to you, and you take it. You hide, you let them bully you, over and over. I'm telling you – you need to stand up to them and let them know the game is over. You're not going to take this anymore. You're going to take charge and stand in their face and tell them what you think of them. I'm here; I'll back you."

"Nup. I can't." Paulo stood slumped against the wall of lockers.

"You can. You have to! Just pretend you're a tough guy. Threaten them, tell them you'll make their lives hell if they don't stop."

"Nup. I know you think I'm weak, but I can't do it. Sorry."

"Shit, mate. I'll do it then. I'm gunna spread a rumour that the pricks that did this have until this afternoon to wipe it off or else…"

"What's the 'or else' part?"

"Dunno. I'm working on that bit," she planted her feet down hard. "If anyone asks, can you at least say you've heard that there's some bad shit gunna go down?"

"Huh! If I have to."

"Believe me, you have to. We both do."

The next week Lily and Paulo were discussing why people do what they do.

"I can't believe it's happening again," Paulo said. "I don't think I can take it anymore. I've tried to ignore it but it's just getting worse. I hate those pricks. I'm over it.".

This time felt different. He was distraught, inconsolable.

"It was really bad when I was younger. I didn't get it. Why would you treat someone like that? One time they ran up from behind and pushed me so hard I went flying along the lino floor into the lockers split my chin right open. I didn't know what hatred meant until that day."

Lily said the only solution was to call them out; call them out for who they were and forecast who they'd end up being. She said, "I knew I'd reached the threshold and there was no more I could take. No matter what they said, no matter what they did, I was taking it to them. They could never be sure if I was around, listening, because I wasn't letting it slide anymore. I'd tried that and it didn't work. You know the funny thing, mate?" She stopped walking beside him, put her hand gently on his shoulder, and he turned to look at her. "Once I'd had enough and I knew I wasn't going to take it anymore, they did too. The meek, hiding Lily was gone and she wasn't coming back. All I had to do was have faith in myself and stand up to them. After that, it stopped."

"Is that how it ended? You just told them it was over, and it was?"

"Yep. I had to gather all my anger and rage and let them have it verbally. To the point that they didn't want to mess with me, because I'd unleashed – and they were scared that maybe I'd become unhinged. From someone who kept their head down, couldn't look people in the eye, to someone who not only called them out as cowards but told them I wasn't going to cop it. Something had snapped in me, and I wasn't going to play their game. I wanted to level the score. All they had to do was to keep pushing me and I was going for them. I would've gone for their miserable throats – actually, the thought of that was quite a satisfying one. Good for me, they took me at my word, or poor Meredith would be trying to place me in some God-forsaken school for juvenile delinquents!"

They laughed and kept walking.

"Why don't you fight back, mate? Why don't you smash them one? I don't get it. You just stand there and let them harangue, belittle and humiliate you. Why? Why don't you stand up for yourself?"

"Lily, I'm a pacifist. Whenever there's the next war, I'm going to be a conscientious objector. I don't believe violence is the solution to anything. No matter what, I won't fight."

"But you're defending yourself. You're the one under attack. It's called self-preservation. If you don't, they'll just escalate this. Please, I'm scared for you."

"Don't be scared, mate. I'm going to keep ignoring them. They'll eventually move on to some other poor prick."

"Nup. You're wrong. They're vindictive cowards. I know their type."

"I've seen what violence does to people. Look at my old man. Apparently, he was a caring guy before the war. Look at him now. I'll never fight. Not ever."

Lily tried again to persuade him. "Whilst you eschew violence, I threaten to use it. I believe I'd resort to it to defend you, or someone I love – huh, these days, maybe even myself. When I think of all the shit I went through in the last few years, and I passively just took it, I feel angry. It's like I've bottled it up inside me, and now it's ready to explode. The other day, when they'd set you up like that, it triggered something deep in me, and all the pent-up rage I've ever felt was just about to escape. They're frightened of me now; they don't know how low I'd go. That's exactly where I want them. I'm going to stick up for you, mate, but I won't always be there when you're picked on. I need you to stand up too."

"I can't. I've told you. I'm a pacifist."

"A *what*? What even is that – *really*?"

"There was a show on TV, and they spoke about people who objected to serving."

"Well, I'm no pacifist. If they dish out shit, I'm gunna serve it back to them. Even if it's just with my tongue."

"Poor bastards. Your tongue's worse than any punch in the head, I reckon."

"Oh, piss off." She tried to whack him. Paulo side-stepped, out of her reach, and pushed her gently back.

TWENTY-SIX

Franklas Mentharl-Cruister stood menacingly close to Paulo with an ugly expression, while his gang's vacuous stares were as plain as their uniforms. Franklas started by whacking Paulo across his head, making Paulo's curls fling from side to side. Then he went in for the push, which hit Paulo on the side of his face, just as Lily came around the corner.

"Hey dickless, get your hands off Paulo!"

"What did you call me?" Franklas's pasty white face flushed pink.

"*Dickless* is what I called you." Lily watched as red prickles travelled steadily up his neck and over his face. He looked at his mates and, in exaggerated tones of sarcasm, said, "Oh, did we hear what the mole said? She's looking for trouble. Not only does she sleep with gay boys, but she insults us. Better teach her a lesson."

Stomping over with his tree trunk legs and heavily shoed feet, Franklas grabbed her by the jumper and yanked her head back as his gang slapped her face hard, one at a time. Paulo grabbed Franklas by the shoulders and pushed him off. Alexa and Mot came from the other direction. Mot was airborne as he threw each one of them in turn towards the common-room wall, where they bounced back like rubber balls, yelping in pain. Alexa thumped Franklas from behind with her schoolbag whirling like roter-blades. A crowd had gathered, encircling the group in anticipation of the escalating drama.

Miss Lemotte, the yard teacher, ran to break it up.

"Enough!" she shouted. "Stop it this minute." Then she

proceeded to march Franklas to the corner and order his mates to wait with him.

Paulo, Lily, Alexa, and Mot were commanded to huddle in the opposite corner.

Miss Lemotte was as sweet as her name, but today she was angry. She ordered both groups to, "Line up and apologise this instance!" When this was delayed, she threatened the principal's involvement.

The two warring parties lined up like reluctant football players after a grudge match. Never were more insincere words spoken. Not one student on either side looked at the others as they spoke, except for Mot. Mot stared hard into each face as if etching their image into his brain. Apologies were said, hands were limply shaken, except for Mot's vice grip (which left each one wincing).

The crowd dissipated as the those involved gathered their belongings and Lily responded under her breath to Miss Lemotte, "It'll never happen again," finishing the sentence with, "...and we get caught," whispered only to Paulo. "That's for sure."

He responded with, "Too right."

TWENTY-SEVEN

Nini gave Lily four dollars from her red purse and said, "Take Paulo to Sandy's Kiosk and buy yourselves some fish and chips for lunch."

Lily gave Nini a bear hug. "Are you sure, Nini?"

"Yes, I'm sure. You've both had a tough week."

Lily flew to Paulo's with Bessie and banged on his window. "We're in the money!"

"Bullshit." he yelled out from the bathroom window.

Once they were at Sandy's, all the tables were taken, so they decided to head off. They even had enough for a can of Fanta each, so there was a spring in their step and the warm package against Lily's windcheater felt comforting and precious.

The wafts of crisp saltiness drove Paulo wild, as he begged to sit anywhere and attack the parcel.

"God, you're impatient. The food's not going anywhere. There's nowhere to sit here; let's go to the lighthouse, out of the breeze."

"What about here on the sand?"

Lily knew that while she held the goods, he'd have no choice but to follow. She kept walking.

Once seated at the lighthouse, their backs against the warm, peeling white walls with the heat of the sheltered western side, Lily opened the prized package, and the smell of the salt and vinegar filled their senses.

Paulo dove right in as Lily selected chips, one at a time. She held them aloft like cigars and, after her third, asked, "What do you see?"

Paulo kept munching on his third potato cake then licked the greasy salt from his fingers. "I see a great big sea. Not much else, looking this way."

Lily kept waving her chips like blackboard pointers and said, "I see potential."

"Huh! That doesn't even make sense. Like, how you can *see* that?"

Lily drew her legs up to her chin, maintaining her focus on the horizon line. "I see the choppy waves way out to sea. The depths we can't fathom sitting here. Like when I swim, I see the jagged lines in the sand, all perfectly uniform, the manta ray that floats underneath with its black-spotted wafting wings, the emerald and blue starfish in the rock pools, the squid that the old Italian fishermen haul in with their inky black trail like leaking blood..."

"Sorry, I can't see any potential in all of that..."

"What I'm trying to say is that we only know so much, and there's a lot more to know. Like potential. It's there, just out of sight, like the bottom of the ocean, the sea urchins, or the crayfish, or the snapper or flathead or whiting... I dunno. Think of Sandy's fish menu – It's huge, and all those fish are from *this* sea!"

"You know what your mind reminds me of?" Paulo looked at her.

"What?"

"The tunnels the old fart Gertram was banging on about in European history and all those poor bastards had to hide out in those tunnels and they never knew when they'd see sunlight again."

"Yeah, but what's that got to do with me?"

"You know, your brain in running around in those tunnels,

thinking of crazy ideas that have no answers, and all you have to do is start spruiking them to poor old Paulo-boy to drive me nuts."

"Well, I drive myself nuts too. I think of all these things that I'm curious about and I want to know the answers to. Some nights I lie in bed and think about why we are here and where did we come from and where do you go when we die, and I think on and on and I fall asleep, but in the mornings, I feel tired 'cause I reckon all night I'm trying to work this stuff out."

Lily remembered the food and watched in horror as Paulo went for the last potato cake. She whacked it out of his hand – "Mine!" – and started munching on it. Paulo picked up the package and emptied the last remnants into his hand.

Lily kept eating and commented, "I wish I could gorge myself like you do."

"Oh, piss off, I do not."

"You bloody well do."

The wind started to flutter the newspaper that had been wrapped around their fish and chips and, with their Fantas drained, the pair stood to leave. Paulo burped loudly.

"You're disgusting," Lily said.

"Thank you. At least it's not the other end." Paulo licked the residual greasy saltiness from each finger.

"True! Small mercies."

"*Take what you can get* – a quote from Ronaldo. Thank you, Nini! Bring on tough weeks every week, I reckon."

"Ha! It's worth it, for sure," Lily said as she held the scrunched-up empty papers.

TWENTY-EIGHT

Two rainbow lorikeets dashed in front of Lily as she trouped home. They raced each other along the dirt road like ribbons, their colours splashing light across the dust.

Nini was relaxing on the back deck with the *Women's Weekly*, enjoying the last rays of weak sunshine, when Lily slammed the front door closed. She told Lily that this was one of her "not-guilty pleasures". Lily thought, *As well as a brandy or two.* Other times, Nini loved to knit, and she'd take a pot of tea, resplendent with the psychedelic tea-cosy she'd knitted, to the back porch. How something so small could have a kaleidoscope of colours Lily found extraordinary.

"Hi Nini," Lily yelled.

"Hello there, Lily-pily. How are you, darling? Did you have a good day?" She tried to crane her neck to the left but recently it only smoothly turned right, so instead she moved her whole body towards Lily's voice.

The flyscreen door creaked, and Lily collapsed onto the old outdoor couch, her feet and legs splaying as she did. Bessie bounded up to hustle in.

Lily wiped her eyes.

"Nup," she said as she hugged Bessie tight. "It was rotten. Again."

"Oh well, darling, there are days like these and then there are magical ones too. I'm sorry it was a stinker." Nini dropped the knitting into her basket and patted Lily's knee. "You okay?"

Lily curled up on the couch and Bessie put her obligatory paw across Lily's chest. She held Bessie's paw and closed her eyes.

"I'm okay, Nini. I'm just tired." The parrots shrieked as they flew in a pack across their yard and out of sight. "I get tired of fighting. I fight with the teachers; I fight with the mean kids... I'm sick of it." Her voice faltered on the last sentence.

"Oh, you dear little girl." Nini breathed out loudly as she helped herself out of her chair. "I'll go and put the kettle on."

She came over and stroked Lily's hair before she went to make the tea. When she came back with a tray, she said, "Lily, are you still using your diary?"

"No, I've got distracted." Lily sat up. "I *was* using it."

Nini poured the tea as Lily took a cream-laden scone. "I had a diary when I was young. Actually, I found it just before I moved in with you and Meredith. Oh my, it brought back some memories. Not all of them pleasant, may I add. At the time, I thought some things were the end of the world... but they weren't. They were stepping stones, little bridges to take me to a new place, a new stage in my life."

Lily wasn't used to Nini talking like this. Her grandmother's tissue-paper wrinkly face softened momentarily as she wistfully looked to the end of the yard and up to the cloudless sky as if searching for something.

"You see, darling, none of us know what's around the corner. We think we do, but we don't. Some of the worst days can lead you to the best stage of your life. Some of the best days can do the opposite. So, don't despair; better times are coming, believe you me."

Lily slurped her tea and nodded her head. They sat in an easy silence. Nini spoke about winning the Intermediate English award and the elation and pride she felt – then returning home to find that her mother, who had been unwell, had suffered a heart attack and had passed away. "My father was not able to cope with the farm and the domestic duties, so I was told to leave school," Nini told her. "I dutifully did so. The resentment and regret stayed with me for years."

"I didn't know that." Lily shook her head. "Thanks for reminding me, Nini." Lily went inside to find her diary and took it out to the porch swing. Bessie curled up at her feet. "There's a lot I have to say," she called back to Nini.

"Good for you. Tell it like it is, warts and all. Get the frustration out on the page. Then you'll make extra room in your heart for all the good things to come. And believe me, they'll be coming, my darling." She gave Lily the longest crinkly smile.

Well, hello, you,

Enid Mary Walters, or Nini ALWAYS takes my side. Even when I know that she knows I was in the wrong! Especially when she knows I was in the wrong. Maybe she feels Mum will deal with the rights and wrongs of stuff but, then again, Meredith makes the odd comment to correct me, but she isn't as on my case as she used to be. Thank God!

Nini gets me. If I ever think of her not being here or "dropping off the twig" as she likes to call it, my heart hurts so much I have to think about something else. She was the legend who told me to pour my heart into this. Well, for better or worse, that's what I'm gunna do.

Today was shit. Really shit. First, I'm late getting to class. The teacher, Mr Powle, had great delight in singling me out and then giving it to me. A bit of public humiliation goes a long way for him. Then Richo Neddleton spills his hot chocolate on my work. Okay, admittedly he didn't mean to, but he's such a clumsy dork. So I swore at him. Not that I'm proud of that. I'm not, but God almighty – my work's smudged and ruined, so I'm bloody furious. Paulo is not in my Politics class, just as well as he wouldn't be pleased with me. I complained to the teacher again and expected his help. He ignores me. Then tells me to see him after the class. But I don't want to waste the whole class. By the time I do speak with him, I tell him what happened, how I feel anxious that the class has been wasted, and how unfair I thought it was that he didn't help me. Then he has a field day. He's off and running with verbal diarrhea and telling me that I'm a prima donna, that I'm demanding and I have a bad temper. That's it. I storm out. He comes out of the classroom and yells at me to come back. In my mind I'm telling him to get stuffed he keeps yelling my name. I wanted to say, "Get stuffed old man". I see myself walking away, gathering my belongings and this middle aged, bald, potbellied man gesticulating wildly. Ms O'Frankhety, the school principal, walks straight into me. Ohhh that's not good. So, I'm in her office, and she's explaining how I can't disrespect a teacher, ever, even if I think they're in the wrong, and I can't walk away, and I can't pack my belongings... I listen with my hands as fists underneath my thighs, "What do you think of injustice, Ms O'Frankhety?" She answers as you'd expect rah, rah, rah, and then I ask, "How would you feel?"

Then she sighs, exasperated, and shakes her head, "Look, Lily, you seem to assume that life will be filled with fairness. Every person you come across will treat you with dignity, respect, kindness, and patience. Is this correct?"

"Possibly."

"I hate to smash this fantasy world; life does not work like that. Unfairness, injustice, intolerance, bias, lack of patience abounds, everywhere we look. Your job as a student is to work against that, not add to it. While yes, you may at times feel unfairly treated, you need

to show restraint, respect and discipline, not to take each issue on, or you'll see yourself in endless trouble. This is the way to get on in life."

"But it's not easy. Some teachers are so mean, and they say things they shouldn't and Mr Powle..."

"Mr Powle is your teacher. He is in charge, and that is whether you like what he has to say or not.'

"It doesn't seem fair."

"No, not all of life is. But if you make a fight out of everything you think is unfair, you'll be fighting a lot, and getting into trouble all the time. Now do you want that?"

I looked at my shoes. "No."

"That's what I thought."

"Okay, Ms O'Frankhety."

"Channel your energy to go for gold. You've got something special in you, Lily. I believe you'll make a difference in this world. In a good way."

So that's what I'll hang on to. Her last couple of sentences; not the detentions, not the obligatory and insincere apology for Mr P; not the fact that I'd now missed the guts of the class that I needed for my assignment. No, just her last sentence, and the look on her face. I knew she meant it.

I'll try again tomorrow.

Sweet dreams,

Me x x

PS I slept on this, and the idea struck me that maybe I love to write because I've tried to keep my emotions in at school and it turned to shit. Now I can tell it like it is and it feels bloody good!

TWENTY-NINE

The lapping water was translucent through to the corrugated sand below. Lily watched the golden light kick up when she waded along the shallows. The frothy foam encased her feet as she walked. In the deeper water, snippets of runaway seaweed danced in tune with the tide. Bessie ran ahead with her tail spinning and sand shooting golden from her paws. The warmth of the sun lightly skipped across the water towards them. Lily's mind wandered back to the last walk she had with her dad.

Many nights, especially in summer, they'd head to the beach after dinner. Bessie would charge ahead, which always made her dad laugh, *Oh, a dog's life – not a bad thing, huh, Lily?* That particular night, as they strolled, the hot pink sunset exploding over the western sea, he spoke about his own dad. Lily had never met him, but Frank said he was *a great bloke, Arthur Richard. A bit of a loveable larrikin. Salt of the earth.* Lily wished she had asked him more, but the conversation moved to his mum. Her dad looked all misty-eyed when he spoke of Heather Agnes. *She was the best. Dad was lucky to have her; we all were. Dad always treated Mum like a queen. She used to laugh at him and wrap her arms around him from behind. She used to do that with me, too, except her head couldn't rest on my back like it did with Dad.*

Lily remembered her dad doing that to her, which she found mildly annoying at the time, but how she craved it now.

In recent days, she'd started talking to Frank out loud. She had read, in an old book on grief from the school library, that talking out aloud to our past loved ones was helpful. It said it was a positive thing to do because it made you feel as if the person you'd lost was still there. From then on, she asked Frank for help, or to give her a sign, or just to listen.

The next day, she was asking Frank what to do about the school bullies as she dragged herself towards Spray Point Secondary. That was the first day that the kookaburra appeared. It showed up every day after that. The first day, it was perched way off in the distance on the fence. The second day, it moved closer to the log that lay across their front garden. On the third day, it sat on their fence and looked her straight in the eye. It tilted its grey and white crew-cut head and looked curiously through her. Initially, she felt confronted, scared that it might peck her. The following day, it appeared on that log and turned its face to stare directly at her. When it started to fly towards her, she turned her back and it gently lifted to a higher branch to stare down at her. The connection with this kookaburra became her own private world. After school, she couldn't wait to get home to see if it was there – and, for a whole week, it was.

Each afternoon, the kookaburra was waiting there on the fence, staring straight at Lily. It held her gaze all the way past the fence. When Lily looked back, the bird shook her tail feathers as if to say, *Don't take it so seriously,* before she cawed her inimitable laugh. *Just because it doesn't make sense, doesn't make it bad. It just is.* Then she flitted off, darting up and down until she zoomed up and over the banksia, she-oaks and moonah bush and out of sight. Until she was gone.

Lily hoped this bird was giving her a signal – a message. She felt lighter, and not so weighed down every time the kookaburra appeared. It was if the bird could see her pain. If only she could figure out where she was going, who she was, where she fitted in, how to make sense of her life.

It was a new day, there was a crispness in the air, and she needed to be in class on time.

Later that term, whenever she heard the kookaburra's distinctive laughter early in the mornings, she wondered if it was hers and exactly where it was. She hoped it found its family.

The more she looked as she walked, the more she saw what she thought were signs from her dad. Now and then, the little blue wren would appear and flutter around her long enough for her to talk to Frank in her mind, and at times out loud, as if he was walking next to her. Some days, once she'd got a whole lot of worry off her chest, she'd listen and see if anything came up. Usually just the wind rustling the leaves, the heavy thrum of the ocean, a dog barking, a truck or bus rattling through the streets. Occasionally, she'd hear his voice in her head, *You'll be okay, Lily-pily. Don't worry. You're stronger than you know. One step at a time.* Whenever this happened, she'd close her eyes, as if to drink it in.

It was Friday, the sky was dull, the road was dull, the asphalt path was dull, and Lily felt drained and exhausted. In her mind, she was complaining to her dad, saying she couldn't stand another fight with those nasty girls, or with one of the teachers, and then she noticed a sprightly young magpie hovering around a low fence as if waving to her with its wings. The stark black-and-white dinner-suit moved to follow her. Mesmerised, she kept walking, and it hopped over to the next fence – keeping stride with her. Her dad's steady voice came, calmly telling her everything was going to be alright. She entered the schoolyard and observed the girls' group huddling and giggling as if she was snorkeling and looking at weird creatures beneath the sea. She floated past them. The usual stuff happened, but it happened at a distance, as if she was looking at it through a glass-bottom boat or in an aquarium.

She told Paulo, as they sat on the bench for lunch, and he said, "Hey buddy, are you on something?"

"Like drugs? Yeah – cool, man, I'm out of it," she said, and staggered around for effect.

"Yeah. The stoners say that they feel like that – not really in this world. I'd be a good stoner."

"Yeah, you'd be a natural. Me – well, maybe calming my manic ways down could be good, but first I have no *spondulix*. Second, I wouldn't even know where to get them. So, I hate to tell you, but it's just the new me." Lily stood up and spun her arms out wide. "I'm feeling good – I can't explain it." She whispered, "I reckon Dad's helping me", as she sat back down.

"Hmm, really? Maybe. You feel good, so that's good."

"No. For me, I need to know why. I reckon it's him. I really do. Do you believe in the afterlife, reincarnation, spiritual stuff, ghosts or angels...?"

"Nup. I don't believe in any of that shit."

"What about a guardian angel; you know – the ones that rest near your shoulder and make sure you're safe and stuff. Do you believe in them?"

"Nup. I believe in Tinker Bell, if that's what you mean."

"No, that's just Walt Disney make-believe. I mean real angels sent down from upstairs – heaven or somewhere."

"Nup. Sorry."

Lily looked over at her friend, who was swallowing the last bites of his sandwich. "I do. I think it's lovely to have a guardian angel follow me around all day and then even at night to keep me safe."

"Well, I believe in keeping my head down and my mouth shut, except if I'm at your joint, and then I believe in keeping my mouth wide open and shoveling anything in that Nini provides! Now that's something I believe in. Her!"

"Yeah, we agree on that one."

They laughed as they foraged for more snacks amongst the lunch Nini had provided for the day – which, as usual, did not disappoint.

THIRTY

At school assembly on Monday, Ms Mary O'Frankhety launched a new award for "students helping students", to encourage fellowship and good community spirit. The Form Five students were allowed to make this award, and had to stand before assembly for five minutes to explain why their chosen person should win it. There were four nominations.

Lily was the last to stand, and Alexa was her chosen recipient. Lily started saying how unselfish and kind Alexa was on Thursday when she helped Lily retrieve all her English sheets, which had been knocked out of her hands. She then looked directly at Nastacia and recounted the whole story. "Just as I was packing my English folder into my bag, I was pushed hard from behind and all of my work went everywhere. My work was being stomped on by students, and I was distressed trying to gather up my sheets. The only person to help me was Alexa."

Alexa stood up. "Yes, I did help Lily," she said, boldly, "after Nastacia Smythton pushed her hard and all her work went flying across the corridor."

Paulo, Mot and several others stood up and confirmed Alexa's claims. "We saw Nastacia Smythton do it."

Ms O'Frankhety took the microphone and told Nastacia to meet her in the office directly after assembly. Nastacia's face was a searing, blistering red, as if she'd been badly sunburnt. She was swiveling her neck to her cronies to back her but, one by one, they looked away, or became fascinated with the floor or the ceiling.

Nini's suggestion for how to deal with Nastacia had worked. In fact, many other students made appointments with the principal to tell her of things she'd done to them or their friends. Her cronies deserted her like rats jumping off a sinking ship.

THIRTY-ONE

It was a *dare to come in and I'll spit you out* type of sea, and this was Spray Point's bayside beach. The bay's roar filled Lily's ears; the salty bitterness assaulted her lungs. She turned south hurriedly from Tea Tree Road to Southern Ocean Road and the northerly lanced her back. She braced herself against the wind and the thought of another school day. The windows rattled in their frames and the musky draft from under the classroom door was a chilling blast. The morning droned by until it was time to scamper to a timber bench with as much clothing as she could gather. Once settled, her crocheted hat and scarf around her head, she folded her arms across her chest and stared at her feet. Her scruffy black shoes were unusually large, the laces never matched, and she had ended up with her left sock up near her knee and the right one collapsed over her shoe. In crowds, she stared at her feet; she'd become accustomed to doing it, perhaps believing that by hanging her head she'd diminish her size and therefore be less of a target. Wrong. Over many years, she came to understand it didn't work that way.

Nastacia transformed into a funnel-web spider as she stroked her thick black hair over her shoulder. Lily's stomach tightened. *Just breathe and say nothing.* Nastacia was on the furthest bench seat, on the side nearest the science room, well out of view. Her beady eyes narrowed to a dark glint as she zeroed in on Lily, who sat sweating at the opposite end, preparing herself for the assassination by words. And so, the game began. Nastacia stood in front of Lily with her feet planted wide and her face slanted at an angle as if she was looking at a rare species in the zoo. She made fake small talk and Lily responded guardedly, aware that her facial expressions were too obvious to shield her true feelings.

"Wow, nice scarf. Hmm, and beret. Looks, umm, really *homemade*," Nastacia said.

Lily clutched at her purple scarf and put it in her lap even though it was cold. She left the beret on as she knew her hair stood up when she took it off.

"Yeah, my Nini made it."

"Huh, your *Nini*. What sort of name is *that*?"

"Her name. She's my nana." Lily made herself look at her nemesis. The image of Nastacia as a funnel-web spider, wicked, ready to pounce, was startling. All she could see was the black hairy legs and arms and poppy black eyes. Lily shivered and looked back at her feet, waiting to hear the true reason that Nastacia had come to talk to her.

"Look, Lily, it's like this. The students in our year level don't like you. Actually, most of them can't stand you." Nastacia took a breather, put her delicate hands on her petite hips, and watched to see what type of reaction she was getting. Lily kept inspecting her tapping feet, although both socks were in line now, pulled up against the cold.

"I just thought I should warn you. They're saying some pretty nasty stuff about you. Not that I want to repeat it. I mean, I can if you want." Again, she scanned Lily for a response. "I mean, I don't know if it's true — not that I'd care — but I get the feeling they hate you. I mean, what they've said — it's spread throughout the whole school." Nastacia folded her arms tightly across her chest and sneered with pleasure at Lily's impassive face.

Lily was silent. She thought of her dad and what he would do. She bit the inside of her lips as the ball in her stomach intensified.

"Wow, that's interesting," Lily said, feeling her peaches and cream complexion become a blazing red. She could feel it start in her chest and creep up her neck until it exploded across her furious face. "They're confiding in you and telling you all this rotten stuff then?"

Nastacia's ice-green eyes became fluorescent as her spider's web tightened. "Yeah, I'm sorry to have to be the one to tell you the truth, but I guess someone has to. It's sort of got to the stage that, you hanging around them, well, ah, is sort of an embarrassment." She nodded her head for maximum emphasis. "Not that there's anything wrong with you. You're just different. We all know it. You know, you're just not like *us*." Her patronising tone sounded increasingly desperate to Lily. "We're all the same, and you're just, um, well, you, you don't fit in." Nastacia fondled her hair, twirling and tossing it back. It was an obsession she had, as if she believed that it added to her beauty.

Lily just thought she looked vain. She sat quietly. Still. Looked up to the sky, and across to a massive old ghost gum nestled close to the entrance of the school. Her hands were sweating, her body burning hot under her clothes. Her face was on fire. She breathed hard and loudly. She kept looking far away at the old tree. She moved forward and gripped the timber bench until she feared it might split in two.

A fresh breeze tingled across her face as she saw the shimmering colours of a rosella as if its wings were waving to her. She closed her eyes and looked again to make certain. Lily became aware of Nastacia's agitation. Nastacia kept clearing her throat and fidgeting. She placed her black patent leather shoes together and apart, together and apart. She started to wring her sparrow-like hands. She resumed her hair fondling and tossing, pushing it up and over, twirling it around her fingers. Lily thought it was fascinating, nearly freakish, and she lavishly extended her silence. It felt powerful. She thought of her dad. What would he do now? Eventually, Lily took a slow, deep, deliberate breath and exhaled slowly.

"Thanks Nastacia." Lily stood up and looked down into her cold green eyes, set hard in her bewildered face. "I could never work you out. You know — what made you tick. Now, thanks to you arranging this little *tête-à-tête*, I know who you are." Lily held Nastacia's stunned expression and gazed at her hanging mouth. "Don't ever speak to me again."

At that, Lily waltzed off, as someone who had shed a burdensome coat, the weight of which could no longer be tolerated. Watching the rosella, Lily understood the point: it was a conniving way to divide and conquer. Lily's popularity was becoming a threat, so Nastacia needed her to remain an outcast, with only a couple of friends, little confidence, and no threat to Nastacia's reign.

After a few steps, Lily started to skip, her arms swinging like batons. She swung them wildly, unburdened. She did a few twirls, bursting to tell her best mate what had just happened.

THIRTY-TWO

She missed Paulo in the throng after school and rang him as soon as she was home. Ronaldo answered the phone, which was unusual. He grunted that Paulo wasn't at home and promptly hung up.

The next day, she ascertained that Ronaldo hadn't passed the message on, and she poured out every detail of her encounter with the funnel-web spider, Nastacia. She even did the hair twirling and tossing and gave Paulo her best evil eye. He watched her with his mouth agape.

"What's up?" Alexa pointed at Lily as she and Mot lumbered up beside them.

"I had it out with the funnel-web," she said, and proceeded to do the whole act again.

"She won't be givin' you grief no more," Mot said with satisfaction.

"Love it, and good for you!" Alexa reached her arm up to high-five Lily as she sat down. "She's a shocker, and she's the one who's been spreading stuff about you. She even lies to your face. Nup, you gave it to her. Well done!"

This story allowed them to talk about the bullying they had all suffered that year. None of them knew how bad it was for the others. The only one who didn't get picked on was Mot, because the first time Bryce tried it, Mot had grabbed him by the throat and shoved him hard against the brick wall outside their form classes, barking, "Say that again and I'll smash your face in."

When Bryce was trembling, he added, "Now say, *Sorry, Mot.*" He didn't loosen the grip around Bryce's neck until he said it.

The teachers had given him grief. Not all of them, but most.

"That's why I hate school," Paulo said. "They treat me like shit."

The rest of them agreed.

For the rest of the break, they shared what the girls had in their lunchboxes. Mot ate half of his curled-up peanut-butter sandwich and Paulo offered up his stale vegemite one. They also shared the avalanche of slights, slurs, exclusion, ridicule, false rumours and insults they had endured. They spoke of Nastacia and the many vicious lies she'd spread about them over the past two years. Alexa and Mot both said they didn't want to pass the horrible rumours on, so they just never mentioned anything.

The four of them decided to defend each other from then on. "To call it out," Alexa said. "I thought it was best to ignore it, you know, not to add fuel to the fire. That's what I do at home. I never thought that maybe being silent might make it seem like I agree. But hearing all the bullshit that's been spinning, I'm speaking up more from now on."

"Yeah, me too." Mot's face was flushed from realising how bad things had got. "Not that I didn't. Like, I used to tell them to shut up or I'd shut them up, but that wasn't enough. I'm sorry, Lily. If there's any more crap, they'll cop it from me — especially that germ, Nastacia. I'd love to make mincemeat of her."

They all laughed.

"We're sticking together," Alexa said as she ran off to class.

"Bloody oath," Mot called after her.

"You bet." Lily high-fived him and headed in the other direction.

Paulo gave them his thumbs up as he trudged back towards the school for mathematics.

It was the first time that Lily raced through the front door after school singing. She hurled her bag towards her bedroom door, followed closely by her hot pungent school shoes, and slid across the linoleum floor in her socks to the kitchen table.

Nini came in from the back door. "Well, well, you do seem like a happy little Vegemite today, Lily-pily."

Lily's head was in the fridge before she gulped down a large mouthful of milk straight from the bottle. Nini put the kettle on and gathered the cups.

"Yep, Nini. Today was ace." Lily fossicked for food as Nini placed the rockie biscuits on a plate.

They sat on the back porch with Bessie, and Lily went through all the events that led to the showdown. Then, she acted out the interaction with Nastacia with gusto (having done it three times already that day) and described the realisation she and her friends had had as a group.

Nini watched Lily, transfixed. "Wonderful, my darling. Firstly, my word, you can act. Secondly, there's strength in numbers. You can mull things over, talk things through and, in the end, come up with an effective plan of attack." She laughed. "So to speak, of course."

"Always remember, they are usually scared people who think this will raise them up. But only the good Lord can do that!" Nini laughed again as she dunked another piece of biscuit into her steaming tea. "Nastacia sounds like a complete non-entity to me."

"Touché." Lily dunked the rest of her biscuit into her tea for emphasis.

That night, as Lily lay in bed, watching the full moon beaming through her window, she felt as if she'd had a heavy belt strapped around her chest that had finally been removed, and now she could breathe. She closed her eyes and listened to the surf droning, the squeaking of the tea tree with the steady breeze through the branches, the final call of the grey gulls, until all she could hear was her breath. Slower and slower, her inhale, her exhale, matching the rise and fall of the waves, lifting up to capacity, emptying out to the ocean floor. She dived beneath the water, dawn approaching, the sunrise breaking through the clouds. Her dad appeared beside her, surfing each wave, holding her hand in between sets, laughing loudly as Bessie came out to join them. "Hey, get off! Christ almighty, Bessie, stop it. Stop it."

Lily was woken by the warmth of the sun, Bessie licking her face with her stinking dog breath.

THIRTY-THREE

As always, Bessie was bolting ahead, Lily and Paulo watching her hit the rise of the sand dunes and stretch out like a thoroughbred, down to the indigo sea.

The sharp air gushed into their lungs as they ran to the ocean's edge. The noise of the waves was loud, with the whitewash swirling and receding like memories. Or were they dreams? Sometimes she wasn't sure.

Lily took a deep breath. "Mate, it was as if I was having an out-of-body experience today with Millicent. I was levitating between my mind and my body; I was looking down at myself and I looked powerful, intimidating – scary, even. I didn't know where or how it was going to end. I was bubbling over with rage." She looked at Paulo's expression to see if he comprehended what she was saying.

"Wow, buddy, that's full on. I mean, she had it coming. You let the steam escape and, bang, she got it in the eyeballs – the little slime bag. I think you've rattled them. I overheard them talking; they think you're a pyscho."

"Great. I want them to think that. Today, I was. I think maybe I was dangerous. God help the little germ if she ever does anything to me, or you for that matter, ever again. I only threatened to hurt her today, but I wouldn't stop next time."

They walked on in silence, captivated by the thunderous waves.

"That's bad, isn't it?" Lily continued. "Maybe I'm a bad person. I never thought I could hurt anything or anyone, but now I think maybe I could. Like I've been pushed to the edge – the edge of goodness – and below is the dark, meandering valley of badness."

Paulo pushed her from the side, towards the sea. She had to hop to miss getting wet. They laughed.

"I mean it. Do you think I could turn bad? Like some people say they can. I mean, you could never turn bad because you are soft and gentle. But maybe I'm a tough hard-arse and, underneath it all, I'm just a seething mess."

"No, you're not. You were just protecting yourself. She's attacked you for years. Serves her right. Bet she pulls her head in now. Better than having you pull her hair out."

"Good one. Very funny."

They laughed and watched Bessie chase the receding waves, only to be drenched with a new one.

THIRTY-FOUR

"Bet you don't even have a brother, you ugly mole, Mango." Stuart was smirking at Lily, his mates Adrian and Brian egging him on from the sidelines. Paulo hovered beside his friend, hoping he wouldn't have to get involved.

"You'll wish I didn't," Lily sneered.

"He's not even around."

"No, he's not, dumb-arse. He's six years older than me. You think I'm big – you wait until he steals your sunlight, you snivelling germ. He's six feet, 7 inches, and built like a brick shithouse."

"Bullshit. Where is he, then?"

"He's in Pentridge for aggravated burglary. He's been in for two years already, but he's meeting with the parole board this week. So, here's the deal. You piss off now and swear never to come near Paulo or me again, and I won't tell him your names and addresses. But if you do, I'm going to give him all your details."

"You what? You wouldn't do that."

"Oh, I bloody well would."

"Would you? We were only mucking around..." Stuart glanced at his mates, seeking back-up.

"Not only do you have a filthy mouth but you're a liar," Lily continued. "You weren't mucking around and we're not copping it anymore. So, you want the deal, or not?"

"Okay. Shit, we get it. We don't want any trouble."

"You should have thought of that before you started all this shit."

"You don't have to go that far. Okay?"

"Oh no, I do need to go that far. And I will. I don't like bullies – and you, Stuart, are one of the worst. My brother is a big, soft teddy bear, except when he's angry. Then he becomes a mean bastard. The three of you against him would have no hope. He'd pulverise you. But you can't say I didn't warn you."

Their eyes widened in their anguished faces, their upper bodies started to lean back before the rest of their bodies followed. Adrian and Brian looked as though they were shaking.

"Hey, Adrian. Tell your sister to back off too. My bro doesn't like mean girls."

"Okay, Lily. No problem. I'll tell her," Adrian stammered.

"Good. I'm just telling you like it is."

After they skulked away, Paulo looked at her. "What just happened? Where did that crap come from? How do you know so much about jail? I was petrified of you, and I'm on your side." Paulo shook his head. "Whoa, you looked scary and the real deal."

"Paulo, it's all a matter of what TV you watch," Lily said. "Don't you watch *Prisoner*?"

"Nup."

"Well, normally, I go to bed and read, but last night I stayed up and watched it. Everything I said came from that show. It's scary shit. So, I knew we had to threaten them. But as I was staring that weak prick down, the show came flooding into my mind. I felt like I was on stage, the words just poured out of my mouth."

"You were fantastic, buddy. Incredible. I'm blown away."

"I was believing it myself by the end."

"No wonder. Wow, how many lies do we need to keep going?"

"All of them. The 'brother in jail' gives us the fear factor, and the romantic relationship gives us distance and cover."

"You're one smart bad-arse. And you just saved *my* arse. Thank you."

"Anytime. Anytime at all."

They high-fived each other and walked lightly back to class.

There was no more trouble from Stuart or his allies. No word from Nastacia, either, but Lily wasn't sure whether that was because of their earlier chat or the new threat. Maybe word about Lily's 'brother' had got around. Lily figured, why not include her?

School became a new experience. People looked at Lily and Paulo with trepidation and they kept to themselves. They took on their new roles and, once the heat died down, they dropped them.

THIRTY-FIVE

"We had to write a creative piece today on 'home', and it could be a place, a thing, a feeling, a memory... What do you think of when I say the word *home*?"

Lily and Paulo were sitting on her verandah, looking out at the garden.

"39 Southern Ocean Road."

"Why?" she pressed.

"'Cause I've always lived there."

"Yeah, but does it feel like home?"

"Yeah, I guess. I haven't had another one."

Magpies, wrens, miners, and sparrows darted in and out of the neighbour's ghost gums, like a race to find their own branch first.

"I reckon I felt at home with Dad. He made everything better. I struggle now to think of exactly what he said, but I know how he made me feel. You know, like you're the centre of the universe or something. Nini does that too."

They swung their legs as the old swing-seat squeaked in competition with the evening birdsong. It was a heavy load with Bessie snuggled up between them. Paulo always got her head on his lap and Lily got the rest.

"I don't know how that would feel, but I reckon it'd be good."

"I guess this old joint feels like home, or it did. Sometimes I want to get as far away from here as possible, and then other times I want to hide out in my room forever. Strange, I guess. I don't think Meredith knows where home is anymore." Lily rearranged her legs and her runners dropped off her feet in the process. "What about Ronaldo?"

"Well, he sure ain't houseproud like those women in *Days of our Lives*."

"That's for bloody sure."

"I don't reckon he feels much anymore. Like he's at work, or he's at home, but he never seems to be where he wants to be."

"Maybe, he wants to go back to the old country."

"I doubt it." Paulo finger-combed his locks and lent far back on the swing. "No one's there for him to go back to. Anyway, he's lived at 39 for decades now. No point moving."

The night was still and sultry. After dinner, Lily retreated to her bed – clammy and exhausted – to be soothed by Gladys Knight & The Pips' *Midnight Train to Georgia*. As she hummed the tune, she wrote in her diary. Lily never wanted to re-read what she'd written, but after a hard day she wrote so much that her hand hurt, and the pages creased beneath her fist.

THIRTY-SIX

It started in the night with the she-oak banging on the roof. The windows rattled and the walls felt as if they'd had a massive push. Lily tossed and turned.

The next day, the wind whipped her body as it roared its annoyance. The walk to school was a gritty one, with the swirling wind and stray hairs flicking into her watering eyes. Once she was through the gates, the usual crowd pushed their unruly way in front and, without any regard for others, darted along the corridors, through doorways and up the stairs.

Mot brooded. Paulo dreamt. Alexa floated. Lily ruminated. The distant kookaburras were trying to outdo each other. Their screeching laughter resonated across the valley. They sat on the grass, Lily with her back resting on Paulo's muscly shoulder. Mot lay, starfish style, face up to the sky, and Alexa folded into herself as a small human ball with a swaying black frizzy top.

They were each deep in their own daydreams when Lily said, "The four of us are a great team."

Alexa's face popped up and she said, "Mango-style to get us motivated. That's the motivational stuff we need from our el Capitano. Love it!"

"You bet. All for one and one for all!" Mot proffered as they rose for class.

"Where do you learn such crap, Mot?" Paulo pushed Mot's shoulder, laughing.

"The idiot box is a great teacher."

"Yeah, a couple of the moronic teachers here could learn a lot from the idiot box," Lily said.

"You betcha sweet bippee. Signing off, Captain!" Mot saluted as he trudged back towards the school.

That afternoon held an endless blue sky. Being Friday, they headed to Lily's after school, as was their weekly ritual. Nini made them muffins and tea. They'd loll around on the back porch and chat as Lily poured the tea. Bessie snuggled up to Mot as soon as he sat down, and he gently patted her golden head. Mot had an affinity with Bessie. If he was around, she was with him.

"What beautiful hands you have, Paulo," Nini commented as Paulo delicately chose a warm blueberry muffin from the plate. "I had a friend with lovely, slender fingers once. He became a magnificent piano player. Not like my dear Alf, God rest his soul – he had hands like a wharfie's labourer, but with a heart of gold, of course."

They laughed and examined each other's hands. Alexa's delicate palms were nearly half the size of Paulo's or Mot's.

Lily nodded to Paulo as she spoke. "Our friend here, with the elegant mitts, has some exciting news to share. Mr Rotondo, over to you..."

Paulo looked embarrassed as Nini sat down in her tapestry-cushioned chair and said, "We're all ears."

He ruffled his hair, finished his mouthful, and cleared his throat. His face turned a burnt brown as he looked at Nini. He did a nervous laugh, "Oh, I dunno really – hmm maybe dance, like a dancer or something. Maybe."

"Wow! That's great. You've got the music in you, that's for sure," Alexa piped in, as a flash of Paulo's mother singing Linda Ronstadt filled his mind.

"Oh, good for you, Paulo. I admire anyone following their dream. *To dream, the impossible dream...*" Nini started to sing.

"What a wonderful dancer you'll be."

"There are many nights now that he's got to practice and I'm all for it. If you're going for gold, you've got to put yourself under the hammer, I reckon," Lily said. "I really admire you, mate. You've found your thing."

"What about you, Lily?" Alexa spoke in her deep, resonant voice. "What's your thing, your dream?"

Lily looked startled. She glanced towards the backyard. After a while she spoke, quietly. "Hmm, I love to write, so maybe a writer or an actor, or a teacher. Maybe. I'm not sure yet."

"Yeah, I reckon with all that diary stuff you do, you'll be a writer. An actor... yeah, I can see that. But a teacher would be good, too, because you'd be a good one and not a dickhead. Oops – me and my big mouth. Sorry for swearing, Nini." Alexa took a long sip of tea.

"Oh, no, dear. No offence taken." Nini looked at her granddaughter. "Wonderful, Lily. How exciting. You'll be fabulous, whatever you choose. You, Alexa – what's your dream?"

"I want to live overseas. Maybe do some charity work – you know, an orphanage in India, or somewhere exotic. I can see myself working with naughty, out-of-control kids. Let's face it – with my family, I've had years of practice."

They all laughed.

Paulo turned to Mot. "Now – leaving the best to last. Mot, what about you?"

Mot blushed and stammered. "Oh, I dunno. Um, nothing jumps out at me. Haven't worked it out yet." He looked away.

"You will. Just don't put it off too long – so long that you wake up years later and the dream has evaporated."

Nini smiled faintly as she pushed down on the arm of her chair, steadied herself and waddled back into the kitchen, balancing her cup and saucer, and singing, *To dream, the impossible dream...*

THIRTY-SEVEN

Glide, roll, stroll, amble, strut, teeter, scramble, scurry, slide, slink, sway, leap frog, float, hover, bolt, dart, dash. Lily made a list of words for her creative piece, *Vanish*, for Mrs M-S. She was dreaming of all the ways you could disappear. Her piece was about a young girl who floated through the world, half girl, half angel. Half divine, half cheeky. Half here, half there. Until she vanished. Lily thought maybe she could go to another realm, another world. Maybe an underwater world. She saw herself as this creature. She floated, she swayed, and she glided through the beauty of that world with its patterns, shapes and shadows; with its kaleidoscopic colours and the omnipresent danger of what lurked nearby.

Lily found Nini kneeling on her cushion at the rose garden bed. From this angle, Nini looked like a gnome who had fallen face first into the dirt. She wore her old floppy green hat that made her soft face look childish.

"Hi Nini, it's little old me," Lily said as she hugged her from behind.

At the *me,* Nini turned and patted Lily's arm with her dirt-covered gloves.

Nini loved her roses, and she planted different coloured ones in one garden bed on the way to the Hills Hoist in the backyard. Now there were always bright fresh flowers inside. Their scent mingled with delicious aromas of cooking, velvet soap, clothing to be folded or the steamed scent of ironing. The house was an oiled cog in motion, though Meredith didn't seem to notice. It was a relief for Nini and Lily to see that she had returned to work. As Lily overheard Meredith say to Nini, "We need the money but, also, I need a reason to get out of bed."

On one of the rare occasions that Meredith went into Lily's room since Frank had died, Lily found her seated on her bed, reading Lily's diary.

"*What* are you *doing*?" Lily demanded.

"I'm reading your beautiful poetry."

"You shouldn't read my diary." Lily marched over, grabbed the diary out of her mother's hands and snapped it shut. "It's mine, and it's private. It's not for you to go snooping around in."

Lily stormed to the bedroom door.

Meredith looked at her through watery eyes. "I'm sorry, I just needed to know how you are." She sat motionless.

"I was okay until I found you doing this!"

"I'm sorry. I know I shouldn't have."

"You need to promise you won't do it again."

"I won't, Lily. I just worry about you sometimes." Meredith breathed out and let her shoulders drop. She clasped her hands in her lap, as if she didn't know what to do with them.

Lily came back a few steps from the door.

"I love the one, *Where are you, my dad*," Meredith said, sadly. "It's truly beautiful."

Lily opened the diary to that page and, after a while, said, "Yeah, me too."

"Could you read it to me?" her mum asked. "I'd love to hear it in your voice."

Lily sat down on the bed close to her mother and read the poem aloud.

Where are you, my dad?
Where are you, my dad,
Where have you gone?
I've been so lonely and sad.
For far too long.
It's not the same here anymore,
Without your smiling face coming through the door.
A big hello from Mr Moon
I pray every night to see you soon.
Dad, you were my sun and you were my laughter.
I hope so hard that we meet in the hereafter.
I love you forever and ever and ever.
You were my greatest treasure.

Meredith put her arm around Lily and gave her a gentle squeeze. "I know how much you miss Frank. He was wonderful." As she silently walked towards the door, she said, "Thank you, darling."

When the door closed, Lily sat for a long time and re-read all her poetry, and then closed her eyes and listened to the late afternoon birdsong. The sweet chatting of one bird to another. She saw herself on stage, reading her poetry with a commanding voice. She felt herself sit straighter on the bed. She decided that one day, she'd read them all to Nini. One day in the future.

THIRTY-EIGHT

It was sports afternoon and Paulo went to get changed. He always waited until the other boys had left for the oval before he went in. It was soccer and the good ones were being as vicious with their kicking as they could be without teacher detection. Paulo tried to hang around within the teacher's sightline. But after ten minutes, Big Red Manifold unleashed and kicked the ball right at Paulo's head. Upon impact, Paulo dropped to the ground and did not move. The siren blasted and the kids ran for their buses. Mrs Lederidge blew her whistle irrelevantly as most of the kids had already run off. When the teacher noticed Paulo face down on the oval, she ran to him. Turning him over, Mrs Lederidge called out to some kids who happened to be sauntering by. "Run and get the nurse immediately!"

Paulo had concussion, a black left eye, and massive swelling around his cheek and eye socket. When the paramedics asked him, he couldn't recall his name or where he was. He had a severe headache and was trundled on the trolley to the sick bay.

Lily was waiting for her friend at the school steps. When he didn't arrive, she went to his classroom where his form teacher told her that Paulo was in the sick bay.

"Oh God, no," Lily said. "They've got stuck into him big time today."

Mr Frenet looked puzzled. "Who do you mean by *they*?"

"The sports jocks – you know."

"Well, I don't think you should be jumping to conclusions, young lady. Paulo is not the most agile student and he probably just tripped over his own feet."

"I doubt it, Mr Frenet." Lily closed the door and ran down four steps at a time to the sick bay. When she saw Paulo's head wrapped with ice and saw the purply blue around his swollen eye she thought she might throw up. She went into the corridor and breathed out hard, thinking, *What good would that do him – me in one bed and him in the other?*

Returning to the sick bay, Lily sat on the edge of the bed. "Those pricks. What happened Paulo?" She said, leaning towards him and patting his hand.

"I dunno," he answered, groggily. "The last thing I remember was, I turned to see where the ball was coming from and Big Red was kicking and then Mrs Lederidge is yelling in my face, *Can you hear me, Paulo? Stay awake. You mustn't fall asleep.* Bit bloody stupid, if you ask me; I was in agony and she's telling me not to nod off. As if."

There were no repercussions for Big Red. When the sports teacher asked him what happened, he played dumb and said he'd kicked the ball towards the goal, the siren went, and he left for his bus. Lily couldn't believe that Mr Frenet and Mrs Lederidge didn't watch Big Red more closely. They seemed completely oblivious to his antics. A kid they didn't know well told Lily and Paulo that the teachers had been warned off Big Red because his father was the mayor, and he had threatened to make life hard for the school if there were any complaints. So they turned a blind eye.

THIRTY-NINE

In the last term, when afternoon walks were frequent, it was a big-sky day, where the clouds were banished and the blue enveloped you. Lily sat with Paulo on the point.

"Do you know the day you asked me for a walk?"

"Yep, I do." Paulo nodded.

"I mean, we knew each other to say 'hi', but we weren't mates."

"Yep."

"I was feeling friggin' bad that day. All the smartarse comments had added up. I just wanted to fit in somewhere – anywhere. I wasn't welcome anywhere. I felt alone." She looked far off into the vast blueness. "I didn't know if I could hack it much longer..." Her voice trailed off.

"Wow, that's bad. What shitheads. I've had crap too – pushed around and stuff – but I can go into my head. It's weird but, since mum left, I can go inside my head and be somewhere else." He scratched his head as if that might tell him why.

"How do you do that?" Lily asked. "I wish I could."

"Dunno. If it gets bad, I just do it." He spoke as if it this had just dawned on him.

Lily stopped talking, unusually lost for words. After a long break, she said quietly, "What you did for me that day, I reckon saved me."

A streak of silver appeared dazzlingly on the rim of the water. Transfixed, they sat looking out in the same direction. Paulo turned his face to one side and looked at her as he dropped his arm around her shoulder.

"I wish I'd known, buddy. That day, I saw your face and it looked so bloody sad. Your eyes were all swollen, your face was red and blotchy."

"Oh, thanks mate! Kick a dog while they're down, why don't you? Geez, I sound absolutely hideous *and* I looked like shit!"

They laughed.

"No, sorry I didn't mean it like that. You just looked sad." His long, olive fingers gave her shoulder a gentle squeeze. "Anyway, we're best buddies now, so they can all go and get stuffed."

"Yeah, I don't give a rat's arse about them anymore. I feel a bit sorry for them. They're petty, small-minded and boring."

"Shitheads. May all the shitheads hang out together to make the biggest pile of shit the world has ever seen, so all the awesome people like our good selves don't have to waste time wading through the dung-heap to find each other." Paulo raised his arms and proclaimed to the big blue sky. "Shitheads United! Long may they stick to stinking together!"

The pair laughed all the way home.

FORTY

The rockpools at low tide held a special allure for Lily. She delighted in gliding her feet through the translucent water. The starfish were often hidden well underneath the rocky ledge. The anemones were dotted in the moss next to the seaweed and kelp. Rust, tan, black, maroon, cream, olive, honey gold and lime green – the colours beneath the sea.

The further out she waded, there was more hazel and bronze kelp and less green-black seaweed. The greens were as vast in variety as the blues of the sea and sky. Today, the rock pool was an emerald green, set apart from the pearling deep blue of the ocean. Set after set, the waves charged across the sea to shore. The rock pools were left intact, calm and still, until the tide changed, and they were again flooded and belted by the incoming sea.

Lily's feet were leathering over the summer. From the moment she hit the sandy track, her shoes were off. The only problem was, if she didn't bring her thongs and the sand was blisteringly hot, she had to lunge – hurl her towel, hop a few paces, and repeat — all the way back to the water or the shaded track, depending on whether she was arriving or leaving for the day. It was a manoeuvre that she taught Paulo when he started to join her.

"Jesus, this track is killing my feet!"

"I told you to bring your thongs, mate." She laughed and threw one of hers at him. "I learnt the hard way too. They're good protection from bull ants, heat, and snakes."

"Snakes? Are you kidding? I'd die if I saw a snake." Paulo

looked back down the track as if to flee.

"Nah, only joshing," she lied. "Come on." She pulled his arm. "Never seen one." She lied again.

Once at the emerald shoreline, Lily ran and dove in. The waves were gentle rollers and the spray was light. It was the type of day where you clearly saw through the green water to the rippled beige sand beneath. The sunlight threw out jagged lines under the forming wave. Paulo stood waist deep, jumping up and over the small waves as she beckoned him out.

"Come out, mate!" Lily swam hard and bodysurfed the next wave. "It's so much fun," she called as she swam out. Another wave rose up and she rode in effortlessly and tumble-rolled to greet him.

Breathless, her wet hair all over her face, she said, "It's gentle today. Come on. You can do it. I promise." She swam way out the back, duck-diving through wave after wave, until all he could see was her arm waving.

Tentatively, Paulo swam further out, until he lost his footing. He ducked under three consecutive waves and caught his breath before realising that he was being dragged away from the direction he was headed in. He searched for Lily, but she was nowhere to be seen. The waves were coming from all directions, as if the wind and tide were constantly changing their minds. He took in a mouthful of water; he was tired, and treading water. Another wall of water rose and he tried to dive under, but he was too late. It was on top of him. The gentle, smaller waves had become larger, meatier ones, some waves doubling up. He panicked, took in more water, and started sobbing. Another punch to the head from a sideways wave, followed closely by another one appearing from the opposite direction. He was bobbing like an untethered buoy. He couldn't fight against the powerful vacuum coming from the inky blue-black water.

The shore was getting further and further away. He had never been out this deep and he believed he was going to die. Still searching for Lily between the waves, he started to pray – not that he believed in it. He prayed that he didn't get eaten by a shark, before, during, or after his death. He prayed that if there was a heaven, he would go there, and not to hell.

Lily was desperately trying to swim to where Paulo's dark hair was just visible above the water, but the waves were fierce, and she kept being pushed back towards the shore. His head was heavy and started to loll, and he was swallowing mouthfuls of salty seawater. Gulping, struggling to breathe, he took in the water from the side waves that kept belting him. Paulo started to drift sleepily. Each time he took another mouthful, he woke up. His limbs felt like weighted steel, and his eyes started to close. A thunderous wave roared its descent and Paulo was hurled and smashed as if he were a ragdoll in a washing machine. He rolled around and couldn't see daylight. His lungs were on fire.

Finally, his body was flung back to the surface and he heard her. "Paulo! Paulo, I'm coming. Keep treading water. I'm nearly there."

Whack! From nowhere another monster hit him. This time he hung on. *He had to hang on until Lily found him.* He was thrust out and there she was, just out of arm's reach, paddling strongly towards him on a surfboard. She dragged his limp body up and he lay slumped, motionless, along the board.

"Mate, you've got to hang on," Lily told him. "I'm gunna push you and you're heading for shore. Hang on."

Push, bang, he felt a massive surge and then he was airborne, flying along the wave. He gripped the board so tightly that when the wave broke, he eskimo-rolled with the board on top of him before it shot off like a slingshot and he was slung into the foaming whitewash of the shallows. Paulo crawled and dragged himself along the sandpaper shoreline, where he collapsed on the sand and rolled onto his side, coughing and spewing up what felt like litres of seawater. He could not move. A couple of surfers came running up to him.

"Mate, we thought you were a goner. Those waves were munchy."

"Yeah, you got caught in a bad rip. Nasty stuff," the other surfer said as he put his towel around Paulo's shivering body. Lily had retrieved the surfboard and ran along the beach to where Paulo lay shaking.

His teeth were chattering so loudly Lily thought he could smash them. His eyes were blood-red, and his body looked the sickly grey colour of a dead person's.

"Oh my God, mate, are you okay?" She knelt next to him. "I'm sorry. I'm so sorry," she said shakily as she pushed his errant locks from his face. She sat next to him and patted his back until Paulo stopped vomiting.

When he could finally sit up, the surfers gave him a drink of water and helped carry him up the beach to their car. Then they drove them home.

Lily helped Paulo inside, where he collapsed onto a kitchen chair, Lily calling out, "Hello! Ronaldo?"

When there was no reply, she made Paulo a cup of tea. Leaving him to run him a bath, she saw Ronaldo leaning in the doorway of the television room, where Lily could hear the horse races. She told Ronaldo what had happened. His eyes slid over to where Paulo sat, hunched and shivering, at the kitchen table, and said, "More fool him." He shook his head and returned to the horse races.

Lily brought Paulo another cup of tea. "Please forgive me." She patted his back. "That was totally my fault. I'm such an idiot. I'm so bloody sorry."

"You didn't mean it – I didn't have to go out," he said into his shaking cup."

I pushed you into it. It could've been so friggin' bad…" she stammered, choking back tears.

He gulped down the tea and looked directly at her. "You saved me. If it hadn't been for you…"

"Don't think about it. I should never have badgered you to come out. What a shit thing to do. When I couldn't see you, I was so shit-scared I was going to lose you. I couldn't live with myself if…"

"Hey, hey, you didn't lose me. It's okay." His large brown eyes floated in their red rims. "I'm just not into the surf." He let his head rest on the pillow she gave him and closed his eyes. "Does this mean you owe me? 'Cause, if it does, you may need to produce a lot more food for Paulo-boy."

"As good as done."

He lifted his weary head and they linked pinky-fingers before he headed to the bath.

It took a few weeks for Paulo to go to the beach again. Eventually, he joined her at the Spray Point back beach.

"I'm only staying at the water's edge, buddy. I mean it."

"Yeah, I know."

"I mean it," he repeated.

"For sure. I may be stupid, but I'm not *that* stupid,' she said as she launched herself towards the water.

Later, they sat on the beach and watched the sets rolling in. Some of the waves were clear and their spiralling lips were fringed with fluorescent foam, spraying diamonds and stars in their wake. Lily thought they looked too enticing to be lethal.

"Apart from nearly drowning my best friend, you know what I love about the ocean the most?"

"Nup. Everything?"

"Possibly. In the ocean, you know you're alive. No matter how numb you feel, in there, you're fully awake. Apart from the other day, when I thought I'd done the worst thing in the world – to insist you swim out way beyond your capabilities just because I wanted you to be with me. So bloody selfish. That is the most stupid thing I've ever done. I still have nightmares about it. Believe me, I'll never do that again. *Ever.*" She looked at him.

"It's okay. Don't say sorry anymore. It was a mistake but look, I'm *okay.*"

"Thanks, mate. I won't push you again."

"Yeah, that's a start."

"I guess I've got to start somewhere." With their knees under their chins, they watched in silence as the ocean discarded wave after wave.

"You know, I reckon I'm a better person on the days I swim. I don't get as angry."

"That's good." The next wave thrashed itself to the seabed. 'I'm happy just to watch."

"Fair enough. I can be the lunatic that takes it on."

"You are the lunatic. Period."

"Oh, get stuffed, mister – I'm just perfect in every way."

They pushed and shoved each other, staggering and collapsing into the sand, until they hit the homeward track. As they left the beach, the blazing sunset threw the wildest pink and orange hue across their faces as it lit up the western sky.

FORTY-ONE

As Lily ascended the crest it felt as though an arctic block had melted into the writhing cobalt blue. The sea-spray needling her face made her feel electrically alive. The closer she was to the beach, the more vibrant she felt. She ran hard, tossing her towel and clothes across the gritty sand, and forged through the biting wind into the barrage of waves until she was under. Her brain threatened to explode from her ice-aching skull and her limbs were weighted down with pulsating blood. *Another five*, she told herself.

She swam out to where the breakers were brewing, one threatening wave after another steadily gaining momentum. Bang, it was on top of her, and she was paddling with everything she had. She knew she wasn't the strongest bodysurfer, but today she was determined. It didn't take long before the second breaker bore down on her and, this time, she was heading for the sandy reef below. She steadied herself and waited until the roaring noise subsided and the black shadow passed, then she exploded like a cork from a champagne bottle. She shot back down to a mouthful of salty water when a monster wave descended. This time, she had to talk herself through the levels of darkness towards the reef. *Now, don't panic, little one, hold your breath, you're nearly there.* Frank's soothing voice was in her head, but this was too hard. She felt the constriction in her chest, like bricks, a desperation for air, a limpness infecting her limbs until, dreamily, she closed her eyes. She awoke as she was being ejected from the ocean as if from a taut sling. Her body was shooting towards the shore. Landing hard, she staggered to the beach and fell face first into the cold, coarse sand. Shivering with shock, she started the long, exhausting walk home. Her legs ached with fatigue. *Never treat the ocean casually, Lily-pily. It is in charge, and you must pay it due respect.*

After a long, soaking bath, she went to bed. She awoke to gunfire – bombs and guns – and found herself in a warzone. She shook herself towards the light-show streaming through the cracks in the blinds over her bedroom window. It rolled and stormed and lit up her bedroom like an operating theatre. Bessie was barking insistently from her laundry bed. Lily got up to retrieve Bessie and snuck the shivering dog into her own bed. More for herself than Bessie.

Her limbs ached from the evening's swim and her legs were jelly-like. Wearily, she started clearing out her dresser-drawers. She had promised Meredith that she would sift and sort old stuff next time a heavy blanket of melancholy descended. The more she found, the more she stopped and read, dropping back into a time now lost. She uncovered Meredith's handwritten notes preceding the birth of their only child. *Her.*

There were kindergarten forms, young children's paintings and drawings, special Mother's Day cards and Father's Day cards. *You are the best Dad I ever had...* It was a ricochet she wasn't expecting, as if she was paddling against a stream and, inadvertently, she had gone over the waterfall and cascaded into locked-away memories. She was clearing cupboards and, in the process, uncovering certain objects that took her back, way back, to another time.

FORTY-TWO

The roar of the ocean filled Lily's ears as she trekked down Southern Ocean Road. The ghost gums stood solid among the tea tree and moonahs, their pale limbs twisted and protruding like pink-veined fingers. The sky was littered with wispy clouds the colour of wet sand, its colour shifting from the weakest aquamarine to Grecian blue the closer she got to the smashing waves. Large chunks of pungent seaweed lay scattered across the sand, like the discarded remnants from a late-night wedding. As soon as she arrived, the waves started to lose their potency, but the sea's mist and frothy, white swirling edges were fascinating to her. The slant of the ocean from shallow to deep was treacherous, moving just like the sandbanks beneath. Not the place for beginners. Then she remembered Paulo, shook her head as if to remove the bad memory, and watched Bessie jump at seagulls, bark at waves, and dash ahead.

From the carpark she could see a couple of seasoned surfers way out to sea while others straggled in, knowing that by nine am they'd had the best of the day. The deepest blue-black outline met the horizon. Nini's words from last night ran over and over in her mind: *Be true to yourself, Lily. Never lower yourself to their level.*

Lily knew Nini was right. But it was one thing to say it, another thing to do it. Meredith only ever proffered tough love. Lily felt exhausted just recalling her disinterested expression as she interrupted Lily mid-story. Meredith had a habit of suddenly appearing and joining in when she wasn't wanted, usually having missed most of the conversation, and being entirely absent when she *was* actually wanted. *Why bother to interrupt when you've got nothing to offer, and why never show up when you're needed?*

Lily started to take off her windcheater as she followed Bessie to the sand. Trudging through the water as if through quicksand, her breath got heavy and her heartbeat drummed in her ears. She lumbered on and kept her eye on Bessie, still darting ahead, watching to keep her anchored on the shore, safe from a rogue wave.

By the time she got to Durga Rock, Lily's face was burning hot, though her arms and legs were chilled. Her body felt tired, and the last spray of ocean mist helped her turn for home, ready to hit the bath and take a large Milo in with her.

FORTY-THREE

The morning was shades of gold in an incendiary sky. Lily hopped down Paulo's side path and yelled from his back step. She proceeded into the musty, rancid fat, and sour-beer-smelling kitchen until he answered.

He staggered out the back door after her, as if his schoolbag was full of rocks.

"You really try to be late, don't you?" she scolded.

"No reason to rush to hell, is there?"

"Very friggin' funny, smartarse. You can laugh when we get three detentions from Frog-face," Lily said, her annoyance easing slightly.

"Okay – I'm just not a morning person."

"Ain't that a fact." She dragged Paulo along by marching just ahead of him.

"Why do you appear so calm when we're on the verge of more shit going down?" Paulo asked as they waited at a red light to cross the road.

"Before we were best mates, I was calm on the outside, but a sad-sack underneath," Lily answered.

"If the old man did or said anything I didn't like, I'd retreat like a turtle. Hide until the cloud passed. The teachers at school, I didn't like them. Just because. Then the kids, well, there's good reason to loathe some of those lowlifes. So, I can seem calm, but maybe I'm nervous underneath."

"I'm nervous on the top."

"Nup, you're over the top." Paulo pushed her from behind. "But you, Mot and Alexa make everything better."

As the lights changed to green, she smiled and said, "Sure, but I still reckon, no offence mate, that you could sometimes fire up. Stand up, hold your ground. You've got a big heart, but remember we were warriors back in the cave days."

"I thought we were hunters and gatherers – or something like that. I think I could rev up if I had to, to protect my dignity. Or you! Yes, I could fire up if they attacked you. That would get me."

"Good. That's the way. I knew you had a flicker of mongrel in that pooch-type heart of yours. I'm a rottweiler and you're a basset hound. Maybe we should both be labradors or golden retrievers like Bessie."

"Or a stuck-up manicured poodle, or a sweet Aussie terrier like some of the kids around here."

"They smell like dogs but aren't as attractive. We do our canine friends a terrible disservice."

Their laughter diluted the sting of passing through the steel gates.

At lunchtime, the air was still, but the noise was unbearable. They walked to their favourite spot under the clump of ghost gums. Lily laid out the contents of her lunchbox between them. Mot and Alexa ran over to join them, and the lollies were shared for entrée.

On their walk home that afternoon, Paulo said, "Hey buddy, I'm sorry, but I told the old man that I wanted you to come for my birthday dinner and he said no. I was so pissed off. He said he needed to talk to me privately about something. He said it had to be just him and me. What an old prick. I feel so bad."

"Nah, don't feel bad. I get it. He wants to make you feel extra-special and he's planned something. So, I'll catch you the next morning. We'll celebrate together then. Besides, you can come for dinner that night. Nini will have her specialty roast lamb and apple pie, just the way you like it."

"Yeah, that's better anyway. You'll only miss burnt snags, mashed potatoes, peas and possibly, maybe, melted Neapolitan ice cream if Ronaldo's gone shopping. And, as you know, that's a very big *if*."

Lily had spent several nights making an enormous birthday card for Paulo. Straight after dinner, dishes dried and put away, she'd raced to her bedroom to create it. She wrote poems, ditties, and added photos of the two of them, as well as some with Mot and Alexa. She interspersed dried seaweed, shells, and sand she threw onto Clag glue, as well as every colour of the rainbow – sunrise, sunsets, and the sea in between. Her canvases were two huge project sheets, sticky-taped together. It was the story of their collective lives, from when they met until this momentous birthday. Paulo was slightly older than Lily. She felt so excited that he was finally sixteen.

Early the next morning she was ready: card; green thongs wrapped in silver cellophane; two towels. She had a mission to accomplish that day – to get Paulo to overcome his fear of the deep sea. She banged on his window. Nothing. She went to their back door, which was never locked, and banged there. Nothing. She opened the door and called out. Nothing. She went in. She ratter-tat-tatted on his bedroom door. Still nothing, and no sign of Ronaldo either.

"Okay, Mr Sixteen-Year-Old, if you won't come out, I'mma comin in!"

The stingy, airless room was pitch black, with only a sliver of light around the edges of his worn blind. He had all the bed covers over his head, so she nudged him firmly. "Hey there, big boy, I'm here to take you on a mission. Plus, I've got your present with me. Come on, get up!"

He stuck his head up like a turtle who'd been woken from a deep slumber.

"I'm sorry, buddy, I can't."

"What? Why not?"

His disheveled hair and his crinkled face made him look like a wreck.

"I haven't slept." He stuck his head back under the covers. "I couldn't."

Lily sat on the end of his bed, trying not to sit on his feet. "Listen, you were just excited, or anxious, or something. Once we're at the beach, you'll be fine." She nudged his legs. "Come on, Buddy. I've been planning this for weeks. I need you to get up. You'll love it. I've made you something really special."

He didn't move for a long time. Lily grew concerned. He was normally sleepy in the mornings, but not like this.

Eventually, he pushed the covers off, sat up, and folded his long arms tight across his chest.

"I'm not leaving until you say what's wrong." Lily stared at him.

"The old man-made dinner. We sat at the table, and when the ice-cream was in our bowls he started to talk." Paulo pointed to a worn-out shoe box on his desk. "He told me that he'd been waiting seven years to give me that."

Lily looked but didn't move.

"It's full of letters and cards that Mum wrote to me – since she left." He gestured to Lily to have a look.

When she opened the box, she gasped. "Oh my God! I've

never seen so many letters." Her hands strummed the edges of the old envelopes held together by an elastic band.

"He decided that when I turned sixteen, he would give them to me to throw out, make a bonfire with, or ignore. He said it was up to me. Now I'm sixteen, I'm old enough to decide." Paulo rubbed his red-rimmed eyes hard and then re-folded his arms.

"Oh, this is incredible. She was writing to you all this time, and you never knew. See – there was an explanation for her just disappearing from your life. It'll be in the letters for sure..."

"Nup. Too little too late. I'm never gunna read them."

His face was one of the saddest she'd ever seen, except Meredith's face the day of her dad's funeral. Lily felt lost. She couldn't believe what he'd just said.

She put the box down. Paulo's eyes seemed to be searching for something in Lily's expression. He looked haunted, hopeless, and helpless all at the same time. Lily was speechless. Paulo was immovable.

She knelt by the side of his bed and put her arms up to hug him. He slid down the bed and collapsed onto his pillow, face down. Lily lifted her friend's wet, blotchy face into her arms as he heaved and struggled to breathe. It reminded her of when her dad passed away. She didn't remember collapsing but the next thing she had known she was rocking and wailing into Nini's soft bosom. Her face had been red and blotchy like Paulo's; her body heaving and gulping for breath like all the air itself had been sucked out of her and all that was left was a suffocating numbness.

The room's insipid yellow light was creeping around the edges of the blind, like a thief. When Paulo's breathing finally evened out, Lily moved quietly to the window and gently lifted the rickety blind. Pushing the thin window open, she asked him, "Ready for that swim?"

"Not yet." He slid back under his old brown-and-green tartan blanket. As he turned away from the window, he said, "Maybe later."

"Sure. I'll come by at lunchtime." She pulled the blind back down and gently tried to close his door. As usual, it scraped along the floorboards where the paisley carpet had worn out. Lily wondered how long it would be before the door handle fell off. Maybe the door would unhinge first.

When she returned, his large frame was resting on his small brick fence. He stood up and gave her a hug. "That card you made for me is the best present I ever got."

"Oh, good! I'm glad you like it."

As they turned to walk towards the beach, he dropped his arm around her shoulder. "These green thongs are ace. Thanks buddy. You're one in a million."

For weeks afterwards, Lily did not let up about the letters. At every opportunity, and inopportunity, she begged him to read them. She even promised not to ask what his mum said in them – not that Paulo believed her. Nor did she believe herself. She suggested he go back to the earliest ones by checking the date they were posted. Maybe he could read one dated March 1976.

FORTY-FOUR

It was the dull time of day – not the full glory of morning or lunchtime and not the dreamy state of pre-dinner; just the nowhere lull between school and dinner. As Lily walked to Paulo's, she was thinking about what happened just before she left school.

Lily had been walking along the corridor near the staff room and passed Lucille-Heather – who stood to the side picking scabs from her scarred arms, as usual, as if waiting to get into trouble – when she overheard two form teachers chatting.

"That one has the name of an angel that lives in heaven, not the name of a wretch that lives in hell," the first teacher said.

"Oh, my, that explains a lot," the other one said before closing the door behind them.

Lily relayed the incident to Paulo later that afternoon as soon as she got home.

"Shit! I just thought she was a weirdo," he said as he stood up from where he had been sitting on her front step.

"Yeah, I reckon everyone did. Maybe she's just sad."

"I feel bad."

"Yeah, me too."

As they walked through Lily's door, Paulo kicking off his shoes and lying down on the couch, she said, "Have you decided what to do about the letters?"

When he ignored the question, she continued, "Mate, you don't know her side of the story. You were only nine. If you read the letters, I reckon you're going to get to know her more. Then you can wipe her if you want to – but, otherwise, you're just listening to Ronaldo's side. You said he can be bitter about her. Maybe she'll tell you things you don't know yet."

Paulo turned away from watching his favourite show, *Get Smart*. Lily got up from the couch and turned the TV off.

"You're nagging me," Paulo said.

"I've got no choice."

"They're still under my bed." His body folded in on itself like an anemone. Lily waited until he eventually looked up at her. "What if she says something really bad?"

His soft face with its watery golden-brown eyes resembled those of the saddest basset hound. His strong body seemed smaller as his fingers repeatedly threaded and twisted around each other.

Lily wasn't sure what to say. "I just reckon it's worth the risk. At least you'll know."

He sighed hard. "You always ask me the hardest friggin' questions. I was feeling good before you brought this up." He ran both hands through his long hair and twisted his curls into tight clumps.

"That's what I'm here for." She knocked his shoulder gently.

"I don't want to do it. I'm scared." He breathed out hard. "Maybe I should."

Lily went to the fridge to make them cups of Milo.

"Okay. I'll do it," he said. "But if it turns to shit, I'm blaming you. It'll be your fault."

"I'll cop that if I have to," she answered as she made their drinks. "Wouldn't be the first time it was my fault."

"Oh, shit yeah."

They sat in a heavy silence as they drank at the table. Lily didn't look at him in case he changed his mind. The dog came and stood at her side, always patiently waiting.

"Good work, Bessie," Lily said, patting her dog's soft head. "Let's run. I'm sick of sitting in this dump."

"Yeah, me too." Paulo lifted himself up off the couch.

"Thanks a lot, mate," Lily laughed, as she walked towards the door. "39 Ocean isn't exactly a palace."

"I'll pay that."

Lily grabbed her worn runners from the back porch, remembering how much homework she had. She pushed the thought from her mind.

Over the following weeks, slowly, Paulo ventured into the box. He sorted the letters by the dates on the envelopes. It took a long time, and even more emotion, for him to read them all. But late into the night, night after night, he read and re-read each one. He told Nini – and no one else – one afternoon, saying, "It feels like Mum is coming back to me."

"Well, she's been with you all along," Nini told him. "The power of a mother's love."

It was the first day of summer and Paulo strode up to Lily as the students scrambled into the building for their English exam.

"You're not going to believe this," he said.

"Can it wait?"

"Nup." He looked at her directly. "I read them."

"Shit! Really?" She paused. The exam was starting soon. "Good?"

"Later." Paulo strode ahead and, for the first time, he was the one to walk into the corridor before Lily.

Afterwards, the squeals, yelling and chatter of the jubilant, relieved and sweaty students were reverberating around the solid stone-yard walls like the sound of birds released from an aviary.

Alexa ran up to Lily, flush-faced, with her hair bouncing from its high sprouting ponytail. "One down, four to go. Reckon I did okay. You?"

"Hard to tell. My hand's aching and I didn't stop. But, then again, I never stop,' Lily said as Paulo wandered over.

"A good sign – unless you spent three hours writing your name over and over," he said.

They all laughed.

"How'd you go, mate?" Lily asked.

"We'll have to celebrate when the last one's over," Lily enthused.

"Yeah, I hope so." Alexa waved as she ran for the swelling bus queue and was absorbed into the waiting crowd.

Paulo and Lily walked to Lena's Fish and Chips, where she shouted them two potato cakes and fifty cents worth of vinegar-drenched, salt-laden chips. They dropped down on the patchy lawn as the grey gulls greedily waited, squawking and hovering.

The pair ate in silence and only when a handful of chips were left did Lily speak. "So, cough up the details."

Paulo swept up the last handful and finished them off before answering. "She didn't hate me. The old man wouldn't let her see me, so she used to come sometimes and watch from her car as I'd walk out the St Jude's gates, just to see how I was. When I came to this school, she was living out of Sydney and didn't have enough money or a car to come and see me. She wrote every week all these years – didn't miss a birthday or Christmas; five-dollar notes in every card. She said she wanted to take me, but he wouldn't let her. She didn't want to leave me, but she had no choice. She couldn't stay with him anymore."

"Oh, your poor mum!" Lily exclaimed. "She would've been

devastated not being able to be with you."

"She wants me to call her. Says she can't call me, 'cause the old man will hang up on her."

"Are you going to?"

"Dunno. Not yet. It's strange…"

"Why is it strange? She's your mum."

"It's like she's come back from the dead."

"But she's not dead. You're so lucky. I'd do anything for Dad to come back." Lily dusted the salt from her uniform.

Paulo got up and scrunched the newspaper wrapping into the bin as two resting pelicans took flight from the pier railing. They glided into the mild afternoon breeze and the warm glow shimmered off their large, flapping wings. Lily watched them cruise along the shoreline until one headed straight beyond the Point and the other turned left to Sandy back beach.

Paulo knelt and took a worn, folded aerogram sheet from his school pants pocket. He handed it to Lily.

Dear Paulo,

My heart has been torn in two ever since I left you, my darling boy. I know you must have suffered terribly without your mum all these years. I can only imagine what Ron may have told you. I have suffered too with a broken heart from missing you.

I hope you are okay and that we can see each other when you are able.

Your always and forever loving mother,

Mum x x

Lily patted his arm as she handed back the letter. "She sounds lovely. Now will you give her a ring?" Lily spoke tenderly.

"Maybe later." Paulo folded the letter carefully and placed it back in his pocket. "See how I go."

"Have you spoken to your dad about what's in the letters?"

"Nup. He said I had to promise to never mention her name. Anyway, he's started drinking more now. He's using the pile of newspapers next to his chair to rest his empties. I used to take out a couple; now I take out six or more." Paulo stood up to leave. "The only time the old man did say anything was the night after he'd given them to me: *She tried to destroy us once, son. Don't let her do it again. She doesn't care about anyone, except herself.*"

Lily walked off with him. "That's *his* opinion." A dog barked persistently in the background, possibly trapped in a yard somewhere nearby. It made Lily's heart hurt. "This time, you get to decide who Valerie is for yourself."

FORTY-FIVE

It was a still day. The ocean was as quiet as breath. The sky was a cool green. The bay had a chill emanating from its centre, with warmth around the edges. The light was cold silver. The stillness crept into the day, hushing all that moved within it. People spoke quietly, even the grey gulls squawked in a muted way.

Lily ruminated. *How could Paulo not forgive her? At least she was alive. I'd give anything for Dad to be alive. Maybe there's a reason she had to go away. She's his mother. The only one he'll ever have.* These circular thoughts swirled around in her mind, and she walked further, trying to sort them out as she went.

By the time she reached Paulo's house, she couldn't hold back her thoughts. As soon as he let her in, she blurted out, "Can't you forgive her? I mean, sure, for the first few years she wasn't around, but now she's got her shit together, can't you forgive her? Like, let her be a part of your life. Even a small part?"

"Nup. You don't understand." He got up and walked out of the room, with Lily following.

They left the house in an uneasy silence. She sensed his determination, but eventually she broke the silence. "She's the only mother you've got, mate. Can't you give her one more chance?"

"No. Not when the person who's meant to nurture you just pisses off and leaves you. I'll never forgive."

Lily listened and didn't interrupt. Paulo looked towards Beach St and turned the corner ahead of her into Main.

"I cried myself to sleep every night for three years after she left. I was nine years old. The old man went into his shell, and I didn't have a Nini to turn to." His voice broke and he coughed to clear his throat. "You should have seen me when she was still there. I was a totally different person."

"What do you mean?" Lily saw the depth of the sadness clouding Paulo's face. He didn't answer for a long time and kept his head turned away.

"You know, like, I was a happy, fun little kid when I was with her. I used to dance and sing and make up plays and get dressed up, and life was a blast. Until it wasn't. Once she left, there wasn't anything to be happy about. Nothing to look forward to."

"That's sad, mate. That's bloody sad. A shame Ronaldo couldn't talk to you."

"Yeah. He spoke to the stacks of newspapers next to his armchair in the darkened room, TV blaring with empty bottles on the floor. That's the help he got. I didn't get *any*."

"Wow, there's still so much we don't know about each other. Even though we spend most days together and have, ever since we met. I can't even remember when you weren't in my life." She pushed his shoulder gently. "Front and centre! I guess that's where all good dancers should be!"

They laughed.

"Yeah, that's true," he said. "You're so loud, you'd think, even if I hadn't met you, I would've at least heard you."

"Oh, shut up. Anyway, what were you like as a little tacker? Don't tell me – *a goodie two-shoes*," Lily teased.

"I dunno about that but, according to the old man, when he *did* speak, *I don't do public affection,* and, as Mum used to respond, *Nor do you do private affection.*" He shook his long hair and, when it was back in position, continued, "I was a *mummy's boy* and a *crybaby.* If I was sitting on her knee, or next to her, I was happy. If she went away, or I couldn't find her, I'd cry and cry. That used to bug the old man, so he'd scream at me to *shut up you little sissy*. Now, isn't that weird?"

"No, that's not weird. That's just really shithouse," Lily paused for a moment for emphasis. "Poor old Ronaldo didn't realise what it was doing to you. If you feel it in your heart, like Nini reckons, you've gotta let it out. Otherwise, she says, it eats away at you. I'm so sorry that happened to you when your mum left."

"Yeah, well, thanks. I learnt to become a bit of a fake. I wasn't ever who I felt I was. So, in the end, after Mum left, I didn't know who I was. I just knew who I pretended to be; was like wearing a mask that covered me up and wasn't true. Now, looking back, and hearing Mum's point of view, I don't think it helped me. I just needed someone to talk to, but with her gone and the old boy, you know..."

"Oh, God, you're making me cry." Lily wiped her face hard. "I thought I did it tough after Dad died, but nothing like you. When Meredith was off the planet, I had Nini to turn to. But I can't imagine your mum moving away and your dad not talking and having no one to turn to. No one. That's too bloody sad." She kicked the pavement as they walked along.

Once they got to the pier, they walked out to the end and looked back at the jagged rocks, which had broken down over millennia, and watched the passive waves lap over and around their edges. "Would you ever talk to your dad about this?"

"Are you kidding? He'd just get all awkward, change the subject, turn the telly up louder, or leave the room and get another beer..."

"Might be worth a try."

"Nup. It's not worth it, and it tears me up a bit too, so best to forget it. I reckon Mum'll get it. Wrote that he did that to her, too."

Paulo got up, shook his head right down to his knees, his hair draping over the concrete. Then he pushed it all back and fanned it out. Straightening his back, he cleared his throat and said, "Catch ya later, buddy."

"Sure thing, mate." Lily knew he needed to think, so she sat on the pier and watched for what seemed like the longest while as her best friend headed home. She watched his figure get smaller as he slogged down Beach Street. He looked preoccupied. She thought she would never know the depth of Paulo's sadness. When he'd finally disappeared, she left. Her heart felt heavy as if his burden was also hers, somehow. She couldn't wait to get home to share it with Nini.

The next day, the streets were quiet, and the sunlight floated around the pavement and fences as if it had nowhere to be. She walked past the clump of ghost gums in the corner of the schoolyard, a family huddled together with their pale limbs intertwined, legs reaching up to arms, reaching up to fingers.

Lily walked to the side gate of Paulo's house. Predictably, no one answered the front door. She'd rung a few times that morning, but Ronaldo often just let it ring, and if Paulo was outside, no one answered it. As she passed the covered windows, she sensed movement in the backyard. There, in the corner, was an old timber table with one unbroken seat. Paulo had his back to her, and she stayed motionless, watching him hunched over a letter, with the plastic bag of letters nestled on the overgrown lawn next to his feet. He had his head in his hands and his elbows on the table.

"Hi there," Lily called.

He turned, waved, and slowly got up and walked to where she stood, with the letter still in his hand. "I need to put these away." He motioned to the bag of letters, the one in his hand fluttering as he walked back. He slid the letter back into its envelope, stretched the old elastic band around the bundle and dropped them into the plastic bag. "I'll just hide them in my room."

To watch this big, strong boy creeping into his home with his precious plastic bag was a sorrowful image.

The route to Durga Rock was comfortably silent. They headed straight towards the old cemetery to the side of the lighthouse and walked along the beach. Theirs was an unspoken, yet shared, chasm of loss. Once they were in their usual positions halfway up the rock, planting themselves on the flattest parts, the gentle sea breeze filling their senses, they spoke.

"I never knew what I'd missed all these years, until today. I thought I was just a sad, lonely boy. But, after reading letter after letter, there is some light there somewhere."

Paulo's words hung in the air. Lily nodded but did not speak, as if they had entered a sacred dark tunnel where Paulo was leading and, if she spoke, she would break the spell and he'd never get to find out where he was heading. She knew he was processing what he'd read and, as much as she was desperate to know more, she only asked him, "One day, will you share with me some of what your mum says in the letters?"

"Yeah. One day."

FORTY-SIX

Too hot in the kitchen, so you thought you'd piss off, then? or *Too scared to stand up for what you believe in?* or *You're not a coward, are you? 'Cause I don't want to hang around with a coward.* That was by far the worst. If she said that, she knew she would have gone too far and she'd cut him to his core. She knew later that day, or that week, or in the middle of the night, when her mind was plagued by all those familiar questions. *Why do I say such mean things? I don't know why I say it. Maybe I'm just a horrible person. I hate myself when I hurt him.*

On a quiet Saturday afternoon, when they were hanging around together, Lily and Paulo walked to the kids' park and sat on the old timber swings that squeaked, kicking up the sparse tanbark and dirt with their runners.

She wanted to apologise. She knew she should. She'd hurt his feelings. But the *sorry* word seemed impossible. So, instead, she chatted about mundane school stuff.

Paulo was silent.

Without preamble, she blurted out, 'I shouldn't speak to you the way I did. I am a shit friend.'

He didn't say anything, which made her feel worse.

"Can you forgive me?" She stopped her swing. "Please?"

"When you say that stuff, I feel *like a low life.*"

"I know. That's my mouth running away from me. I don't even mean it. I just want to get you to protect yourself."

"That doesn't work."

"I'm not going do that anymore. I promise."

"Really?"

"Yeah. *Really*. You're my best mate and I'm a big fat horrible shit."

"Nah... Just *shut up* sometimes.'

"Yeah, I need to shut up big time. I'm going to do that. I've got it now."

"Good." He stood up to leave.

Lily followed him as the birds chased each other through the bushes and the magpies started their chortling. A siren blared in the distance, and she remembered her English project. "I gotta go! I've got the assignment due on Monday and I've barely started. Nini asked if I could help her with some housework this week, and I didn't do any of it. I better help."

"Yeah, I know the feeling." Paulo walked from the dying grass to the broken bitumen path. "I'm outta jocks, socks, school shirts, shorts... I hope the old man's bought some food for dinner."

"Well, you know where to come if he hasn't."

When they got to the corner, Paulo's hound dog eyes crinkled as he turned to cross the street. "See ya!"

"See ya, mate." Lily turned in the direction of her house. "Sorry!" she called out to him.

"No worries, buddy." He waved his hand behind his back and kept walking.

Later that week, on a windless and sky-blue afternoon when the sun shone weak streaks of warmth through the bitsy clouds, Paulo and Lily were sitting on the asphalt at school and talking about some of the nastiest kids, as well as some of the vindictive teachers.

Lily asked him, "How come you don't care?"

"Care about what?"

"You know... What they say to you. How mean they are."

Lily looked around the yard, as if to make sure no interloper could eavesdrop.

"Oh, I care. But not about them," Paulo answered. "I take my mind somewhere else until they've finished. Then, when it's over, I come back and their crap washes over me."

She was mesmerised. "That's incredible! What a skill."

"When Mum left, if I felt too bad, I'd sit on the back step and imagine I was somewhere else. It made me feel better, so I kept doing it."

"Shit! I didn't even know that was possible. I mean, to do that. It's so smart." Lily uncrossed her legs and flexed her feet. "I'm going to try and do that. Where do you go?"

"Anywhere. Rivers, mountains, the city... I go dancing... I dunno know. Different places."

"Could've used that earlier this year when they were putting me through the wringer." She looked as if she'd left something behind.

"Oh, yeah. That's for bloody sure." Paulo stood and stretched lazily. As she watched him, she noted how he was changing. He looked different, he seemed different, and she wasn't sure why.

Paulo was such a good guy, but Lily rarely knew what he was thinking. When she'd ask, he'd often glaze over, or not really answer. He was a master at keeping his feelings to himself. Even his closest friends sometimes didn't know how to read him. He could divert the conversation so quickly, they didn't even notice he'd done it, until they found themselves prattling on about themselves again. Paulo was a great listener – but if the limelight moved to him, he was startled, disconcerted and visibly uncomfortable.

Later that term, Lily was telling Alexa and Mot how she was

trying to do Paulo's disappearing trick sometimes, especially when she was in trouble. Paulo lopped up to join their circle, which that day reeked of wonder, Vegemite Saladas, and stale cordial.

"Nup, it's real. I knew he must do something extraordinary, because otherwise he'd be a mess from the crap they gave him. Don't ya, mate?"

"What?' Paulo leaned into Lily's lunchbag and unwrapped another section of Vegemite-and-cheese biscuits. He'd only overheard some of what Lily was saying as he nuzzled his way in.

"Take your mind somewhere, if shit's going down?"

"Yep, I did. And I still can." He looked away as if there was nothing more to add.

Alexa raised her eyebrows at Mot.

"If I need to," Paulo added through a mouthful of biscuit.

"Well, why not?" Alexa said, nudging Mot good-naturedly. "I mean, between the two of us, we have heavy shit going down daily."

Lily noticed their transfixed expressions. The screeching bell pierced the conversation and she stood to leave. "You should try it. It works." Lily rushed towards class.

Alexa and Mot sat for a time before anyone spoke.

"I'm gunna practice tonight when the tyrant starts yelling at me for all the things I either didn't do or didn't do properly." Mot said. "Yep. Think I'll go to Hawaii when the pig goes off his nut just because he can. Maybe I'll leave early and settle in. Might go and live there."

Alexa stood straight up from sitting cross-legged. "Make room for me," she yelled back as she bolted to class. "We need a four-bedroom joint!"

"Bring it on, baby.' Paulo added.

FORTY-SEVEN

Lily came through the flywire door and onto the porch with a thud, carrying another plate of Nini's rockie cakes.

"In my life, Paulo, I've always found it harder to hold a grudge than to forgive," Nini had told him. "In the end, it's kinder, not only to the other person but to yourself. A person full of hatred or spite can't be happy. That way, you make room for good things in life to come in."

She squeezed his shoulder as she went back into the kitchen, whistling an old song that Paulo didn't know. Lily returned with two cups of tea, handing one over to her friend.

"I just asked Nini if I should meet up with my mum," he confessed as Lily sat down beside him.

Lily looked at the side of his face. "And what did she say?"

"I reckon she said yes. Like, it's harder to hold a grudge than to forgive." He dunked a broken piece of biscuit into his tea. "Yep, she said yes," he confirmed, lifting the crumbling biscuit to his mouth.

"Well, are you?"

"Dunno. Maybe." Paulo shrugged.

"You're killing me. Seriously."

Paulo started tapping his feet, finished two more biscuits and drained his tea. "Catch ya."

"What? You're leaving when I don't even know what you're going to do. You've gotta be kidding me.""

"You wanna try living in *my* head! I don't *know yet*. I gotta go." He took the last of Nini's biscuits, stood up and went inside.

Lily heard the thunk of his teacup landing in the kitchen sink and Paulo saying something to Nini that she couldn't make out. Lily got up and, once she was inside, he'd gone.

Two weeks later, after their swim, they sat outside the kiosk with $1.50 worth of chips.

"God, Meredith's pissing me off lately," Lily whined. "She's so friggin' annoying."

"Buddy, you are full of advice for me to see Valerie when you don't even bother with Meredith."

The grey gulls came, as they always did. Paulo threw the burnt chips at them, which made them scatter and fight.

Lily's shoulders tensed and she said, "*Me*? She's the one who should make the first move. She's an adult. Actually, she *is* the mother, and I'm the child, remember."

Paulo pressed the point. "Yeah, but *she's* been sick, and you haven't. If you care about her, you should try and be with her." He watched as the birds regathered, hovering above them. "Maybe you don't bother because you've got Nini."

Lily brushed the salt of her hands on her towel. "God, Paulo, you can be pretty hurtful when you want to be."

"Nah, I'm just being honest."

"Well, *don't be*. How dare you say that! I think you're jealous because you don't have your own nana. Anyway, how I relate to my own mother is my business."

"That's a bit rich. You've been telling me for months how I should relate to *my* mother."

"This is different."

"No, it's not. It's the same."

"And you telling me all the things I should and shouldn't be doing with mum, the old boy, life in general... and I make one bloody suggestion and you fire up."

"I'm trying to help you. You're just criticising me because you're jealous. I'm not going to listen to this." Lily got up and stormed off.

As she marched down the street, Paulo called after her, "I'm not jealous! You just don't know how lucky you are."

She heard him but didn't reply.

They didn't speak to each other all weekend. On Monday, they avoided each other. It wasn't until the end of lunch when they were walking back to class, Lily walked over to Paulo and said, sheepishly, "Hi."

"Hi."

"Guess now's the time I should say *sorry*."

"Yeah, probably."

"I just get upset about all this shit," Lily said quietly as they approached their lockers.

Paulo didn't answer.

"You and me still mates?"

"Yep, I guess so." He sighed.

"Thanks, mate." She opened her locker and, with her head down, said to him as he walked past, "Sorry."

"Okay. No worries." He said as he walked on.

She took a deep breath and felt the tightness in her chest release for the first time in three days.

Another Life
Frank, my dad, you've gone from my sight.
The tears are endless, especially at night.
When you were here, everything was okay
Come out in the sunshine, Lily, you'd say.
But the house is now quiet – lonely and sad,

I want Mum to smile, I feel so bad.
Nini is gentle, funny and kind,
She understands me; she doesn't mind.
Your clothes are hanging above your shoes all
Lined up,
As if we should make you tea in your favourite cup.
I'll never forget you, Frank, my dad.
Nothing about you, no matter how sad.
Love,
Your Lily-Pad

<h1 style="text-align:center">FORTY-EIGHT</h1>

It was a sizzling March day. There had not been a cloud in the sapphire sky for days, and not a breath of wind. Lily could not concentrate in class. She was dreaming of diving into the ocean, the relief of her body being subsumed and soothed by the cold waves.

"Grab your bathers mate. I'll meet you at mine at four." Lily skipped off home after school.

"Yep, it's a bloody hot one," Paulo limply called at her swinging ponytail.

At exactly four o'clock, Lily stood impatiently in the shade of Paulo's porch and banged on his front door.

Paulo sauntered down the concrete path along the side of his house.

Lily was already out the gate. "Come on! We're here for a good time not a long time, mate."

Paulo was slow, walking along the shriveled and dusty nature strip.

Lily turned around. "What's the hold up?" She threw one of her thongs at him. "You are gold star at forgetfulness."

"You hurried me."

"Yeah – because I was growing old waiting."

He grabbed her thong and shoved his big foot into it.

At the beach, the sand was so hot they had to use the throw-your-towel-down-hop-step-and-repeat until they reached the shoreline.

Lily threw down her belongings and ran. Her pale, strong, agile body dove straight through the first uncurling wave. She swam hard, way out beyond the smooth, cylinder set. For the first time, she looked back to see Paulo popping up from a wave and laughing. "First time I went straight in!"

"About bloody time. Now keep diving in!"

She caught a wave in to join him, as he never liked to go too deep. She was thinking how grateful she was there was no undertow when he said, "Hey, look at the seaweed. It's moving." He pointed to an approaching black mass.

"Seaweed doesn't move like that." Lily panted. A large, dark form shimmered, morphed and glided over the waves. As a wave rose, the shape flashed though the translucent crest. Treading water, Paulo and Lily watched on. And then it was around them, moving like fabric, gliding and turning, as if they'd rubbed their hands both ways along a black velvet rug. A school of thousands of tiny fish – enough to make a huge, black shadow, fluttering around and through them – tickling their skin as it moved across their limbs.

"That's the coolest thing I've ever seen!" Paulo exclaimed.

"Can you believe it? It's amazing."

They stayed for the longest time, calling "unders and overs" for each rising mound of water, before the crush of the breaking wave. In between waves, they kept searching for the glittering shadow rolling across the sea.

The seabirds gathered, hovered and dove to where the mass was. The dark shadow of fish rose and flickered away, out beyond the breakers until it was gone.

"How do they know who to follow? Like, who is their leader? How could they tell?" Lily said.

"Someone shouts *left or right* and they bolt, I reckon."

"Hmm. Did I tell you, last night, when I went to the

lighthouse, I saw a pod of dolphins? Instead of swimming and playing, they were just hanging out. I mean, maybe they were fishing, 'cause they just hung together like they were at a barbecue or something."

"Cool. Good thing they weren't at Ronaldo's barbecue last night; he burnt the crap out of the snags again. Seriously, I don't mind the burnt bits, 'cause I drown 'em in tomato sauce, but when they're charred and black, they're rotten."

"Yeah, I reckon! Did you eat them?"

"Yep, every blackened one. Hard and tasteless, but swimming in sauce and squeezed between two slices of white bread. The sauce and the bread saved the day. I bought a fresh loaf. Then, for dessert, I had three rounds of honey sandwiches."

"You and your tomato sauce and bread. Seriously, I reckon if you didn't know me, you'd have scurvy or rickets. Probably both."

"Yep. I ate an apple last week. Hmm, and an orange. They were left in your lunchbag."

"Oh, well, fair enough. You know how Nini hates waste."

They crunched up to their towels with their shivering bodies all wrinkled and shriveled like prunes.

"God, my hands and feet look a hundred!" Lily said.

"Yeah, yours always look worse than mine." He pointed at her off-white fingers, all shriveled up.

"Thanks, mate. Yours look pretty RS too."

"Yeah, I'm just saying... Anyway, your food's the best. Invite me over this weekend. I need a decent feed."

"Done."

FORTY-NINE

It was Easter Saturday, and the Point was jumping with people. Lily and Paulo had decided to do the long walk and grab an ice-cream from Sandy's kiosk on the way. As they strolled along the esplanade, families were setting up picnics with laden baskets, fold-out chairs, checkered rugs, dogs, elderly relatives, pushers, prams, and exuberant children with every type of ball game imaginable. Even a couple of kites getting entangled with the trees, and people side-stepping stray balls.

Mothers and fathers were setting up on any spare space as all the old wooden tables were taken by organised early arrivers. Once they each had their ice-creams in hand – butterscotch for Lily; chocolate-fudge for Paulo – their usual debate ensued.

"Mine's superior," Lily said as she licked the trail from her cone whilst expertly twisting it around.

"Everyone knows chocolate's better," Paulo responded. "Even the old girl knew that. That was my Sunday morning, after-mass treat. Never quite worked out why we went to mass. I mean, she wasn't a religious type. Anyway, maybe it made her feel like she was doing a good job or less guilty for cheating on the old man. Who knows?" He dismissed the subject by turning to watch the colourful yachts out on the water.

"Do you miss being a family? Like your mum and dad at home together..."

"Yeah. But, more than that, it's made me realise how much I want what I'll never be able to have." Paulo's deep voice trailed off.

Lily stopped walking. "What do you mean?"

"A family – a husband, a child. I reckon I'd be good at it, too."

"Wow, that's amazing. I never knew you felt that way. Maybe one day you'll be able to do that. Like, get married and adopt some kids."

"Yeah, and we might fly around on comets in outer space like *The Jetsons*. I'm not holding my breath."

Lily resumed strolling along the path. "I never want to get married, and I don't want kids either."

"Why? Why not?"

"Because it's too bloody sad. If you get married and it doesn't work, or one of you dies, then you've got to look after a child just when you can't even look after yourself. I mean, look at Meredith." She raised her eyebrows and shook her head. "Nup. I'm going to be as single and selfish as I want to be."

"Wow, every day you drop a bombshell. Everything that you can have, you don't want; and everything I want, I can't have."

"Yeah, how stupid is that? Life can be shit sometimes." Lily popped the last piece of ice-cream cone in her mouth. "Here's to living our best shit lives – whatever they are!"

"Straight to the top of the shit pile, here we come!"

FIFTY

Mr Hammerington was immersed in Ballarat's 1850s gold rush. The class were disinterested, with a few of the usual boys throwing paper airplanes across the room whenever he was reading to the class. A few of the girls took to whispering under their desks. Sally, across the aisle from Lily, got out her lunch and started eating it with her desk lid up. Matilda, next to Sally, started to paint her nails. This was Mr Hammerington's third class in a row in which the students who weren't up the front just did their own thing.

Lily put her hand up. "Mr Hammerington, is there another topic we can move to?"

"I beg your pardon?" His face grew red.

"This whole gold rush-era thing doesn't seem to appeal to anyone. I mean do we really have to cover it?"

When he didn't answer, she continued, "I was just asking, do we..."

"Do not make the mistake of asking the same question twice, Miss Mango. Who are you to question the curriculum?" The teacher stood up, his pale veined face pulsating, and pointed to the door. "You may sit in the hallway. Your impudence and ignorance do not serve you well. Pack up and high-tail it out of my class. Your presence, as well as your face, offend my sensibilities."

"What do my looks have to do with my question of a class topic?" Lily spat back in outrage. "You shouldn't speak to me like that."

"Don't you dare answer me back." The veins in his neck where now protruding. "I'm in control here, not you. Ignorance is where you came from, and it's where you'll stay." His voice was now yelling. "You, hallway, now!"

Gathering her belongings, Lily muttered to herself, "This isn't fair."

As she left the classroom, slowly closing the door behind her, she heard him thunder, "*Out!*" at her retreating figure.

Lily burst through the front door and told Nini what happened immediately.

"Your intelligence is an affrontery to Mr Hammerington." Nini joined Lily at the table, patting her hand. "Such an overreaction. You're a brave girl, Lily-pily, and I admire you for standing up to him." Nini put both of her sun-spotted, gnarly hands on top of Lily's and gave them a squeeze. "I wish I had your confidence when I was your age. I would never have left school early if I did. Meredith's done a fine job bringing you up – and, of course, your dad, too." She touched Lily's heart with her hand. "You have a pure heart, darling."

Lily gave her Nini a warm hug. "But he humiliated me. He put me down, he put our family down, he bloody-well kicked me out of class because I asked a genuine question. I can't go back to that class. I can't!"

"Do you want me to intervene? I can call a meeting with him, or I can go to see the principal?" Nini looked concerned.

Lily didn't answer. She held her head in her hands, looking at the floor.

"I'll put the kettle on. We'll have a cuppa and let the dust settle before you decide. Huh? I've got some chocolate brownies still left."

On cue, Bessie started to scratch on the flywire to come in. Lily lay on the floor with her eyes closed and Bessie nestled in with her paw across Lily's belly.

After dinner, Meredith popped her head into Lily's room, to see her girl hunched over her book-littered desk with her head in her arms.

"Night, darling. Nini told me about your day. I'm sorry that happened."

Lily turned to see her mother resting her head against the door with her hand on the knob.

"Maybe if you've got a question or a suggestion, even though it's probably a good one, it's better to ask the teacher after class." Meredith sounded weary.

"Why?" Lily turned her whole body away from her desk to face Meredith.

"They won't feel threatened or criticised then," she said.

"Well, that's pathetic. You ask a question, and they go off their nuts because they're insecure."

"Irrespective, it's better not to upset them," her mother concluded. "Good night." And with that, she quietly closed Lily's door.

Lily looked at her strewn books and decided it was bedtime. Once under the covers, she tossed and turned, thinking, *Nini tells me to take it to them, Meredith tells me not to. I don't know what to do.* After a fitful sleep, full of strange dramas unfolding at school, Lily was happy to get out of bed the next morning. Nini's kettle was whistling, and the radio was on. Lily smelled the toast.

"Good morning, little one. How'd you sleep?" Nini asked as she applied the butter and jam thickly across Lily's toast.

"Rotten, Nini." Lily grabbed the Weetbix and stood with the fridge door open. Nini handed her the opened milk bottle.

"Oh, sorry to hear that. You'll sleep like a baby tonight, for sure."

"How come?" Lily shoveled in her cereal.

"Because you'll be tired, and because you'll know how you're going to deal with Mr Hammerhead."

Lily chuckled. "It's Hammerington, not Hammerhead, Nini."

"Oh, yes. Well, he sounds like a shark, so may as well call him one."

They laughed.

"Remember – don't put him down to the other students; he's doing that all by himself by losing control in class."

"That's for sure." Lily put her bowl in the sink. "Thanks, Nini." She kissed her grandmother goodbye and ran to pack for school.

"Have a good day, darling," Nini said from the kitchen sink.

"I will if I can keep my big mouth shut." Lily called from the front door.

"Just be respectful. He holds the trump card," Nini warned. "Maybe ask for a meeting with him. Explain your passion for history – that you didn't mean offence; that you thought suggestions would be welcome in his class. However, from now on, you will reserve your opinions and let the examiners do the judging instead."

Lily stood in the doorway with her mouth open and put her hands up to heaven. "Oh, God help me, that sounds like an apology!"

"Lily, you're not apologising for your views; you're reassuring him that you won't publicly disagree with him. That way he maintains self-esteem, and you get to resume your studies –

which is the whole point. Remember?"

"Okay, okay, you're right."

"It's not that I'm right; it's that I've had decades of experience dealing with people like him. You've got bigger fish to fry than him. Keep your eyes on where you're heading, darling."

Lily let out a huge sigh and grabbed her bag, blowing kisses to Nini before the front door slammed.

Later, Lily met with Mr Hammerington. He had his arms folded tightly across his chest and an etched scowl upon his lined face. She stayed on script, trying to remember word for word what Nini had told her. She'd rehearsed it in her mind all day before the meeting.

After more finger-pointing and the usual *You, young lady, have no right* speeches, he finally acquiesced with the promise that she would keep her views to herself, unless she was requested to give them. That didn't matter to Lily. It afforded her more reading time, which she loved.

As she stood to leave, she said, "Thank you, Mr Hammerhead... oh, Hammerington, I mean," she stammered.

"Off you go, Miss Mango." As she swiftly closed the classroom door, the giggles escaped her as she imagined telling the others, especially Nini and Paulo.

FIFTY-ONE

Form 5 started with gusto. Lots more choices. The plays were out, Paulo was dancing daily, Lily was writing in her diary, and most days were spent with Alexa and Mot. Alexa had shared with them stories about her family, how a few of her six brothers would often punch on and how, when it got out of control, she had to run and hide with her eldest brother, Antonio.

Mot seemed to understand.

Lily said, "I blamed Dad for 12 months. It's only now that I know he didn't choose to leave." She looked awkwardly at Paulo. "Sorry, mate, I didn't mean…"

"Nuh. It's okay."

"Anyway, I thought I'd never be happy again." Lily looked relieved to be talking.

Mot nodded silently.

Paulo said, "I'll never forgive Mum. Never."

No one spoke after Paulo said this.

"What about your dad?" Alexa asked him as she ran her hands through her curls.

"He still drinks. It's like he's not here. He doesn't say much. Maybe I'm like him. Shit, I hope not."

They all laughed.

"Nah," he continued. "I'm not like him 'cause I want to be a dancer and he hates music, dancing and anything that could remind him of the old girl. You know, she was a singer in a band."

"Wow! How amazing," Alex said. "We never knew that. Maybe you're like your mum. You like to dance and she liked to sing."

"Nup, no way." Paulo shut down the conversation. "I'm

nothing like her." And he shook his head vehemently.

Alexa asked Mot, "Hey, what about your family? There's heaps of them, that's for sure, eh?"

"Yeah, twelve. Nah, there's too many; too many for them to look after." Mot picked up a handful of gravel from the playground and started to throw the pieces one by one at the broken paling fence. "Except Tommy and Alice. They're little and good."

That night, Paulo met Lily and Bessie at the front beach just before dusk.

"Mate, what do you reckon about what Mot said?" he asked. "Why won't he speak about his family?"

Lily searched Paulo's face for the answer. "Shit, I don't know. I was listening to Alexa talk about her brothers and their full-on fights. I didn't notice what Mot said."

"Yeah, more what he *didn't* say. He sure got a mean look on his face when he started to hurl those stones around."

"Oh yeah. I wonder what's wrong with his family. The only ones he'd talk about were his little brother, Tommy, and his baby sister, Alice. Seems bloody strange, doesn't it?'

"Yeah. Maybe they're bad. He calls his dad 'the pig'."

"Shit, that's right."

"Not exactly a term of endearment," Paulo said, the sand squeaky and still warm under his feet. "Alexa reckons she's never been into their house. Reckons the mum comes to the door and always says Mot's busy. Even though Mot goes to the milk bar. Her mum likes him 'cause he picks up the drink crates if the delivery truck comes when he's in the shop. Alexa reckons her mum says Mot's hungry. She gives him leftover pies and stuff. He reckons her brothers are ratbags, but he likes Antonio. He's the one Alexa likes – the good one."

As the term went on, Mot started to forget his books, forget to do his homework, not hand in forms that needed signing from his parents. He was ordered to go and see the principal.

"What if they call me folks?" he stuttered at recess. "The pig would kill me." Mot's face went beetroot when he spoke.

"Just say you're sorry and you'll never do it again," Lily advised him. "Try to look *really* sorry. She's alright; I reckon she'll understand."

"*What's* she gunna understand? That I'm an idiot. That I can't do anything right. That I'm a no-hoper like the pig reckons.'

"Come on, buddy, it won't be that bad," Paulo said and patted Mot's arm.

"Oh, yeah? You don't know how bad." He stormed off without any warning. An awkward silence enveloped the others. No one knew what to do or say.

Towards the end of term, Mot started to skip classes. Just one or two here and there, so as not to be noticed. Then he started to miss whole days. When he did come to school, he'd anxiously ask the others, "What have I missed?" or "What's due in?", until he advanced to "Give me your homework, will you?" More a demand than a request.

Lily and Alexa shared some of their homework with him.

Paulo said, "You're welcome to mine, buddy, but I get Ds and sometimes Es."

"Ha! Thanks, but I don't need any help to get a D or an E."

It was a freezing July day, and the rain was horizontal, landing in icy sheets against the shelter-shed roof. The four of them huddled together with their shared food – which, in fact, meant that Lily and Alexa ate half of what they brought. Alexa always had exotic

Greek food, with eggplant, vine leaves and spices they'd never heard of – all of which Paulo devoured, leaving Lily to give half of hers to Mot. His stale peanut-butter sandwiches were not appealing to any of them and usually ended up in the bin.

The detentions were weighing him down. He struggled with schoolwork as it was, but having more schoolwork heaped on him week after week in detention was hell for him.

"What do you say to the teachers when you don't have a letter from your parents?" Lily asked.

"They don't write letters. So, the teachers don't expect one."

"Where do you go when you're wagging, Mot?" Lily asked.

"Nowhere." He looked at his hands.

"You must go somewhere."

"Um, some days, if the weather's good, I walk to the Point and sit there. Sometimes, if I've got any coin, I go to Lina's for fish and chips. I pinch the money from the pig's drawer. He hides it in a tin, but he blames the old girl if he thinks he's light on."

No one said anything.

"Or, if it's really cold or wet, I go to the cemetery," Mot added. "There's a shelter near my nan and pa, Eileen and Victor Woolsely's, graves. Mum's folks. They used to take me in a lot when I was little. If the pig was drunk, Nan told me to run to their place; it was safer than hiding under the bed or in the wardrobe."

The wind picked up and Lily's loose hair lashed her face. The only memory she had of hiding in the house was when her dad played hide and seek with her. Lily looked at the others and Mot kept his eyes on his hands.

"I used to spend a lot of time with them. They were really good."

FIFTY-TWO

Mrs Montgomery-Smyth pranced into her English class as a lead actor would walk onto centre stage for opening night. She'd turn theatrically on her heel and, with expansive arms, command her audience. Her long flowing dresses, bright scarves and jewellery would swing around and waltz behind her. Her booming, polished tones would bounce off the back wall, reverberate and linger above the students.

Once on the platform, she turned on her heels and tossed her wild, long grey hair. She epitomised theatrical passion, adoring every text more than the last. Today's text was Shakespeare's *Othello*. She liked to read out loud to the class, employing hand actions, bodily movements, and appropriate voice intonations. The class were captivated from the moment she entered the class. She was the actor, and they were her adoring audience. Her voice had a mesmerising quality, like they'd been tranquilised upon her entrance into the room.

If Form 5 English could be described as a cult, it would qualify: unquestioning compliance, trance-like followers, a charismatic and impassioned leader. If any student attempted any part of her class with genuine interest, she wholeheartedly congratulated them. Right or wrong, it made no difference to how she responded.

"Bravo, Lily! Bravo. You're interpreting the text with fresh eyes and elucidating the themes within. Do you think themes such as betrayal, jealousy, evil, lust, power, are still relevant for people reading this in 1977?"

"Yes, I do Mrs Montgomery-Smyth. I mean, you only have to

read the newspaper, or watch the news on TV, or listen to the wireless, to know that those themes are in our lives today. Just as they were in the lives of Shakesperean times."

"Oh, I love the way you're thinking, Miss Mango." Mrs M-S (as the students knew her) clapped her hands hard. "What about anyone else? This is a juicy topic. What do you think? Is this relevant? If so, how?"

She beamed her wide-faced smile to encapsulate every student. The hands and arms were waving madly. It was if she was sharing a conspiracy theory, and this English class were the first to discover it. Perhaps it would change the world forever. The more verbose and voluble the students became the happier she was.

"This is rich, this is art, and we celebrate that art reflects life back to us. What a dull existence we'd endure without the insights of artists. You, my friends, are artists. Let good literature be your ally through your life. You'll never be lonely, you'll never be bereft of ideas, and you'll be transported to places and thoughts that you'd otherwise not experience."

The class would finish with extra zest. "Congratulations for your valuable and insightful contributions today. You are a wonderfully enthusiastic and talented class." Mrs M-S would outstretch her arms and boom, "Bravo to you, one and all!"

The students would leave her class bursting with ideas, wanting to do their homework, unafraid to read in class. It was like no other class Lily or Paulo ever went to.

"I don't even like reading, but I'm gunna read everything she sets," Paulo enthused.

"I love her class! I love the way she speaks, the way she encourages us. Ha! Even when we're wrong."

They both nodded.

"I think I may even *love* her," Paulo's said. His dark eyes were wide and glistening.

"Yeah, it's weird. When I'm in her class, I'm under her spell." They laughed hard.

That afternoon, Lily took Bessie down to the bay. It was a sleek sea – midnight blue. The day had been hit with a north-easterly, but just before dinner the wind dropped and, with each step, the calmness filled her body. Even Bessie sensed the change and walked next to her, rather than dashing on ahead.

Elenor Montgomery-Smyth in full flight was something to behold – so much so that if she caught a glimpse of her reflection in the glass door or window, she would sensuously run her elegant fingers through her mane, wearing an imperceptible grin of admiration, before resuming where she'd left off. Her views were numerous, and she espoused them with passion and fervour – yet, mostly, she encouraged student participation. Curiosity and counter-views were welcomed.

"I am here to teach you, but you will also learn from each other, and from getting things wrong and especially by being curious. I will also learn from you." She said this in such an irrefutable way. The students had never heard a teacher say such things. She was enthralling.

Lily, who loved to ponder life's questions, was in heaven in Mrs M-S's class. Questioning the ideas she knew about, and the ones she didn't know about – this would allow her to form a view during the discussion and then proffer it openly with no thought of the consequences.

This sultry Tuesday afternoon, as the weak sun filtered feebly through to the dusty floor, Mrs M-S spoke of DH Lawrence's

Lady Chatterley's Lover. She walked across the platform, arms waving, fingers throwing her hair from side to side as if she was tossing a salad, hands thumping on her heart and occasionally wiping her brow with her embroidered lace handkerchief.

When Lily thought it was a good time to break her teacher's performance, she asked, "Excuse me, Mrs Montgomery-Smyth... I think this is outdated and irrelevant for people of our generation."

Mrs M-S spun on her heal to deliver an indignant stare at Lily. Her nostrils flared, her chest, neck and, finally, her face turned a crimson pink. She waved her copy of the book high in the air, and said, "Interesting, Lily... You dare to question one of the all-time classic authors. His expertise with the written word is lauded by all the literary critics. On what basis do you think the text is outmoded and irrelevant?"

"Well, he speaks of the eventual love scene. We've just passed the 'Swinging 60s' where free love and bodily expression were invented. No one today would take the time they did in the novel to have an intimate relationship."

"Lily, remember, we must be very careful when we use absolute terms – that is, *no one*. Yes, you're right that we are all products of our time and, yes, you're right when you say every text is set in a period which, by virtue of that fact, means it is set into a value system, mores of the time, cultural expectations, understandings, social and political frameworks etcetera. So, you're making very valid observations here. However, if you were answering a question such as this in an end-of-year exam, you'd have to have several relevant examples from the text to back up your contention. And *never* use an absolute term, because the examiner can refute your contention, even if it is a worthy one, with copious textual examples by disproving what you say. Tonight, re-read the text, let me know if there is any relevance to today in how they felt – what were their separate motivations, what were the risks, how did the drama build up, did the story arc engage you, was the humanity of the story still relevant today? Then let's see what we uncover. That's tonight's homework everyone. The jury will decide tomorrow – relevant or irrelevant?"

Every student was quickly writing in their homework diaries.

"Thank you, Lily," Mrs M-S signed off. "Your questions and observations enrich our discussions and our analysis of texts."

Lily couldn't wait to get home to tell Nini about Mrs M-S's class. Of course, she would imitate her teacher, and Nini would giggle along.

Mrs Gigory was stomping around the class in her solid black ankle boots, snatching sheets from students as she barged down the aisle. Paulo, as usual, had his eyes downcast, even more so when Mrs Gigory was on the warpath. She let out a huge sigh as she grabbed his sheet from under his nose. "You haven't answered *one* of these questions, Paulo. *Not one.* What excuse are you going to give me today? Huh?"

"I... I... I don't understand algebra. Sorry, Mrs Gigory, I did try."

"Try? Are you kidding me? Do you take me for a fool?"

"No, I don't think you're a fool."

Someone tried to stifle a laugh and Mrs G glared around to catch sight of who it was.

"What is the answer to 1? Huh? What is the answer to 2? 3? 4? For God's sake, Paulo, we've been learning this for three weeks. What is wrong with you? Are you a simpleton?"

"I don't know."

"Well, you just answered my question in the affirmative. You should not be in this class, wasting my time and holding the other students back. Pathetic. Absolutely pathetic." She threw the empty sheet back at Paulo, who retrieved it from the floor with trembling hands. She stomped her way back to her desk as Lily raised her hand.

"Yes, Lily?"

"I don't think you should speak to Paulo that way, Mrs Gigory."

"I don't care what you think, Lily. So, because you don't know when and when not to speak, you can go to the principal's office and speak with her."

"He said he was *trying* to do the work. It isn't his fault if he can't understand it. You're meant to be teaching him. It's not right what you said to him."

"Get out! Get out and take everything with you. Straight to the principal's office, you smart-alec. Let's see how smart you are then. Get out."

"You should apologise to Paulo, Mrs Gigory."

"I said, get out!" She picked up a heavy book from her desk and threw it towards Lily's head. It missed, landing heavily against the door as Lily slid behind it.

Paulo put his hand up.

The teacher sighed and jutted her chin at him. "What do *you* want?"

"Please don't get Lily into trouble, Mrs Gigory," Paulo pleaded. "Please. I'll take the suspension instead of her."

The class was eerily silent. Their heads turned nervously between the teacher and Paulo.

She smiled and said, "Oh yes you will, Paulo Rotondo. Pack your desk, your bag and everything in this class that belongs to you. You go down to the principal's office and be with your only friend, Lily. See where this sticking up for each other gets you. Get out."

As he gathered his things and tried to hurry out the classroom door she screamed, "Now!"

And that was the tone of Form 5 mathematics. Lily received two weeks detention and Paulo one week. Lily was made to apologise to Mrs Gigory. When she went home, enraged about the injustice of it all, Nini was there to make tea. She listened and said, "Well my darling, some days are balloon and some days are stinkers. You've had a stinker.' Nini patted Lily's knee. "I'm glad you're enjoying the chocolate cake, but I think you're going to be eating humble pie for a while."

"What do you mean, Nini?" Lily broke off a corner of the chocolate cake and bit into the icing.

"Mrs G's wrong, but the principal is not going to admit that to a student. You're going to have to play the game. Apologise, say sorry, and don't speak in her class unless she calls your name. The last thing you want is for her to target you."

"But she was horrible to Paulo. It wasn't fair. She was calling him an idiot. I felt like swearing at her."

"Oh, well, I am pleased you didn't do that. Just say sorry, that you won't do it again, and move on. Otherwise, she can make your life hell. And you need to be in class to do well. Paulo isn't academic like you are. He'll find his way with his dancing. Just keep your own head down."

Nini got up to refill the kettle and said, "You'd think the people in positions of power would be full of goodness, but they're not always."

Lily heard Nini say to herself as she followed her through the back door, "No, they're certainly not always."

"I couldn't look her in the face and say it. I'd throw up."

"Okay, then write it. But remember, it's a game, and the people who play it the smartest win. Fighting with a teacher is not a winning proposition – fair or otherwise. If they feel you've humiliated them in front of the class, God help you."

Lily walked to the back step and threw the hard part of her cake to Bessie who caught it in her mouth mid-air. "Wish I was a dog." Lily picked up an errant tennis ball and threw it for Bessie to catch.

"Yes, not a bad life, I agree," Nini said.

The sky lightened as the streaky clouds floated away and revealed the soft pastel blue. The sunset threw an orange-pink across the horizon which shone through the tea-trees.

FIFTY-FOUR

Lily raced through the door and threw her school bag towards her bedroom door as it ricocheted off the hallway table.

"Hey, Mum, Nini, you're not going to believe what happened today!" Lily was standing with the fridge door open, sculling milk straight from the bottle.

She heard the flywire door close and Nini's humming floating up towards the kitchen.

"Nini, I need to tell you about today," Lily called in between gulps. "Is Mum home?"

"Well, a warm hello to you too, my darling." Nini beamed a smile at her granddaughter from the laundry door. "And no, Meredith's still at work. She should be home around 5pm."

Once Nini had made the tea and Lily had piled Anzac biscuits onto a tray, they nestled down for some serious storytelling.

"You know how I told you about Mrs Gigory? Well, she's so hoity-toity and she bangs on about everything for the longest time. Well, today she's complaining how some of us, me included, Paulo and, of course, Mot, were not reflecting the school well with our disheveled school uniforms, hair etcetera. So, we just sit there being embarrassed and belted until she goes to start the class and turns her back to us. Unbeknown to her, she's tucked her dress into her pink bloomer undies. We can see her saggy bum through the paisley nylons! It was the funniest sight. The whole class was uproarious. I laughed so hard I thought I was going to be sick."

Lily started to cry with laughter and Nini was laughing with her.

"Oh, the poor woman! Now that is *embarrassing*," Nini said, egging Lily on. "Take her off. You're such a natural actress."

Lily, not needing any encouragement, got up and tucked her school dress into her undies, put on her best plum-in-the-mouth voice, and started talking about the lack of dress standards, pointing out the culprits – Lily herself being the first. Then, she turned on her heels and revealed her half-cheek bottom. Nini was crying with laughter.

During the retelling and performance, Meredith sauntered in. "Hello, Mum. Hello, Lily," she said as she poured herself a cup of tea, kicked off her shoes, and took a biscuit.

"Hi, Mum.' Lily pulled her dress out of her underwear.

"Hi, Meredith. How was work?" Nini asked.

"The same as usual." She silently padded to her bedroom and closed the door.

Lily and Nini looked at each other and acknowledged Meredith's drifting off, then resumed their conversation as if nothing had happened.

Over time, gradually at first, Lily went more and more to Nini. Meredith may have been there, but her presence had no traction, no matter what was happening or being discussed. It was as if none of it had anything to do with her; as if she was a vague observer of a play or a scene that she did not belong in.

Meredith, did you hear what happened with Mrs Gigory today? Or *Meredith, Lily got great marks in her English test.* Or *Meredith, Lily gave her speech to the class today.* It didn't matter how Nini phrased it, Meredith would faintly smile her dim acknowledgement, perhaps say something brief, and make her quiet departure as soon as she could. Work was all Meredith could manage, and she was utterly depleted when she came home. So much so, that she often ate lightly and went to bed. Or, if she joined them for dinner, she ate little and excused herself when Lily started the dishes.

On better days, she'd manage a weak smile at Lily, like the sun peeking through the gloomiest clouds. Sometimes, Meredith retreated to the backyard with a cup of tea, looking at the sky for hours. Lily often saw a magpie on a branch nearby. Her mother was always looking for it, although she never mentioned this. One day, Lily went and sat with her. Though Meredith didn't speak, Lily chatted away. Then Meredith patted Lily's leg and got up and went to her room.

The silence was hard for Lily to bear. Despite the pain of those early days after Frank died, at least Meredith still had *some* words back then, through her tears.

Lily recalled an evening, just a few days after the funeral – her mother overcome with remorse at not ever having comprehended her own mother's grief before that point. They were sitting at the dinner table, the three of them, Meredith weeping over her barely touched meal.

"I never acknowledged your pain, Mum, after Dad died," Meredith had said. "I ridiculed you at your lowest point, with all your superstition, signs, and symbols. I didn't understand it until now." She placed her cutlery together over her half-full plate.

Nini's pastry-soft face creased towards Meredith, and she took her daughter's hand.

"I'm sorry, Mum," Meredith said. "I deserve this pain. It's my turn to suffer and I'm suffering dreadfully." She stood up and as she passed Lily, she looked at her and said, quietly, "I'm sorry, Lily." And patted her on her head.

Lily had felt lost and invisible. "Mum, you think you're the only one grieving!" she had shouted. "I'm grieving too! He was *my* dad and I loved him *so much*. You only think of yourself. What about *me*? I'm left with you when all I want is him." Lily ran from the table and slammed the back door.

"I'm sorry, Lily. I'm so sorry," Meredith had called after her, between tears.

From the porch, Lily could hear Nini comforting Meredith. "Here, here, darling. I understand. Lily's struggling too. Dear girl. Dear, dear girls." She saw Nini walk towards Meredith with her arms open and watched as her mother collapsed into her own mother's embrace.

FIFTY-FIVE

The ocean sounded like an engine left running. It was rarely silent, so when it was, it unnerved Lily. The background thrum soothed her, as if a friend was just around the corner. She left home early with Bessie and walked the long way. There was the usual Saturday buzz of drivers, and the morning was mellow. Lily felt she had all the time in the world; she'd handed in two assignments the week before and, apart from reading, didn't have too much homework weighing her down. From up on the path to the lighthouse she watched the waves being pushed by the onshore westerly in lines like troops in an army line-up.

Alexa, Mot, and Paulo had said to meet at the basketball courts behind the milk bar. She could hear them yelling out to each other, especially Alexa's low, gravelly voice. She ran lightning-fast to grab the ball in mid-air as Paulo stood with his arms up expectantly in the goal ring.

"Hi!" Lily yelled as she ran and caught the ball from Mot and sped towards the opposite end of the court.

"Here! Here!" Alexa and Mot yelled, before Lily turned and slammed a basket.

"Yay!" Paulo shouted and they high-fived each other.

After half-an-hour of running and playing hard, they sat on the bench seats at the side. Paulo, who had been playing in bare feet, scrunched his toes into his thongs.

"Huh, finally you wear both." Lily pointed at his feet, remembering that he'd told her and Nini that he'd outgrown his birthday thongs.

"Yep. The weirdest thing happened. I emptied the mailbox

last night and inside the ring where the paper goes were these little babies – brand new and my size." He put his feet up to show the others. "Later, I tell the old man, and he says, *Huh, never accept a gift from someone you don't know.* I think bullshit. These are for Paulo-boy and I'm-a-keepin-em."

They all laugh between pants, still puffed out from running.

"What's on this weekend?" Lily asked the group.

"I'm meant to mow the lawn, clean up all the broken rubbish in the backyard, and then chop the wood for our fire. Not bloody likely," Mot said.

"Well, I'm currently unpacking about 12 boxes of stuff in the storeroom for the shop," Alexa said.

"I've got to help Nini do the shopping and maybe some vacuuming. But I don't mind..."

Alexa interrupted Lily. "Oh, shit, that's Ricardo and Dimitri", and she sped off and out the gate towards the milk bar.

"What's up?" Paulo asked Mot.

Mot stood shaking his head and watching her flee. "The brothers dob her in. She's like a prisoner. She's either helping her mum or working in that shop."

"What, like she's not allowed to do anything else?" Paulo asked.

"Nup. She's not allowed to do sport, hang out, nothing."

"God, that's cruel," Lily said. "What's wrong with her folks? She must be scared of her brothers, too."

Mot started to thump the basketball hard against the brick wall of the building next door.

"I can't imagine not being able to do stuff. That's probably not even legal."

"It's their culture," Mot said. "Plus, her dad makes the rules, she reckons. Her old man is tough, and they all do what he says.

When he's out, the boys are in charge. The mum's okay but she's not in charge."

"I gotta go." Mot smashed the ball one last time and it bounced way off into the basketball court.

"Why?" Lily asked.

"The pig'd kill me if he thought I was having fun. He's piled up so much work, I better start. Sure hope he's not back from work early. Check ya later." Mot grabbed the ball on his way past and threw it to Lily. He hurried out the gate with his head down.

Lily thought it didn't seem real that for an hour or so you could have such a great time and then, in a flash, it felt scary.

FIFTY-SIX

Sullenly, Lily ate her Weetbix and milk next to Meredith, who kept yawning into her steaming cup of tea. Nini had started to sleep in recently and was often still in bed when Lily left for school. Having breakfast at the same time as Meredith was a new dynamic for the two of them. It felt uncomfortable to be the only ones at the table. Lily never felt at her best in the morning; and after the night shift, Meredith definitely wasn't at her best, either. But that day she looked, as well as acted, completely worn out, hardly able to keep her eyes open. She rested her elbows on either side of her plate and cradled her face in her hands as if stopping her head from falling onto the table.

"Mum, you look terrible. Are you alright?" Lily asked as she sat down with her mug of tea.

Meredith looked up. "Thanks, Lily. I must remember to have breakfast with you more often." She stood, walked over to the sink and poured the rest of her tea down the drain.

"I wasn't being rude, Mum."

"Well, if you think telling someone they look awful first thing in the morning, even though it is actually night-time for me, is not rude, I don't know what is."

Lily dropped her spoon back into her cereal bowl, causing a wave of milk to splash over the side and onto the table. "I was only caring about you. You take offence at everything I say."

"Argh. Okay. I'm tired, Lily. I can't help that." Meredith's slumped frame shuffled off. "Have a good day. I'm going to bed to hopefully get some sleep. Let Bessie out before you go," she slung over her shoulder before she closed her door firmly.

Lily threw her breakfast out. She grabbed the lunch Nini had made the night before from the refrigerator, let Bessie out, and slammed the back door as she left.

By the time she got to school, the ruminations about Meredith were running around and around in her mind. *Why is she so mean? I'm sick of her. Sick of her complaining. Sick of her bad moods. Why doesn't she ever think of anyone else? She's so bloody selfish.*

Paulo wasn't there, which felt like the last straw. Lily stormed past Nastacia.

"And good morning to you too, Lily," Nastacia said sarcastically.

"Get stuffed, Nastacia," Lily snarled.

"Oh, how charming."

"Whatever, Princess." Lily stuck up her rude finger and smiled back greasily.

These acidic exchanges were rare, but Lily couldn't resist the odd one. She threw her bag at the outside wall and snatched her books ready for roll-call.

Paulo was extra late today. Mrs Greenshmit, who was humourless at the best of times, requested he see her after class. Paulo looked like he'd slept in his uniform, with his hair wildly haloing his face and cascading down onto his shoulders. Big mistake. Lily motioned to him about his hair. Terrified, he rummaged through his bag for an elastic band. They tolerated girls having messy long hair, but no slack was ever permitted for boys. Lily threw him her hair-tie, which he had to drag towards himself across the linoleum floor with his shoe.

"What on earth are you doing, Paulo? First, you're late, then you start mucking around. Behave, or you're out." Mrs G took great pleasure in her threat. There wouldn't be a second one.

Lily knew he either got that band or he'd be ordered to cut his hair – the equivalent of a slow death to Paulo. When Mrs G turned to the board, Lily crept over, picked up the band and dropped it behind her on Paulo's desk, just as the teacher turned around.

"Lily Mango, get out! No excuses – I'm not in the mood." Mrs G pointed at the door. "Out!"

Paulo stared wide-eyed at her, which meant, *I owe you*. She stared back, which meant, *You certainly do*.

At lunchtime, Lily found Paulo loitering around his locker and muttering obscenities under his breath.

"What's the problem?"

"I can't find my bloody history assignment. It's overdue, and he said if it's not in today he'll fail me." Paulo kept rummaging but to no avail.

"Why are you so absolutely hopeless?"

"Don't know. Just lucky, I guess." He kept siphoning through rubbishy bits of paper, dog-eared overdue library books, folders with papers half torn and falling off the binders.

"No, I really mean it. Has anyone ever told you you're hopeless? You're late, you're forgetful, you're messy..."

Paulo stopped and stared hard at her. "And you, of course, are perfect." He forced his locker closed and thundered off.

Lily stood with her mouth agape. After a few minutes she shook her head, as if that would erase what she had said, and returned to her next class.

By the time Lily had returned from school, Meredith was showered, dressed, and in the laundry. Nini had the tranny on talkback in the kitchen. Lily gave her a peck on the cheek and retreated to her bedroom before her quick exit to the beach.

"Hello, Lily." Meredith sheepishly entered Lily's room while Lily was getting herself ready to leave. "How was your day?"

"Not flash, but better than your night, I reckon." Lily did not look at Meredith as she bent over and laced up her sandshoes.

"Lily, can we just let it go? I don't want my time with you to be one long argument. I get tired sometimes. I don't *want* to be grumpy. I'm sorry. Okay?"

"Yep. That's okay."

Meredith stood expectantly in the doorway. Lily walked past with her back to her.

"Nini, I'm off to the beach," she called.

"Okay, darling. Be safe."

"I will. Bessie!"

The tension in the house rarely eased. Meredith tried, but Lily kept her distance. The odd conversations they did have were peppered with one of them yelling at the other, storming off and slamming their bedroom doors. Mostly it was Lily but, sometimes, in exasperation with Lily's lack of interaction or respect, it was Meredith.

One afternoon, when Meredith was out shopping, Nini sat with Lily as they ate their afternoon tea. Nini patted Lily's thigh. "You feeling okay, little one?"

Lily kept her gaze down and twirled her teacup. It was a pink flowery one of Nini's and she loved using it. "I've been fighting with Paulo. I was mean to him. I don't even know why. He never says anything nasty to me."

"What did you say to him, darling?"

"I told him he was hopeless. I mean he stuffs everything up. He doesn't put his homework in on time, he's always late to school, he loses things..."

"Do you think he does that deliberately?"

"Maybe. Ah, no, he's just forgetful and hopeless."

"No, he hasn't got a mother, or a father for that matter, to guide him."

"But he is late, always late. He forgets assignments. Sleeps in when I'm meant to go to the beach with him. Borrows stuff and doesn't return it. It gets annoying. Really annoying. Like he's deliberately trying to piss me off. Sorry, Nini, didn't mean to swear." Lily breathed out loudly and threw her head back.

"He's lost and is trying his best, but sometimes he can't make the mark, poor boy."

"Maybe. I never thought of it like that. I mean, the dirty dishes and his piles of clothes everywhere... You'd have a fit if you saw their place."

"Don't be too harsh on him, darling. He's left to his own devices a lot of the time. He's doing a good job of it. The best he can do, without any adult to help him."

"Oh, I feel *bad*. I shouldn't have said what I did. It was mean of me." Lily scrunched up her face. "Sometimes I speak before I think. Like, I said what I said to him and, when he stormed off on me, I thought, *Oh God, why did I say that?*"

"Then say sorry. You know, *love* and *sorry* are two of the most powerful words in the dictionary." Nini took a big sip of her tea. "Those two words can change the course of a relationship. Forever." She poured them both another cup and sat back with a faraway look on her face. The blackbirds chirped happily, and a couple of blue wrens darted from the gum into Nini's pink camelia. A willy wagtail bopped up, flashed his tail at them and raced off. The sky was streaky white with an insipid blue background like a watercolour with too much water.

Lily listened and didn't speak for a while.

"Never be afraid to use those words when you mean them," Nini said. "Be very afraid of not using them. Without love and forgiveness, a relationship will wither and die – like that old cyclamen pot I've just noticed..." Nini put down her cup and tottered off the verandah to salvage her plant.

FIFTY-SEVEN

Lily could hear the kookaburras on the electricity pole in the distance. The night before, there had been a cacophony of them laughing and the circle of their laughter whizzed around her as she brought the washing in. It felt as though they were chortling at a shared joke. She remembered her dad pointing them out to her on the telephone lines and saying, *We should all spend our days like them – laughing and hanging out with our mates.* It had been a lazy Saturday afternoon and she and Frank were strolling into town. As was his way, he pointed out gum trees, the shape of leaves, the different greens, the drift of the clouds from a clown to a king and back to a sheep. There was so much to take in when she was outside with her dad. Lily swung her hand in his. *You know who has the best laugh, Lily-pily? Apart from you, of course. My old mate the kookaburra.* As they walked on, *You know why they laugh so much? Because they think life is ridiculous. Because they think if you don't laugh at yourself, you're in big trouble. The more you laugh at life, the happier you are.* Snippets of conversations floated through her memory at times when she least expected.

Then she thought of how awful she'd been to Paulo, how critical, and she didn't know why. Like she was looking for a fight. His sad face was in her mind as she remembered the way he had tried to stand up for himself.

As soon as she saw him that day, she said, "Are you speaking to me?"

"Hmm, maybe," Paulo said and didn't look at her.

"I don't know why I say what I say. I mean, you do forget stuff and I know – I know I'm not perfect either."

"Yep, you sure as hell are not perfect."

"I didn't mean to hurt your feelings."

"Well, then shut up. Sometimes just friggin' shut up."

"Yeah, I'll try to."

He walked off.

"Sorry," she said to his back.

"Yeah, yeah, okay," he said as he kept walking.

After school, Paulo seemed to have thawed, so Lily told him about the conversation with her dad, and how it explained why she loved kookaburras so much. How she kept noticing and hearing them since her dad died.

She looked at Paulo's soft eyes. "They're not beautiful like you, though."

"Huh, like me?" His face looked incredulous.

"Yeah, you *are* beautiful. But that doesn't bug me – I mean, I know I'm not beautiful but I'm okay with that."

"I don't feel beautiful," Paulo said. "You're tall and strong; I like the way you look.'

He nudged Lily's arm, his gentle expression resting upon her face. His long eyelashes almost reached his eyebrows. She thought, *You are beautiful – but maybe more so because you don't know it.*

"If you were a girl, you'd be pretty," she said. "It's your face. But I think it's mainly because you're good. You're a good person."

"Oh, thanks buddy." He looked around as if he needed somewhere to hide. "You're good too – in your own way. Well, not all the time, but sometimes."

She pushed him hard and he nearly tripped.

"See what I mean?" He shook his head and his wavy hair flounced around his face. "Pretty, my arse."

"Your arse? As if!" She covered her eyes for dramatisation. "I've never even looked at your arse, pretty or not, and I don't intend to!"

He stuck his bottom towards her and did a duck walk. "I don't want to look at your arse, either. Although you are a very big smartarse."

"My arse? You don't want to look at my arse?"

They laughed all the way to the Point.

FIFTY-EIGHT

After the drenching rain, the droplets hung on the she-oak thistles like the Myer Christmas fairy lights. Lily wondered why what Paulo said didn't match how he looked. She couldn't read his expression, or why his usual slouched walk was replaced by a stride.

He fidgeted and twisted his fingers. They reminded her of the twining ropes she saw on the fishermen's boats. His foot-tapping habit had recently become foot-stomping. Paulo would sit cramped over and one foot, usually the right, would take off. He never seemed to notice. Lily thought about the way Paulo played with his hair. There was a lot of it to play with. Then she thought of the way it hung over his face, like a shield. She tried to imagine him bald like Ronaldo, but she couldn't.

Alexa flitted. The more Lily watched the willy wagtails, or especially the blue wrens, sometimes the darting sparrows or blackbirds, the more she thought of her. It was somewhere between being chased and hunted – quick, unpredictable movements which seemed so fast that you second-guessed whether they had happened at all. They seemed misaligned with what was happening around her. She started to eat less. For such a small girl, Alexa always had a great appetite. But not this year. Maybe, Lily thought, it was to do with the exams. She was under pressure from both of her parents to do well. Her mother thought Alexa could aim for a better life than she had. Her father didn't want his money to be wasted on her education for nothing.

Mot, on the other hand, ate when food was offered but never

seemed hungry or that interested. It seemed as if he needed to be somewhere else, but he didn't know where. As he ate, he looked around as if someone might swoop down and grab whatever morsel was in his hand. A cheeky magpie did just that one spring – except it was Paulo holding the prize. As they divided up Nini's corned beef sandwiches, the bloody maggie swooped and took Paulo's share. Everyone was stunned, until they laughed – everyone but Paulo, who stood swearing and shaking his fist as if the magpie would hear and give it back.

One day, when Paulo was raving about Nini's roasts and Alexa was enthusing about her mum's famous lasagna, Lily asked Mot: "What's *your* favourite meal?"

"Ah, there's not many," he answered. "My nan used to make Chicken Maryland or roasts, but that was when I was young. She's not here anymore."

Everyone else was changing, Lily thought. She didn't know why, and she couldn't work out if she was, too. Things were moving in different ways and Lily wondered why things couldn't just stay as they were.

Lily's left eye started to twitch. Sometimes she bit her lip, and she didn't realise that she was doing it. Nini asked her, "Why do you do that? Are you worried about something?"

Lily was shocked that Nini thought she was doing these things on purpose, and when she went to answer, she couldn't, because she didn't know why. That was when the headaches started too, mild ones to begin with, thumpers on bad days. Meredith usually bore the brunt of these. Everything seemed to be weighing Lily down.

Lily, will you do something to help? Lily, clean the bathroom, hang the washing out, do the vacuuming, put the bins out. Help

Nini. Meredith would make these demands before closing her bedroom door.

Why in the hell don't you? Lily would retort. Or, *All you do is give me orders.* Or, *Do it your bloody self.* Or, *Here's an idea – why don't you shut up?*

Nini often interrupted. *Now, now, darling that's not how you speak to your lovely mum. Why don't I run you a bath, or make you a hot chocolate?* Or, *Why don't you take Bessie for a walk?* Anything to diffuse the situation.

The chill of the road rose to meet her body as the edges of her face tingled. It was before sunrise and the flywire door creaked enough to speak of her leaving. Once she turned left into Southern Ocean Road, she felt the southerly whistling down upon her. She didn't feel like swimming. She'd had a rotten night's sleep. Too cold without the eiderdown, too hot with it, her legs couldn't get comfortable, and then the dream, the nightmare, came. She awoke in a panic. She had lost something, she'd lost someone, and she couldn't change it. Her dad. This propelled her out of bed early and Bessie was already in the hallway, ready to go. She walked determinedly around the cemetery, the lighthouse looking ghostly white at the Point, and turned into the relief and protection of Spray Point front beach. The water was silver, the sky was a harsh white, and the crest of Wallawee in the distance was a murky brown. Fringing the crest were the softest rose-coloured clouds, a tiny hint that it would be daylight soon. She watched a large sea bird glide, stop and pin-drop into the sea. She drank in the sharp sea air and the stench of seaweed clinging underneath the pier with its vivid green tentacles.

Lily thought of her mother and how mean she was – old, tired, grumpy, demanding, unfair and tough. She thought of their most recent fight. It was pretty much like most of them. She had never fought with her dad. He used to whistle, hum, play games, read to her, nothing like Meredith. She remembered her mother tickling her on the couch one night after dinner and laughing, her hair thick and healthy-looking, her face fuller and happier. Not the way she was now.

She saw a peep of orange come over the crest. Then an explosion of fluorescent orange as the sun burst through. Lily let out an audible gasp and thought about how she'd write about this in her diary. The best part of her day.

FIFTY-NINE

The rain had washed the bitumen road, and the trees took on a wet iridescence, the damp air felt clean and soothing. Lily's pace slowed as her mind raced. Paulo did his usual slide shuffle, more laconic than usual, encouraged by the weather.

As they turned into his street, Lily said, "Nini reckons you've got great rhythm."

"Really?" He sighed his long curious sigh. "Why?"

"She reckons some people just have the music in them. She said, *That boy can move. He's got the music in him,*" Lily enthused, doing a poor imitation of Nini's voice and an awkward twirl.

"Ha ha. Sometimes I put on Mum's old records; I dance like crazy and sing at the top of my lungs. Only when the old boy's at work, 'cause there's no music, no dancing, nothing fun allowed when he's around."

"Yeah, I know – you've said that before. Why, though? Like, does he just hate a good time?" Lily scrunched up her nose as if it was a horrible thought.

"Maybe. But mainly because it reminds him of Mum."

Lily shook her head. "Oh yeah, that's right. Wasn't she the lead singer in a band?"

"Yeah. *Valerie and the Swinging Dixies.* I found a crumpled-up old pamphlet advertising them playing at the Criterion hotel the year she left."

"I'd love to see it. She must've been good."

"Her older brother, Leonard, came to visit us once after Mum left, and he reckoned that she was a good jazz singer. Ronaldo never went to watch. He thought Ronaldo was jealous of her."

Paulo did an extra-long sigh. "Anyway, now I'll never know..." He studied his feet as he walked.

"Your mum sounds incredible."

"Yeah, well... Some things are hard to forgive." He wiped the back of his hand across his eyes.

The mood shifted like the light dimming when a dark cloud passes across the sun. They were approaching Paulo's house.

"Hey, buddy, don't forget I'm here." Lily patted his olive-skinned arm. "Always."

"Yeah, thanks." His body seemed to crumple in on itself. "Sometimes everything feels like shit."

"I know. I feel like that too sometimes, but since I started running and swimming it doesn't seem as bad. I run until the rage comes out through my grunting lungs. When they're about to explode with pain, I feel okay. Then I hit the sea. The cold does something to my aching brain. It takes the headaches away. I feel weightless, like an old friend is carrying me. Weird, isn't it? I can't explain it, but I know I need it. I don't feel sorry for myself when I swim. I just survive one wave at a time."

They sat on his low brick fence, the tips of their shoes scuffing the pavement.

Paulo's sad face softened. "The only time I'm happy is when the old man is at work, and I can dance. I turn the stereo on full blast. Listening to Mum's old music makes me forget everything. I go into the lounge room and play cassettes. I go into another world. I float and spin in a trance. There's me and the invisible crowd. It's electric! That's when I feel alive."

Valerie was where he got his gorgeous looks. It was a shame he was gay. Lily thought of all the girls who swooned when they spoke to him. Paulo never noticed. It was embarrassing. Lily loved the fact that some of the students thought they were a couple. While she was tall, athletic and strong, with Irish colouring, Paulo looked like his mum but taller. His mother smiled broadly out of the photos; she had huge hoop earrings, massive jewellery, close-fitting clothing of brilliant orange or red, her thick brown hair swept up into messy buns and a very cheeky look on her face.

Lily thought of the conversation she'd had with Paulo about his mum. He had shared Ronaldo's version with her. When Valerie told Ronaldo she was leaving, it came as a total shock to him. He thought they were happy. Sure, Valerie was out four or five nights a week with her band, but that was her work. It suited them, given Ronaldo was a mechanic and he could leave the Ford factory by four to look after Paulo.

Valerie had told him that she couldn't stand his lack of interest in music, in her, in anything. She said, "I'm leaving, and I'm taking Paulo with me." Paulo clearly remembered this part. He was nine years old.

Ronaldo had said, "Over my dead body! You can leave, but we are a family, and we are staying. Paulo is not going anywhere. He won't be properly cared for. You've always put yourself first, Valerie. I've been the one to pick up the pieces. He isn't going to be neglected, while his mother the muso lives as if she's single. Pack your bags, take what you want and don't ever contact us again. You've broken our home, now you get to live with that."

Ronaldo told Paulo to give his mother a kiss goodbye, and Paulo whispered in her ear, "Will you write to me, Mummy?"

He remembers her begging Ronaldo, sobbing, holding her son and promising him she would write. "Please, Ray, don't cut me off from my boy. Please I'm begging you..."

"You've made your decision, Valerie. We're going out. Be

gone by the time we come back."

And that was the end of what Paulo knew of his mother. The sadness of the story seeped into Lily. They were quiet for a long time until she said, "*Bingo*! Found it. There's your passion. You're a dancer. That's what you've gotta do." She looked deeply into his excited face and clapped her hands.

"Yeah, dunno. I mean I love it, but the old boy would be against it. He thinks I'm too much like Mum as it is, let alone me wanting to be a dancer." Paulo stood up and grabbed his bag. "Plus, I can't afford the lessons or the shoes and all that shit."

"This isn't about what Ronaldo wants; it's about you. It's your life, mate. I'll help you with what the lessons cost. I've got the money that Dad left me. Right... where's a good dance school near here?"

"I can't let you do that."

"Yes, you bloody-well can. Besides, you can pay me back when you're famous. Back to the question of where..."

"Miss Cherie Dimontina is the best. I've got her brochure. That's my dream – I'm on stage, twirling faster and faster from corner to corner, and the audience is going nuts." He beamed and did a formal bow in front of her. "There's a standing ovation and I'm holding flowers and taking several bows." They had reached Paulo's house. He sighed and turned to open his squeaky little gate. "But then I wake up."

"Let's make the dream real. There's no point saying why you can't do it. We've gotta work out how you're *going* to do it. You've *got* to enrol. You've gotta chase your dream. You *have* to." Lily did some twirls and nearly fell over. "I'll go with you tomorrow," she declared.

"How will I pay for it? The old man won't give me a cent.

Not that I'd tell him, anyway."

"Well, if you won't take *my* money, what about the money your mum left in your birthday and Christmas cards?"

"Oh, yeah. I forgot about that."

"That's a start, and then the Star Bakery are always asking us if we want a job. You can do both. We'll call in on them after the dance part is sorted. Bring it on, baby. You can be the dancer and I'll be the romancer." Lily ruffled his hair as they bounced in step together towards his side gate.

The next day, when the scream of the afternoon bell had finally ceased, Paulo and Lily grabbed their bags and flew down the stairs. They ran to the bus stop and were the first to get on. The dance academy loomed after five stops. It was an old red-brick building with a long timber ramp leading to the first floor. Jazz music blasted from the studio. The heavy maroon timber door screeched as they pushed it ajar. The smell of dust, wax, cool stale air and dreams greeted them. They stood expectantly in the corner of the room. Students were dashing past them in their ballet outfits and laughing, en route to their next class. There, Cherie Dimontina stood – resplendent, tall, statuesque, with a long dark ponytail, distinctive make-up, large earrings, and a broad smile.

"Hello. May I help you?" She smiled at them.

Paulo froze. He looked back towards the door as if perhaps he should flee.

"Hello, Miss Cherie. I'm Lily and this is my best friend, Paulo. He's wanting to join your school. He is a very talented dancer and has heard so much about you."

Even Paulo's tanned skin couldn't hide the sudden redness in his face.

"Well, that's good to hear, Lily." Miss Cherie turned her

eagle-eyed stare to Paulo. "Now, Paulo, what type of dance have you done? Where and for how long?"

He stared at her, and nothing came out.

Lily broke the prolonged silence. "He mainly does free dance in his loungeroom to very loud rock and roll. His mother's old albums. She was a lead jazz singer – in a band. His mother's not there anymore, but Paulo loves to dance to her music."

"So, I take it you'd like to do modern dance?"

"Yes," Paul said nervously, "I think so. Please. How much would it cost?"

"Why don't you stay now and watch a couple of classes? This is tap and then modern is after that. See what you're interested in. We can talk about the fees later."

Paulo was mesmerised with the action surrounding him. He watched the girls move and practice in their pink wraps, ballet shoes, tap shoes and leggings. They were stretching by the bar, limbering up and laughing. The mirrors lit the main room, which was an old stage, and the large leadlight windows streamed colours across the hall. There were also two side rooms, which held the other classes, which Miss Cherie didn't teach. Lily sat at the edge with Paulo throughout the first class. His head rested in his hands and his elbows were on his knees. He didn't speak or look at Lily once. His face looked so excited as he watched and listened to the rhythmic tapping.

At the end of the class, he walked up to the teacher and asked her a couple of questions. Lily waved to him and left. Paulo didn't notice.

SIXTY

The beach was strewn with shells, crunching loudly under Lily's worn-out runners. She stopped abruptly to collect a superb one, cream-laced with silver and curled like the smoothest wave, its fawn back melding into mauve, then soft blue, then into its pearl-pink interior. She held it to her ear; the ocean whispered soothingly back.

Her swim today was in the bay – an oily, slick, smooth sea. The clear water showcased the ocean's sandy base, sprinkled with a multitude of tiny silver fish, the occasional larger one weaving through. She dove amongst them as they scattered.

Lily's mind was full of the memory of Paulo's words as they walked back from the basketball court.

"What type of fish do you think you'd be, mate?" Lily asked.

Paulo winced. "Buddy, does your overactive mind ever have a day off?"

"I prefer to think of it in terms of my deep mind; however, whichever it is, back to the original question. Big or small, would you be a deep-sea dweller or a shallow small fish? I mean, there's the whole ocean to inhabit, so which would it be for you?"

"You make my brain hurt. Seriously, you do." He ran his hands through his hair.

"C'mon. Which? Painful brain is not an adequate excuse for not answering."

"Small fish. Fast and flashy. Great moves, shiny, shimmering, and electric."

This made Lily happy. "Plus, you love silver!" she enthused. "For me, I'd be a deep-sea fish – large, considered, and wanting to know more about the depths of the vast ocean. What truly lies beneath."

"Fair enough. The fish I'd be would be like a marine dancer. The shallow water's my stage. The sky," he said, lifting his arms skyward, "my audience."

"Exactly. Now you're getting the hang of it. Me – the depths. I want to know more and more – the colours, the nooks and crannies, the hiding spots for the deep-sea life. When nothing make sense, I want answers; I go looking for more."

They looked out at the depths when they noticed a black mass moving towards them.

"Is that seaweed?" Lily asked.

"Where?"

Lily pointed as an enormous black sheet floated past them, parallel to the shore. "Oh my God, that's a manta ray! Look – it's friggin' huge!'

It slowly drifted and draped across their line of sight.

"Shit! Another reason I didn't want to swim today," Paulo said.

"You never want to swim any day."

"Yeah, and now I know why."

Lily pushed him and he fell into the sand, charging back to grab her ankles. But she was too fast.

"Speaking of all things gargantuan," Paulo panted, "I'm starving. Do you reckon Nini'd care if I crashed lunch again today?"

"Nup. She reckons you're family. She's factoring you in every Sunday."

"Oh God, how I love that woman."

They laughed and ran back to Lily's place. The scent of

succulent roasted lamb and vegetables, spuds crisply crackling and – the *pièce de résistance* – the promise of apple pie with lashings of cream for dessert.

SIXTY-ONE

Lily and Paulo's afternoon walk was under a sultry, sunken sky. There was a tiny brilliant blue patch, but a threatening dark mist gathered and loomed way out to sea. Beyond the waves, a black form moved.

"Look, Paulo – dolphins." Lily pointed. "Whoa, there it goes!"

Paulo strained to see it. "It's a baby. Where's its mother?"

"And its father?" she said. "The other day, when I was here after a swim, I saw a pod of them way out. Twelve, I reckon, I'm not exaggerating. Hope this little one wasn't left behind."

"Yeah, me too. Come on little fella, swim faster and find 'em," Paulo said, pushing his arms through the air as if to propel the calf along.

They crunched along the length of the back beach and didn't speak, their eyes on the calf, which was moving in and out of sight, in the hope that an adult would soon appear beside it. The sky blackened as the first raindrops fell. They ran the whole length of the beach back to the track as the rain intensified.

Drenched, trudging and squelching up the sand-dune path, once they'd regained their breath, Paulo said, "Poor little bastard is on his own now."

"So sad. Maybe his mum and dad found him."

"Hope so."

They ran all the way home to get out of the rain.

SIXTY-TWO

The old path had become overgrown with stray tree-branches littered along the way, hiding the steep narrow concrete steps that Lily ascended. By the time she reached the last step, where there was a timber seat, her breathing had become laboured.

Only perching there for a moment, Lily decided to forge on. She started to puff audibly, and her trek became slower. She had to get to the top. Her legs were slightly wobbly, and she was perspiring profusely. She chastised herself for taking the hard route and forgetting to bring water on such a hot day. Annoyingly, she could hear Meredith's voice, *Never go on a long walk without water.* Once the slope started to level off, she knew she was nearly there. The overgrown track to the side was now disused, apart from the greenies clearing it once a year. And there the old lighthouse stood, defiant in its decay, its use now defunct, the white flaky paint lifting off like old, dry skin all the way to the top. Lily put her hands against its surface and felt the warmth of its thick exterior, heated by the afternoon sun. On the bayside, the wind whipped her hair, and the white caps peppered the blue-black sea. Her lungs filled and her jacket flapped like unhinged sails.

No one came here, or rarely at least, and yet she never felt lonely up there. At that height, she felt close to the sky and the clouds; the sea had a magical allure for her, and their little township appeared like a doll's house in the distance. She imagined living in the lighthouse. Never missing the changing mood of the weather or the sea – becoming one with them. Her mind whirled with the stories the old girl could tell, the tragedies it averted, the escapes it had witnessed, the sinking boats it had observed, the wild and treacherous weather and, always, the ever-changing sea.

SIXTY-THREE

It was just on sunrise as Lily banged on Paulo's filthy window at the side of his house. Even with his blind firmly drawn, she knew he was there. "Mate, get up. It's a cracker of a sunrise." Further insistent tapping, which sounded more like banging. "*Please*... Get up."

"Lily, go away," Paulo mumbled, his bed squeaking as he rolled over. "It's too early."

"No, it's not even that early. You need to get up, 'cause we're going swimming. There's no wind. It's gunna be awesome."

"Go yourself." More squeaking from the relic of a bed.

"No. I'm staying here and I'm not going to shut up until you get up."

"Come back later."

"No. You need to come *now*." She kept the banging going.

Finally, she heard some rustling, staggering and swearing as the back door slammed.

When they got to the pier, the sunrise was a burst of orange through fluorescent purple streaks and the rays were shooting outwards like a star-show towards them.

"See, I told you," Lily bragged.

"Yeah, it's good." Paulo's face was lit up orange, too.

They dropped their towels into the seagrass and Lily headed straight in. Paulo shuffled as Lily ran ahead and dove into the water. The sea was a cool mint green against the blinding sunlight. She swam to the furthest yacht as Paulo breast-stroked towards her.

"Put your head under. It's incredible!" she yelled.

He kept swimming gently and called back, "Nup. Drying this mane is a nightmare."

Lily waited for him, panting. "Was it worth it? Huh?"

Paulo's drenched face glowed, golden, the sunrise reflected in his eyes. "Yep. Bloody good."

The rays of the fully risen sun were now casting a dazzling diamond carpet all around them.

"Don't you reckon it's amazing how the sun's rays always shoot to where you are?" Lily asked.

"Nup," Paulo answered, holding on to the side of the cream yacht.

"I mean, if we move, it moves. Like it is beaming something directly to us from above. A message from the angels or something."

"Nup, I reckon it's just its reflection; you see it where you are."

"Really? No, I think it's far more magical than that. The heavens are beaming light towards us and there's some mystical message, just for us."

"I dunno. You and your crazy ideas. I'm cold." He started swimming for the shore.

Lily harangued Paulo most days. Some days, especially if it was cold or raining or both, he begged to sleep in. Sometimes, she let him. Some days, he refused. Most days, her persistence won him over.

The following week, when the wind was squally and the air was chilly, she dragged Paulo out of bed for another swim. He complained to her the whole way to the beach. She ignored him, saying, "It's worth it when you're in."

He didn't reply for fear of encouraging her.

Once there, Paulo swam out deep to meet up with her and hung on to an old yacht called *Serenity*.

"Do you believe in heaven?" she asked him.

"Nup."

"Why not?"

"Dunno, just don't."

"But why?"

"Because I think it's just something they made up to make sad people feel better."

"So, when we cark it, that's it? All over. Game, set, and match?"

"Yep. I reckon."

"Not me. I believe in heaven. I believe the stars, the moon, the sunrise, the sunset, the sea, the mountains are all telling us that upstairs exists. I mean, what's the bloody point, otherwise? We suffer all this shit down here, struggle through and then, bang, no warning, you're dead. Nup. I'll never believe there isn't an afterlife. That would be too cruel. I won't ever believe that."

"You, buddy, can believe whatever you want. Believing your dad is upstairs makes you feel better – that's good. I wish I could believe but I can't. It doesn't seem real to me." He started to swim back to the shore.

"I wish sometimes, just sometimes, that you would agree with me." Lily looked at the sky before joining him through the now choppy water.

"No, you don't wish *sometimes*, you wish *every* time. But I'm not gunna lie. Besides, if I always agreed with you, you might talk more than you already do."

She turned her hands towards him and bucketed his face as she swam off. He coughed up the water and joined the race.

Alexa called in to see Lily at home one night after school. She was meant to be helping one of her brothers move some crates, but he told her he had footy training that night, so she ducked out quickly. When there was a knock on the door, Lily expected a neighbour calling in or Nini's friend, Beatrice from around the corner. She was surprised to see Alexa.

Lily sat her friend down at the kitchen table and made her a hot Milo.

Twisting her hands around the mug, Alexa blurted out, "I'm worried about Mot. I used to call around to his joint but, if his folks were home, they wouldn't let me in. The last time I visited, his dad opened the front door, gave me a greasy, and slammed the door, yelling, *Bloody foreigners, should go back to where you come from.* I don't know where he is. But something's wrong." Her emerald eyes pierced Lily with their intensity. "I can smell trouble. Something bad is happening there." She finished her drink, stood abruptly and said, "Thanks. I know you care about him too."

At that, Alexa vanished out the front door as if she hadn't really been there.

Lily thought about Mot all weekend. *What did she mean, something bad is happening there? Bad as in sad, or bad as in really bad?* Nothing made sense. Paulo had no ideas. Alexa seemed fidgety and nervous.

On Monday, the dreary weather had settled in, not freezing but chilly and gloomy, as they sat around for lunch.

Alexa swung her legs from the old timber bench and repeated the story to Lily and Paulo. "Huh!" she said. "I thought, *You were foreigners once! Besides, you bloody idiot, I just happen to be your son's best friend."*

She folded her legs tightly and said to no one in particular, though watching out for interlopers, "I wonder who he talks to now." She knew the feeling of not liking your parents, Alexa told them, but it was worse for Mot. "He hates his dad. He says so all the time."

Her eyes darted around the playground as if she suspected his dad could be lurking somewhere. "The only way I used to be able to speak to him, was to call when his dad was at work. If one of his siblings answered the phone, I could talk to him, but if either of his parents answered or came into the room, I knew, because he'd hang up. Now, I never can."

"Wow, that's shit," Paulo said.

"Sounds weird," Lily added, and looked to Alexa for more information.

"My life is a fight – maybe that's why I'm good at it – but there are some good bits. But his life is *bad*. I reckon it's worse than he tells me."

No one said anything. The wind picked up the chip and lolly-wrappers and thrashed them around the fence line.

Alexa changed tracks unexpectantly. "You know what Mrs H said to me – *I'm not here to attack you, Alexa. I'm here to help you.*" The smile dropped from her face. "No one's ever said that to me before." She looked down at her shoes and her dark eyelashes blinked. "Maybe Antonio does kind of say it, in his own way."

"Yeah, she's a good one,' Paulo said of Mrs Helpin, who was Alexa's English teacher.

"For sure,' Lily added. "Antonio must be, too."

"If they could all be fair like Mrs H, I'd try my guts out in every class. But they're not. So, I'll fight them instead," Alexa said.

Lily and Paulo wondered if she was really talking about the teachers. Lately, Alexa laughed and smiled less – not even when Lily told her that Paulo burped loudly in class and went blood-red when the emergency teacher said that he was disgusting. It was as if, now that Mot was not around much, she'd lost her guiding star.

"Mot relied on Alexa, because he had *no one* else," Paulo said to Lily one day when Alexa wasn't around. "At least she has Antonio – and her mum, at least a little bit."

Alexa had become agitated, on edge, jumpy. When Lily walked up behind her, she started, as if the building was on fire. Her eyes looked wild, searching in all directions as if she was being hunted.

One day, just before the mid-term exams, Paulo approached Alexa and playfully pushed her birdlike arm as they headed out the front gate. "How goes it, Alexa?"

"The same, unfortunately." Alexa swivelled her neck and snatched up her bag.

"You alright, my friend?" Lily asked.

"Nup. I've had a gutful. *Listen to me, young lady, I'll have you know... For your information... At this rate you'll never amount to anything... You'll be a nobody.*" She brushed her petite, bony hand across her eyes. "If it's not here, it's at home. I'm friggin' over it." Alexa darted towards the overcrowded bus and swung onto it as it pulled out from the kerb.

SIXTY-FIVE

The wind howled like the Southern Aurora. The house shook like a ship in a storm. Lily got up early to walk Bessie and see the violet shades of the sky lighten. When they approached the peak of the dunes, the trees shivered violently as if they were made of rubber.

It was Saturday. The morning turned into a lazy, nowhere-to-go, nothing-to-do afternoon. Lily thought it was a good day to attack her homework. While setting out her books on the table, Paulo phoned to ask what she was doing. "Nothing. Come over," she lied.

Ten minutes later, he arrived, trembling. He went straight across to the gas fire, where he stood, hopping up and down. Lily put Jim Croce on the cassette player and went to make mugs of hot chocolate. Once settled, they listened to *Operator,* one of Lily's favourites.

"Do you think good thoughts or bad thoughts most of the time?" Lily shot out without preamble.

"Dunno. Don't know what I think."

"Haha, very funny. No, really."

"Hmm, how many times do I have to say it – you make my brain hurt." Paulo rubbed his hands hard through his hair. "Mainly shit, I reckon. I mean, so much bad stuff has happened, I guess it…"

"So, you reckon bad stuff will just keep happening? Like, to the two of us? Like before…" Lily peered earnestly at him.

"I dunno. I just reckon bad stuff happens and good people like us have to cop it."

"Why?"

"There isn't a *why*, it just *is*."

They lay opposite each other on the floor, their faces cupped in their hands, as close to the gas heater as they could tolerate. The wind battered the windows, making the handles rattle.

Lily sat up and pressed her back against the bricks of the fireplace, her knees close to her chest. "Do you reckon we ever get *there*?"

"Get *where*?"

"Get to where we're meant to be. Like, to feel we've made it in some way."

Paulo frowned as she continued.

"You know, like, feel we're accomplished or finished, or that whatever it was we needed to find out about ourselves, we found it. Maybe, if we're striving for who we really are, or who we're meant to be, that we find it." Lily closed her eyes as the trees lashed the side of the house. "Ever?" she said, opening her eyes.

Paulo rolled away from her, grunted, and covered his face with both hands. "Hmm, as per usual, you're diggin' too bloody deep for this thick-as-a-brick brain." He sat up, rubbing his temples. But, once at her eye level, he continued. "Find it? I don't think so. I mean, we can strive for who we want to be, or what we want to do, I reckon, but *make it*? Don't reckon."

"That's the difference between you and me; you may be okay with that, but I won't ever be okay with it."

"You're okay, buddy." He patted her knee. "We'll be okay – don't worry."

The loungeroom was now draped in darkness, the wind's roar reduced to a whimper, and the orange flames gave their faces a haloed, golden aura. Wafts of roast chicken and sizzling potatoes drifted across their consciousness.

"Need a hand, Nini?" Lily called.

"You could set the table, darling."

"Paulo's joining us, okay?"

"Of course."

"Thank you, Nini – you're the best," Lily said as Paulo raced to help her set the table.

"I'll wash all the dishes and the pans," he said.

"So you bloody-well should," Lily teased.

SIXTY-SIX

After the ferocious winds and bullets of rain that had lasted a full week, the day was still. The light took centre stage, shining brilliantly as silver in the middle of the bay. The crunch of Lily's feet and Bessie's panting was interspersed with birdsong on their descent to the cove. The earth was damp, and every green thing was weighted with moisture.

The sharp briny air reassured Lily that tomorrow a brighter day would come. Once they'd reached the beach, each wave receded, quivered and hovered just before a new one unfurled. *The ocean, my lungs*, Lily thought. *Each lap, my breathe. Soothe me, help me, heal me. Just breathe and step, breathe and step. It's gotta get easier.*

The well-known view held her attention with its ever-changing manifestations. On the eastern walk, the light stretched out across the cove like a lover's embrace; on the western return, mere slivers of silver-grey beamed straight at you. Each time she reached the point, the angle of the sun made the view of the cove, the frisson in the trees, the tinkering boats and the creaking pier seem new. Clouds cast long dark shadows across the sand. Patches of blue stood out against the white clouds. Same beach; different perspective. *Was one more real or worthy than the other?* Lily thought. The light moved across the water, beneath the horizon – a line of hope.

People were coming down to the shore. Some were in couples, some were alone, some with dogs, some taking their kids for a walk or a bike ride to the pier. The ferry's horn droned whilst it was backing in, the dull moan of the engine, idling, ready to reverse. The upturned boats on the shore; their Neapolitan colours. The crunch of the maroon seaweed was pungent underfoot – slimy, slippery, its unmistakable dried-sea scent. The fish shop on the beach. The smell of the salty, oil-drenched crisp chips. The cove as big arms, east and west, welcoming you home. Bessie sprinting, bounding around the other dogs, swimming, and roaming wild.

SIXTY-SEVEN

Lily swam early, when the light was muted and the bay was full of pesky waves. The inky indigo chill assaulted her body piece by piece, until it was too late, and she ducked under to escape the bitter winter wind. She swam hard and fast to the yellow fishing boat left abandoned by its mates, which had been safely retrieved from the water months before. The boat felt abandoned, and the joy had gone from its colour. The sky was undecided in its variations: clumpy white cumulonimbus interspersed with insipid blue patches. In the distance she saw the dark, brooding hills near Wallawee. She started to tread water. There was not a bird in sight and her body throbbed with the cold. Her wet face ached in the wind, and it took her breath away. She plunged in again and dashed for the shore.

Later, as arranged, she met Paulo for lunch at the kiosk bench. She felt famished. She shouted him some fish and chips. The salty, oily vinegar mix ran down their fingers and she tried not to feel ripped off. Sharing chips and potato cakes with him made her want to eat fast, but he was always way faster.

"Do you think I'm a 'plucky disruptor'?" she asked.

Paulo frowned and kept eating.

"I saw a show on this last night. You know, someone who just swims against the tide for the sake of it?"

"A *what*?' he muttered between mouthfuls. "I can't even say it."

"Like someone who seems to know what they're on about – but scratch beneath the surface and they're just a pretender. They don't fit in, but they stand out for all the wrong reasons. They put on this bravado – like they know what's going on –

when they haven't got a clue about anything. They just make trouble for trouble's sake. Like a pain in the arse."

Paulo shook his head and kept eating.

"I've also discovered there's a term for people like me, like us." She appeared certain of her newfound knowledge. "We're referred to as social misfits."

"Man, you do my head in. Now you're telling me there's a term for us? You're a plucky something. We're out-somebodies… I don't know what these mean and I don't care. I've been called more than my fair share of names. They can all go and get stuffed. I'm me, like it or lump it." Paulo took the last potato cake.

Lily snatched a couple of chips. She took the longest ones as Paulo resorted to handfuls.

A few grey gulls hovered and squawked. Paulo thought about it and then inspected the bag. "Nah, piss off." He waved his arms at them. "You're the one who tells people what you think. Don't let 'em label you."

"That's the whole point. Why don't we – or, in particular, *me* – fit in? I'm contrary, or maybe I make my life difficult because I always see things a different way to most people. Maybe I should make a concerted effort to shut up and just bloody-well fit it. To cop their bullshit and let it slide, rather than argue every friggin' point. Sometimes I get tired. It's exhausting, even when I know I'm right and those deadshits are wrong. It's still bloody tiring." She let Paulo pick up the parcel and drain the contents into his hands.

When he finished eating, Paulo licked his fingers. "Just be you. Forget the bullshit categories. You weren't born to shut up. You never do." He raised his eyebrows and nodded his head.

"Even when you should."

"No, *especially* when I should. I act all smart with the questions and theories, but I haven't got a clue. You've got it all sorted in your head."

"Nah, I haven't. But I'm trying to be me. I hid for too long. I can't do that anymore." Paulo looked at Lily in a way that made her think that he knew her, and she loved him for that.

"You make life simple. I don't know how to do that. I wish I did. Anyhow, thanks mate.' She winked at him. "You're the best."

"Oh, thanks, buddy."

Bessie bolted ahead as they headed for home.

SIXTY-EIGHT

Paulo and Lily were sitting on her bed with the cassette recorder blasting out Fleetwood Mac's *Go Your Own Way*. Paulo was singing at top note and letting his hair fall towards the floor then whipping his head back for dramatic impact. Lily was belting her thighs as if she was playing the drums and occasionally standing to smack her hips as a tambourine.

She had made a cassette with all her favourites: Fleetwood Mac, Joan Armatrading, Leon Russell, Gladys Knight and the Pips, James Taylor, Carole King. Bessie started to bark for a walk – maybe the music got to her – so they begrudgingly took her outside.

It was a blustery, chilly day. The sky was a sickly white. The horizon line was lost. They dug their arms deep into their coats as the wild spray hit their exposed faces. They found a protected spot at Durga Rock behind a sand-dune, facing north, away from the bitter blast.

"Tell me about your classes. I've heard she's the best dance teacher around."

"Yep, she's all class. She's a hard taskmaster, but she gets you to lift. She doesn't mind telling you when you're slacking off or not listening properly."

"Haha, no more astral travelling for you, boy." Lily playfully shoved his shoulder.

"No, seriously, buddy, I'm loving it."

"That's great. Good for you."

"It's weird to say, but I know you *get* weird... I used to think I'd never be good enough. I'd be too fat, or too un-co or too dumb or too lazy or too useless..." He pushed his arms out in front of him as if accepting a gift. "But, I dunno why, but now I believe I'm meant to be there. Like I belong. Like a tribe or something. That's not being vain, is it?"

"Vain – you? Never," she joked. "Like *a tribe*? What do you mean?"

"It's where I feel at home. Who I am meant to be with." Paulo looked at Lily for understanding.

"Don't you feel at home with me?"

"Yeah, of course I do. But I'm never going to *be* like you. I'm different. When I dance, something inside of me explodes. It's like my heart's going to burst through my ribs. My blood is electricity shooting through my veins." He stopped and, after a few moments of silence, said, "I feel like I've found *me*." His gleaming eyes lingered on her face.

"Wow, mate. Sounds as though you've found your future. I'm bloody happy for you. You deserve this."

"Thanks, buddy. You'll find your thing too. You've got so many talents. I reckon it'll be something to do with writing or drama... You could do anything."

Lily glanced quizzically at the sky. "Maybe. I sure don't feel like I've found my one thing yet. I love to talk – God knows I'm bloody good at that!"

"Yeah, you could say *too* good at."

"A harsh assessment but probably a true one. I do love to act and write. Nothing concrete yet, though."

They braced themselves as they left their protected spot. The sea whipped up into a frenzy of froth, foam and spray. Starting the march back along the beach, the roaring wind belting their backs, they tried to yell to each other but ended up using a kind of sign language until they hit the quiet of the narrow dirt path.

When they were within earshot of each other, Lily asked, "If I can't find who I'm meant to be, could you help me? Like, point me in some direction or something? I'm scared I might be left behind while you go forward and develop into a rockstar dancer." Paulo turned around to face her as she continued. "Daggy old me, stuck in this small town with no one, doing nothing, going nowhere..." Lily didn't look at him while she spoke, but the last word caught in her throat.

"Hey," Paulo said. "You'll never be a nobody doing nothing. You're amazing. I mean it. You're a dead-set legend. You just have to *believe* it."

They kept walking, side by side. When they got to Lily's driveway, she turned and looked into Paulo's soft eyes. "Thanks a lot, mate. That means heaps to me."

"Anytime, buddy. That's what besties do."

"Yeah. You may be the strong, silent type, but when you do speak, you're worth listening to. If only I'd shut up more."

"Well, we both know that's never gunna happen."

They briefly linked pinky fingers before walking off in separate directions.

SIXTY-NINE

The weekly school assembly was long and boring. Then the principal declared a new rule: *There will be no touching between male and female students. A new school policy.*

"What a bloody joke! We're best mates, so what are *we* supposed to do – bow to each other?" Lily complained as they left the hall.

"They're stupid. Not all male/female relationships are sexual," Paulo agreed.

"Some of them still think we're boyfriend and girlfriend, apparently."

"Yeah, let 'em think whatever they want."

"Yes. I like to be risible."

"What in the hell does *that* mean? I swear you make these words up."

"It means what I do makes you laugh," Lily chuckled. "Okay – try this. I'm the sand and you're the sea."

"Why? Why not the other way round?"

"I'm gritty and scratchy, yet I can be soft and warm, or cold and harsh. I can make a lovely bed and a pillow to rest on, or I can be a sandstorm that'd scratch someone's eyeballs out. You, on the other hand, are fluid, soft to touch, broody, silently captivating and powerful."

"Maybe I'm the sand, and you're the sea," Paulo suggested. "Who likes to stay near to shore, who wants to travel and see the world, who can whip up a storm, and who holds the shore together? They've both got their strengths in different ways." He put his hands up to the sky. "I dunno who I am."

"I don't know who I am, either. Maybe you're just the yin to my yang. Or I'm the yang to your yin."

"You think too much."

"Yeah, I know, but I have to tell you what's coming up for me."

"Sometimes, maybe, let it come up, and then let it go down. You know, like a wave. Up it comes" – he pointed to the crest of a wave breaking – "and there it goes. Gone. Sometimes I *can't* talk."

Lily walked ahead of Paulo and didn't speak on the way back to their lockers.

"Buddy, I didn't mean to offend you," he said, opening the door of his locker and taking out a stack of heavy books. "It's just... my brain needs a rest. I can't think fast like you can. Half the time I don't even know what in the hell you're talking about."

"You didn't offend me. I know I talk too much. But, with you, I can be myself. That's pretty *out there*. So, the stuff that I talk about is just stuff, but it can make me understand my life a bit better. Are you getting sick of me? I'm sure you are. *I'm* getting sick of me. Would you prefer a new bestie?"

"As if." He put up his pinky finger. She hooked hers around it.

"Lucky you said that." Lily smiled, and she was off to her next class.

SEVENTY

Mrs MacKenzie – or Mrs Mac, as she was known by the students – was Lily's form teacher. Form 5 had been bearable because of her. She was a slim woman, with short brown wavy hair and an expression that you wanted to pour your heart out to. During that year, there were too many times to mention when she had supported Lily. She seemed to always give students the benefit of the doubt. Even when she didn't agree with *what* had happened, she always wanted to know *why* it had happened. This led to much less angst in the class, and a kinder atmosphere.

In the last week of school, prior to the exams, Mrs Mac discussed the student awards and what was involved with applying. She took the time to explain why each one would be important to the student's development, not only academic, but in general: confidence in public speaking, debating, clear thinking, constructing an argument and a professional approach to representing ideas in a public forum. Everyone was silent in the class as she answered questions and openly encouraged participation in the selection process.

"It's not about whether you win the award, it's more about how you conduct yourself during the process. What you'll learn about yourself could change the course of your academic life."

After the bell sounded and everyone left the classroom, Lily tentatively walked up to Mrs Mac's desk. "Mrs Mac, do you think there'd be any point in me applying for the English award?"

"I absolutely do think so, Lily. You have great potential. I see it in your essays. The way you approach your studies. There is much you can offer. Believe in yourself."

"You really think so?"

"I do. You can do this. I think you'd be a wonderful candidate. You've got nothing to lose."

"Thanks, Mrs Mac. I'll miss you next year."

"And I'll miss you, Lily. Good luck with the exams. Remember, go for gold! No holding back."

"Thank you."

Lily skipped out of class. She ran home, flew up the front steps and threw her bag at her bedroom door. "Nini! Nini, you'll never guess what's happened."

SEVENTY-ONE

Lily and Paulo swung in through the back door and spied Nini dancing to Perry Como's *For the Good Times* with a brandy in her hand. When they entered, Nini asked Paulo to join her. Lily laughed and made the tea. Paulo took Nini in his arms and they waltzed around the kitchen. Lily glanced back at their happy faces and couldn't believe how well Paulo moved. *And I Love You So* was the last song on that side of the album and Nini sang every word.

Lily assembled the tray of tea and cake on the kitchen table and watched her beautiful grandmother move slowly and gracefully around their loungeroom. Paulo's height and strength were magnified, like tall, dark timber against a pale, old, curved tree. He gently swayed and moved in rhythm with Nini. Lily imagined her as a young girl dancing with her Alf. She saw them at a dance with a big band playing and Nini's dress swishing around her ankles. Lily watched Paulo's large feet in his runners next to Nini's dainty stockinged feet.

Meredith walked in, stunned, stopped, and threw her keys in the bowl. "Mum, stop that! What on earth do you think you're doing?" She shook her head vigorously, marched over to the record player and took the needle off before the song had finished. Paulo stood still with his arms straight by his side.

"I'm dancing, Meredith. Singing, dancing, and having some fun," Nini said as she curtsied, thanked Paulo for the dance, and carefully took her brandy glass towards the sink.

"I thought you weren't meant to be drinking," Meredith said, following Nini into the kitchen.

"I don't drink much. Just a little brandy in the afternoon sometimes to settle my nerves." Nini kept her back turned away from Meredith.

"Just don't embarrass yourself – and us." Meredith walked towards the tray of tea. "It is not fun to make a young boy have to dance with an old lady."

"Nini isn't an embarrassment," Lily cut in. "We were having fun. Just because you never do, doesn't mean we can't. If Dad was here, we would have fun. You're so mean."

Paulo slowly edged his way out of the room and closed the back door without making a sound.

"See?" Lily pointed to the back door and then back at Meredith. "You have to ruin *everything*. I wish Nini was my mum and not you!"

"Now, now Lily, don't speak to your mum that way. You don't mean that." Nini turned towards her daughter. "Meredith, there's a reason I asked Paulo for a dance."

"What? Because you're tipsy and felt like it?"

"No. Because one day he'll be dancing for a living, and I don't know that he's got anyone else to practice with."

Meredith nodded but she didn't smile.

"And there's nothing wrong with a bit of fun," Nini added gently.

Meredith turned her stare to Lily like the old lighthouse once beamed its light across the treacherous waters. "How dare you speak to me like that," she hissed. "You can stay in your room and miss dinner."

Lily ran from the room, the slamming flywire providing testament that she had gone. She ran after Paulo as the wind picked up, blasting down Southern Ocean Road. Breathless, she called out, "Please come back."

Paulo stopped and turned, his hair moving wildly around his face. When Lily had caught up to him, he said, "No, it was time for me to go anyway."

"I'm sorry. Mum's so nasty. It's no fun when she's home."

"Don't worry about it."

They walked together back to his home.

"Meredith is always picking on Nini for drinking. It's not as if she drinks that much. Like, a couple of brandies at night. Sometimes, if she goes to Beatrice's to play cards, she buys a bottle of sherry."

"Good on her, I reckon. She doesn't touch the stuff compared with the old boy. He'd have more to drink in his first hour than Nini does in a week."

"Yeah, Mum's so prickly about it. Her face goes red, and the veins pop out in her neck whenever Nini's had a couple. She's like the grog police. I found her the other day marking the brandy bottles."

"Shit, that's full on."

"Yeah. So, I told Nini. She puts a bit of water in the bottle to keep it at the mark for a few days."

"Oh, the games we play…"

"Even when we're old."

They high-fived each other and Lily headed for home, braced against the north-westerly and hearing the crashing surf just beyond the car park.

The following week, Paulo was at Lily's home in the afternoon when she had to go to the bakery to buy some bread. The next day at school, she asked him if he had stayed on to chat with Nini after she left.

"Yep."

"What about?"

"Me."

"What about you?"

"Oh, just stuff."

"You can be so annoying sometimes. Just tell me what…"

"Argh… Nothing. Just, like, personal stuff."

"What personal stuff?"

"God, you're nosey."

"Yeah, it's a problem I've got. I've always been nosey. Can't help it."

"Yeah,' he agreed. "I want to talk to Mum about stuff, and Nini said I should. She said, *We are who we are*."

"I'm not following. What stuff?"

"Doesn't matter. It's just stuff."

Lily exhaled in annoyance. She thought of Paulo being named after some flamenco guitarist that his mum was taken with. Valerie told Ronaldo that she loved the name 'Paulo' because it reflected her South American heritage (which he later discovered did not exist; rather, her dark skin came from her Spanish ancestors three generations back). Lily thought how different Paulo's upbringing was to hers, and that she still didn't know much about him. Valerie looked stunningly exotic in the photos Lily had seen of her. Thick auburn curls, olive skin, heaps of jewellery and colorful clothes. She was smiling and surrounded by musicians. Only a few photos of her with Ronaldo and fewer with Paulo. He had a faded picture in his room of her holding him as a toddler. When you looked closely at her eyes, they were unnervingly sad. As if she wasn't certain why she was there.

"But I'm your best mate and you don't tell me something

that's so important you need to talk to Nini and your Mum... I don't get it. Why not?" There was an uncomfortable silence. Another exhale from Lily. "Well, if you're not going to tell me, are you going to tell Ronaldo?"

"Nup. I told her he wouldn't understand. She said secrets can be bad if you keep them to yourself and that I've got nothing to lose."

"So, will you tell Valerie whatever *personal* stuff you need to?"

"Maybe."

"Will you at least tell me how it goes?"

"One day."

"Oh God, you piss me off and drive me nuts sometimes."

"And you drive me crazy most of the time."

"Thank you."

"The pleasure's all mine."

SEVENTY-TWO

The following week, in a dilapidated shelter-shed, Paulo told Lily that he'd found an old video of his mum hidden in a cupboard underneath his childhood toys. She was singing and dancing wildly at a fancy-dress party. She was wearing a rock 'n' roll party outfit, a white sailor's suit and cap, and sang *YMCA*. Lily had never heard of it, so Paulo got up and impersonated his mum.

Lily said, "What a hoot! I want to watch it."

He told her he'd watched it over and over, until he knew every line by heart. He sang with gusto, twirled his choreographed arms and feet – *It's fun to stay at the Village People's Y-M-C-A!* – when LSA walked past and muttered, "You're so gay, Paulo."

"What if I am, Lincoln? What's it to you?" Paulo stood motionless, hands on hips, locking eyes with LSA.

"Piss off, Lincoln, you germ," Lily said, standing next to Paulo.

Lincoln's eyes bulged and he turned away. His body couldn't keep up with his head as he bolted like a pea from a sling shot.

Lily nodded at Paulo, and gave him the thumbs up. "Bravo, mate." She high-fived him as they wandered over to an old timber seat outside the English department. Then she asked without thinking, "Are you gay?" She turned to look more closely at her friend. "I mean, I don't care if you are or not."

"Maybe." He looked around the yard as a group of boys wrestled, pretending to play football. "I don't know. I only notice boys. I don't look at girls. Except you, of course, but not like *that*." He blushed. "So, maybe."

"Exactly. We love each other, but not like *that*." She watched the group of boys wrestling and rolling around the yard. "You're my BF and you can be into whoever you like."

"Oh, thanks, buddy. You, too. Haha, imagine if we ended up going for the same guy. That'd be bad."

"Friggin' bad. Actually, Ricardo Massoni's a bit of alright."

"Nah, Mark St Peters is hotter."

"Nup, I reckon Mark's too bulky, big muscly legs and hairy everything."

Lily looked around the yard and spotted the boy in question.

Paulo followed her gaze. "Not that I've seen his *everything*," he added. "Hairy everything. Ooh, Lily, *you* want to see his hairy *everything*."

"You're disgusting. I don't want to see... assuming he has hairy *everything*."

"Assuming or dreaming? You're dreaming of his hairy everything. Now *that's disgusting*!'

They laughed all the way back to class as the bell rang out across the yard.

SEVENTY-THREE

As the word spread on the school grapevine, Paulo had a few more accusations to deal with, the latest one being that he was a *pansy,* a *poof,* a *cream puff.* As Nini said, Lily told him, *It's impossible to argue with someone who agrees with you.* His standard response to the accusations became, "Well, you know what – you might be right." That seemed to shut them up. The first few times he said it, they became so aggravated by not knowing how to respond that they stormed off. The grapevine slowly dwindled and eventually died out on the topic. As Nini told him, "If they don't mean anything to you, Paulo, who cares what they think? The only person you have to please in this world is yourself. Before you go to bed at night, look yourself in the mirror and see if you're happy with the person looking back at you. If you are, then you're okay. If you're not, you can change."

On a Friday afternoon, as they wandered home along their usual route, everything felt different, somehow lighter. The shrubs and trees were more vivid, the flowers brighter, like a plain canvas with a pencil outline, now filled in with the most vibrant colour. Every step of that walk was like staring into a face they'd known forever, only to discover for the first time that the shade, shape and sparkle of the eyes were utterly captivating.

As they crossed over the old bridge that straddled the canal, Paulo turned to Lily and said, "Buddy, thank you."

"What? Me? What for?"

"I've always known that you've had my back, Lily. I knew it, but I took it for granted. But the difference now is, I've also got *your* back."

On the other side of the bridge, they stopped, and Lily looked at him curiously.

"What is this? You don't need to thank me. I'm your best friend; that's just what we do for each other. Right?"

"No. You've gone above and beyond to defend me. You were the only one who did that. I need you to know that I've found my courage. No shit – now I know I can stand up. I can be me. I didn't before, not because I didn't care about you, or myself for that matter, but because I was too scared. Shit-scared, in fact. I believed I didn't have it in me. You made me believe I could be strong too." He stood tall and tapped her on her arm. "Being with you made me brave."

"No, mate. I didn't make you brave. You did. I knew you had it in you all along." Lily nudged him in the ribs. "Now there's no holding the gentle giant back, is there?"

"Nup. Not anymore. I decided that if I can stand up against those useless pricks, nothing's going to hold me back. I feel like I've been let out of jail. Shit, it feels good. Yay!" He pumped the air and did three massive twirls as they left, beaming.

It was a mild summer evening, with the waft of next door's jasmine drifting in on the breeze as Lily sat beside her grandmother on the porch swing. Nini had brought her brandy with her, and Lily sat crunching her apple.

As the cacophony of birdsong filled the air, Lily asked, "Do you think differently about life, now that you're old?"

Nini crinkled her eyes as if she would burst out laughing. "Thanks for reminding me!" Nini grinned, and added, "About some things."

"Like what? Like the meaning of life, or what makes a good life or...?"

A truck grumbled past in the distance, replaced by whooshing through the she-oaks. Nini watched the movement of her roses. "Oh, how I love the way your brain works. Wish mine worked like that." She tapped her head for effect, her soft grey curls lit up with the afternoon rays. After a pause and a sip, she said, "I think differently about being old, now that I'm old." She smiled at Lily and continued. "When I was young, I dreaded being old. I thought it would be lonely – boring, meaningless. But I'm not lonely, I'm not bored, and I do have purpose." She took a long sip of her brandy and, holding the glass in her lap, continued, "Hmm, also, when I was young, I felt too busy – like there was never enough time. I raced everywhere, never feeling like I'd achieved enough. I felt this deep sense of a lack of time. But now, I have plenty of time. I never have to rush anywhere. I suppose that's 'cause the old body can't." She laughed. "And yet, I'm more attuned to the passing of time. To the wonders of life. Like this sunset. Ironic that when I've got plenty of time, I'm so aware that there isn't much left. That life is the greatest and most fragile gift, all wrapped up in one." She stared at the powder blue sky, as the evening birdsong chirped on and a lonely car on the distant road made its way to where towards its destination.

"Is that because of memories? Do you think back to how things were because you've got more time to?"

"Perhaps. Memories can be deceptive. Maybe we wash over the hard parts and glamorise the good parts, who knows? Things can seem better in retrospect. Except love. Love doesn't lie."

"Yeah, I know that too. Dad was loving – that wasn't a lie."

"Frank was a beautiful father. He absolutely loved you so much – his little Lily-pad." Nini squeezed Lily's hand.

"Yeah, he was the best. Wish he was here."

"Keep talking to him, darling. He'll be listening."

"I do, especially at night."

They sat in silence as the evening crickets started up their chirrups and the birds flitted through the bushes.

"But, what else? Do you think about life itself the same way you did?"

Nini's gaze was steady on the halo of the western sky. It illuminated her face, making her look angelic. "The preciousness of life. That strikes me now, far more so than before. Maybe because I've lost many people who were close to me over the years. You learn a lot from dear friends and with each sorrow you understand the preciousness of life a little bit more. Life is fleeting. It's just a series of moments. If you embrace them, they last longer. The way these moments make you feel. You just don't want to waste a second because this moment sitting in the golden twilight with you is all I have. And there's no better feeling than the feeling I have when I'm with you."

Lily tried to speak, but she couldn't, so she looked away and nodded. She turned and watched her grandmother's kindly, beautiful, weathered face. Her watery pale green eyes had red veins running through them. Lily didn't speak. She stopped pushing the chair, allowing it to come to a halt. "Do you think I'm wasting time? Not noticing the moments. Like I'm racing through life?"

"Oh no, darling, not at all. You notice the little things. In life, it's always the little things that matter. The big things smack you in the face, but the little things linger." She patted Lily's hand. 'You'll never waste your life, Lily. Not a second. It's a gift, and you are too intelligent to waste the most precious gift of all."

They sat together until the chill descended. Then, as the light faded, they wandered back up into the house, arm in arm, to the unwashed dishes that they'd left in order to catch the last rays of the sun.

Later, well after bedtime, Lily lay awake. She thought of her conversation with Nini. The passage of time. There was a gentle murmuring coming from down the hall. Without realising how she got there she found herself kneeling at Nini's bedside, listening to her breathing. She sat with her back against the bed and as if listening to the passage of time itself. Each long, audible, exhausted, open-mouthed breath. Lily closed her eyes. *This is all we have, a moment in time.* She thought of all the times when she was scared and she'd run and hop into Nini's bed. When Frank was alive, she'd snuggle in between her mum and dad. Now that she was grown up, she was relegated to her own cold lonely bed, which made childhood look appealing forever. Lily felt constricted in her breathing. With stinging eyes, she took Nini's hand, its knuckles swollen, and watched as her chest rose and fell. She wished she could stop time. Shivering, her legs going numb, she reluctantly let go of Nini's warm hand, placed it gently across her chest, and crept back to her own bed.

SEVENTY-FIVE

On the day of the vote for prefects and school captain, Lily saw her wren. It had been raining overnight, and the ground and branches were laden with water. He was dancing along the arm of a she-oak, the tree's nettles glittering in the faint light. Mentally, she asked the wren a question: *Could I become a prefect?* He jumped off the swaying branch and flitted around her. *If I could, I need you to circle me three times.*

The blue wren stopped on the branch and shook his tail-feathers. Lily walked on. Then a flash of blue whizzed around her. Shocked, she looked to see what it was, when the wren darted out from a tee-tree shrub and flashed by her again. She kept walking and once she got to the corner where the school was in view, the bird flew slowly at first and then darted off fast and over the ghost gums in the distance.

There was an excitement about the voting that Lily had not expected to feel. The following Monday, she was on gate duty first thing. Paulo was dancing up to the entrance until Lily's expression met him like a stop sign. He immediately halted, put his broad shoulders back, checked his hair, straightened his uniform, and marched into school, pretending he wanted to be there, with only a slight nod of the head towards Lily as he passed.

SEVENTY-SIX

The vegetation enduring the summer heatwave looked sick and disinterested. Lily's long, thin hair was plastered to her face in wisps as she swatted away the bushflies. She remembered the swarming black mass on the back of Paulo's drenched white shirt. The skin on her forearms were an inflamed red just from the walk home, and her heels were forming painful blisters. *Summer,* she thought. *If it wasn't for the ocean on days like these, it would be unbearable.*

Once home, she unlocked the front door and hurled her bag into the hallway so hard that it bounced off the wall. She drank three consecutive glasses of water, kicked off her shoes and socks, flung them at her bedroom door, and went to lie on the loungeroom floor. Meredith had left all the blinds down in a vain attempt to keep the heat out.

Lily discarded her clothes as she walked to the bathroom to find her bathers. Distressed, Bessie lay panting under the lemon tree. Lily waited an eternity for the water to cool in the hose before drenching Bessie's coat, then herself. She gathered a towel, stiff as a board from drying on the clothesline, put her thongs on, picked up Bessie's lead from the back door, and headed out along the searing driveway.

The bitumen track crackled under her feet. The air was thick and cloying. There was nothing to inhale or smell but hotness. As she looked for the entrance to the beach walk, she saw the quivering mirage of heat, wafting up like a genie from a bottle before dissipating into the belting Grecian sky.

No running today, just get in, Bessie old girl. Even the dumping of the waves was listless. Once Lily had dumped her towel and thongs she bolted for the water's edge, and Bessie darted straight in ahead of her. With the first liquid smack, she felt the pressure-cooker of her mind release slightly. She gasped for air and dived under the next wave and felt her mind loosen a bit more. She stayed in the water until her limbs felt spent and her mind clear. As she luxuriated between sets, her legs methodically kicking to keep her afloat, her dad spoke to her. *Just always be the lovely you.*

Lily heel-hopped back to her towel, the sand scorching, hot as coals. She lay back and closed her eyes. Bessie, dripping and reeking of wet dog, collapsed alongside her. Lily floated like the absent clouds, heard the crash of each wave, felt weightless and hovering. As she soared along the coastline, she came to a bay further on, Lavender Bay, where a young girl lay drenched and peaceful next to her loyal dog. Her burning eyelids broke the dream. She lay on the sand, unable to choose between the pain of staying and the effort of moving. Eventually, thirst and the burning heat won out, and she stood to go.

There wasn't a bird in sight; it was as if Lily had landed at the end of the earth. Not another soul was nearby, just the heaving, heavy lull of the sea. As if it was the last day and the sun was torching all it saw. Resting on her elbows, she breathed in the ocean. The movements out at sea reminded her of a whale rolling and lolling. The hum of the waves had a voice – a melodic and soothing sound: *It'll be okay, Lily, it'll all be okay.* The smell of the salt filled her mind, the searing, dry wind prickled her reddening, blotchy skin. She was bone dry, even her long hair.

The light was shifting. Bessie's panting quickened and it became all that Lily could hear. The heat within her body was feverish. She hopped from foot to burning foot back to the ocean's edge. Bessie dashed straight in. Lily followed and dove through a clear wave and the shock of the chill brought her back to life. *Oh God, I'm never leaving this water.* Bessie felt the same way. Lily could tell. She looked towards the Point and saw the hissing sea-mist wafting up like clouds. The longer she dove and swam, the better she felt.

The pair stayed in long enough to feel cool again and, as Lily tired, she remembered she was very thirsty and hungry. Again, hopping back to the sanctuary of her towel, she looked at panting Bessie and felt guilty. Home seemed like the only proposition.

As they walked home, the sun was taking its final bow, casting shadows over the stinging sand. The majestic glow of hot-pink and orange lit up their faces – until they were home, and the sun morphed to a soft silver before it slipped out of view.

SEVENTY-SEVEN

Lily believed the best part of Spray Point Secondary College was that the students in Form 5 voted for head prefect. The teachers, and especially their principal Ms Mary O'Flaherty, thought it was a coming-of-age privilege.

At the start of Form Six, the school hall was packed with anticipation, chatter and anxiety. The last year of school was so daunting that most of the students felt a degree of nausea just sitting in the hall.

Paulo was late, as usual, and Lily reserved his seat, as usual. She waved to him, and by the time he sat down, the hall was silent, interrupted sharply by his shuffling shoes before he dropped his bag unceremoniously on Lily's foot. She stifled an *Ouch! Shit!*

Once Paulo was seated with Lily, Alexa and Mot, Lily noticed Alexa's legs shaking in her tiny school shoes. Her own knees were jumping up and down, so she placed her hands firmly on her legs to keep them still. She thought how good it was that Mot was with them. He wagged so often now that Lily realised that she missed him. The faint beam of light coming in through the upper windows cast bruises on Mot's legs in a spectrum of metal grey, off purple and sickly cream. Lily looked away.

The school band played a drum-roll as Lily noticed the dust falling in the shafts of sunshine that crept into the cold hall. Ms O'Flaherty started proceedings.

"It is now time to open the envelope to read the prefects' names for 1978 and, lastly, the extremely important and coveted role of Head of School."

As the names were called, eleven in total, Lily's heart sank.

Not that she thought she would be chosen – but, secretly, even secretly to herself, she desperately wanted to be a prefect. Alas, it was not to be. Paulo didn't look sad; he didn't look interested. It was as if they were talking about something that had nothing to do with him. Alexa looked nervous and then disappointed, but Mot looked as though he didn't want to be there.

Ms O'Flaherty stood at the microphone. "Now, drum-roll…" She said and afforded herself a little giggle.

"This is a most prestigious role, as this student is voted for solely by their peers," her voice echoing around the assembly hall. "During the course of their year, they will be trained in public speaking, they will be on boards representing the school, they will meet with me and the vice principal, Mr Geoff Kelly, and discuss ways in which we can improve the school and, in particular, the concerns of our Form Six students. We have found in years gone by that the student chosen for this role is someone who will go on to make a positive impact in the world… Without further ado… Mr Kelly, if you could please bring me the envelope." The principal extended her arm theatrically, displaying her perfectly manicured hand, resplendent with red nail polish.

At that point, the air became quite suffocating in the hall. Lily felt the airlessness constrict her throat. The silence was heavy, cloying, only a gentle tweeting audible from outside.

"And the Head of School for 1978 is… Lily Mango."

Sitting there, crimson-faced, Lily was shaking as Paulo turned to hug her first. The entire hall clapped rousingly as Lily stood and was swept up in a group hug from her three closest friends.

"Great stuff, Lily!" Alexa said.

"That's a bloody ripper! Go *you*, buddy." Paulo smiled so broadly you'd think it was him who'd been chosen.

"Me? I didn't think many of them even liked me."

"They do, and so they bloody well should. You're ace!' Mot said and did his classic two-fingered wolf-whistle.

"Get up. Go you good thing!" Paulo enthused.

There were even some pats on the back from a few students she passed and a couple of high-fives as she made her way up to the stage. Lily shook uncertainly as the applause hit her, walking to the podium as if in a trance. Ms O'Flaherty and Mr Kelly both shook her hand, but she could not take in what they said as the microphone was handed to her.

"Ms O'Flaherty, Mr Kelly, and Form Six students – thank you," she heard herself saying. "I will try my best in the role. Thank you, everyone."

That night, when Meredith sat down to dinner, Nini passing around the steaming gravy boat, Lily blurted out, "I got voted Head of SRC for next year."

"You what?" Meredith asked.

Lily looked at Nini. "I was voted as Head of School today."

"Oh, my golly, that's wonderful! We are so proud of you!" Nini said and got up to hug Lily.

Meredith had a faraway look in her eyes, but they shone more than usual. "That's well done. I'm very pleased for you," she said.

The next day, Lily described the scene to Paulo. "Nini starts jumping up and down and gives me a hug and tells me she knew I'd be chosen and how wonderful it is. Meredith says, *Oh, that's good. Well done.* Seriously! With her as a mother, it's a wonder I have any self-belief at all."

As promised, public speaking courses were arranged. Lily sat on different boards and got a feeling for who spoke well, who seemed impressive and persuasive, and how to best conduct yourself while pushing an agenda.

At one point, there was friction between the parent body and the sports department. The parents were riled that the students had to attend three training sessions per week, when the study workload was intensifying. Ms Gildebrant, the sports teacher, a no-nonsense type, chaired the meeting in the small meeting room to the left of reception.

Miss Rollindson, the receptionist, winked at Lily as she entered and whispered, "Good luck, kiddo. Should be a doozy."

In the room, Mr Kelly sat next to Ms Gildebrant and Lily sat next to her. Two men and two women came in with crossed arms and furrowed brows. A cursory hello as they sat down heavily in a row.

"Good afternoon, everyone." Ms Gildebrant opened proceedings. "Now, what can we do for you good people today?"

One of the fathers started in, tapping on finger on the table. "Look, we're sick and tired of the ridiculous emphasis on sport. You expect the students to be here three times per week, for God's sake. It's too much. I've been talking with other parents, and they all agree. This needs to be sorted."

He pointed his finger at the teachers, his offsiders all nodding in support.

Mr Kelly took over. "I hear what you're saying, Giles, and I appreciate there are a lot of competing pressures on our Form 6 students. Let's face it, matric can be a bit of a stinker."

The other three parents smiled.

Giles forged ahead. "As I was saying, I've done a ring around, and all the other parents are on board. Once a week is acceptable."

"In such a dynamic year, I think we'd all agree that the health of our wonderful young people need to be attended to." Mr Kelly sat back in his chair, his relaxed tone both confident and disarming. "Firstly, the need to get adequate sleep and rest. This is hard when you're seventeen or eighteen and the world is just opening for you. But limiting phone calls and late-night television helps. Secondly, they need good quality nutrition to feed their ravenous, not cavernous, brains." Again, the other parents smiled, one of them offering a small chuckle. "Which, of course, I know you're providing. Thirdly, they need purposeful work – well, they have that in spades. And, last but not least, they need to move. They need exercise. Would you all agree?"

All the parents, including Giles, muttered their agreement.

Ms Gildebrant stepped in. "Now, if we break up the week and look at how much of the students' time is actually allocated to sedentary activities such as study, rest or sleep, then we see that exercise is vital. When we factor in three sessions of one hour's duration, that is not a great percentage of time overall. The rationale here is that, at the very least, they get some consistent exercise in their week. In an ideal situation, they would get much more than that. However, this is a minimal requirement and, as a school, we believe it helps with their emotional, mental and physical wellbeing. This is why we incorporate it into the curriculum, and we feel it is necessary to do so."

The teachers stuck to the facts, keeping their voices modulated, and rounded off the argument. *Wow, that shut them up*, Lily thought. The parents thanked them for their time, told them what a great job they were doing, and the praise went on. Giles looked miffed, but conceded in the end that he would offer no more resistance, even when Ms Gildebrant suggested that if he had any further concerns, he contact her directly. *Huh, subtext: don't contact every other parent and start World War Three.*

The other matter was to do with the valedictory dinner

planned for later in the year. This one had momentum, and the parents were on a roll. Graduation was always held at a posh place called The Regency Room. Everyone looked forward to the night and it was an expensive affair. Luckily, Lily's mum had been saving for it all year, so they could afford to go, but it was a struggle for some families and then, to add insult to the expense of the evening, the powers that be decided there would be no alcohol. That set off a cascade of trouble. Parents were calling each other, accosting each other at bus stops, in cars outside the school. There was a tidal wave of fury, and the parents weren't standing for it. The best night of the school calendar, the celebration of the completion of their little darlings' secondary education and a quiet acknowledgement of all the effort and sacrifices the parents had made, and this was the best they could have – *chilled water*? Lily saw a group of agitated parents gathered outside the school fence, gesticulating wildly, pointing their fingers into each other's faces and vehemently arguing the point. *Well, it's an insult. It's as if they're treating us like children. How dare they charge $35 per ticket and think it's a celebration drinking bloody water!* Lily overheard as she left for the day.

The meeting was held in Ms O'Flaherty's office. Again, Mr Kelly was in attendance, this time along with Mrs Fitzweiben, the school counsellor. Three parents were there, all speaking and shouting at once, words tumbling and spewing out incoherently. This went on for about ten minutes, Ms O'Flaherty observing the parents as if she was meditating, nodding her head calmly as they carried on. When they finally stopped to breathe, she interjected. Her considered and courteous voice cut through their rabble like a soothing balm over a burn.

"Well, I can see that you're upset. Last year, we had trouble with a group of students who decided to drink until they were drunk. Some vomited in the toilets, others smashed some pot-plants on the way out, and a couple of them had a physical altercation out the front of the venue. As you can understand, this was a totally unsatisfactory situation and one that did not do justice to the great reputation of our school." Ms O'Flaherty frowned.

"While, on the one hand, we are celebrating the students' graduation and all that they have achieved, they have not done this on their own, and parents and teachers need to be acknowledged as well as celebrate the contribution they've made to the successes of these impressive young adults, most of whom are eighteen and thereby legally permitted to have a drink. What do you think would be a mutually acceptable solution to this problem?"

After that, she had them eating out of the palm of her hands. She could have led the conversation anywhere and they would have rolled over. It was agreed that parents could drink if they fully supervised their children. If it was deemed that any student was drunk, or acting inappropriately, the parents and the child would be asked to leave. If any parents did not sign a form stating so prior to the night, they would not be permitted to attend.

To listen is the greatest compliment you can give another person. Also, do your research before a meeting; know what you're talking about. When you've got to give a speech, any speech, practice. This is what the year taught Lily.

SEVENTY-EIGHT

The culmination of Lily's learning came in the form of the end-of-year speech, delivered as the highlight of the valedictory dinner. There had been an English award offered to any student who wrote a piece under the heading: *If I Was the Leader of the World*. Lily worked tirelessly on her submission and, to her astonishment, she won.

"Oh my God, Paulo, you are *not* going to believe this. I won! I friggin' won. Yeeha, baby – here I go! Launch, lift-off, I'm on my way."

Paulo started to shriek. He grabbed Lily and they danced and jumped up and down and around in circles at the school entrance.

Lily had set her sights on this prize. All through school she'd been told to be quiet. Many of the teachers were not interested, let alone encouraging of her enquiring and ranging mind. It was all *Do it my way, shut up, don't cause trouble* and, above all, *don't make a spectacle of yourself, or worse, of me*. There were a handful of golden exceptions, but the majority of them took Lily's outspokenness to be disrespectful, brattish, and a threat to their authority.

Motivated by this, Lily decided to interview her contemporaries. She drafted a template and quizzed them about their views on the world. She said it was research, for a school project, which it partially was, and that she'd be using their answers but not their names. She interviewed two-hundred students.

Once she sifted through their anonymous answers, a couple of topics stood out, as if she'd inadvertently scratched the top of a deep and weeping wound. Injustice came in many guises and took more forms than she had ever imagined. Hope for the hopeless was what she saw as lacking. Not that most of these students *looked* hopeless or defeated. They had learnt early on to cover up, imitate, play the game, or to retreat or go on the attack. What a cost.

If she was the leader of the world, what changes would she make, who would be her role model, who could she emulate while being true to herself? Now, *truth* – there was a tricky topic.

"Hey Paulo, tell me about truth. What do you know about it?"

"Lily, dunno. That's too big for me to manage."

"Well, you know, what do you understand *truth* to be? In the world, I mean. What matters? What's important? What's irrefutable?"

"School Capitano sounds like big stuff! I believe in what I think is the truth, but maybe I'm wrong. I mean, we can't say my truth *is* the truth; it's just the way I see it."

"Like, say we were racist, prejudiced, sexist, right-wing supremist or left-wing Communists, we would come up against an issue with our bias. So, then, our truth would be flawed?

"Yeah, I reckon." Paulo stopped and inclined his head. "Like, even with the old girl and me, my truth said she didn't care about me, but I was wrong."

"And when dad died, I was angry because I thought he chose to leave me. Like, that's totally untrue."

"Yep."

"So, then, how do we come up with a universal truth? Like, one that doesn't diminish anyone because they're different, or individual, or have different life experiences, culture, beliefs, etcetera?"

"Dunno." He scratched his head hard. "Maybe people want to be *right* so much that they change the truth."

"Shit, you piss me off."

"Now you know how *I* feel."

Lily continued. "Because when I've got a good idea, you come in with something left of field and blow mine away. You, with your artsy, airy-fairy, head-in-the-clouds ideas. Couldn't you just once agree with whatever I say and not come up with something better? It'd do my confidence a lot of good."

"Nup. I'll never do that. But whatever I say could be wrong!"

"Oh God, this is ridiculous. I'm not getting anywhere."

They fell over, laughing.

Lily thought about their conversation and why Paulo *would* say what he thought when he was asked but didn't care if he was *right*. He would change his mind; say *he didn't know* and often just listen. She didn't know anyone else who did that.

One day, he told her, "Looking back too much can drag me down. So, I try to look to forward and hope for the best."

Lily thought a lot about his attitude. She had such a loving home, Nini always there, cooking, cleaning and listening. Her mum, working hard but, underneath, full of love and strength, especially before Frank died. Her dad used to say, *If more women were in charge of this world, it would be a better place. Be proud of who you are and speak up. You're as good as the next person. Better in my view.*

In her diary, Lily started to think about what it would be like to be in charge. *I've got every advantage, and I'm determined to do well. As Nini would say, 'It is shameful to waste an opportunity.*

Some only come by once. You have a great brain, Lily-pily – use it. If I had the chance to have the education you're getting, I would have grabbed it by the horns. Fly towards the stars, darling, and if you only reach the sky, you're still flying.'

The rain painted the garden green. The filigree lime leaves hung heavily outside Lily's bedroom window. The morning birdsong was lost amid the pelting on the tin roof. It was a day to hunker down. The garden changed colour as the day went on; the trees drooped more, as if too heavy to hold themselves up.

After two solid days of earth-soaking rain, in the night it ceased. Lily gazed at the new growth on her favourite trees. In the morning sun, she saw shimmers like mirrors on the leaves, swaying on the sodden branches. The air had a new, clean, just-after-the-rain scent. It was sweet, fresh and dewy, the earth was sighing, *Thank you*. She saw the tiniest red-breasted wrens darting in and out between branches. Spring was here and it felt good.

Lily ruminated on her new role. She kept asking herself questions about how she wanted to be, what she brought to the role, why was it important, in what way could she be her best self. She had always been competitive – mainly with herself – but this role represented something deep within her that she could not fathom. All she knew, with every fibre of her being, was that it was important. Like the completion of a recurring dream, when you want the dream to end well. This was her chance to make her own personal dream end well. Or was it just the beginning? So many unsolved questions, so much to work on, so much to learn. She could feel the excitement building, like a drug she wanted to get addicted to. The excitement of possibility. It seemed infinite.

EIGHTY

It was Saturday morning and the house was abuzz. The washing machine was noisily humming from the laundry, the kettle's whistle gathered steam, the sizzling waft of bacon and eggs filled the house.

"Oh, the lovely romantic songs of our era," Nini said. She sang the Vera Lynn lyrics, *I'm dancing with tears in my eyes, because dah dah lah lah lah,* as she turned the breakfast, cooked the toast, and made the tea. As she brought the breakfast to the table, which Lily had laid, Nini sang at top note, *We'll meet again, dah lah lah lah.*

On queue, Bessie started to whine at the back door. She did this every time Nini sang. Lily wasn't sure if she was trying to join in or stop Nini mid tune. The calamity, plus the irresistible aromas, drew Meredith from her slumber. She didn't work weekends, and sleeping in was mandatory for her.

They sat in their usual spots and Lily told them about her morning swim.

"It was incredible," she said between mouthfuls. "The sea mist drifted across the beach and you could seed the funnel-shaped clouds. On the walk back, the mist had lifted, and the sea was blindingly silver. Like someone was reflecting a mirror in your face and you couldn't stop blinking."

Nini listened and nodded, and Meredith seemed to come to life after eating and having her second cup of tea.

"You've always been a beach-baby," Meredith said as she took some dishes to the sink.

"Too true. When you were little, you wanted to live at the beach," Nini added.

"Oh, how funny. Dad loved the beach," Lily said.

"He sure did." Meredith sighed. "He was a great swimmer, like you are now."

As Lily and Nini chatted and poured more tea, Meredith left the room.

That night, after a couple of brandies, Nini sang in a voice that did not match the Village People's song, *YMCA. It's fun to stay at the... la la la la la.*

Paulo taught her that one, on a Sunday night when he stayed for a lamb roast. Nini thought it was wonderful, with all the arm actions and the limbs representing letters. She could never get that part right, but she had a lot of fun trying.

"Nini, your arms are meant to go like this." Lily tried to show her.

But no matter how often she tried, Nini would always mix them up. Her 'Y's became her 'M's, and her 'C's became her 'A's. The more she mixed them up, the more hilarious she thought she was.

"I just don't think your limbs are made for these moves." Lily giggled.

"Darling heart, my limbs are not made for any moves; however, it's fun trying."

After the dishes were done, Nini put on her old-time favourites tape.

"Paulo, now it's my turn to teach you. Do you know how to foxtrot?" she said.

"No, Nini. I can't even believe that's a real name – *foxtrot.*" Paulo swung his arms wide and rolled his mouth around the name. "*I'm a foxy trotter.*" His broad grin had a mischievous edge to it.

"Alright, Mr Foxy Trotter, let me lead the way." Nini showed Paulo how to fox trot and Lily imitated them. That brought peals of laughter as they repeated the moves.

"You're a fast learner, Paulo. Lily?"

"No, thank you. Just watching you two is as close to any foxtrotting I ever want to try."

"You don't know what you're missing, Lily-pily." Nini wandered off to get another brandy.

Lily resorted to dancing with Bessie, who obliged and was gently led by her two front paws in Lily's hands, leaving her hind legs wobbling behind. Occasionally she let out a bark, especially when the music gathered pace.

EIGHTY-ONE

At five bells from the grandfather clock on the mantelpiece, Nini would pour herself a little brandy.

"Why do you do that every day, Nini? Why do you drink brandy every day?" Lily asked her.

"I don't. I drink sherry when I play cards and other days I have a brandy. Sweetheart, when you get to my advanced years, you need something to look forward to. A treat, if you will. Actually, five o'clock is my treat hour – the work of the day is done, and I can potter around the kitchen, have a little sing to myself, reminisce and enjoy the mellowness of a little tipple."

"Good for you, Nini. I never thought of drinking like that. I've had a couple of sips of beer and champagne at Christmas, and on my birthday last year, but I don't see the point in it. Maybe when I'm older."

"Yes, you'll enjoy a glass or two when you're older, I'm sure. I like the taste of it but, more than that, I like the idea of joy. As life goes along the track, Lily-pily, you need to grab moments of joy like sun-kissed apples on the tree. If you ignore them, they'll get pecked by birds or drop to the ground to rot, but if you notice them as they ripen, you'll savour every bite. That's what I decided to do once Alfie left. He was pure joy just by being there. I didn't have to search for it; I bathed in its light." Nini had a sip of her drink and continued, "After he'd gone, I had to make a choice – to be miserable or search for moments of joy. I decided on the latter. Hence, apart from you, my darling girl, and all the endless joy you bring me, I started the five o'clock ritual, which I find rather civilised."

"What are you reading, darling?" Nini asked Lily as she flipped through her magazine.

"*Cosmopolitan*, Nini."

"Oh, does it have saucy bits in it?"

"Nini, I don't read it for that. Anyway, I didn't think you'd care about sex…"

"Ooh la la, sexy Rexy." Nini did a little sidewards movement with her hips. "Just because I'm old, doesn't mean I *think* old."

They laughed as Lily showed her the male model centrefold.

"My, my, my, if only I was fifty years younger…" Nini said, and she took a long sip of her brandy and shuffled across the room to change the record on the player.

Lily laughed and wrapped her long slender arms around her grandmother. "You're the best, Nini. A living legend." And she turned and bounced out the back door.

EIGHTY-TWO

Mot dragged himself into class late, disinterested, disheveled and disorganised.

"Oh, we do gratefully acknowledge your presence, Wheatleigh. Fifteen minutes late – I think, even for you, that's quite something. What's your reason today? Huh?" Mr Turmach glared at Mot.

"I dunno, Mr Turmach, I'm sorry. I didn't mean to be late. It just sort of happened."

"I think it's about time I brought your parents into the equation. See what they think about your incessant tardiness."

"Oh no, please don't do that," he blurted out. "I'm sorry. I'll take whatever punishment you want. Please don't tell them." Mot was stammering and shaking, his hands dragged through his wild auburn hair as he spoke. He looked wide-eyed at his teacher. "Please, Mr Turmach."

"Sit down, Wheatleigh. You've made enough of a spectacle of yourself for one day. See me at recess."

It was a scorching hot March day. The air was thick, and the simmering heat lifted off the asphalt yard in breathless wafts. All the class windows were open, hopelessly seeking the nonexistent sea breeze, and the one government-issued fan always faced towards the teacher. This heatwave was the precursor to Easter.

At recess, there was a desperate rush for the water-taps. Each student bent over the steel ball too long when the trickle of water did not satiate. Mot took his turn, even splashing water over his face and hair, only to be bumped off and on his way. The water had dried on him by the time he found the others.

He was the only student with his sleeves fully down, shirt buttoned up to the neck and mismatched long socks pulled up to his knees.

Paulo asked him, exaggeratedly fanning himself. "Hey Mot, what are you trying to do buddy? You got a death-wish or something? You need to get some air circulating around that body of yours."

"Nah, I'm good. I don't get hot."

But Mot's puce face dripping perspiration said otherwise.

"Have a drink, Mot." Paulo passed him his semi-frozen cordial. "I reckon you're gunna pass out."

"Mot, undo your buttons. Roll your sleeves up. Seriously, you'll keel over in this heat," Lily said.

But Mot held his ground. "Nah, I told you, I'm good. Just leave it, okay?" He turned his back on them to indicate case closed when Lily saw the back of his drenched shirt and beneath it the hideous reddish-purple streaks. As her eyes cast down, she noted the lines between his socks and his shorts and on the back of his hands, and an angry black bruise like a dark shadow across the back of his neck.

Mot eventually accepted a drink from Paulo, but he didn't speak, and they didn't ask any questions.

After school, Lily asked Paulo if he had noticed. "Remember he said he could fight? Maybe because of his old man. That'd be why he never invites us over."

"The old man must rule with an iron fist. Poor Mot. Geez, he must have got stuck into him badly. No wonder he never talks about home. What a thug," Paulo said. "If I had a choice of a dad like him, or not one at all, I'd go for not one at all."

"Yeah, me too. No wonder he hates *the pig*."

In the days after, they started noticing various bruises on their friend, but the worst instance was on Friday when Mot turned up to school with an angry black ring around a swollen bloodshot eye and was walking gingerly.

"Don't tell me, the fridge. No, the bedroom door. Or was it that you fell down the back steps again and landed face down on the concrete? You've taken being unco too far, Mot." Paulo was smiling until Mot put his head between his knees and kept it there. "Oh, sorry, buddy. I didn't mean anything by that; I was just trying to be funny." Paulo apologised. "God, I'm so stupid. I'm sorry. Please – this was just me trying to make you laugh. I'm such a dickhead. This isn't about you being unco, is it?"

Mot didn't answer and didn't move. Paulo sat with him silently.

Lily walked over, saw Mot bent over, and looked at Paulo's distressed face. She placed her arm gently around Mot's back. "You okay, mate? What's wrong?" She sat next to him. "Can we help?"

"Yeah, you can get me a new father." He took a long, halting breath and looked up. "The only thing we have in common is that he hates me, and I hate him. But I hate *him* more."

There was silence for a few minutes until Mot started to talk. Once he did, he spoke without looking at them, as if he were speaking about someone else's life, not his own. Mot told them that he had being suffering bouts of inexplicable abuse from his father ever since he was twelve years old. On his eighteenth birthday, his family were gathered around the birthday cake and his father came in late and drunk and began yelling, swearing at him incoherently, grabbing him by the shoulders and shaking him. He had fallen silent as the family stood back from the kitchen table and his father had placed his sweaty boxer's arm around Mot and with rancid breath slurred these slow, quiet and deliberate words into Mot's ear: *I never loved you. I don't believe you're mine, you useless bastard.* Words that explained the unprompted rage. Words more hurtful than the beatings Mot had endured.

Mot had stepped back and, realising he was the same height as his father, had looked directly into his father's bleary, blood-stained eyes and said, *Good. I hope I'm not. And I never loved you either. I hate you.*

Processing Mot's retort, his father had punched him fully in the face, Mot reeling backwards and cracking his cheekbone on the side of the table before collapsing on the linoleum floor. It was a miracle that his dad hadn't killed him. Gideon was a solid man with hairy arms like clumps of gnarly twisted rope. They hung out from his body like handles on a mug. No one, including Mot's mother, came to Mot's defence, although he heard his eleven siblings crying as he came to. Being the eldest child, he was the one who bore all of his father's frustrations – but now, for the first time, he knew why. Mot believed he was protecting his mother and his eleven siblings by being the target of his father's attacks. His mother was terrified of Gideon's drunken outbursts. While she was never nasty to Mot, she never protected him either, to the point that she often said, *Well, you don't hit girls. Gideon would never do that.* Mot took that to mean she accepted that her angry, violent husband had to vent his explosive rage somewhere and on someone – and better Mot than on his mother or his sisters. The only thing she did when her husband's unpredictable fury spilt over was to gather the other children and hurriedly usher them into her bedroom where they'd drag the wardrobe across the doorway and sit in front of it for protection. Mot was regularly left to accept the onslaught alone.

On Monday morning, the week before the Easter exams, it was a stormy, swirly, gritty day. The heatwave had passed, which left the blustery northerly in its wake. Mot arrived at school early. He smiled at Lily as his blue eyes darted, walked up to her, put his large, freckled hands flat on her desk, leant in conspiratorially and said, "He's dead."

"Oh, my God, Mot," Lily said.

Paulo lent over and said, "What's that, buddy?"

"The pig's gone. Choked on his own vomit after a three-day bender. He was found slumped over in a mate's garage." He showed no emotion, just nodded his head and stated the fact. "Good effort, even for him."

Lily and Paulo were stunned and speechless. They sat looking at Mot, overwhelmed by the horror of what he'd told them and discombobulated by his total lack of emotion, uncertain of what to say.

"We're sorry, Mot," Paulo said as he lightly patted his friend's arm.

"I know what it's like to suddenly lose your father. I'm really sorry." Lily's eyes were moist as she spoke.

"Nuh, don't be. I'm not." He held their eyes. "The old girl will be the only one who'll miss him, and the younger kids'll look after each other. I'm the one who copped it from him and the one he couldn't stand, and now I don't have to stand him either." Mot looked wistfully out the windows to the grimy-grey clouds as a flock of black ravens circled and shrieked. "He got what he deserved. Couldn't have happened to a nicer bloke really," he snarled sarcastically.

The afternoon before his father's funeral, Mot followed Lily, Paulo and Alexa out the school gates, which was unusual, as he lived in the opposite direction.

"I just wanna say thanks for being good mates to me." Mot couldn't hold their gaze. He kept twisting his hands.

"Of course, Mot. That's what friends do for each other," Alexa chirped in and patted his muscly back with her bird-like hand.

He swallowed hard. "It's meant more than you'll ever know."

Lily placed her hand on his arm, as Paulo said, "No worries, buddy. Anytime."

"See you tomorrow, Mot," Lily said.

"No, I'm not going to the pig's funeral. They'll say nice lies about the him and I couldn't stand it."

Mot seemed calmer. He looked at them intently with his electric-blue eyes for a long moment, as if he wanted to say more. They waited. Eventually, he nodded his head at them one at a time, turned and strode in the direction of home. His stride was long and purposeful and, shoulders back, for the first time he seemed to command his full height.

His words hung in the air for hours after he'd gone. Alexa stood speechless and then waved as she ran for her packed bus. Lily and Paulo walked home in silence. Lily kept thinking about what had happened. She couldn't talk about it. Throughout the night, she woke up, either reliving her dad's funeral, or imagining Mot choosing not to attend his own dad's.

It wasn't until the next day that they could speak about Mot's decision. Lily felt compelled to ask him if he was really sure that he didn't want to attend the funeral. She was worried that he might regret it forever if he didn't go. After breakfast, Lily and Paulo walked to Mot's house to check whether he had changed his mind. Mot was the sort of person who didn't say much, but he reassured them that he had meant what he said the day before at the school gates.

It was the last time they spoke with him.

As arranged, the entire school attended the funeral. Mr Gideon Wheatleigh was a Catholic, a parishioner of the St Jude's Church, and a well-respected plumber in the area. Mot said the only reason they didn't go to the Catholic school was that they couldn't afford the fees. Given his father had so many children at Spray Point Secondary, the school thought it a mark of respect to have the whole school attend his farewell. The stifling church was packed with mourners.

Everyone respectfully queued and walked somberly into the church. In the lonely front pew sat Mrs Marjorie Wheatleigh – motionless and expressionless, head covered with a mantilla – followed by eleven of her twelve children. As the organist started to play *Nearer my God to Thee,* she turned around and looked down the aisle, as if expecting someone. Lily, Paulo and Alexa searched the church for Mot, still thinking that, surely, he must have changed his mind at the last minute. But true to his word, Mot did not attend his father's funeral. The priest spoke about what a fine, upstanding character Gideon was – a wonderful role model for young men who aspire to live a good, faithful Christian life. In the eulogy, one of Gideon's brothers spoke of what a hardworking man his brother was, an *all-round good bloke, a man's man,* even mentioning that *he liked a drink or several. A good husband to Marjorie, the kids never went without.* The congregation was overheating inside the church. Its pungent incense lay heavily across the room, irritating their dry throats. Most were agitated, fanning themselves with the hymn books, dabbing their brows with handkerchiefs and looking weak, on the verge of distress, in the heat of the day.

There were prayers, hymns, candles lit, and incense strewn around the solid mahogany coffin with its brass handles. After what felt like hours, the priest, sanctimonious, with his heavy cross swaying in time across his swishing white robes, offered his closing rites and led them in the final hymn, *The Lord is My Shepherd*. Six of Gideon's brothers were pallbearers. Mrs Wheatleigh, a small thin woman with a pinched expression, was held up by two of her elder children as the others filed into the aisle, stony-faced and dry-eyed, to follow the coffin. The airless church made the whole ceremony feel surreal.

That day also marked the last time that Mot's family saw him. Apparently, as they had been making their way to the church, he had packed his meagre belongings, gathered the money he'd ferreted away under his mattress, and caught a train to Sydney. Later, there was word from one of the form teachers that he'd joined the navy there.

On the day of Gideon Wheatleigh's funeral, Marjorie Wheatleigh buried not only her husband but any relationship she had with her eldest child, Mot.

The slate grey day had quietly seeped into Lily's being – slowly, steadily, silently. Above held a smudged mascara sky. The glassiness of the bay reflected the heaviness of the sky.

The soft daylight was weakening as they strolled along the ocean towards the cemetery. Not that they intended to go in. The smell of the biting sea soaked into their pores and the breeze pricked their cheeks. The waves seemed sapped of energy, meekly lapping the shore. A rhythm, nonetheless, that reminded Lily to keep breathing deeply.

"Why do you think we're mates?" she asked Paulo.

"Dunno.' He kicked a mound of sand. 'We just are."

"Nup. Not good enough. I need you to dig deeper. Like, what *makes* us mates? Why, do you think?"

"We just are because we are."

"That's not answering the question. I mean, we have so little in common."

"It's enough to just be mates because we are. We don't need to know why."

"You maybe, but I need to know why. I mean, we're insanely different; you sleep in, I get up early, you go to bed at midnight, I go to bed at eight-thirty, you move slow, I move fast, I speak fast, a lot and loudly, and you hardly talk, and when you do it's quietly. It's what we eat, how we move, what annoys me never annoys you... I can fire up. You wouldn't fire up if there was a gun at your head."

"Yeah, because I'd be too shit-scared!"

"Yeah, yeah, but on paper we don't look like we'd get on at all, let alone be best mates. It doesn't make sense." She peered at him. "Does it?"

"Hmm, yep. Maybe no one else could put up with you. I mean, *us*.' Paulo laughed and broke into a rendition of Supertramp's *Quite Right*. "I accept stuff. I'm lazy."

"Maybe. Except your mum. You don't accept that."

"I'll never accept that."

"So, why? Why do we get along? Why don't we argue and drive each other nuts? Why, do you reckon?"

"I dunno. You *do* drive me nuts, but I can't be bothered arguing. You're smarter than me, so even if I don't agree, I shut up, change the subject and hope you'll shut up too."

"Ah, very strategic. If you do change the subject, I'll just change it back to where I was. I mean, I didn't notice you did that – but I will from now on! I'm not *that* smart. You *get* things. I get bogged down in crap. You don't."

"Nup, I don't. I'm smarter 'cause of you, and maybe you're more fun 'cause of me."

"Yeah, maybe that's why we're mates. That's it. It makes sense. Wow, I never thought of that. Thanks, mate. See, I *told* you that you get stuff." Lily patted him on the back.

"No need to tell me to *get stuffed*." Paulo opened his palms up to the sky. "Now, can you shut up, so I can sing?"

"Ha ha…" She did a little skip and hopscotch. Paulo twirled with arms expansive and resumed *Quite Right* with Lily joining in.

Their walk along the front beach was under a wispy sun, the earlier darkness had lifted. A flock of pelicans flew above them, majestic in their perfect 'v' shape – all seven of them. Lily and Paulo watched them glide way out to sea until they morphed out of sight.

"Do you think there's a difference between knowing and understanding?" Lily asked.

"Not really. If you know something, you understand it.' Paulo turned with his arms outstretched as if remembering a new dance move. "Not that I've thought about it."

"Yeah, I get what you're saying, but I reckon they're different. Like, for example, I *know* Dad is dead, but I don't *understand* it. I'll never understand why. So, I can't get how it happened or why. Like, shit happens, but unless you've lost someone you love, you don't get what the not understanding does to you." Lily took a deep breath and folded her arms tightly. "It does your head in – literally. You saw what it did to me, let alone what it's done to Meredith. She's a shell of who she was now Dad's gone. Does that make sense?"

"Hmm," Paulo slowed down as he considered Lily's question. "Like, I knew Mum had gone, but I didn't know why. So, I didn't understand it, but I knew it."

"Yeah, that's *exactly* what I mean. I was talking to Nini about it, and she reckons we don't have to understand something to accept it. Like, sometimes you just have to accept, even though you don't want to."

"Oh God, now my brain really hurts. Do you know how much you hurt my small brain?"

"Ha ha, no, seriously. She reckons that with my pa, until she accepted it was his time, she thought she was going mad. She even told herself that he was just away on a holiday to pretend to herself that he was coming back. She said she saw him everywhere, heard his voice when she was out somewhere or even in the garden. She thought he was going to walk through the door, that there'd been some terrible mistake, even though she saw his body after he'd passed away. It was driving her crazy. She kept turning around to see him, as if he was standing there. She couldn't sleep, couldn't eat... She reckons she struggled to breathe. She lost a heap of weight. She said you become a different version of yourself when you lose someone you love. I asked her about me with Dad, but she said I was always a wonderful child and I'm still blossoming, whatever that means." Lily watched as the colours of the sunset cast purplish hues across the water and the clouds turned mauve, mutated, and floated off. Lily seemed to come back to where she was. "But ages later, she dreamt that a voice told her it was as it should be, and it was his time – there was nothing to worry about because he was happy, content, and he was where he was meant to be. Waiting for her." Lily crinkled her nose as she looked directly into Paulo's eyes. "Can you believe that?"

"That's weird. What does 'his time' even mean? I don't get it."

"His time to leave this world and go into the next. Nini believes in the afterlife; Meredith doesn't. I reckon Nini's thinking is better – happier and more peaceful, 'cause they haven't gone, they're just in a different place to us. I think that's where Dad is. Thinking that makes me peaceful. For the first few years, I was so angry, but now I don't feel like that. It's still so sad, but I'll see him again whenever my time comes, and I can live with that." She unwrapped her arms. "But maybe I'm just trying to make myself feel better."

"Your time better not be for a bloody long time. If it makes you feel better, then think that. Me, I dunno. I mean, I dunno about a lot of things, so maybe you're right. I just don't *believe*. That's just me."

The last rays of morning disappeared, leaving only the faintest hint of what had been.

EIGHTY-THREE

The morning held two skies. One side was black, ominous, leaching its darkness into the light blue that hovered above the horizon, promising that morning was on its way. The translucence looked tropical, with a tinge of summer, but it was July, winter, and the air was cold and lifeless. The birds were quieter, their tweeting intermittent, feeble. The ocean was uneasy, its rhythm interrupted. Still, as Nini often said, *always welcome a new day. It's a gift and it beats the alternative.*

Lily waltzed home, tired but thrilled. The usual smell of baking didn't greet her, but the droning talkback radio did. Always a tad too loud. "Hey Nini. Whatcha doin'?" she called out.

After calling and calling Nini's name and checking and rechecking the rooms, Lily's voice became more urgent. Yelling from the backdoor, she saw the upturned washing trolley at the back of the yard. She jumped down the four steps, still calling out, and there she saw her, face down, one arm broken into an unnatural angle and her apron askew. Bessie was whimpering and licking Nini's face. Lily dropped down next to her. She felt her neck. She was cold. As cold as the concrete she lay on. Lily put her face next to hers. "Hey Nini, it's me. It's your Lily-pily. Nini, wake up. *Please.*" Nothing. No breathing. No pulse. Nothing.

Lily started to scream. "Help! Help me. Please someone help."

Their neighbour, Brian Drewsome, came running down the side path. He knelt next to Enid, did the textbook First Aid, got up, put his hands on Lily's shoulder. "I'm so sorry, Lily. Your Nini has gone."

Lily screamed, ran and called her mother at work, and then

the ambulance, but it was too late. Bessie was howling the most sorrowful dog sound. Lily was an adult, and her guide was gone. No more life road map to follow. No wise and comforting words. No one ever again to always take her side. No one ever again in life to say, *Hello, darling Lily-pily.*

Paulo was a mess. For such a big guy, he was a blubbering, snotty, red-cheeked, mess. He sounded shocking when he cried, Lily thought. In fact, he sounded so bad it was nearly funny. Except it wasn't.

"Hey, Paulo, I'm the one who's grieving here. She was my Nini, remember?"

"Yeah, but if I ever had one, I would've wanted *her*. I mean it. She was everything a Nini..." He was off again.

Lily waited. Once he had regained his composure, Paulo draped his arm around her and said, "I'm here for you, buddy. I mean it. You tell me what to do and I'll do it."

"Can you age seventy years? Can you become a woman? Can you be my wise counsel, life-coach forever?"

"Piss off! I already am. I can dress in drag if you want me to. Actually, I loved Nini's clothes..."

With that, they were laughing. It felt good. Lily hadn't laughed since Nini died. It was as if they kept flipping between laughing and crying as if the emotions were two sides of the same coin.

And yet, things had to be done. People had to be told – the notices, the funeral, the burial, the flowers, phone calls made by Meredith. People came with food. It was Lily's job to open the front door and greet people. She made endless cups of tea when the mourners offered consolation, which she did not want. Cards arrived, phone calls were taken, flowers were delivered. It felt surreal. For all people's kindnesses, she felt nothing. All this again. Déjà vu of the worst kind. Lily thought she and Meredith were drowning. They couldn't help each other. All they could do was divide the tasks and do them slowly. They could not have done without each other, and yet the affection and care they needed the most, they couldn't give. If one of them was slumped on the couch or lying under their eiderdown on their beds, weeping softly, Bessie would come in and snuggle up to them. One night, after a terrible dream, Lily woke to Bessie lying on her bed with one paw across her. Lily patted that paw and listened to the dog's breathing until she finally drifted back to sleep.

Meredith asked for Father Gerard to officiate, but still argued with him that she did not want a requiem mass, as it would be too drawn out and sad for them. Plus, the only remaining friends of Nini's were too old to sit for that long. They held the wake in the parish hall, and the ladies of the parish helped with some food. Lily served the tea. Meredith ordered the scones from Star Bakery which Paulo brought. She said Nini would never forgive her if there weren't fresh scones.

The funeral was small and Meredith arranged it all. Paulo did all the flowers and music. *I've Got the World on a String*, sung by Ella Fitzgerald, and *Someone to Watch over Me*. These were some of the songs that Nini used to hum or sing to herself all the time. She loved the romantic words, which reminded her of the war era, and the yearning, loving letters that Pa used to write. She used to write back, and spray rosewater on them, so he could still smell her. Her eyes got watery when she spoke of Pa. *You didn't know him, but he was the sweetest man that ever lived. He never raised his voice. He just would say, 'I'm happy if you're happy, Enid.'* He adored Meredith May. He always said, *'Thank God for you, Meredith May – you're the best there is.'* After the shock of losing her dad and then Nini, Lily was unable to swallow properly. She was breathless, sleepless, she shook and felt chilled. In her mind, she played out the *what ifs – what if she did this, what if she did that, what if you didn't do this, or you did do that?* It didn't change anything. There was an inertia from the grief, too, the languid lying around, uncomprehending, unable to think clearly or complete the simplest task. She dreamt of a tidal wave sweeping over her, submerging her, and keeping her pinned down. Grief felt like that to her. It kept you within its clutches as if something unthinkable had put you in a foreign land. Nothing would ever be as it was.

After the funeral, Lily and Meredith went straight to the cemetery, but they didn't invite the other mourners, except Paulo. Meredith said the smaller the better. Father Gerard said prayers and there was a basket of pink rose petals to throw on the grave. Lily kept Nini's lavender-scented handkerchief with her, and Meredith wore Nini's gloves and soft woollen hat. Meredith was bent over, shaking, as she threw a couple of petals in. Lily knelt by the side of the grave on the soft, loose earth, closed her eyes and whispered, *I'll be loving you...* but when she got to the *always*, her voice broke and she couldn't talk. She stood up unsteadily as Meredith put her arm around her and Lily threw her petals in. Paulo stood to the side, ready to catch either of them should they collapse.

Each night, Lily wrote in her diary the questions that kept looping around in her mind. Nini used to say, *Remember, darling, our problems are bigger in the night.* Lily tried to remember this and wrote down anything that she couldn't stop thinking about. *Why take her when I need her so much? Where was Nini? What bird will she be? Is she with Pa? Would her dad be with her too?*

A vast emptiness greeted them, which only intensified once they were home. There, Meredith settled in her lounge-chair and kicked off her black high-heels. Bessie went and nuzzled into her lap as Meredith leaned her head back and closed her eyes. Lily offered to make tea but once the sound of the kettle started to whistle, she froze, and ran wildly into the backyard sobbing. Meredith followed forlornly.

"I couldn't turn it off," Lily wailed. "That's what Nini did. She made everything better with tea and *a good old yarn.*" Lily ran to the beach and Meredith understood. This was such a massive loss. It was going to take a long time for them to adjust. Lily didn't stop to think of how her mother felt. She couldn't console her. She was consumed with, *Why did the people she loved the most leave? Why did she have to keep going on her own? Why?*

That night Lily wrote in her diary.

Hello you,

It's little old me. The saddest me. I can't believe she's gone. Nini the one and only. We had the funeral today. Meredith spoke. She said, 'Farewell our beautiful mother and Lily's Nini. Thank you for your constant love throughout our darkest days after we lost Frank. We will miss you every day. We will look out for you. Will you be a kookaburra, a blackbird, a wren, or a rosella. Whatever bird you are, we will find you. Thank you for everything, Mum. We loved you so much.

*It was a good eulogy. Nini would've loved it. I wrote a poem, but
I was too upset to read it. Mum's sister read it for me.*
Good night sweet Nini,
You will meet your Alfred and my dad soon.
There will be angels and the old music you loved
From the war era.
There will be rainbow sandwiches, scones, jam and cream and
Even some brandy.
I hope there's some dancing.
As the song goes, 'I'll be loving you
Always. Always.'
Sweet dreams and thank you my Nini.

She was a little leaf tossing in the wind with no direction, no way
to control what was happening or where she was going, with no
sense of home.

Lily grabbed Bessie roughly by the collar and let the flywire back door slam hard. They ran to the beach. Lily could not see where she landed her feet, she could not hear the cars, or the birds or the ocean, only the crashing sound of her own breathing. She hurled herself down the sand dune and she ran until she could not run any further. At the bottom of the dune, she curled up into a small human ball. Bessie nestled in, panting, placing her hot paw across Lily's self-protective arms.

Before leaving the house, she had yelled at her mother. "Do you even care about me? You're not the only one who's sad here. Nini was my *everything*. And she was not like *you*!'

When the ocean grew quiet and the sharp chill descended, Lily and Bessie walked home.

There, Meredith was sitting at the kitchen table. Lily sat down next to her.

"There's nothing to live for now." She crossed her arms on the table and lay her head onto them. "My Nini has gone, and my best friend is going. That just leaves you and me, and that's not working out very well, is it?" She kept her head down as she spoke.

"Lily, I'm trying. I'll try to be more like Nini. This is new for me, too. Nini took over. I couldn't help her. I wanted to, but I couldn't. I mean, before your dad died, I think I was a good mother. At least, I thought I was. I wasn't able to get over the sadness; it overwhelmed me. Mum understood. And now my anchor has gone too..." Meredith stared out at the trees lining the side driveway. She looked beyond them and up to the sky.

Lily lifted her head, "I don't want to fight with you anymore, Mum. I'm tired. I'm tired of fighting. You're a good mum and I know it's not your fault that Nini's gone. It's not your fault that Dad died, either. It's just you and me and Bessie now. Like you said before, it's sad enough as it is. Maybe we can try to be friends."

Meredith looked at Lily's face as if for the first time. She looked deeply into her eyes, at the wonder of her uniqueness. She saw Frank's curled mouth, his freckles, his strength, and she saw a glimmer of Nini, too. A soft crinkling around her mouth; her quizzical look. And then, for the first time, she saw a shadow of herself. A young girl lost and struggling, vulnerable and pleading. Meredith shuddered at the thought, and she reached out her arms, unable to move the rest of her aching body. Lily fell into her mother's embrace.

The feel of Lily's velvet skin, her muscled arms, the straightness of her back and the sweet warmth of her breath, was a tonic beyond her knowing. They swayed in a way that only family can: two bodies who are one. One in their hearts; one in their longing.

EIGHTY-FIVE

Just after lunch on Sunday, Lily and Paulo went to the basketball court and threw some balls for a couple of hours. They sat on the wooden side-bench and Lily shared her drink with Paulo.

"I had a dream last night," he told her.

"I dream every night – and in colour, too." Lily walked over and picked up her ball.

"I don't dream like you but last night I did."

"Hmm, were you extra tired or frightened, like a nightmare? Oh God, after Dad, I used to have these drowning dreams over and over and wake up in a mess. I couldn't find him and it was so bad. The feeling of not being able to breathe and the weight of the water, it felt so real. Dreams are our subconscious – or was it our unconscious minds – trying to process the thoughts from our days. I read something about that in class one day."

"Yeah. Anyway," Paulo pressed on. "Last night was incredible."

Lily waited. "What? *What* was incredible?"

"My dream."

They stood to leave, Lily bouncing the ball as they walked. "My dream last night was of exams," she told him. "I was trying to cram and study, and I got caught with cheat sheets. It was humiliating, and I was thrown out of the exam hall, hysterical."

"I gotta go," Paulo said suddenly.

He walked off, Lily standing there, unsure of what had happened.

"Hey!" she called after him. "What about your dream?"

"Doesn't matter." He crossed the road and yelled back, "But

it was really bloody good." Then more loudly, "Insanely good."

"Shit!" Lily yelled to him across the road. "Why didn't you tell me about it?"

"Because you didn't shut up long enough for me to." A truck screeched its gears down the main road, and again he called out, "Check ya later."

When she got home, she rang him, but no one answered the phone.

The next morning on the way to school, Paulo finally told her about his dream. "It was as if the doors to wonderland had opened," he exclaimed. "It was like a runway to the stars. I had angel's wings and a sparkling gold in-laid cape. Once I arrived in this magical place in the sky, the music started with this great beat and my body moved like it was liquid. I was jumping, pirouetting and cartwheeling. The crowd were screaming for me. It was the best feeling. Then I woke up because the old boy yelled out, *You'll be late again.*"

"That sounds incredible. It felt like I was up there too!" Lily smiled.

"Yeah, you were the one with the screaming lungs." He laughed.

"That'd be bloody right."

EIGHTY-SIX

Friday afternoon smelt of sultry humidity and relief. While Lily's bag was heavy, Paulo's was not. Every spare moment she had, she had to study. Every spare moment he had, he danced. She grew tired with the hours of reading and revision. He came to life with his practice. The more Paulo danced, the more he wanted to dance.

"What are you doing on Saturday?" she asked.

"I've got an audition."

"A *what*? Did you say *audition*? What for?"

"Miss Cherie has the head guys come down from Sydney School of Dance if she feels there's anyone who is worth it..."

Lily stopped in her tracks. "Do you mean *worthy*? Like, worthy to go there?"

"Yeah, that's what she said. So, I have to go for this private audition. It's for kids who can't afford to go up and back." He did a little twirl and pointed at himself. "That's me."

"Oh my god, that's incredible!' She jumped up and down on the spot before they kept walking. "Why didn't you tell me? I'm so excited! This is incredible. You'll blitz them!"

"We'll see." He did a little soft shoe shuffle and then a tap, and then a rolling turning point down the street to Nancy's café, which was closed. He watched his reflection as they passed.

"See? You've been practicing." Lily clapped her very loudest clap. "They'll think you're great because you've *got it*. You nervous?"

"Shit scared," he admitted, as he tap-danced in step with her.

"So, how will you overcome your nerves, Fred Astaire?"

"Miss Cherie reckons if you're not nervous, you don't want it enough. She reckons nerves are good." He clapped his hands at the side of his head like a Spanish matador. "Makes you try harder."

"But what if the nerves make you freeze and you can't move, or remember what to do, or you feel sick and shaky, like I did in the trial English exam? Oh God, that'd be so bad…"

Paulo kept dancing around her and said, "I'll think of putting the old boy to bed every night and how desperate I am to get away."

"Oh, sure." Lily fell silent.

The audition was on Saturday morning at Miss Cherie's Dance School. Paulo told Lily she couldn't go with him; she'd make him more nervous. He said he'd meet her for lunch at Nancy's afterwards. Lily got there early, grabbing the best table outside and putting in their order. She knew that, whether he was happy or unhappy, he'd want to eat. A few lonesome grey gulls hung, squawking, as a fishing cruise-boat chugged by, rods jolting in anticipation at the back of the boat. Bessie snuggled into Lily's leg as an errant English sheepdog flew in the opposite direction of its aggravated owner. Lily found it humorous, thinking, *Bessie would never do that*. She decided to give Bessie a few more chip-ends today.

Lily waited for what seemed like an eternity, the hot-chip parcel before her now only warm.

The audition was nerve-wracking and, yes, he did feel sick, but the judges nodded to him at the end. One of them said, "You'll be hearing from us, Paulo." When Lily saw him skipping towards her, she knew. It was the most excited conversation she'd ever had with him. Even while devouring the fish and chips, he spoke more than she did, giving her a detailed account of all that happened that morning.

The following weeks flew by. The audition hung heavy in the silences between them, but Lily decided not to hound him about it except to make Paulo promise to tell her straight away when he received their letter. "I don't want to ask you every day, but if you don't promise, you know I *will* ask every day."

"Yep. And I sure as hell don't want that."

Thursday morning and they had HSC assembly. Paulo joined her amid the mash of students waiting to squeeze through the school gates. Boy, was that blazer of his getting too small. His shoulders were broader, and he was a lot taller than her now. She noticed his paunchy belly had disappeared and he stood straighter.

He leant in close to her ear. "I told Valerie that I've applied."

"You *what*? *When*? Oh, my God!"

"I rang her last night."

"You didn't tell me..."

"Actually, I've rung her three times."

"That's incredible. You bloody ripper! How was she?"

"Good."

"Good for you! What'd she say?"

"That it was a great idea."

They had to leave their conversation mid-stream and resume it as soon as they were clear of the throng of students pushing through the gates.

"Have you told Ronaldo yet?"

"Nup," Paulo whispered.

"Why not?"

"'Cause when I told him I was trying out, he said dancing was for pansies."

"What a stupid thing to say. As if."

"He said dancing lessons were a waste of money – he knows it's from the money mum sent me, but to audition for a career he said was a waste of my life. He said he didn't want a son who was a pansy." Paulo furiously rubbed the backs of his hands across his eyes and looked away from her.

"What a shitful thing to say and it's not true," Lily said. "I don't even know what a *pansy* means. What would Ronaldo know? It's not as though he's exactly made a huge success of his life. I mean, there's nothing wrong with working as a mechanic, but…"

"It's just him."

"Just ignore the moron. I mean, sorry, but really? No offence, but he's old enough to know better. What did your mum say?"

"That she always knew I had talent – even as a little boy, I'd twirl under the clothesline, pretend to tap-dance after watching Shirley Temple. I don't remember any of this." Shaking his head, he added: "Wants me to stay with her if I get in… Not that I ever would."

"Of *course*, you would. Good old Valerie. She gets it. She's an artist herself, a singer…"

"I don't know anything about her except for her letters. The old man reckons she's no good, but what would he know?"

"Exactly. He wouldn't know. It's up to you now. Another artist in the family."

"Maybe she's a bullshit artist." He smirked. "A bit like you."

"Oh, good one. That's a bit rich coming from you."

They pushed and shoved each other all the way to Nancy's.

"My shout,' Lily said, once they had reached the café. "This is to celebrate you being famous one day. You better not forget me when you are. I mean, I was the one who went to Miss Cherie Academy with you. I was the one who watched you practice all those bloody dance steps over and over."

"So you bloody well should." They joined the queue at the counter. "When, or *if*, I make it, they'll charge people to see me. You should be bloody grateful." Paulo said, laughing at his own joke.

"Pay to see *you*... oh, *please*." Lily turned to order their food.

They sat on the bench and ripped open their parcel of chips and potato cakes. They spoke about Sydney and how exciting it would be for Paulo to live there, and how Lily would save up to visit as if they were planning another life entirely in another country.

EIGHTY-SEVEN

"Wow mate, you look like shit," Lily said as soon as she saw Paulo come down the corridor.

"Thanks, buddy. Anytime I need a pick-me-up I'll remember to come to you," he yawned.

"No, sorry, I didn't mean it like that – but you look sick or something. What's wrong?"

"That's what a whole night awake does to you. I couldn't sleep. Not a wink."

"That's bad. I read you can die from not enough sleep."

"You're a classic. I'm not dying; I'm just dying to *tell* you…" Paulo yelped. "I've been accepted into Sydney Dance Academy!" He waved his arms into the air as if accepting the Lord Jesus himself.

"Oh, my God! That's the best. *Really*? Really truly?" Lily hopped up and down on the spot wildly clapping her hands.

"Yep, little old me. Who would ever have believed it?" His grin was the largest she'd ever seen.

Lily put her hand over her mouth. They hugged each other and danced around in a little circle, whooping and hollering.

It wasn't long before Alexa appeared and joined their circle. Paulo was beaming. Ghostly white for a swarthy Italian – but beaming. He had used up all his joy by lunchtime, though, coming down with a thumping headache. He told the nurse he thought he had the flu, went home, and slept for sixteen hours straight.

Lily was in bed that evening when she realised that, at the end of the year, Paulo would really be leaving Spray Point. The idea of saying goodbye filled her with an aching terror. That night, she tossed and turned, repeatedly jolted out of a disturbing dream. She dreamt of standing at a corner and walking in a different direction from Paulo, him waving and laughing, her unable to turn around to say goodbye, her yelling, *Please don't go*, and him not hearing, or not caring, and her being distraught. She woke to the thought, *Why are the best people always leaving me?*

EIGHTY-EIGHT

There was a spotlight centre-stage in the ocean – a shaft of light beaming out like veins. One lonely fishing boat bobbed about way out at sea.

Lily sensed something behind Paulo's silence. She felt uneasy. It was Friday afternoon, and their usual buoyancy was lacking. Lily tried to chat, but Paulo didn't answer, and after a few attempts she fell silent too. When her curiosity eventually bubbled over, she asked, "Something up, mate?'

Paulo chewed his cheeks and scrunched up his mouth. "How do you reckon the old man's gunna cope when I go?" His voice was barely audible.

"The same way he copes now." Lily kept her gaze on the fishing boat drifting towards the lighthouse.

"Well, how's he gunna get to bed, make dinner and stuff?"

"Get to bed?" She thought he was joking, until she saw his troubled expression.

Paulo also watched the faint outline of the boat as he spoke. "Yeah, it's old Paulo-boy who puts him to bed every night. He gets pissed, leaves the idiot-box on, passes out and snores, crumpled up in his chair."

"Wow, I never knew that…"

Paulo interrupted, "Yeah, it's either me doing it or he wakes up with a crook back – or, at least, crooker than the one he's already got."

The breeze started to lose its sting as the meek sun warmed their backs. A couple of laughing kids raced each other down to the water's edge. Their dad followed behind. "Ay, you two – not too close," he said, as he stumbled down the dune, spraying sand as he ran to catch them.

"You can't worry about that, mate. You've done enough. It's up to him now. He's a grown man, for God's sake."

"Maybe I shouldn't worry, but I do. He's all I've got."

"You're bloody devoted to put him to bed and look after him the way you do. I mean, your cooking is shithouse, and you could poison him, but at least you make him eat." She elbowed Paulo gently in the ribs.

"You can talk. What about *your* bloody cooking? Last time you boiled eggs, you burnt the crap out of the pot."

"True." Lily grinned. "That was an experiment, and it didn't turn out well. Anyway, I'm learning. I reckon I'm improving. Best I practice on you. I'm getting sick of Meredith's spaghetti Bolognese. I did try to do the Chicken Maryland out of Nini's recipe book, but not much luck there. Burnt them, too. Didn't look anything like the ones Nini used to make. She never burnt anything."

They walked on.

"Right," Lily continued, "come around for breakfast tomorrow and I'll try not to poison you. Pancakes?"

"Great! Never one to knock back a free feed."

They turned to wander up the long path to the main street. Lily took off her windcheater and tied it around her waist.

"Where do you reckon Mot is?" Paulo wondered. "Nothing's the same now he's gone."

"I heard he was working as a labourer or helping unload trucks at the Sydney market or something. One of his brothers said he'd gone into the navy, like Mrs M said, but I don't reckon they have a clue."

Lily made long strides and Paulo leisurely kept in step.

"I heard one of his brothers is smacking around one of the little ones. He must've picked up his old man's evil habits."

"Mot'd really hate that."

Paulo watched as a family of four walked towards them. "I feel sorry for Alexa, studying all the time now, what with her dad giving her grief."

"He yells at her and her mum. They're scared of him, for sure. Her brothers are pretty rough, too, except Antonio. Alexa reckons she's moving to the city when the exams are over and she's never coming back – not even to see her mum. She said she can come and visit her away from that stinking milk bar. I don't know how she's meant to study when the buzzer goes all the time, even when they're cooking or cleaning or hanging out the washing. Don't think her brothers do much around the house. I guess they have to help in the shop, but so does she."

"Yeah." Paulo stuffed his long arms into his jean's pockets. "Mot's gone, and Alexa can't hang out anymore."

"And then there was one," Lily said, sadly, when they had reached the town. "You're off soon, too." She looked at the cars banking up for a Friday night out. *In a hurry going nowhere,* she thought, as Nini used to say. She bit down on her lower lip and turned away from him.

"Not for ages, buddy." Paulo nudged her.

She nodded. "It'll be here soon. Anyhow, I've got to help Meredith when I get home. She said, since Nini's gone, the housework, laundry, endless cleaning, shopping and crap is too much for her. I can't be bothered fighting. So, guess who's got be a domestic slave?"

He laughed. "Not likely. Maybe you could come and give our

pigsty a once over every now and again."

She rolled her eyes at him. "Good try and pigs may fly. Our place is bad, but yours is worse. *Much* worse. Sorry, you have sort out your own filth." She gave him a quick hug. "Catch ya tomorrow. Come at nine. You can have the usual three rounds of peanut-butter toast. Or pancakes."

"Sure will. See ya, buddy."

EIGHTY-NINE

Lily was grappling with her mathematics homework.

"Knock, knock." Meredith waited for a response and entered. "A letter for you, darling."

Lily rarely received mail, but as Meredith passed her the envelope, the writing was unmistakable. She took the crumpled and dirt-stained envelope to the back swing-chair. Opening it, Lily had an overwhelming sense of Mot.

Hi you Form 6 losers,

I hope this finds you studying, reading and basically living the most boring life imaginable, when you should be free and living with me!

I'm sorry it has taken me 6 months to write, but you know I never was much good at writing (Lily can you correct my spelling mistakes? Ha ha). I trained it to Sydney with the money I had stashed away. Anyway, I had enough to get by and find a hostel to live in. It was in a place called Ryde, The Gold Hostel – stupid name when it was such a dump. It smelt, it had strange old men in it, and I got the last room. Lucky me! But 'beggars can't be choosers', I guess.

After looking for work for a couple of weeks I got a dishwashing gig in this pizza place. A guy who came in regularly was chatting to me one night and suggested I try the navy. You don't need Form 6 to get accepted, so I did it. I sent in my form, went for the interview, a bit embarrassing because I had to tell them I lived in a hostel, but they were cool with that. I got a call three weeks later to say I started on the Monday.

So now I'm on a boat called HMAS Sydney and I'm junior crewman. It's good going out to sea, you have to work hard and sometimes they treat you like shit but hey I'm used to that. Some of the crew are good, the rest well – at least the old man taught me how to fight. No problem with sleeping. When I hit my bunk I'm so stuffed I sleep like a dead man.

Good luck with your exams. Say gidday to the good guys and to Mrs MS.

Tell the rest to get stuffed from me! Miss you guys.

See ya round,

Mot XO

PS If you see the old girl you can tell her I'm okay and doing good in the Navy. I'm not writing to her, figure it's better this way. A big hi to Alice and Tommy from me. Tell the others they better look after them or else. XO

PSS Can you show this to Paulo and Alexa cos I don't remember their addresses? Ta, XO

Lily sat for a long while holding the letter in her hands and imagining Mot writing – knowing how much he hated it and feeling his loneliness seeping into her heart. She thought of times the incredible loneliness swamped her after her dad died. The nights she'd stare out at the stars to Mr Moon and beg her dad to tell her where he was, as if he was hiding from her, cruelly. Her mind slowly drifted back to the young seaman with the vivid blue eyes, wild red hair, Irish skin, and a broad back. A young man who had no one, who had to start again.

There was no return address, so Lily wrote to the navy headquarters in Sydney.

Hi Mot,

It's so good to hear from you! We talk about you all the time and wonder where you are and hope you're doing okay. We miss your cheeky grin and your 'they can all go and get stuffed' daily comments!

Paulo has been accepted into the Sydney Dance Academy. He's pumped and because he's in touch with Valerie, he will have a couch to crash on when he gets there (she lives in Sydney). Maybe when you're in dock you two can catch up. The sailor and the dancer... just need the romancer up there and we could have a blast! Alexa's studying hard. We reckon her parents are giving her grief, 'cause she's gone quiet. You know how she does that sometimes.

I don't know if you've heard my bad news, but Nini passed away. It's so sad and I'm adjusting to life without her here. It was quick, a stroke they said. So at least she didn't suffer.

We all send our love. Bessie misses your hugs big time. Meredith is still the same, but she hopes you're keeping safe and well.

I called in to see your mum after school last night. I told her what you said. She sent her best to you, said everything was the same at home, told me to tell you not to be a street brawler, not to become a drunken womaniser, and to write to them.

Take good care Mot.

Your friend,

Lily XO

PS. If I do well enough in the exams (which is a very big maybe) I'm going to the city to Victorian College of the Arts to study acting and writing. You always said I was a drama queen!

PSS We do think you're a lucky shit to have escaped the exams, but more than that, we all miss you!

NINETY

It was a blistering northerly. Bessie forged down the narrow beach unperturbed, her fur waving sleekly in the wind.

"Jesus Christ!" Lily muttered to no one as her shoes filled up with water from an errant wave. She felt relieved that Nini wasn't there to hear her say that. She squelched on through the clag-like sand. It had a mealy, moist, meanness to it, and she kept thinking, *I'm only doing this for you, Bessie.*

Cutting Bessie's run short, Lily turned and felt almost airlifted by the updraft. *Gale force winds*, she overheard on the six pm news. Bessie darted towards a grey gull that hovered in the air, only requiring intermittent flapping. By the time they got home, Lily felt the day was already presenting as a chore.

Since Mot left, Alexa was even quieter. In their shared classes, she never put her hand up, and if she was asked anything she'd answer fast, in a quiet voice, keeping her eyes on the floor. Lily remembered when she first became friends with Alexa. She thought she resembled an exotic gem, sparkling, flashing and edgy. Lily found the passionate way she spoke, her humour and her sparky anger captivating and, especially, the way she wouldn't back down.

But recently, Lily had found herself avoiding her old friend. Watching Alexa just take whatever the mean teachers dished out was disheartening. It was as if her feisty spirit had left with Mot. Maybe Mot leaving made Alexa not feel as strong. Lily couldn't work it out.

Paulo, on the other hand, had found his zing through his dancing. He couldn't talk about anything else. He was always humming, tapping his feet, swirling around or just trying a new move he'd learnt. Lily got accustomed to it, so that she kept talking and he'd listen and dance at the same time. Sometimes he would answer, sometimes he didn't – but irrespective, Lily kept talking.

Saturday was hot, and because of Bessie's barking, Lily dragged herself to the sparkling bay. She dropped her oversized tee-shirt and thongs and followed Bessie across the burning sand. Lily dove under the water and saw the zigzagged lines in the sand and the tiny pieces of filigree seaweed that floated up in front of her. She took her first breath and swam hard until her limbs loosened and the tautness in her muscles released. Her arms strained and ploughed through the chilling water, she blew bubbles, breathing hard. It had been a long time since she had swum. The last time was the day before she found Nini collapsed under the clothesline. She remembered what a beautiful day that was. She had swum the length of the cove towards the old lighthouse and back.

Nini once told her that she was a natural; that when Lily was a baby she took to the water like a little ducking. She had no fear; she'd just walk straight in. Her parents had a hard time looking after her because as soon as they'd retrieve her from the ocean, she'd waddle straight back in again. Lily and Nini often spoke about their shared love of the sea – and how, as a young girl, Nini went to the beach whenever she could. On their second cup of tea, on the back porch, she said, *Always look for the light, darling. You can't always see it, but eventually you will.* Those lines played over in Lily's mind as she swam. At the beach, she found herself constantly searching for a glimmer of that joy she felt when sitting with Nini on the porch or the hours spent hopping across rockpools with her father.

Nothing was the same since Nini had gone. Lily didn't hang out with Alexa, or even with Paulo much now that he was distracted with practicing for dance competitions. Everything and everybody were wrong. She was in a bad mood every day. She knew it, and her mother frequently commented on it, as did her teachers, who liked to remind her how rude and disrespectful she was. Lily didn't care. Life wasn't any good anymore. She couldn't see how it would ever be good again.

Once she got to the end of the cove, she was in the rhythm of her swimming. The water caressed her skin and she felt weightless. She became a creature of the ocean, once again belonging there. By the time she got back to the beach, Lily felt serene. Her tingling, tired body felt good. It felt like the sea was a part of her. It was the strangest feeling. Her mind drifted back to her conversation with Nini about always looking for the light. Maybe Nini meant it was a sign to say that everything's going to be okay. Eventually.

Lily floated home to cook the first decent meal she and Meredith had shared in a long while, and the first meal she'd looked forward to for a longer time. After the last lamb chop was chewed down to the bone and all the mashed potato and peas were gone, they sat at the table, not speaking. After a while, Meredith made tea, as Lily washed up. A family friend had dropped around some fruit cake, so they had tea and cake, and chatted quietly. A feeling descended over Lily that she couldn't make out. It felt old, comfortable and familiar. She didn't leave the table until Meredith said, "It's probably time for me to hit the hay."

Her mother kissed her goodnight and Lily slept a deep slumber. She couldn't remember her dreams, but she wasn't disturbed by them. Something to do with being at home, or feeling at home, or going home. She didn't care – whatever it was, it felt good.

The next day drifted by and, later that night in bed, she could not remember walking home. She only recalled yesterday's swim – and not really the first part, but the return part. Something shifted in her as she strode, flexed, kicked and breathed for home. She wanted more, and she longingly dreamt of tomorrow's swim.

It was Friday. Alexa was not allowed out as usual, and Paulo was at his two-and-a-half-hour dance lesson, so Lily took Bessie to the beach and sat on the bench, watching the way-off surfers, who resembled raisins bobbing in between khaki sets. She walked to the Point, where she sat hypnotized, studying the surfers below as Helen Reddy's *I Am Woman* floated out of the spluttering, metallic blue Torana that had just swung into the carpark. She thought, bitterly, *Not in my world*. Four girls fell out of the doors, laughing, as Lily turned her head.

She ambled home, arms wrapped tightly around her chest against the rising chill. The lines from *Fire and Rain* about loneliness and trying to find a friend spun around in her mind. *I wish he'd never given me that bloody cassette*, she thought. *I didn't even know who James Taylor was before* Fire and Rain. Her body trembled. She decided it was too painful for her to listen to.

NINETY-ONE

The wind was cyclonic. It lashed the trees like twisted ropes against a flagpole. The banksia swayed and the tea tree shook. Lily attempted to put on her runners, sodden from being left on the back verandah. The wind whipped her hair and pushed her back towards the flailing flywire door.

She was determined to get out of the house. The tension between her and Meredith was escalating. They now argued about the smallest things: *Who didn't hang all the washing out, why the dishes weren't done, whose turn it was to buy some groceries, put out the bin, bring the bin in, water the garden...* Their bickering seemed endless – but, worse, also pointless.

This morning, Meredith yelled back as she went out the front door, "Make sure the dishes are done before I get home. I mean it."

When the front door slammed, Lily sneered, "Get stuffed, Meredith, and, by the way, I hope you have a great day too."

These dealings with her mother always left her with a stomach-ache. Now it was likely she'd end up with a headache, too. She shook and shuddered in the sideways rain in her flimsy raincoat.

Once she turned from Tea Tree Road into Southern Ocean Road, Lily faced an ugly sea, its ferocity scary, and there was no differentiation between sea and sky. The foam was the only indication of the waves, and the sandbanks were a murky yellow. Lily trudged on towards the Point, but the southwesterly had other ideas. She turned and huddled sideways back to Paulo's where she thumped on his front door.

"Oh my God, are you mad? What are you doing?" Paulo

said as he ushered her into their dark, dusty hallway, the door slamming in the wind as she entered.

Lily stood drenched and shivering, water pooling under her feet, her face a livid red. After she took off her shoes, Paulo handed her a towel. She thought how much their house smelled but was relieved to be in it. In the hallway, she dried herself off, then went to the kitchen to fill up their kettle. She started to clear the table of dirty cups and plates, dumping them into the sink. The clattering of the cutlery against the crockery was loud but her freezing hands were grateful to be immersed in the soapy warmth.

"Hey, buddy, you don't have to do the dishes," Paulo hovered awkwardly in the doorway. "Sorry, we live like pigs..."

She turned fitfully and said, "She's *so* nasty. I can't do *anything* right. She tells me off for being lazy, not helping enough, not doing enough homework, my room being a pigsty, it just goes on and bloody on. I slam the door and she opens it... I just want to scream that I'm sick of her and if Dad and Nini were here I'd never have to speak to her again or put up with her bullshit friggin' moods..." Lily snatched a cup off the side of the sink, knocking another one, which smashed on the lino floor. "Oh, my god. Sorry. I didn't mean to break it..."

Paulo bent over to pick up the pieces. "No worries, mate. Sit down and I'll make *you* a tea, for once." He went to the cupboard to search for teabags, but there was only an old tin of Milo. He hacked at the congealed powder with a spoon, filled the tin with boiling water and found a small amount of milk in the fridge. He found some sugar and heaped it in, put the lid back on with a bang of his fist and shook the contents like a maraca.

As he shook the tin, Paulo did a Jamaican dance that he'd

seen Peter Allen do on TV. *Life is a shit. Let's face it.* He made up his own lyrics, singing out of tune. *Life is a shit. Let's face it. A bit of a shit and you just want to hit someone and get over it.* Lily started to laugh.

They slurped on their very sweet Milo from chipped mugs and Lily thought that she should buy them some mugs for Christmas.

"I always feel better when I see you," she said.

"Yep, you do."

"Oh, brag, boy, why don't you?"

"Well, it's a fact. Now, go home and do your work." Paulo playfully pushed her towards the door.

"You shouldn't have stopped me in my manic cleaning before." She waved her arms toward the piles of dishes. "I mean, I was making some ground there..."

"Yeah, but we only wash what we need. The rest can wait," he said, as an uneven pile lost its balance and slid haphazardly across the dirty bench.

"Maybe do a few more, just to balance out the piles."

"Yeah, yeah..." Paulo pushed her out the door as she pulled her raincoat back on.

Outside, the rain had ceased, which left a kingdom of clouds drifting aimlessly.

NINETY-TWO

Lily hammered Paulo with her questions and complaints about Meredith in the following weeks. "Do you know how much weight she's lost?" she said one day as they walked to school. "She looks like a walking ghost. She creeps around sniffling with red puffy eyes and hugging herself in her old dressing gown..."

Until one day, Lily's mood seemed to have lifted. "Today, she got dressed. She even made me breakfast. I couldn't believe it! Scrambled eggs and not too bad, either. I mean, not as good as Nini's, but..."

Paulo scratched his head and shook his hair back. "That's good, buddy." He smiled, his eyes crinkling at the edges.

"I mean, she's started doing stuff, making phone calls, a load of washing, cooking... she even cooked lamb shanks last night. And surprise, surprise, they were good."

"Haha, now that's a bloody relief! When can I come for a decent meal? I'm missing Nini's food *so much*..." He stopped and saw Lily wipe her eyes. "Oh, that's shithouse of me, sorry. I didn't mean to talk about food. You know I really miss Nini, too."

"Yeah, I know. Anyway, you always talk about food."

"That's because I'm always bloody starving!"

"Well, you don't look like someone who's starving."

"Oh, shut up. I don't look too bad."

"Yeah, only kidding."

Lily started to see occasional glimpses of the mum of old. The corners of her mouth sometimes turning upwards at some quirky or disparaging comment Lily made. The rare and unexpected hug. The kiss goodnight was becoming more regular. The greatest change: *I love you,* as Meredith gently closed Lily's door behind her after she wished her goodnight.

She remembered her mother in the days when her dad was alive. Meredith making the rules, and Lily and her dad often breaking them. Often, when she'd catch them, Lily would notice a small smile on her mother's face, or a wink to her dad, or a twinkle in her eye. Lily remembered nestling into her mother when she had read her a bedtime story. Frank usually did this, but not always. She thought of the times in the old loungeroom, when Lily would pretend her couch was an island and Meredith was a tickling fairy. These memories made her feel a golden warmth right through her body.

NINETY-THREE

The night before her speech, Lily had a soothing bath and went to bed early. She said goodnight to Meredith, who had fallen asleep in front of the TV with Bessie at her feet. As Lily stared at the full moon and said goodnight to her dad and Nini, she hoped they would be pleased with her composition.

It was misty with a warm breeze blowing. She was sitting very high up on a crest, which could nearly touch the clouds. The bay twinkled below, and the village snaked around the headland.

After a while, she closed her eyes, and Nini spoke to her. "Lily, we wish you strength and self-belief. All the Mango women are in your heart. This speech matters: what you have to say is important. Speak your truth from an open heart, Lily. We are all with you."

When she opened her eyes, the sun's brilliance on the water was dazzling, so much so that her eyes watered and they closed once more.

Then she heard her father's voice. "My darling Lily, the hopes and dreams I had for you will culminate in your speech tomorrow. Let your light shine, my beautiful one. This is your time. Be true to your beliefs and know I am standing right there with you. Tomorrow and forever more. I love you."

She stood up and felt on top of the world, and ready.

When she woke up, Lily vividly remembered the dream. She remembered every word, the tone of their voices and the whimsical vision of their incarnation. She sat on the edge of the bed, and as she dressed for her run, heard the words, *We are all with you. I'm there. Tomorrow and forever more.*

Lily ran like the wind, effortlessly gliding. *Stay with me. Stay with me. Stay with me.* And as she turned up the dusty, sandy bush track home, *Go shine your light, Lily. This is your time.*

She couldn't tell anyone about the dream. It was too real. She didn't want to risk it dissolving in her mind. She wrote it in her diary. She knew the words like a mantra.

The rest of the day she floated and, as the time for her presentation approached, she stayed centred. Meredith asked if she wanted to practice one more time in front of her and Lily did – perfectly – only glancing at the notes every now and again, and looking ahead, speaking calmly, confidently and coherently. Meredith said it was brilliant. Compliments from Meredith were rare, so Lily drank this one in.

NINETY-FOUR

Good evening, Judges, Ms O'Flaherty, Mr Kelly, teachers, parents and students, My name is Lily Mango, and I am honoured to be accepting the 1978 Form Six Australian literary award.

When I was a young child, my father read to me every night. It was our special time to snuggle up together and escape to a world of magical adventures and memorable friends. These books took me to places I'd never imagined before: Enid Blyton's The Magic Faraway Tree *and* The Secret Seven, *with people who were wildly exciting and on rollicking adventures.*

Unfortunately, my father passed away suddenly when I was fifteen. Bereft and lost, I sought the comfort of books. I would retreat to my bed and take myself to a happy place, to another world, to my faithful friends, who never left me, not even when the book was finished.

Secondary school is not for the faint-hearted. I was someone who didn't fit in. Someone who was different. These were not the happiest moments of my life. But it taught me how it feels to be on the receiving end of injustice, unfairness, humiliation, degradation, and brutality.

I was fortunate to have my beautiful mother and lovely Nini to go home to.

Then I made a friend. My best friend, Paulo. He was on the outside looking in, too. In time, it became easier, because we could share our loneliness. It lessened the hurt. As the years went on, we made more friends, especially Alexa and Mot. Before long, there were more. By the beginning of this year, most of the year level had spoken with me at one time or another about their own times of despair at not being accepted for how they looked, or what they had, or the colour of their skin, or the shape of their bodies, or their sporting prowess or lack thereof, or their academic achievements, or where they lived, or their sexuality, or if they had a boyfriend/girlfriend... The list seemed endless.

The more I heard these stories, the more I noticed this playing out in the world, by world leaders. In the pursuit of power, they aimed to dehumanise others; reduce others to a construct of what someone should say, think, look like, their heritage, their culture, their religion, their beliefs, their sexuality, their income, their experience of the world, the border of their country... 'I have the power, so you will do as I say, and I will defend my position any way I want to because you threaten me. If you threaten my sense of power or my world view, you'll be sorry.' Sounds infantile – like a school yard bully – doesn't it?

The topic for this essay is, 'If I Was the Leader of the World...'

If I was the leader of the world, I would stand for justice. I believe fear and anger do not solve problems; they start wars. Wars do not solve problems; they feed fear and anger. This becomes cyclical.

If we do not listen to each other respectfully, allowing that we have different points of view – deeply listen to the other person – hubris and ego will be in charge.

You can be you, and I can be me. No better, no worse, no competition, just acceptance. My rights should never come at the expense of your rights. I need to listen to you. You need to show me the same courtesy. In difficult situations, we need mediation, where a peaceful solution is the goal for both parties.

There is a better way. Conflict is a flawed model. It keeps repeating itself. There is racism, sexism, discrimination, pollution, brutality, violence, war... and these issues are not going away.

You do not have to follow any faith or religion to understand the impact of the breeze in the trees, the birdsong in the morning, the glory of the sunrise or sunset at day's end, the fierceness of the ocean, or the air in the forest, to know that we are a part of something beyond our imagination, beyond our understanding, something that keeps unfurling, changing and instructing. The only peace to be fully realised in this life comes from respecting nature and acting in accordance with that. To do otherwise will cause not only disharmony, but a denial of ourselves as humankind.

Society should not reduce us to the lowest form of ourselves but raise us up to our highest form.

The current world status is demanding we go inward, to reflect, to reimagine, to reevaluate, to prioritise... It's time. It is the right time for peace, justice, humility, encouragement, education, passion, creativity and hope for a better future. This is our birthright. For all of us. When we think of the best world leaders who do we think of? Mother Teresa, Martin Luther King, Rosa Parks, the Dalai Lama. What do these people have in common? Were they passive? No. Were they submissively shrinking into themselves? No. Did they say and do nothing, so as not to cause offence? No, not one of them. They were the beacons for change. They did not accept the status quo. They demanded a better way. They were forthright in their fight against poverty, repression, violence, and injustice.

It's our turn to unite. My generation is full of hope. We are the torchbearers, and the advocates for a better way.

Let your heart speak your truth. Creativity can help us access this through freedom of expression, the ability to stand up, speak up, act, sing, dance, make music, become involved, write, paint, converse, make films, create, create, create. Do not sit in silence and think it is someone else's responsibility to make change.

When we see injustice, we need to call it for what it is. You be the change that the weeping world needs desperately. When we say 'no', mean it. Be who you were born to be, who the world needs you to be. For the sake of humanity.

A new dawn is approaching, and the power is in our hands. Let's join as one to make the world one of tolerance, inclusivity, justice, and peace. For you, for me, for everyone. Above all for the children of tomorrow.

In the words of the great artist and advocate John Lennon, 'Imagine' – that is what we need to do – to imagine all the people, sharing life in peace...

Be inspirational leaders in your own lives. Be dreamers, risk takers and action makers.

If we don't act now, humanity and the world may die.

This is our time. The time for world peace.

Thank you.

There was a pause before the clapping thundered into a standing ovation. Lily searched the front row where her mum and Paulo stood in their new outfits, crying, waving, and applauding. Behind them stood Alexa, Ricky, Norma, Gayle, and some of the other Form Six kids. There was hollering, wolf-whistling, jumping up and down. Lily was stunned. She kept saying, "Thank you, thank you all so much. Thank you..."

It was the best night of her life. She was euphoric. She, Paulo, Ricky, Norma, and Gayle went dancing at their favourite pub, The Trusty Anchor, where Genie and the Girls were weaving their spell. The place was humming – full of smoke and grunge, dark and fabulous. Even Alexa stayed for a little while. After a few cocktails shouted by the crew, Lily was electric. Her hair was as loose as her mind and body. It was as if everyone was celebrating her, and she couldn't contain her joy. They staggered home late after the pub closed, arm in arm. She slurred to Paulo, "Hey buddy, we won. We friggin' did it!"

"Never in doubt, mate." He grinned back at her. "Had your name written all over the chalice the minute you met me."

They laughed all the way home, where Lily collapsed into bed and fell into dreams of parliament and being the leader of the Pacifist Party. She was giving an impassioned speech when Bessie came bounding in far too early. Dusty and croaky, she pushed Bessie off and dragged herself out of bed.

Meredith took the next day off work. Lily leisurely strolled out of the bedroom, resplendent in her worn chartreuse dressing gown. Meredith made bacon and eggs, and the toasty smell lured hungover Lily towards the stove, wrapping her arms around Meredith as she tended the frying pan.

"Well, well, old girl, what do you think about your Lily-pad? Huh?"

"I think you're amazing, spectacular and stupendous, a passionate orator, and a provocateur, and I'm so bloody proud of you I can hardly stand it."

Lily whizzed around the kitchen.

Meredith laughed. "Also, Lily, I hope your head can still fit through our humble front door with all these accolades."

The phone rang. Meredith answered. Someone was telling her something important, and she kept nodding and saying, *Okay then, thank you very much* and *we'll have a look. Thank you for calling. Yes, she was, wasn't she? Absolutely. We are very proud of her. Yes, indeed. Thank you. Bye now.*

"Who was that? God, Mum, you sounded so formal!"

Meredith put the TV on. "It was Ms O'Flaherty. Your speech

will be broadcast tonight on the ABC, as well as on the ABC breakfast show. Now! They called Ms O'Flaherty to tell her."

They sat together on the couch, spellbound, and watched it play on the morning news. *Young Lily Mango takes the stage for peace. A force for good in the shape of a girl. Her impassioned speech spoke of injustice and amply answered the question, 'If I was the leader of the world...' Lily is the 1978 winner of the prestigious Australian English Essay Award.*

It was as if they were watching someone else – someone older, wiser, more poised and considered, whose timing in delivery was immaculate and whose green velvet dress shimmered in the spotlight. Her sparkling eyes glistened with light.

NINETY-FIVE

The day after the event of her speech, Lily hung out with Paulo. In the late morning, they walked for two hours from Spray Point lighthouse to Lavender bay, had lunch at the Beachboys Deli there and meandered back. They laughed so much that day – a processing of the incredible night before, the speech – which they felt they shared – and the TV coverage. It felt surreal, and they were the only two people who fully understood where they had come from and how far they'd reached. Even Paulo's acceptance into the dance school still seemed ridiculously implausible, given all he'd had to overcome. Lily kept any reservations she had to herself that day. The covers that Genie and the Girls had played at the pub the night before included two of Lily and Paulo's all-time favourites. As they turned the corner of the last point before Spray Point Beach they belted out *YMCA* with interspersions of dance moves, Paulo's being the best and most outrageous. He had fabulous rhythm. Lily just jumped up and down, did some unrelated twirls, missed the beat, and had timing that only she could follow. Followed by a few renditions in scratchy voices, and the whisky-sounding low notes of Supertramp's *School*. "Yeah, baby, that song was written for us. Our dreams are all coming true. Sweeeeeet!"

NINETY-SIX

Lily walked to the couch to read after dinner, and Meredith followed.

"Darling, I need to chat to you about something."

Lily looked uncomfortable. Meredith sat down, "After Dad died—" She continued, "I struggled to breathe after Frank died. He was my rock and once he was gone, part of me was too. I know I wasn't available to you – not in the way a mother should be. I feel very guilty about that, Lily."

Meredith held Lily's gaze until she looked away.

"Dad was the one to lavish you with affection and fun, I was the more serious parent. I disciplined you – not him, never. But when he left us so suddenly, I didn't know how to parent anymore. And I had to keep working – that was all the energy I had. Mum took over my role because she knew I couldn't do it."

Meredith choked up and wiped her eyes. "This has been weighing heavily on me since Nini's death, and now with the end of your year coming up and decisions you'll need to make, I need to clear the air."

Lily was playing with her fingers, and she did not look at Meredith.

"You've been so wonderful. Having lost your beautiful dad, and then losing Nini, who was more like a mother to you than a grandmother..." Meredith was sobbing now. "It hasn't been fair on you to lose so much."

"It's okay, Mum." Lily looked up and patted her mother's arm.

"No, it's not okay, Lily. I need to say how sorry I am for letting you down. You only get one mother, and unfortunately yours was absent for many years. Not anymore. I'm so sorry, darling."

Lily's face was red and blotchy, and she sniffled as she hugged Meredith. It felt as if all the hurt she had stored up came gushing out when her mother apologised. They hugged each other and their tear-streaked faces leaked onto the other's clothes. It was as if they could feel the depth of the other's sadness and, in doing so, they somehow lessened their own.

Bessie nudged the door fully open and pushed her head in between them to be patted. The three of them hugged, Bessie in the middle.

Meredith looked at Lily and said, "I'll be a better mother from now on. I promise."

Lily said, "You *are* good mum, and I'll try to be better, too."

With that, Meredith stood, wiping her hands on her skirt. "Let's eat. I'm famished."

"Yeah, me too."

NINETY-SEVEN

Nini's room always smelt of peace, rose water and lavender talc. Lily had never spent much time in there. Once Nini moved in, it was the only space she could go to with her thoughts. When she was in the rest of the house, Lily followed her and talked. Nothing pleased Nini more than to talk with Lily, but each night after dinner she'd waltz off and gently close her door.

Without Nini, their home seemed colder, smaller, and duller. One Saturday Meredith told Lily that she had to clear Nini's things, or they would linger there and be too sad for her to address. Lily was torn with this – was it too soon? But Meredith was persuasive, and focused.

"No, Lily, a lot of life is hard. But the longer you leave a sad task the more difficult it becomes," her mother told her. "You're here with me and I can face it today. In a little while, I'll be packing you off. I can't bear to think of packing darling Mum's things up then, on my own."

So, with determination in Meredith's heart and resignation in Lily's, they started. Nini's was the smallest room, at her insistence. *I don't need much space. Good heavens – for the few belongings I have, you could shove me in the broom closet.*

A tear fell down Lily's cheek as she thought of how unselfish and undemanding Nini was – not like me, she thought wryly. Nini had a photo of herself with Sis and Son, or Kevin, as was his proper name. She loved that photo. Those three were the closest in age. Both predeceased Nini by decades. She couldn't work out why she lived to such a good age; thought it was because Pa looked after her so well and she was blessed with wonderful daughters, and such a sweetie-pie as Lily for her granddaughter. Even though she lost Pa too early, she maintained a cup half-full approach to life and didn't complain. The medical history of her family was always summed up the same way: *Our blood races too high in our family.*

Meredith slumped on Nini's bed as she tried to place Nini's belongings in piles. Op shop, St Vincent de Paul's, Beatrice Hartwell (Nini's oldest friend), Lily, and herself. The roll of plastic bags was diminishing as each sad grouping was sorted. Lily perspired, even though it was not warm. Her hands shook as she opened Nini's chest of drawers, or *bureau*, as Nini called it. They were sentimental to Nini because they had belonged to her beloved older sister, Lois, or *Sis*, as she called her. When she married Pa, it was the only piece of furniture she took from her original home. Apart from their bed, it was their first piece of furniture.

Lily tentatively glanced inside the top drawer. A lavender scent wafted up from the hand-embroidered *E* on a white linen square pocket, which was nestled in amongst the white lace and floral handkerchiefs, Nini's large pink or cream underpants, sunken bras, beige singlets and a dusky pink rayon slip. Lily rubbed her neck, lifted, and dropped these personal but now irrelevant items.

"Oh God, Mum, what do we do with these?"

"Hmm, oh, those…" Meredith dragged herself up from where she was kneeling, sorting clothing on the pink eiderdown. Her fawn-coloured eyes were red-rimmed and had a greyness to them. She wore an old cardigan of Nini's. It was soft cream cashmere with pink and yellow roses for buttons, one of Nini's favourites, and as Meredith leant in Lily smelt Velvet soap and

Arpège. Nini used to say, *A little dab of French femininity never hurt a girl.*

Meredith peered over Lily's shoulder. "Hmm, no one will want the privates... Oh, I'll keep the hankies and..." She picked up the lavender sachet and breathed it in hard, placed it inside the pocket of her cardigan and patted Lily's back before she knelt to resume her sorting. She took her time with a small, rust-colored book. As she flipped through the pages, some of them adrift, with the cover coming off, she said, "Oh, *Ivanhoe* by Sir Walter Scott. Dad gave this to Mum when they were courting. *Men bless their stars and call it luxury.*"

"Doesn't make sense to me."

"No, I'm not sure... but Mum loved it."

"Nini blessed everything." Lily sniffed.

Meredith inhaled the fanning pages as if Nini's scent still lingered there. Lily watched as Meredith uncovered the brown leather wallet that had been Pa's. It had one button and, on the inside, was a worn wedding photo of him and Nini. As Meredith felt in the pockets, she took out a photo of her own wedding, and one of Lily as a baby: full cheeks, pink lips and soft blonde curls. Meredith passed the wallet and the loose photos to Lily. Its leather surface was smooth and cool, with markings that said many hands had held it. When she passed them back, Meredith placed them carefully in the keep pile.

Lily dragged the lowest drawer open, where the smell of musty neglect mingled with a mix of rose water and stale lavender. There were some neatly folded Burberry scarves inside, a couple of pastel silk scarves, green rosary beads, a tattered blue bible, a worn leather-bound book with an elastic band holding in the contents. Lily did not ask Meredith what to do with the old brown book. When her mother turned away to pull out Nini's shoes out from the base of the wardrobe, Lily took it to her room and hid it under her pillow. A gentle breeze blew through the open window, making her blind tap against the window-frame. The afternoon light left dappled shapes on her pillow and when Lily lifted it, it was warm to touch. She held the pillow to her chest momentarily and closed her eyes before putting it back on her bed and sliding the letters underneath.

Later that night, when the long day was over and the dust mites had settled in the darkening light, they had toast and tea for dinner, without conversation. It felt as if they both had so much to say that it rendered them mute. Perhaps if they started to say what they were thinking, they would unplug something they'd never be able to stop. Lily cleared the dishes, washed them quietly, and patted her mother's shoulder as she went to her bedroom. Meredith sat at the table with Nini's old cup and held it in both hands as one would a piece of Venetian glass.

Once in bed, Lily snuggled under the red satin eiderdown, curled up into a little ball, and took out the old brown book. The inscription on the inside cover was in magnificent ink cursive:

To my darling Enid,

May you write what your heart truly feels in these pages. Until my safe return.

Your loving, Alfred xx

P.S. Your photo is safely tucked away in my rucksack.

Further along in the journal, between the pages with the frayed edges, there was a worn letter, creased and frayed as if handled many times:

To My Darling Alf,
*   In the twilight of afternoon*
*   when the light fades and the memories deepen*
*   I see you.*
*   In the first kiss of light*
*   when the warmth radiates*
*   I feel you.*
*   In the setting of the sun*
*   as the sky becomes emblazoned with all it has*
*   achieved that day*
*   I think of you.*
*   You have left me; you are no longer in or of this world*
*   but you exist, nonetheless.*
*   I am yours; you are mine*
*   the boundaries are blurred*
*   Your spirit is alive, and I feel your presence.*
*   It is a great comfort to know you exist still.*
*   My love for you has not diminished.*
*   Nature reassures me that you go on.*
*   I look for you, and in the garden*
*   I find you.*
*   Go well my love.*
*   Until I meet you again,*
*   I will see you in the clouds, the garden, the sunset or the sunrise...*
*   Love,*
*   Yours forever,*
*   Enid x x*

Within the pages a sealed envelope fell out. It was marked *PRIVATE* and underneath: *To Lily Enid Mango*. The crumpled lined pages looked as though they'd been reread many times.

To my darling Lily,

The fact that you are reading this means that I've gone. I wrote this as a consolation for you in your grief. You and I have been very close for your entire life, but never more so than after your wonderful dad passed away.

Firstly, there's so much to tell you and now that you're in your final year of school or much older, it's time to tell you about my life, so in turn, you may make more sense of your own.

I grew up in a different era to yours. As the youngest child in the family, I was often left to my own devices, my parents being busy raising the family and, of course, running the sheep farm. There was an endless stream of chores for my sainted mother, Collette, and my dad, Hubert. He did the best he could but was a stern disciplinarian. A 'his way or the highway' type of father (the exact opposite of your grandpa or your dad). So, I learned early in life not to upset him and, if I did, to run to either mum, Lois or Mabel (my eldest twin sisters) for cover. I loved my father, but he was distant from me.

As my schooling progressed, which for the most part I loved, the workload of the farm increased due to my older siblings leaving home. For the boys it was a matter of going to the city looking for work, apart from Harold and Spencer, who were expected to stay on the farm. Alma, Gertrude, Lois and Mabel had one by one married early and left. Dear Mum became overworked and unwell. By the time I turned 14, she was mainly bedridden. Now, in those days, illnesses could be vague, so whether she had depression, uncontrolled high blood pressure or another illness,

I don't know. And Dad being a proud and private man did not discuss the specifics with anyone in the family. After a regular visit from old Dr Thornbury, he told Dad to tell us to say goodbye to our mother.

It was a Thursday morning when Dad came to me. "Enid, go and say goodbye to your mother," he said firmly. I told my mother how much I loved her and begged her not to die. I held her little hand as she gave mine a weak squeeze. I kissed her goodbye and felt tears on her pale sunken cheek. I went to school that day and when I came home, Mum's sisters were in groups, weeping with my siblings. I ran to my parents' room, but the bed was empty. The undertaker had been, and she was gone. The shock of losing my mother was profound.

Soon after, my father determined he could not cope with the domestic work as well as the farm, so I was told to leave school. All my hopes and dreams were shattered with that decision. I did as I was told, however the bitter disappointment and unfairness of it seared a hole in my heart. The only person who unconditionally loved and protected me was gone. My sisters, as kind as some of them were, had their own lives to live. My brothers, who showed no outward emotion, drank more and left the farm for nights out in town whenever possible. I was left to cope alone, which made me withdraw. I promised myself that once I turned 18, I'd leave. Which is exactly what I did. I wrote Dad a letter. On the day after my birthday, I took my scant belongings, some money I had saved from the last four years, and I caught the 962 bus to the city.

I met your wonderful Pa, Alfred, at the cafe that I worked in. He had such a lovely smile, and his eyes were a translucent blue with honey-coloured rings. When he spoke to me, I'd get lost in his eyes, to the point that he'd ask me a question and I'd have no idea what he'd said. Your Pa was a character. He was charismatic, funny, witty, kind, loyal and generous. We married six months after we met. Meredith was born in the first year, followed by Jennifer and, lastly, Stephen. I was 19 years old when Meredith was born, 20 years old when Jennifer was born, and 22 years old with Stephen.

Stephen, as you know, was a very unwell child. We had many times racing to the hospital in the night when he would inexplicably stop breathing. He did not thrive as a baby should. He struggled to put on weight, he cried incessantly, and his limbs remained soft and underdeveloped. This was a strain on the family. Alfred's family were interstate, and expected that Alfred was a married man now and his problems were his own. Meredith was extremely kind to Jennifer, always doting on her and mothering her. I, on the other hand, was struggling to juggle all the doctors' appointments, the anguish of Stephen's illness and maintaining a happy home. Meanwhile, Alfred was working three jobs to pay for all the medical costs that kept mounting up. As you know, Stephen passed away suddenly at 10. No doctor had given us a specific diagnosis, but neither had they told us Stephen could die this young. Yes, they did say he may not "make old bones", but our family was totally shocked and utterly devastated when he passed away.

I tell you these difficult truths because I know at times you find Meredith distant and unaffectionate. I blame myself for this. I was distant from her, for the entire journey of Stephen's difficult life. Alfred was a soft, loving father, but he was exhausted. Exhausted from his work, and when he did come home, the work did not stop. Meredith would take Jennifer and keep out of the way. They literally looked after themselves, which of course is not possible for young children. Once darling Stephen had gone to God, I became depressed. No one diagnosed this, I just know now looking back that I would drag myself out of bed, get the girls to school, and return home to close the blinds and stay in bed until it was time to collect them. This went on for years. Eventually, Alf intervened. He insisted I tell the doctor how I was feeling, and how I was spending my days, and this is when I got the help I needed. But it was five years after Stephen had died, and for Meredith and Jennifer it meant that, for most of their teenage years, their mother was not able to care for them properly.

When I first met your dad, I knew he was the man for Meredith. I said to Alf, "There's only one man on earth who can be Meredith's love, and it's Frank Mango." It pains me to say that once Jennifer moved to Tasmania and found her partner, she and Meredith grew apart. Which is a source of deep sadness to me. There are always two sides to every story, we all struggle in our own ways, and we must forgive. Try to forgive in life. Disappointment is a part of life, and we're always disappointing ourselves or somebody else, but if we don't forgive, the only person who truly suffers is ourselves. When you forgive, you lighten your heart. I learnt this the hard way because it took me years to forgive God for taking Stephen. That was another reason I was depressed for so long.

So, I want you to open your heart to dearest Meredith. Life has not provided her with an easy ride. Yes, she may be aloof at times, but she has a reservoir of love and courage that I'm in awe of. Her love for you, Lily, is boundless. The day you were born was the happiest day of her life. She is captivated by you, and she only wants to protect and guide you. Her fear that something could happen to you at times interferes with the immense joy she has, because you are her magnificent daughter. Never doubt her love or her pride in you Lily-pily. No mother could love a daughter more.

Tell yourself the truth, no matter how bad it may be. Then, if you can't change it, accept it. Once you've processed the facts and accepted them, allow yourself to heal. Listen, in the quiet times, to your soul. Your brain will want to get you racing in myriad directions, sometimes all at once. But that is not where the peace lies. Peace lies when you listen to your heart. I've always loved nature for this, as I know you do. Also, God has stayed my constant. I hope you have faith in your life; it makes life easier to bear in the dark times.

Now, lastly, I want you to dream big. Chase the rainbows of your mind. Just because things are a certain way, doesn't mean they have to stay that way. If something is wrong, right it. If you need to change things, do so – even if it's only your attitude. Accept what you can't alter. Be considerate, kind and supportive, firstly to yourself, and then to others. The sky is the limit for you. Dream, plan, and go for your hopes and ambitions. What have you got to lose? If it doesn't turn out the way you'd hoped, you will have learnt from the experience. Honour what you've been given, be grateful, be humble and true to yourself. Don't harbour resentments nor regrets as they don't serve us. Appreciate your uniqueness; not because it makes you better or superior, but because it makes you YOU.

Always know I love you with all my heart. Being your Nini has been one of the greatest privileges and blessings of my life. You have brought me endless love, joy and fascination.

God bless you Lily-pily and until we meet again,
Your loving,
Nini x x
P.S. Please pray for me.
P.S.S. I'll be watching over you little one.

Lily sat at her desk and let the words soak in. *Until we meet again* kept playing over and over in her mind. Could she really allow herself to hope that one day she would meet Nini again? That would mean she could also be with her dad again. She sat and watched the branches of the agonis sway gently and the leaves twitch. She thought she saw a flash of red, then a splash of blue, and then lime green and yellow, until the rosella came out from the depths of the foliage and hopped along the branch nearest Lily. She watched as it played amongst the leaves, the wind dying down, until it was gone.

Lily was glad he was there. "I need to ask you something" spilled out as she shoved her books into her locker.

Paulo held one textbook aloft as if it smelled.

"If you could have anything, what would you have?"

"Done last night's homework," he quipped.

"You're bloody slack. No, really."

"You're friggin' exhausting. Why do you have to know so much crap?" He breathed out hard and ran his free hand through his hair.

"I dunno." Lily kept staring at him.

"Oh, okay, I wanna be a dancer. That's it. Nothing else." He turned his back to her when the siren blared and called back without looking, "Oh, and the most important thing – for you to shut up and stop asking me questions."

"Never going to happen," she called back.

He stuck up the rude V sign and kept walking.

Lily pondered whether she could met her dad and Nini ever again. She had a headache from too much thinking.

If her dad and Nini were alive, then everything would be good. But they weren't. And it wasn't good.

The school days were getting longer. The next day, sitting next to Paulo at lunch, Lily said, "Where has Nini gone? She filled my life – how could she just not exist? I feel so angry that she's gone." She made fists with her pale fingers and punched her thighs.

"I'm sorry, buddy. Nini was my Nana, too. I mean like one

that cared --"

"Yeah, I know. But to lose Dad and then Nini. It's shit. It's friggin' cruel. I... " Lily couldn't speak, and Paulo patted her knee with his hand.

"At least you've got me."

'I haven't got you for long.' She walked off.

After school the following day, as they were wading through the shallows, Lily asked him, "Do you feel better at the beach?" Without waiting for his answer she continued, "Like the ground can collapse beneath your feet, the earth can stop spinning, but the waves keep coming. The sunrise happens and the sunset comes, night follows day, and it goes on and on. The beach tells me that I'm only one insignificant person who doesn't stop the tide, the waves, the sunrise, the day, the night... I'm just living one small life and no matter how bad that life is, the waves keep coming. Like when Dad died and now Nini. You can't believe that normal life goes on when your whole world has stopped." She kicked her feet through the water. "Nothing makes sense."

Lily was navigating the sand between clumps of kelp – velvet swaying sheaths of tan, rust, taupe and gold. Paulo paddled out further. Lily held closer to the shore.

"Where are they?" she implored him. After a moment, "I need to know. Please say something. *Anything.*"

Paulo turned to her. "I dunno." His furrowed face looked at her solemnly. "Maybe they're nothing. Like the wind. I don't know. But I reckon they'd be peaceful, wherever they are." He stopped. "Sorry, buddy, I just don't believe in all that afterlife shit."

Lily nodded as if to say she understood. "Yeah, I don't know what I believe anymore." She headed towards the shore and called back, "I'm going for a walk. I'll catch you later."

"You, okay? Want me to come?"

"Nah, thanks anyway." She saw the faintest silver streaks of light coming through the sea mist. Her back cast a sorrowful shadow.

"See you tomorrow," he called after her.

She waved behind her but didn't call back.

NINETY-NINE

The golden glow of morning made Bessie a black silhouette. The peachy sky was expansive until a clump of dirty clouds hung on the cliffs like a bad haircut. Lily's prickling cheeks ached as she turned towards home. Here, the sky had softened to a glimmer, the softest hue of blue as the day began.

As the grey gulls screeched above, Bessie ran ahead and was lost to the birds, the brisk wind and the pewter water. Her zest for life made Lily feel sad and inadequate. *Oh, Bessie you're so free.* Her stomach tightened as if a distant storm had gathered and was steadily grumbling into view.

The last exam loomed, and she was ready. Ready for this task, but not ready for the year and all her schooling to be over. Not that she enjoyed being there, but there was a rhythm to it, a predictability. Her mind meandered and circled back to what would take its place. A place without Nini; a place without Paulo.

The sickness she felt was stronger when she thought of the time after the exam rather than during it. She'd spent hours hunched over her desk, her books, her notes. She had quotes and slabs of printed work Blu-tacked on her walls. As each exam came, she felt prepared. She knew she could always do better, but she also knew she had tried as hard as she could. This attitude had been the same with her dad, Nini, and now Meredith: *Just try your best*, with no additional pressure. But it was the thought of '*what next*' that sent a wave of terror through her.

Lily headed home in the softest light. A lonely figure with her head downcast and her arms tightly crossed.

ONE HUNDRED

If anyone walked behind them, they would think they were two young lovers leaning into each other against the biting Southern Ocean blast. They were not to know that these two had never been, nor would ever be, lovers in the traditional sense. And yet, for the most part, they had become inseparable. There was no one else either of them preferred to be with. Lily put her arm around Paulo as one would a younger sibling, even though he was so much bigger than her.

They passed Meredith's old home. It struck her that it wore its verandah as a girl wears her make up, enough to be interesting and enhanced, but not overwhelming. The draping bougainvillea, with its bold flash of colour, reminded her of a dancer's purple feather boa. Without the now flaking paint, and the rusty guttering, it still had some charm and a certain warmth. Their current home sufficed but, as Lily knew, their situation over the years had been somewhat reduced.

After dinner that night, Meredith knocked on Lily's door and came and sat on her bed. Lily stopped reading her novel and looked at her mother.

"As painful as it is for me to think of you leaving, Lily, you must live your own life." Meredith patted her leg. The last words were barely audible and coupled with one silent tear. Lily took her mother's hand. She wanted to speak but no words came.

The next afternoon, the wind whipped up to howling. Lily sat beside Paulo, protected inside the hidden dune, with her arms wrapped around her knees. She thought of her mother's words the night before, the sad little smile that flitted across

Meredith's face after she spoke, but mostly Lily remembered the way it made her feel. She heard the whistling wind flying across the scrub above their dune and she closed her eyes.

She took Meredith's lead and spoke while she had the courage to do so.

"As much as my insides feel like they've been ripped out, I know you have to live your own life," she said to Paulo. She stumbled on the last couple of words, just as Meredith had.

Paulo craned his neck to get a closer view of her face and to hear her properly. After a while, he quietly said, "Thanks, and so do you, buddy." In that moment, his chocolate eyes were melting.

"Yeah, that's what Meredith told me last night. It was weird, 'cause she hardly ever comes into my room, so I knew it must be important." Lily hugged herself tighter and Paulo kept Bessie close, snuggled in under his arm. "It's hard to think, if I go, she'll have no one."

"Bessie's not no one." Paulo patted the dog adoringly.

"You know what I mean."

"Yeah, and you're the one who told me that I had to go, and that Ronaldo needed to look after himself."

"Yeah, but it's not the same..."

"It *is* the same. I'm all he's got. I'm going interstate. You might just go to Melbourne and that's only four hours away."

"Yeah. Maybe. I don't know. I can't see myself ever leaving here. When I was young, I wanted to do so many things, and go everywhere, but now I'm just too scared to leave."

"Scared? You? Who are you kidding? You're the one who took on the deadshits and stuck up for me, told a few teachers where to go, and now you're the *head of the bloody school*!"

"Yeah, but this is way harder."

"Nup, you're no coward." Paulo leaned his should against hers. "Besides, if *I* can go, *you* can go."

Lily looked away from him, rubbing her eyes. She looked along the deserted beach. At the Point, she saw the old lighthouse, still standing after all the storms it had endured over the decades. They sat for a while longer, until the wind seemed to lose some of its ferocity.

"Thanks. I needed that," she said to her best friend as she stood to leave.

Nini had told her many times, *Knowing something is not the same as accepting or believing something. First, you need to know it, believe it, and then it takes time to accept it.* Sometimes, like when Nini lost her Alfred, it took years.

Lily tried to accept what was inevitable but found she couldn't. She was told to think of her study preferences for next year. She vaguely considered teaching, or writing, or acting, because she loved reading and writing, but could think of nothing concrete. Her focus kept going to the calendar and the days slipping away towards *doomsday*. Most nights, she dreamt of a rogue wave gathering force, swimming towards the shore and not making any ground, her panic rising with the noise coming at her. Then, she was awake, wet with perspiration, thinking, *Thank God that was only a dream*. Until, lying there in the blackness, she would remember, *No, it's real*. Her dreams darkened again. Sometimes in the dream she was floating, lost at sea, or running slowly in a race where everyone was passing her by, or wandering around directionless, not knowing where she should be.

There seemed to be a well that she'd fallen into, and there was no one with which to share her anxious feelings of dread. Nini was gone, Meredith was sad, and Paulo – the one person she could always rely on – was now the cause of her distress. *How could she possibly burden him with her sorrow at his leaving when it was his one chance to live his absolute dream? The dream that he'd held silently for years, the dream that could lead him to live an amazing life. No way would she let him know. She'd try to live a lie for the next couple of weeks. She'd try.*

The happier and more hopeful he became, the more miserable and frightened she got. They were the light and dark of each other's hearts. Her fear seemed heavier than usual because she had to keep it to herself.

At lunchtime on Monday, Paulo was away, so Lily sat with Alexa.

"How's the study?" Lily asked her.

"Friggin' nightmare. You?"

"It's okay. Bloody constant and can't wait for it to be over. Then, freedom..."

"Do you reckon?" Alexa scrunched her half-eaten lunch back into her bag and said, "Antonio told me that Dad's promise of a car if I do well is not for me."

"What? How can it not be for *you*?"

"He said that Dad told him it was for me to drive Mum everywhere."

"But you'll be in the city! You won't be here all the time, so that can't work."

"You don't know my dad. If he decides something, nothing and no one can make him change his mind."

"God, that's so unfair." Lily tried to imagine her dad not wanting her to study and do whatever she wanted to do. She couldn't. "Like, how will you go to uni?"

"Don't worry, I'm running away. As soon as the last exam is over. Antonio said he'll help me find somewhere at one of his friends to stay. They can stick their friggin' car. I don't want it." Alexa looked so angry, and sad. She bit her lip and a trickle of bloody oozed out like jam squeezed from a donut. Her hands kept twisting around each other. "What about you? What're your plans?"

"I'm not sure. I feel bad. Mum's on her own now. Paulo's going. It's so messed up. I think I'll just stay at Spray Point and see what happens." Lily frowned, and her eyes clouded over. The day suddenly lost its warmth.

"*What*? *You*? Are you nuts? Stay in this shithole? Nothing ever happens here. You know everyone. There's nothing to do. Don't do it! Holy crap, that is *messed up*." Alexa grabbed two fistfuls of hair and turned them like taps. "I'm running away to escape and you're locking yourself in." Alexa ran off as if the thought might be contagious.

Lily thought of earlier in the year when she had watched *Prisoner* while Meredith was out and Nini was in bed. One of the inmates spoke of longing for freedom. Lynne Hamilton's song *He Used to Give Me Roses* floated through her mind.

The bell boomed and the crowd funneled back into their classes.

They sat on their rock like two old sea wrens. Arms wrapped around themselves for warmth, they looked out to the horizon. As they sat, they saw a sliver of sunlight, a silver line on the horizon. Lily broke the stillness.

"You know, I can't think of you leaving. It's so painful that I have to think of something else."

"Buddy, it's not going to be that bad." He turned his attention to the side of her face, the wind flicking blonde strands across her cheeks.

"You won't come back," she said with certainty.

"You don't know that. I don't even know that yet."

"In my heart I do know it. You'll love it. Everything about it'll be what you're looking for. It's a brand-new scene. You can be yourself. The excitement and lure of anonymity. No small-town whispers and no one trying to drag you down. New friends." She was examining her Adidas like a surgeon might concentrate on a complicated operation. "You won't need boring old me anymore," she whispered and turned her head away from him.

Paulo put his arm around her and, after a while, said, "Hey hey, you and I are the best. Good, bad, broken." He paused and breathed out. "I know how you've struggled with losing your dad, but kind of losing your mum, too. Then to lose Nini. And because I know stuff about you, you made it okay for me to say how I really felt about losing Mum." He choked on these words and Lily turned to face him. "And the old man, too. I trusted you and my life got better. I don't know what would've happened to me if I didn't meet you."

He breathed out hard.

"There's a few more things I haven't told you," Paulo continued. "I've read all Mum's letters now, some over and over, but there's one… It was written just before the old boy gave me the bundle." Paulo looked way out beyond the breakers where the ocean meets the sky. "In it, she said, *You've gotta follow your dreams and what's in your heart.* She said, *If you don't, your soul withers and dies.* I couldn't get that line out of my head. That's when I knew I had to go for my dancing. Ronaldo was never going to get it. That's probably half the reason she left him. He didn't want her to be in the band anymore. When I spoke with her, I told her about that line, and she explained that she had to be her, and I had to be me. And it takes courage."

"That makes sense. You're an artist just like your mum." Lily understood why Paulo went for the dancing scholarship. "And you're brave. I used to be brave. But that was before Dad, Nini, Meredith, and all the crap at school. I want to go back to the old me. The old me was better."

"Listen, I leaned on you for the whole of school. It's time for you to lean on me. I owe you. Big time."

She smiled for the first time, and he continued, "There hasn't been one day that I haven't thanked the stars that you're my friend."

"Really?" Lily asked with an incredulous look.

"Okay, maybe a few days," he teased. "I know you're going to be okay, and so am I. We're mates, and it doesn't matter where we live, or who we hang out with, or what we do, we'll always have each other's backs. I promise."

Paulo lifted his left pinkie finger and she intertwined hers with his. The light sky held layers of clouds like streaky paint, and the steel grey was on its way from Wallawee.

"Yeah, you're right. We've been through a lot of shit together, why not get through a bit more?"

"You bet. Together we're inde-bloody-structable!"

"Sure are, mate."

They started the trek back home as streaks of light hit the water in a dazzling silver show.

Lily thought, *Except, this time, we're not together. Recently, I haven't been past Wallawee, and you're going to Sydney.* She struggled to even imagine the mystery of it. It glistened like gold for him with every comment he made about his future. There was an aliveness to him lately that she'd never seen before. It was as if he was awakening, like a bear coming out of a long hibernation, ready to attack whatever came his way.

They strolled towards the avenue of Norfolk pines where the whirring wind vibrated between the nettles. The eerie sound pushed against their backs as if it were hastening their descent to the beach. Paulo was hunched over in his black hoodie, with his arms and upper body folded into himself. Lily yelled against the competing wind; her head stooped to hear. Although this was one of their favourite treks, today felt different. Lily savoured the sharp sea smell, and the pinpricks reddened her cheeks as she strode to leave the looming shadow of the pines. Her gait slowed, Paulo reminding her again, *What's the rush?* The crunch of their runners on the tideline mixed with the dampness and filled their senses. *Polly* and *Pie,* the pelicans, snuggled their noses into their feathers for shelter on the idle, creaking pier. Random dogs bolted past, chasing seagulls, as the curving path to the Point came clearly into view.

On the return journey, the sky was lighter, and the water shimmered a radiant cobolt as the wind died out. Lily's eyes reflected the colour of the bay. Two deep, enquiring pools.

The birdsong was sweet, interspersed with the sound of gentle lapping. Lily's eyes stayed on the red tanker travelling steadily towards the Point. It was not an uncomfortable silence, but a silence that says, *I can't talk yet, because I don't know how to put what I feel into words.*

"Hey, you alright, buddy?" Paulo asked.

Lily dismissed him. "Yeah, I'm just lost in my own thoughts today. I'm good." She cast her eyes to the horizon with her head turned away from his.

"Really? You annoyed with me?"

She looked at him. "Nuh, mate, nothing to do with you." Her red eyes stood out in her pale face. "I just feel bloody sad."

"I'm sorry. I feel it too." He lent his head towards hers as they walked. "But we're gunna be okay." He smiled faintly; she didn't smile back.

"But *you're* the one who's leaving. *I'm* not. I mean, I will leave, eventually but not soon. Every day I hang out with you. What am I gunna do for summer? I'm much more concerned about me than you." She turned and pushed away the tears with her palms. "What a *shit* friend I am."

Paulo slung his arm loosely across her shoulder. "Nah, you're not. You're my bestie. And I promise it's gunna be okay."

"I want to believe you. I just can't yet." Lily wrapped her arms around her chest and as they wandered back to Nancy's café, where Paulo brought coffees, an apple scroll, they sat outside in the sun.

"I'm gunna miss this."

"Me too," he said as he broke the scroll in half – well, nearly half.

"Oh well, you better get a joint with a spare bedroom, or I'll just come up, crash on your couch and cramp your style!"

The squawking pelicans took flight and the seagulls hovered and snapped at each other in anticipation of some easy food. The constant lapping, odd dogs barking, The Wallawee bus crunching through its gears and the hum of traffic filled the air. Some children ran to the water's edge as their mother called to them not to get wet. A passing bus tooted hello to the other and they drove lazily through their afternoon.

There was nothing special about this scene, this day, and yet it felt monumental. In Lily's mind, it was catastrophic. Was Paulo putting on a brave face? Lily wasn't sure if he really believed it would be okay between them, or whether the prospect of dancing was so thrilling that he couldn't waste time being sad. *But what is waiting for me?* she thought. *I'm lost.*

These thoughts kept running through her mind – mostly at night, but recently in the daytime, too. Every day was one day closer to Paulo leaving. Her head throbbed and, in her heart, was a solid boulder. Even her words got stuck and she couldn't speak.

It was the last time they walked and chatted that way. This time, the way life had been, was over. As they separated at the corner of Tea Tree Road and Southern Ocean Road, where for years they had met before walking to school or parted before heading to their respective houses, Paulo patted Lily on the back. "I'll call you tomorrow, buddy."

"Yeah, mate. Sure thing," Lily called back over her shoulder as she headed for home. She did not look back.

Paulo stood and watched until she was out of view.

Lily kept her head low as she sobbed the whole way home. She sat on the back swing as Bessie snuggled in. She reached down and picked up the discarded, well-chewed tennis ball. Each time she threw it, Bessie would run, salivating and waving her feathery tail, as Lily tried to coach her to drop the ball at her feet. Lily thought about how Bessie loved to play, but the security of the ball was hard for her to give up, even though it wasn't possible to have both.

She thought of Paulo, and how strong he seemed through all this change. She wandered inside to the empty house.

"My fine friend, I have an idea! Tonight, we celebrate – beach style – and forget everything."

Rolling Stones' *Dance Little Sister* was playing on the stereo, and Paulo burst into song and moved about the room, his arms swirling and his head swaying, singing, clapping his hands, and gyrating his hips like Mick Jagger. "And tonight, you shall not sit it out; you, my finest buddy, shall dance!"

"I'm your woman." Lily laughed. "After dinner, I'll grab you, and we're off to the beach. All supplies provided by *moi* – nothing but the best Chateau cardboard, compliments of Meredith. Chips, Twisties and even the rock-box. You're responsible for the tapes. Let them be loud, let them be wild, let them run long into the wee hours..."

"See you at eight. I'm off to arrange music extrordinaire! You better be ready for some heavy-duty *rock and roll*!" Paulo pumped the air, did some outlandish swirls, and dangled his thick tangle of hair down in front of his face, playing his air guitar as if his life depended on it.

At eight on the dot, Lily was there with her laden school bag, an old tartan rug around her shoulders and the promised rock-box in her other hand. Impatiently, she walked around to the back of the house. There was Paulo with a dozen tapes strewn over the kitchen table. He was marking each one. He had even ordered their sequence, as if he was running an event. She laughed and said, "Hurry up, mate, or it'll be tomorrow already."

They staggered down to the quietest corner near the Point. There was a soft breeze, and the full moon did not disappoint.

It was phenomenally large, milky yellow, with a haze around its orbit. The light shone straight across the water to where they set up camp. Lily even brought candles and matches. Once their little section of the earth had been prepared, bowls of chips laid out, the music gently started up. Carol King's *So Far Away* set the mood. Generous drinks were poured from the cask's ample bladder. They sat cross-legged on the rug and began to chat.

"Alexa said if she can escape, she'll come," Paulo said.

"Huh! Doubt it. Her old dears are on the warpath. They haven't let her leave her room since her last report."

"True. Poor bugger." Paulo took a large slurp.

"Wish Mot was here." Lily's glasses looked golden with the candle lights.

"Yeah, miss him. Never thought he'd be a candidate for the navy. But I guess he didn't have much choice."

"I was going to ask Ricky, Norma and Gayle, but I ran out of time. We celebrate *for* them. For them, *and* for us.'

Jim Croche's mellow strains in *Operator* floated over the evening tide as the conversation deepened. There was nowhere to go, no one watching them, no one listening in. The hours drifted by, the cassettes changed, the tempo increased, they ate, they drank, they laughed until they cried. James Taylor; Stevie Nicks; Fleetwood Mac; The Beatles; Diana Ross; Crosby, Stills, Nash and Young... A cavalcade of the best. It was as if the world was spinning just for the two of them. Where they would get off, nobody knows – and for this, their farewell night, they didn't care.

Paulo put Supertramp's *School* on the rock-box and that's when the dancing began. Followed in quick succession by *Bloody Well Right*. "*Right, quite right, you're bloody well right, you've got a bloody right to say...*" Paulo sang. He was a fluid, bronze

Adonis in the moonlight, his body mirroring the music, eyes closed, head rolling, body swaying, As the tempo went up, so did his gyrations. Electrifying. He reached out his hand and spun Lily up. She lost herself in Paulo's trance. Tape after tape, The Rolling Stones, Supertramp, Joan Armatrading, Led Zeppelin's *Stairway to Heaven* found them, locked arms around each other, swaying and singing every word to the invisible crowd, to the ocean, to the sky, to the moon, to the universe. She'd never danced like that. Her body was free, and she was the beat. Paulo was a wild animal, melding and expanding into the music. Every word, every lyric, written for them, for this night, for everything they had gone through and for whatever lay in their untold futures. Supertramp's *Dreamer* – they spun and sang as the sand shot stars around them and anything seemed possible. As if as they moved, they felt lighter, and lighter.

Queen's *Killer Queen* had Paulo full-throttle singing to Lily, down on one knee, until she pushed him over and he kept the tempo as an upturned bottle, strumming his air guitar ferociously to the swooning audience in the deep black sea. Diana Ross's *I'm Coming Out* made them euphoric, wild, Paulo owning the song and the moment. *Ain't No Mountain High Enough* was played on repeat. Their stomping made tiny dunes in the sand, and the sand-spray looked like electric shots sparking from their feet.

Exhausted and exhilarated, Paulo started to pull off his clothes and dash for the sea.

Lily was yelling at him – "Oh no! God! I don't want to see anything of yours!" – all the while hurling off her clothes and chasing him in.

"That makes two of us!" he yelled as he leapt into the water.

They laughed, fell over, and sprayed water on each other;

squealed, swam and floated like starfish. The dazzling navy of the water enveloped and embraced their lithe bodies as they went out deeper and deeper. The twinkling diamonds above set against the blackest velvet blanket. As they headed back, the shoreline looked small, far away, as if it wasn't real.

"It felt like we were two little starfish floating off into the unknown," Lily said, gliding towards the shallows.

"Yeah. I feel a bit like an unknowable jellyfish, or a monk fish."

"Why?"

"No reason. It just came out of my mouth. Nothing I say makes sense."

With that, they were hysterical, howling until they were swallowing water. They left their liquid cocoon to gather their strewn belongings and dress hurriedly on the damp shore. The darkness lifted as the sun's brilliant orange rim peeped over the hazy horizon.

The sun was going down on their last full day together. At every step, every reed and clump of pampas grass felt significant, as if they would never see them this way again. Their hearts were heavy, but also full. The feeling from their beach night lingered. It was time to leave their sanctuary post. Forever.

Lily recounted their first walk and how they'd become lost in the sandy scrub for hours, in the heat, with no water, and how wildly exciting and yet terrifyingly suffocating that whole experience had been. Because they were new friends, they didn't want to totally lose their cool – although Lily's swearing and constant complaining had, admittedly, given her away. And during what could have been a complete disaster, they laughed. And in their laughter, they knew they were two of a kind.

When they eventually found themselves back on the beach, they could see the shimmering, majestic Durga Rock, aloof, just out from the reef. It beckoned them. It became their spot. Many walks took them there, across the jagged edges and the steep slope, to the big sky and wild sea, to witness their thoughts, failures, hopes and dreams.

Tell it to the wind, the sky, and the sea; they won't let you down. You'll never know how it pains me not to be with you. But if you talk as if I'm there, you'll feel better. I know I do.

Paulo told Lily that his mother wrote that to him in one of the letters his dad gave him. He focused on those words whenever he felt down. He pretended his mother was with him, loving and protecting him.

"I know it's a strange thing to say, but once I had you in my camp, I didn't miss having Mum as much. I mean, it's been hard not having her, with the old man being so vacant, but I knew you'd take my side. That's what I needed." He had tears running down both cheeks, which he wiped with the back of his hands. "Not that you were always the best listener... but thanks. It's meant a lot."

Lily held his gaze and rested her hand on his shoulder. "Yeah, me too mate. Thanks."

She stood up to leave. "And now, you bloody selfish bastard, you're going to jet set off to sensational Sydney and leave me all on my little lonesome."

"Nup. I'm not worried about you. You're gunna do great. You've got uni in Melbourne –

a whole new scene. You'll make new friends. Me, on the other hand, I hardly know how to introduce myself. So, I'll just pretend I'm you, and amble up to some stranger and say, *Hi, I'm Paulo. How're you doing?*"

She pushed him, "Okay. I was a dork, still am. But you can't say I didn't teach you everything I knew!"

"You taught me more than I ever needed to know." He smirked. "And a few things I never wanted to know."

They laughed and told stories of their awkward school times and how the other would step in, get the teacher's attention, lie for them, be pretend boyfriend and girlfriend, fake an illness to move the attention away from the other one, chat to Meredith or Ronaldo to ease the tension.

The heat wave had left the gardens and the nature strips scarified. They met at the beach. When it was time to go, Lily stood up, hands holding her hair off her neck, and walked away.

Paulo knew better than to follow. "Love ya, buddy," he yelled into the wind.

In the distance, Lily's back was hunched, and she had tied her hair into an unruly bun. Her head thrust forward, leaving only her collapsing hairdo to wave goodbye. He got up and trudged home.

There was only four weeks between him receiving his letter of acceptance and arranging all he had to do. Lily thought Ronaldo was useless. Every time Paulo needed something to take with him to Sydney, she'd tell Paulo to ask Ronaldo to buy it in Wallawee on his way home from the railway.

"Did he buy the jocks and toiletry bag?" Lily asked.

Paulo shook his head. "Nuh, he forgot."

"Shit. I'll ask Meredith to get them for you on her way back from work."

"Nup. It's personal stuff. I'll buy it up there or maybe Mum will offer if I tell her I'm a bit light on."

"Yeah, good one."

Lily thought, *Why not be like* her *mum and just do what needed doing, help him with all the paperwork, loose ends, pack what he needed, and then offer to follow up with a trailer load once he'd found his digs? But, no, his dad just sat there watching TV and had a few 'quiet' beers. Really? Stoic resignation, with no fanfare for his son's departure – and no help.*

The nights that Lily and Paulo had together before he left

gave him the chance to break down how he felt about seeing his mum.

"I'm still angry with her for leaving, but I know she was on the edge of a nervous breakdown when she left. That she never expected to lose me."

"That's so bloody sad. Shit, I feel sorry for Valerie."

"Yeah, it was sad alright. I never thought about it being sad for her, cause the old man let me believe she didn't care about me. Anyway, now she lives with an old musician called Jem." Paulo showed Lily a photo of them – Valerie and a hairy guy with a Labrador named P-boy – and told her they had a shack on the New South Wales coast just above Sydney. "Not sure if it's a step up from the old boy or a step down, but I'll get to know, sooner or later, I guess,' he said as he put the photo back in his wallet.

She hoped Sydney could be an opportunity for Paulo to get closer to Valerie. Ronaldo accepted Paulo's move but never spoke about it. Although, after he knew he was leaving, Ronaldo started to shrink. Even in his car, he seemed closer to the wheel.

Lily helped Paulo pack. Sorted through the gear to follow later – for when he had his own place. Valerie said he could stay with them to begin with, and that she'd try to help him find somewhere closer to the Academy. He seemed to have softened to the idea.

On a Saturday morning, Lily drove her old Datsun to Paulo's place. He was running late, and his room looked as if someone had broken in and thrown all the neat piles she'd created the night before up into the air.

After some stern rebukes, Lily reorganised his stuff to into an adequately packed bag for the car trip. "Thank God I'm a control freak and got here early! Jesus, mate, you've taken it to the wire today."

"Shit, buddy, sorry. After you left, I stayed up drinking with the old man. He spoke more to me last night than he has since Mum left. He probably won't speak to me for the next nine years to make up for it!"

Ronaldo came out of his house and shuffled towards the side of the car where Paulo stood. He held out his gnarly hand and when Paulo took it, he placed his other hand on top. He whispered something to his son and stepped back, nodding his head. But Paulo lent in, forcing his dad into a hug, and his old man hugged him in return and patted his back.

Lily jumped into the driver's seat, tooted the horn, and leap-frogged the car into the main street as Paulo leaned out of the passenger window, yelling, "Bye Dad. I'll call you when I'm there". His dad stood motionless, waved once and followed them with his gaze.

"Good old Ray. Geez, the poor bastard looked sad. I think I detected a little tear, too, as he waved farewell to you."

"Yeah, I know. When he hugged me, I could feel his bony chest and I started to well up too. That's big for him today. As he says, *Never show your emotions in public*, and I say, '*Shit, Ray, you don't even show emotions in private*.' I'll ring the poor old bugger when I'm there. It's sad leaving him, it was sad for him too – huh, I never thought I'd say that."

"That's for friggin' sure." Lily laughed.

Paulo didn't. They swung around a corner too fast, and he gripped the dashboard. "Shit, if we make it to the train in one piece, I'm gunna become a good letter-writer. Even to you, Lily-guts. No, no – *shit* – *especially* to you."

She swerved to miss a cyclist who pulled out without warning, and the car behind blasted her. "Shut up, dickhead." She gave the guy her rude 'v' sign.

As Paulo fossicked in his backpack, Lily tried to concentrate on the gathering traffic. "You *better* write to me. I'm the one suffering here. You get to do all this cool stuff, and become a friggin' rockstar dancer, and I'm at boring old home doing the same old boring shit."

"I will. Deal." He put up his pinky finger to seal the promise, she looked at him as she did the same, drifting slightly into the other lane. The next blasting horn told her so.

Lily swung into the car park too fast, and all the gear on the back seat fell forward.

Once the car had stopped, Paulo asked her, "Hey, two promises? Just try to keep alive while I'm gone." He got out of the car and grabbed his gear. "And no more 'poor-me' bullshit. You'll go to uni like you always planned and life's gunna be great for you too."

Without waiting for her to reply, he strode ahead. Lily kept her sunglasses on. She hurried to catch him. "Who am I gunna dump my problems on, and laugh my guts out with?"

"Dunno. You'll find someone unsuspecting." When he walked to the counter and bought his ticket, she locked his bags properly. They walked together like a young couple setting off on a holiday.

"Let's go!" He said, waving his ticket as if he'd won the lottery.

"I'm a selfish shit. I am happy for you. I don't know why I'm crying..."

At the platform, the Aurora was waiting. An announcement blared over the speakers. It would be departing in ten minutes. Lily heard a train rattling by on another line. She thought of her dad working in the railway office.

They stood at Paulo's carriage.

"At least I got you here on time," she said.

"Yeah, thanks for driving me. God knows Ronaldo couldn't." He put his hand in his top pocket and took out a small envelope.

More announcements came over the speakers for trains on nearby platforms. Rubbish gathered under the seats lifted and spun as one sped by on the opposite line.

"This is for you. Read it later. I started it the day you walked off on me at the beach. It's taken me four weeks to write. There'll be heaps of spelling mistakes, but hey…"

Lily took the envelope from his hand. "Thanks, mate. I'll keep this forever," she said, holding it against her chest.

She took a tan leather book out of her shoulder bag. "This is for you. Maybe you'll write in it. Maybe one day you'll look back and read the inscription I've written on the inside cover and remember how much you mean to me. Then, maybe you'll come back to me and be my bestie again." The tears were streaming down Lily's face, but she didn't turn away. "See – even now I'm being a big fat selfish shit. Thinking about me, instead of you."

Paulo hugged her hard, and she buried her wretched face in his flannelette shirt, which smelt of Old Spice. Lily had given him her dad's old bottle when they were in Form Four. The hug felt like the authentic bone-cruncher that Nini used to give.

He picked up his things and walked up the steps of the carriage. Before stepping on, he turned. "Thanks, buddy, for everything. See you round like a yoyo. Love ya guts."

"Love you too, mate. Call me. Write to me. I won't forgive you if you don't."

He stood and yelled from the gap in his window. "I will." Put up his left pinkie. "Only if you stop driving like a friggin' maniac."

She laughed. He laughed. She put up her left pinkie. The people in the carriage looked on in disdain. "Deal," she yelled back.

The whistle pierced the air and the train exploded into a jolting, jagged movement, and they waved and waved until he was gone.

Lily's feet were leaden, her head didn't move; she was stuck as if glued to the asphalt platform, transfixed towards the abyss. The suction of the air with the train's departure left a tunnel with no light, no exit, no way out. She shuddered and hugged herself tightly.

Suddenly, the wind whipped up behind her with the speed of an approaching, screeching train. She turned and took two steps towards the tracks. As she moved, the image of Meredith's face, the lines etched deeper since Nini died, hovered in her mind. She steadied herself, buried her hands deep in her trench coat, and thrust her head low to watch her feet make just one step at a time.

The man in the guard's box had been watching her. He hoped she was not a risk. He'd seen that once before; never wanted to see that again. Thought it best to walk down to the platform. He took his time. Didn't know what he'd say to her and he had to make the new announcements for the 8:50 to Pakenham.

Achingly slowly, one unsteady step at a time, she left the station.

When the other line was clear, and the passengers had left, he turned to the Sydney line and checked.

She'd gone.

Lily didn't remember driving home. However, once in the driveway, she sat with the Air Supply song *I'm All Out of Love* blaring on repeat. This was one of their favourites – Paulo's, especially. The lines about being lost and what that left the other person to be were too painful for her to sing. She dragged herself out of the car when Meredith called her from the front porch.

They shared a quiet dinner.

Meredith only asked, "Did Paulo get away okay?"

"Yes, unfortunately."

"I'm sorry, love. It's a hard time for you."

"Yes. I can't talk about it, Mum."

That was the end of their conversation. Meredith did the dishes and told Lily to have "a good long soak", which she did. Then she went to bed early.

ONE HUNDRED & SEVEN

There were a lot of footsteps in the sand for such an early hour. But, then again, it was summer, and the day was glorious by six am. Lily tried to step into the footprints that were heading in the other direction. She took perverse pleasure in knowing that she was heading in the opposite direction from the footprint's original maker. She nullified their step. It saved ploughing through the untouched sand and making her own path. Only when the footprints ran out was that what she had to do.

The spinifex grasses fluttering throughout the dunes were thriving, and this was incomprehensible to her. Lily was becoming aware that much of life was beyond her understanding. A large mound of sand had been obliterated by the huge surf over the past couple of weeks, exposing the roots of the grasses. The backdrop of scrubby tea-tree crowned the sand dunes leading back to the road. Many variations of green, brown and cream morphed with the light and shade of the dunes.

Lily thought of the ocean as a survivor. Tumultuous days, calm days, days where the waves petered out, others where the waves were magic, set after set, peeling, lifting, spraying, graciously folding, curling and falling. She loved to surf these waves; to toss and roll and be splayed out across the water's edge. She rolled with Bessie, trying to avoid her paws as she swam close by.

Too many conversations converged in her mind, like the swirl of the water adjoining a rip. It was like putting the contents of her mind into a sieve, hoping something worthwhile would drop through. She'd go home feeling less burdened. The rousing chill of her cheeks, the icy tightness in her chest after the surf, left her whole-body tingling, exhilarated and alive. When she'd held her breath for a long time, it felt good to completely exhale. The waves were her sedative for sleep. In her mind, crashing in, sucking out, repeat.

In the distance, Durga called her on. It rose out of the reef, adorned by shell-speckled rocks and rockpools where the swell spilled over. Durga's expression seemed superior, surveying the sea and beyond. Lily was saddened to notice that it was diminishing in parts. Spikes of sand-rocks shot up until the rock melted away into the dunes.

This was Lily's thinking place, but also a place she shared with Paulo. Private, peaceful, and protected from below. Lily was an adept climber. So was Bessie. Her sure-footedness afforded her the best view. Today, she was alone. No intruders, no interlopers, no interrogators... She stood aloft and breathed in the ocean's salty presence, arms out wide, and pretended she was free. She couldn't solve what she didn't know; the harder she tried, the further it slipped from her grasp. She pondered the thought, *Why is life so hard?*

As they descended the rock, a flock of seabirds swooped low in front of them. So close she could see the eyeballs in their stark white heads and hear the flapping of their wings. *Because it is.* She heard it clearly. *Because it is.*

She got up at sunrise and ran down to the back beach with Bessie. The initial shock of the liquid ice slicing her skin started to dissipate as she swam under each wave. Bessie was right behind her and seeing her faithful face bobbing up, as the sun poked its head above the mauve horizon, soothed her.

Afterwards, they cruised, sodden, up the twisting path, tramped through the last of the sand dunes and sat together at the top of the highest one. Lily wrapped her arms around Bessie and watched as the morning unfolded. It was a kaleidoscope of changing colour – pinks, orange, pale blue and hints of violet. They were in no hurry. Today was a leisurely one and, as the brightness and warmth intensified, they sat listening to the surf, the gulls and the ocean breeze.

When they arrived home, Meredith stood in the doorway with a smile. "Darling, the postman's been." She held out the letter to Lily. "Here it is."

Lily felt sick. She looked at the envelope with its official-looking words, her typed name visible through its little window. Her stomach lurched and she said, "I can't open it."

"Okay. Do you want me to open it?"

Lily stood there, not answering, and not taking the envelope. The hallway seemed too small. There wasn't enough air.

She ran into the back yard, crying. Meredith watched as she sprinted to the end of the garden and sat like she did when she was nine, curled up in a little ball, after Frank died. Arms around her knees, knees to chin, back to the world, rocking. Only, this time, Nini wasn't there to stroke her hair, wrap her arms around her, and say her soothing words. "There, there, my Lily-pily, you dear little pet. Darling girl, darling little one. Dearest little girl."

Meredith never had the soft touch of her husband nor her mother. She wanted to; it just didn't come naturally. Frank always knew what to say, he had a gentle touch. He'd only see the look on Lily's face and he'd crumble into a big soft bear and hold her until she was still. Enid did the same after he was gone. She would miraculously pop out of nowhere if there was an argument, having not said a word, and go and lie on the bed with Lily. Right or wrong, Enid didn't care, she'd ease the storm by just being there. The sting would ease, and the storm would pass. But not today.

Lily stopped rocking as Meredith said, "I'm sorry, darling, for all you've lost. Your beautiful Dad, then darling Nini, and now Paulo has moved. It's been painful to watch. I don't know how to make any of this better, but I need you to know that I love you with all my heart." Meredith stoked Lily's hair and continued. "I know I'm not good at showing it. I don't give you the affection you deserve, I don't express myself well..."

Lily sat up and looked at her mother, who was seated next to her on the ground.

"But I *am* on your side, Lily," Meredith said. "I'm so proud of you – not because of what you do or don't achieve, but because of who you are. You are a wonderful young woman –

you have so much to give, and I'm here to support you as best I can. These marks today, they're just numbers. You've tried your best and that's what matters. They're just stepping-stones to the next stage."

Lily sat up. Meredith handed her one of Nini's lace handkerchiefs. After a while, she hugged her mother – a hug that made them rock and brought their two struggling hearts together, a hug that was felt long after they pulled away.

"By the way, my bum's killing me," Meredith said. "Let's go make tea."

Lily took her hand and helped her mother up. They walked hand in hand back to the kitchen. With the tea made and some muesli slice on the table, Lily took up the envelope.

"Well, I guess it's now or never."

Her face looked so young, vulnerable and lovely that Meredith could hardly bear to look at her.

"Oh, my God. Oh, my *Gooooddddd*. Mum, I got four As and a B that was three marks off an A. That's a 97.5 score! I can go to drama school. I'll get in. Oh, thank you, God. *Woooohoooo!*"

They jumped up, hugged, swirled, and laughed. The little green kitchen whizzed around and around.

ONE HUNDRED & NINE

That night, Meredith and Lily went out to Kettle Royale, a fancy restaurant in Spray Point, to celebrate. They spoke of things they'd never mentioned to each other before. They shared a bottle of white wine. Lily didn't even know she liked wine until then. Meredith laughed and was funny, cheeky and good company. Lily didn't know her mother had a good sense of humour. She was telling jokes, and relating some of the funny things she and Frank did when they were courting. Like the time they went out for dinner, and they ate a feast, then they realised that neither of them remembered to bring their wallets. They'd shared plenty of drinks by then and, when the bill came, they tried to explain but couldn't stop laughing. Then the owner came over, furious – even more so because they got nervous and kept laughing. So, they ended up washing all the pots and pans in the restaurant's kitchen in their finest clothes and sweeping and mopping the floors. The owner said, *You can leave when it's done to my satisfaction,* which took hours.

And the New Years Eve when, again, they again had no money, so they went to the promenade with the cheapest bottle of spirits they could muster. It was a very hot night, so they stripped off to their underwear and a police car came by. They ran into the water. The police called them out and of course their underwear had gone see-though and they couldn't stop laughing. Lucky for them, the cops saw the funny side and let them dress and get going. Mum said the best part was that if the cops been five minutes longer, they would've found them starkers in the water. *Oh, God, no!*

It was a revelation to Lily that her mum could still be her mum, but also be a friend. The walk back home in the dark was magical. The promenade had a golden hue, and the blanket of stars was winking at them. They strolled arm in arm through the avenue of palms, and Meredith told Lily to go for her dreams, no matter what.

"You only get one life, Lily. Make it be what it's meant to be. Just set your mind to where you want to go and, most importantly, how you want to feel when you've reached your goal."

"Is that how you became a nurse, Mum?"

"No, not really. Mum told me to go for it, but with Dad gone I felt lost. The grief sucked the confidence out of me. I didn't do so well in my final year. I couldn't concentrate. I worked at different jobs, but they had no soul. Nothing that let my heart sing. Nothing that excited me or made me feel alive. You know what I mean?"

"Yeah, I reckon I do. I hope I do..."

"Anyway, after a few years of floundering around and going nowhere in particular, I met your dad. He was a natural student. He couldn't understand why I wasn't studying. He kept saying things like, *Don't worry about the money; do what you're passionate about and the money will come. Listen to your heart, Meredith. What gets you excited?*"

"Oh wow, Mum, I never knew Dad encouraged you like that. So, he was the reason you did your training?"

"No. He was the reason I shut the doubt up. He was the reason I took the risk to have a go. If you fail, you try again, or you change track. But if you don't have a go, what can happen to you? Your soul dies. That's too big a price to pay."

"That's powerful. He was wonderful, wasn't he?"

"Yes, he certainly was. In his own quiet, gentle way, he had firm beliefs about life. He didn't waiver. He was never a people pleaser, go-with-the-mob type of guy. He just set his own course, believed in it, and stuck by it. Because I fell deeply in love with him, I found myself. Through his steadfast belief in me, I started to love myself, too. Not in a vain way, but in a courageous way. Mum, of course, loved Frank. He was a force for good. You were lucky to have a dad like him. Even though it wasn't for long enough."

"I wish he was still here. I wish I remembered more about him. I loved his gentle eyes."

"You have his eyes exactly. There was a kindness and an intelligence about his eyes that shine through yours too, Lily. He was taken too soon – but, boy, what an impression he made during his life! To know him was to love him – absolutely. You are your father's daughter. There's such a bright future for you, my darling. Believe it, with every molecule of your being."

The time had come. Lily absorbed the slow creep of her stomach-ache, which had been building all week. The thought of not living at home was scary, but the thought that maybe she never would again was petrifying. Her home would be in the city, four hours' drive from the coast (if you didn't stop, which Lily knew she would). This both excited and terrified her. Every time she thought of Meredith alone at home, she cried. Especially when she thought of her mum at night. Then, she thought of Bessie snuggling into her when things were bad, or sad, or just because. The pit of her stomach knotted, so she couldn't think of it for too long.

As the weeks rolled into days, she knew she had to face it and talk with Meredith. When she emptied her desk drawer, she flipped open the diary to June 1976, and a page that read:

Hi you,

I'm gunna tell you about today. This is what we spoke about:

Going to your joint, Lily, I remembered what home is. After Mum left, the sense of home left too. When I go to your place, I smell and feel home.

I wonder what it would have been like if Mum didn't leave. But she did and that's that.

Nini says, 'Always feel at home in the world, Lily. Even when the world is not kind. I know there were times when I didn't feel at home in my world. After your pa died, I was lost. But eventually I felt at home in the world again.'

So, no matter what, never lose hope. It just takes time and courage, but with those things you do find a better day.

It had been unbearably hot. A heatwave like Spray Point had never known before. The roads seemed to be melting. The beach offered the only relief, and Lily spent every hour there, when she wasn't working.

She had decided to go to college. They lived too far from town to do the commute. Meredith told Lily she'd saved money just in case, and Enid had left a little nest egg for Lily's study expenses.

They'd spent the weekend packing. Bessie knew something was up. She just wouldn't leave Lily's side. The house grew smaller and quieter, like an old pair of favourite runners that no longer fit.

Meredith made a breakfast feast, packed food, and seemed unusually jolly. She was humming and smiling. Lily saw straight through it.

At nine o'clock, Lily had to leave to miss peak-hour traffic and have time to set up her room before classes started the following week. It was 'O-week', and she was nervous, but excited to get amongst it. Meredith had told her to join all the clubs; be a part of it. *You'll make friends that way and keep your public speaking skills up*. Oh, the tips she was dishing out about how to make it a fabulous experience began to make Lily's head spin. It was as if Meredith thought she should be going herself!

"Okay, Mum, I'll try to do it all. Maybe one day at a time, hey?"

Meredith helped her pack the overladen car and gave her one more heart-to-heart hug. Lily had a lump in her throat as she smelled her mother's hair. It always smelled of vanilla and reminded her of when she was little.

She hopped behind the driver's wheel. Her hands were sticky, and her face was red as she rolled down the window.

"Drive safely, love. You're under no time pressure. Don't speed. Keep in the left-hand lane. Concentrate. Eyes on the road. Keep the music down..."

"Mum! Okay! Okay. Enough instructions."

"I'll miss you, my darling, but I'm thrilled that you're going."

"I'll miss you too, Mum. Please give Bessie extra pats for me. She's gunna miss her Lily-pad."

"I will. I promise. Now, off you go. I'll check the road for you. I love you, my baby girl. I love you heaps. Keep safe and call me when you're there."

"Yeah, I will. I love you too, Mum. Thanks for helping me. Bye, Bessie girl." She reversed too quickly and abruptly crunched the gears as she waved out the window, yelling, "Bye! Bye, Mum."

Meredith walked into the middle of the street. Waving both arms and blowing kisses, she heard the drift of Supertramp's *Dreamer...* floating behind the car across the salty air.

About the Author

Anne Olle is the author of Where the Light Shines, and Two Quid Kid. She completed her Graduate Certificate of Writing and Literature at Deakin University in 2020. She has a deep empathy for young people and the struggles they endure. She lives on the Mornington Peninsula in Melbourne, Australia with her family.

Author Contact

Anne.olle.author@outlook.com
www.anneolleauthor.com

Acknowledgments

I would like to thank Sarah Sentilles for her wonderful encouragement during her courses and for being my first mentor. Her kind words, "...you are a great writer..." has been stuck to my computer since 2021.

I acknowledge and thank all the lecturers at Deakin University for their passionate guidance during the Graduate Certificate of Writing and Literature.

A very special thank you to Dr Kate Ryan for being my incredible, skillful and kind mentor throughout the writing of this novel and for her belief in my work.

Thank you to Rachel Power for her superb professional edit of Where the Light Shines.

Thank you to Emma Ring for her brilliant IT-related assistance.

To Ashley Kalagian Blunt, Kate Mildenhall, Liza Boston and the Authors Group, Troy Hunter, Martin Copping, Kym Jackson, Stephen Kok, Colleen Callandar, Corrie Perkin, Veronica Sullivan, Mike Flanagan and Jack Lewis for being supportive of this novel.

Special thanks to Julie Postance for her expert professional guidance and facilitation in every aspect of the publishing process. Thank you to Sophie White for the gorgeous design and layout of my novel.

Thank you to my lovely friends for encouraging my writing.

Heartfelt thanks to Nana, Patsy, Pal, Johnny, Georgia, Marg, Ian, John/Jack and other shining stars for being full of *light* in this life and beyond.

With gratitude to my fabulous extended family for showing interest in my project, and immense thanks for reading my drafts.

To my beautiful family - Rob, Bridget, Myles, Marcus, Johnny, Brooke, Olivia - thank you for always supporting my creativity, reading or listening to my drafts and truly caring about *Where the Light Shines.*

To all my magnificent grandchildren and family thank you for the love, fun and inspiration you bring every day. You are where the *light* shines!

www.ingramcontent.com/pod-product-compliance
Lightning Source LLC
Chambersburg PA
CBHW061615210726
48287CB00001B/140